A FATEFUL REUNION

Alone with the general, Imoshen's breath caught in her throat. She looked up. Tulkhan's eyes, black as obsidian, bored into her. She sensed the force of his emotion barely contained. Would he reject her because she had not fought off Reothe?

He offered his hand, palm up. Her skin looked pale against his, and his flesh felt hot as his fingers closed around hers. Pulling her to her feet, he drew her into his arms. She welcomed his touch. Without a word he sought her lips, hungry and demanding. Tears of relief stung her eyes.

She had been so afraid he would reject her. Pressed to the length of his body, she felt the strength in him, but she wanted more. She ached to share the absolute intimacy of mind-touch. Only when he opened to her would she know how he truly felt. She needed to be absolved by his love.

She gasped as he lifted his head.

His great body trembled and his ragged breathing made her heart race.

Also by Cory Daniells

Broken Vows
Dark Dreams

DESPERATE ALLIANCES

Book Three of
THE LAST T'EN TRILOGY

CORY DANIELLS

Bantam Books

DESPERATE ALLIANCES

A Bantam Book / June 2002

All rights reserved.
Copyright © 2002 by Cory Daniells
Cover art © 2002 by Franco Accornero

ISBN 0-553-58103-1

Published simultaneously in the United States and Canada

Bantam Books are published by Bantam Books, a division of
Random House, Inc. Its trademark, consisting of the words
"Bantam Books" and the portrayal of a rooster, is Registered in
U.S. Patent and Trademark Office and in other countries. Marca
Registrada. Bantam Books, 1540 Broadway, New York, New York
10036.

PRINTED IN THE UNITED STATES OF AMERICA

OPM 10 9 8 7 6 5 4 3 2 1

*To my friends and colleagues who have helped
bring the T'En trilogy to life*

DESPERATE ALLIANCES

One

TORN BY CONFLICTING loyalties, Imoshen knelt by Reothe's bed. With the arrival of evening, scented candles burned in the chamber that had so recently been her prison. The tower room had been stripped of its rich hangings and, in the space of one day, their positions had been reversed.

She should let Reothe die, for if he regained his gifts he would be too powerful to contain. But to stand by and let someone die when she could heal him went against her instincts. All day she had fought to save him, easing his pain with herbs and, when this failed, drawing on her innate healing powers.

"Here, sip this." She lifted Reothe's head and held the tisane to his lips. His suffering had pared back his features, emphasizing his high forehead, narrow nose, prominent cheekbones. He grimaced at the bitter taste but obediently drained the goblet. She smoothed the damp silver hair from his pale forehead, and his hand squeezed hers in gratitude. Her heart contracted.

After what he had done she should hate him, but she could not. He was the last of her kind. Both Throwbacks to the T'En race that had settled Fair Isle, they were marked by their wine-dark eyes, vivid coloring, and six-fingered hands. Last survivors of the old royal line, they were gifted with the powers that were both a blessing and a curse. And since the Ghebite General had conquered their island king-dom, they had both clung to life with determination and, when necessary, guile.

Anger ignited Imoshen, for she had succumbed to Reothe's trickery. Last night he had come to her in General Tulkhan's form, slipping into her arms and planting a seed of dissension that she feared would drive Tulkhan from her. He would never accept another man's child.

The General's bone-setter cleared his throat. "Some warmed wine, Princess?"

With an effort she grasped the bed upright and came to her feet. "Thank you. I think the worst is over."

"I will watch him. Get some rest," Wharrd urged.

"Yes." However, she remained, staring down at Reothe. She had to admire his daring. In a decisive gamble he had kidnapped Imoshen and her son, luring the General into a trap. In exchange for a mercenary army, Reothe had offered to deliver Tulkhan to King Gharavan. The Ghebite king was Tulkhan's younger half-brother and legitimate heir, but any love he bore Tulkhan had been eroded by the General's pop-ularity and military success.

With the mercenaries and his rebel army, Reothe could have retaken Fair Isle. He had come so close to making the exchange that Imoshen shuddered.

This time last year she would have given anything to see Tulkhan in chains, but now the thought brought her no joy. How ironic that after surrendering her Stronghold, she had set out to woo the conqueror, only to fall in love with the man.

Through the partially open door General Tulkhan watched Imoshen tend his deadly enemy. Only last night, when Tulkhan had been held captive in the tower's dun-geon, Reothe had come to him with Imoshen's scent on his skin, boasting that she carried his child.

Fury surged through Tulkhan. As a tactician he knew, if he was to hold Fair Isle, Reothe must die. But it was the thought of another man's hands on Imoshen that made Tulkhan resonate with rage. Reothe would die this very night!

As Imoshen bade Wharrd good night, Tulkhan stepped

into the shadows behind his guards, who were playing dice. Blinded by exhaustion, the last princess of the T'En walked by, her straight nose and determined chin a beautiful mask. The General wanted to break her terrible composure. He wanted her to beg his forgiveness and declare her love for him. But he let her pass, a stiff-shouldered, tall figure with a deceptively fragile air. Something twisted inside Tulkhan. How could she betray him after everything they had shared?

Imoshen climbed the stairs to her room, numbed by the speed of events. Even the knowledge that her life would be forfeit if the Church learned she had used her gifts to kill a True-man left her unmoved. She longed to hold her infant son and rejoice in Ashmyr's innocence. But now that simple joy was a double-edged sword, for she carried a child she had not chosen to conceive.

Resentment urged her to take control. Every midwife knew the herbs. One draught of womansorrow would dislodge this babe and circumvent Reothe's trickery.

She staggered, reaching for the dressed stone wall. In a flash of understanding so intimate that she felt nauseous, Imoshen realized she could not do it. She sank onto the stair, her head in her hands. As a healer she was devoted to preserving life. But it was more than that—she was a mother. Tears burned her eyes. Just as Ashmyr, her son, was an innocent pawn in the game of power, this child was innocent of its father's treachery. She would defend this babe with her life.

But the General would never accept Reothe's child. Taking a deep breath, she stood and straightened her shoulders. Despite everything, she must make Tulkhan understand.

Primed for murder, Tulkhan pushed the thick oak door open, revealing the injured man. Wharrd looked up, a single candle flame illuminating his sun-lined features. Silently, the bone-setter greeted Tulkhan and led him to the canopied bed, raising the candle. By its flickering light the rebel leader lay vulnerable.

"I have never seen an injury like this. The whites of his eyes are blood red. And it is almost as if he can sense the Princess; since she left he has faded rapidly." Suddenly, Reothe's body convulsed. A moan was torn from him and he lay panting, his skin glistening. "He sinks deeper still and radiates heat like a forge. I doubt he'll last the night."

"Then he will save us the trouble of killing him!"

Wharrd met Tulkhan's eyes.

"Not only is he the last male of the old royal line, but he is pure T'En. If he recovers his sorcerous gifts he will unite Fair Isle against me." As Ghebite war general, Tulkhan had made many hard decisions, but betraying Imoshen's trust went against the grain. "Better to suffocate him now and face Imoshen's wrath."

"Why face her anger when you could console her?" Wharrd suggested. "As I watched Imoshen battle to save her kinsman, I felt for her, knowing that we could not let him live. Like you, I sought a soldier's clean solution, but after consideration I offer you a courtier's solution. My herbal knowledge comes from the mainland. Pains-ease is odorless and swift, and in his state a double dose would snuff his flame."

Tulkhan's mouth twisted with repugnance. "A courtier's solution!"

"Imoshen trusts you, and this way—"

"She will not know that I have betrayed her trust," Tulkhan acknowledged. Wharrd was right, yet the General felt this subterfuge diminished them both. He longed for an honorable solution that would not conflict with his warrior code, the Gheeakhan. Finally, he expelled his breath. "So be it. I have fought beside you these eleven years, Wharrd, and never thought to see you murder a sick man. Never did I think I would give you such an order."

Wharrd looked down.

"Just do it and do it quickly," Tulkhan ordered. "I'm going to see Imoshen."

On the mainland much was whispered about the mysterious T'En of Fair Isle. Tulkhan was only just beginning to understand their strengths and weaknesses. They called them Dhamfeer in his own language, and the priests believed them closer to beasts than to True-men.

The General should have been repulsed by a woman who stood as tall as a tall True-man, whose milk-white skin and garnet eyes proclaimed her tainted T'En blood, but he found Imoshen's refusal to admit him her master exhilarating and her Otherness fascinating. He had discovered that this proud, passionate woman was far more dangerous than any mainland myth. Tulkhan could not pinpoint when it had happened, but in the space of one year she had ensnared him, heart and soul. Imoshen was his addiction and he ached to confront her again. As conqueror of Fair Isle he had dictated the terms of surrender. Imoshen had negotiated many concessions for her people. But tonight she would be the one to make concessions.

The soft sound of running feet made him stop.

"General Tulkhan?" Kalleen gasped. The little True-woman wore nothing but a nightgown, and her hair hung loose to her waist, glowing like honey held to sunlight. Though she was no longer Imoshen's maid, she would let no one else serve her lady. "It's Imoshen, she—"

Mouth dry, Tulkhan rushed past her. Striding to the door, he threw it open. Imoshen lay crumpled on the brilliant carpet like an abandoned toy. "What happened, Kalleen?"

"She had just passed the baby to me when she convulsed and fell to the ground."

Crossing the room, Tulkhan spared one glance for his son, who slept in his basket. "Imoshen, can you hear me?"

She did not respond.

He slid his arms under her and stood, fear making the movement effortless. Even as he carried her to the bed he felt the heat rise from her skin. "Did she give any sign that she was sickening?"

"She was very quiet. I thought her tired after nursing T'Reothe all day." In her distraction, Kalleen gave the prisoner his royal title. Kalleen touched Tulkhan's arm. The expression in her hazel eyes made his stomach clench. "I believe this is no ordinary fever. Before it came on, there was that tension on the air. You know the way it feels when Imoshen uses her gifts?"

Tulkhan nodded briefly. For him, forewarning came as prickling of the skin. His concern deepened. Once before, when Imoshen had suffered as only the T'En could, Reothe had saved her. Imoshen had been granted dispensation to forgo her vows of chastity and take Reothe as her betrothed. That was before the General had invaded Fair Isle, and though Imoshen had since bonded with the General, Reothe claimed the last two pure T'En were bound in ways a True-man could not understand. Cold certainty gripped Tulkhan. "Wait here."

He ran down the steps, forcing himself to stride past the guards as though Imoshen's life didn't hang in the balance. He found Wharrd leaning over the unconscious man, trying to get him to swallow something. "Stop. Kill him and you kill Imoshen!"

Wharrd straightened, letting Reothe sink onto the pillow.

"She lies upstairs in the same state. I fear..."

Wharrd gave a grunt of understanding and glanced at the mixture in the mug. Tulkhan realized that with one act of treachery he could be free of both the dreaded Dhamfeer. The thought revolted him.

Grabbing the mug, he strode to the oriel window and flung the potion into the night. Far below the Citadel's tower, where the rocks met the sea, the waves would obliterate all trace of "the courtier's solution."

Closing the window, Tulkhan turned to Wharrd. "Through Imoshen I command the loyalty of her people. Without her at my side, the highland nobles would rise up in revolt. They know that since my half-brother turned on me I don't have the backing of the Ghebite Empire, and without it I cannot hope to put down a rebellion." Battle strategy was second nature to Tulkhan, but in his heart he had to admit that, though he had taken the last T'En princess as his wife out of political necessity, it was not cold necessity that took him to her bed, nor simple lust that bound him to her. "I need Imoshen."

"To hold Fair Isle you need the Princess, but that means"—Wharrd gestured to the unconscious man—"letting this snake live."

They both stared at Reothe. Once Tulkhan would have given almost anything to have Reothe in his power; now he felt no surge of victory. "Come and see if there's anything you can do for Imoshen."

In the room above, Kalleen was sponging Imoshen. "Wharrd!"

"Kalleen."

In that one exchange Tulkhan heard their love confirmed. A stab of guilt assailed him, for he knew Wharrd wanted nothing more than to retire to his estates with Kalleen.

Wharrd examined Imoshen. "She appears to suffer just as he does. I fear there is nothing we can do but watch and wait."

"I will watch over her," Tulkhan said. "Take my son for the night."

He wrung out the damp cloth while they collected the baby. Consumed with fear for Imoshen, Tulkhan hardly heard them slip away. His hands trembled as he blotted the beads of perspiration from her forehead.

She lay unaware of him, her pale skin flushed, silver hair spread across the pillow. She gave a soft moan, and her lids moved as if she was watching events played out on another plane. When he felt the tension of her gifts, frustration ate at him. He was only a True-man. Reothe, however ... But try as he might, Tulkhan could not revive his anger.

"Ahh, Imoshen, how could you betray me?" he whispered. He had to believe that she had not gone willingly into Reothe's arms.

Threading his fingers through hers, the General pressed her hot skin to his lips, savoring the satiny texture. Loving Imoshen might yet be his downfall, but that did not stop him from willing her to live with every fiber of his being.

Imoshen woke with the dawn and silently gave thanks for escaping death's shadow. The last thing she recalled was sensing the approach of the vengeful soul of the True-man she had killed. She had managed to pass her son to Kalleen before the man's shade had latched on to her. Cruel in death as he had been in life, the Vaygharian had tried to drag her through death's shadow with him. Only her fierce will had saved her.

In her study of the T'En, she had never read about this phenomenon. Reothe's experience was greater than hers; she needed—

"Imoshen?"

"Tulkhan?" Her voice was a mere thread. She had not expected to find the General by her bed. His unshaven beard looked dark against the coppery skin of his jaw. His temple plaits had unraveled and his long black hair hung disheveled around his broad shoulders. She longed to smooth the lines of worry from between his brows, but he had avoided her since they took Reothe captive yesterday morning.

Anticipating that Tulkhan was here to argue for the rebel leader's execution, she began to prepare her reasons for sparing Reothe, but the General clasped her hand, saying, "I prayed the fever would break, but when it did you went so cold and still, I feared you would never wake."

"Water," she croaked. He helped lift her head to take a sip. Sinking back onto the pillow, she was touched to see him so careworn. "You stayed by me; thank you."

"Ah, Imoshen." He brushed this aside gruffly. "They will come soon, wanting to know how you are. I must be frank. After Reothe's capture the town seethes with rumor. You cannot deny your powers when your features proclaim your T'En blood. But for my men to accept you, they must believe these gifts nothing more than the useful ability to hasten healing."

"As you see, even my healing gift deserts me if I overextend myself," she whispered, then wished she had not reminded him that she had spent the previous day by Reothe's bedside. Tulkhan must wonder why she hadn't fought off Reothe's advances. If he discovered how Reothe had tricked her, he might march down the tower steps and kill the rebel leader with his bare hands.

"I am no fool, Imoshen. That was more than a passing fever. You suffered something only the T'En can endure."

"True," she admitted, but would not elaborate.

"Very well." He stood, expression unreadable. "When you are ready we will tour Northpoint. I must speak with the captains of the mercenary ships. The people must see that we are united and our heir unhurt."

Imoshen sat up, alarmed. "Where is Ashmyr?"

"With Kalleen. I will send for her."

But the little True-woman was already at the door with a hungry baby, issuing orders to draw a bath. Imoshen hardly noticed Tulkhan slip away. Joy blossomed within her as she cradled her son and bared her breast, marveling at the boy's perfection. His lids were closed, the better to concentrate on feeding, hiding his wine-dark eyes. Thick black lashes formed crescents on his pale cheeks. She touched his hand, and his six fingers closed around her little finger. Imoshen gave thanks for his precious life from the bottom of her heart.

As soon as the servants left, Kalleen climbed on the bed next to Imoshen. She stroked the baby's fine hair wonderingly. "People kept stopping me to touch him. I can't believe he nearly drowned. How could you let . . . I mean—"

"I am not all powerful, Kalleen." The near loss was still too immediate for Imoshen. Her voice shook as she tried to speak dispassionately. "The General was in the boat, about to be rowed out to the ship and exchanged for the mercenaries, when it happened. The Vaygharian was acting as go-between. He always hated me, and in a moment of spite he snatched Ashmyr and threw him into the sea." She closed her eyes, seeing her son fall into the mist-shrouded bay, hearing that terrible small splash.

The shock had unleashed her gifts. In white-hot fury

she had turned on the Vaygharian, driving him to suicide. When Reothe had sought to console her, she'd refused to believe that Ashmyr was dead. Lashing out, she had crippled Reothe's gift. "I ran to the wharf's edge and called on Tulkhan to save our son."

"But Ghebites cannot swim."

"I helped him." How simple it sounded. But only in desperation had Tulkhan dropped his guard and accepted the mind-touch, letting her guide his body.

"My sweet boy," Kalleen whispered, cupping one tiny foot, which had escaped the blanket. His toes curled in reaction, making her smile. "It was lucky Tulkhan reached him in time."

But he hadn't. Ashmyr had been dead when Tulkhan passed him up to Imoshen. In desperation she had called on the Ancients to restore Ashmyr's life. That she held her living son in her arms was due entirely to those old powers, and her willingness to make a bargain.

Servants arrived with the copper bath, and others followed with buckets. In the old tower they did not have the luxury of hot water piped to each floor.

Kalleen took the drowsy baby, tucking him in his basket. Still weak, Imoshen was grateful for her help. It was wonderful to sink into the warm, scented water.

The General returned while Kalleen was rinsing Imoshen's hair. Without explanation he went to stand before the windows, his hips resting on the sill, his arms folded across his broad chest. The light from behind hid his expression, revealing only the glint of his eyes as he followed Imoshen's every move.

Very aware of him, she bent her head as Kalleen twisted her long damp hair into a knot. Kalleen sent Imoshen a questioning look, but she had no answers. She stood with one hand on Kalleen's shoulder for support. The little woman gently rubbed scented soap into her skin.

Imoshen's body grew hot under Tulkhan's gaze. The water sluiced over her, little droplets falling to the floor before the fireplace. Her pulse throbbed through her limbs.

Still, Tulkhan said nothing, neither leaving nor sending Kalleen away.

Dizzy and breathless, Imoshen stepped from the tub. Kalleen wrapped the bathing cloth around her, patting her dry. She undid Imoshen's hair and let it fall heavy and damp to her hips. Imoshen knelt before the fire as Kalleen finger-combed her hair, spreading it to dry.

Hardly able to swallow, Imoshen dared a quick look at the General. He stood rigid, his eyes devouring her.

When Kalleen began to divide Imoshen's nearly dry hair to plait it, Tulkhan straightened. "Leave us."

Kalleen looked to Imoshen, who nodded.

Alone with the General, Imoshen's breath caught in her throat. She looked up. His eyes, black as obsidian, bored into her. She sensed the force of his emotion barely contained. Would he reject her because she had not fought off Reothe?

He offered his hand, palm up. Her skin looked pale against his, and his flesh felt hot as his fingers closed around hers. Pulling her to her feet, he drew her into his arms. She welcomed his touch. Without a word he sought her lips, hungry and demanding. Tears of relief stung her eyes.

She had been so afraid he would reject her. Pressed to the length of his body, she felt the strength in him, but she wanted more. She ached to share the absolute intimacy of the mind-touch. Only when he opened to her would she know how he truly felt. She needed to be absolved by his love.

She gasped as he lifted his head. His great body trembled and his ragged breathing made her heart race. He pressed his lips to her forehead, large hands cradling her head.

Letting her barriers down, she sought his essence. She knew him now, having shared his mind when she urged his body to swim. He had trusted her enough to save his life and rescue their son. But she had barely touched his awareness when his barriers clamped into place.

"No, Imoshen. You promised not to try this."

"I thought with what we had shared..." She hesitated. He was pulling away from her physically as well. "Tulkhan?"

He stood before her, arms out. "I am but a True-man, Imoshen. Accept me for what I am."

"We could share so much more!"

"Where would it end? When I am your puppet king?"

She shook her head, cut to the quick. "Never, Tulkhan. I respect you too much—"

"Then respect my wishes in this one thing." He caught her hands in his. "Imoshen?"

She looked down at his strong hands, scarred by years of battle. Respect his wishes in this one thing... but it was such a central thing. By denying her T'En nature he was denying an intrinsic part of her. Could she live with that? Did she have a choice?

She searched his face, aching for him to hold her.

"Imoshen!" He pulled her close. His mouth was bruising on hers, his hands almost too hard. It was as if he was trying to erase her doubt with the force of his passion. If this was all they could share, then it had to be enough.

Tulkhan stepped off the mercenary ship's gangplank to find Imoshen gone. Wharrd answered his unasked question. "The Princess went to inspect the hospice. I insisted she take three Elite Guards."

Tulkhan was not really surprised. Considering Imoshen's gift was one of healing, she was a natural choice for patron of the hospices, and she had been raised to believe the Empress's duty was to serve her people. Still, he did not trust these people. They had been too quick to support the rebels. "Which way?"

But he needn't have asked. Shouts and splintering wood urged him to hurry. Hastening up the steep lane, he followed the sounds to their source, a grand building faced with the same white stone as the Citadel.

He stepped over the debris and thrust the double doors

of the hospice wide open. The public hall was festooned with market paraphernalia. "What's going on here?"

Tulkhan's Elite Guards greeted his arrival with relief. They were no match for Imoshen in full stride. With their sleeping son strapped to her chest, she was berating a little man.

At the sound of Tulkhan's voice she spun to face him. "This is, or was, the hospice. They have turned it into a market!" Imoshen rounded on the man. "This building was dedicated by Imoshen the Third to serve the sick. The Church should never have allowed this."

"The priests were killed in the invasion, like the hospice healers. Our markets burned down, so we—"

"I heard how your township suffered in the initial invasion," Imoshen said soberly. "But now I want the hospice restored. I will send for more healers." She gestured to the Elite Guards. "See that this building is emptied and cleaned."

Tulkhan's men bristled. They were warriors, not common laborers. Before the silence could grow uncomfortable, the General swung a bale of wool onto his back. "Where do you want this, Imoshen?"

She smiled her thanks. "Outside. They can rebuild their markets."

"Why rebuild? When another invasion threatens?" someone muttered.

Imoshen silenced the traders with a look. "When Tulkhan's army arrives, he will sail across the T'Ronynn Straits to forestall Gharavan's invasion. Thanks to the Protector General, your town won't be a battleground again. You can not only rebuild the markets but your lives!"

Much heartened, the townsfolk joined the General and his men in dismantling the stalls. When this was progressing well, Tulkhan joined Imoshen. "Now I understand why this building bears the T'En royal sign over the door and not the anchor and sword of the great merchant houses."

"Do not mention that symbol to these respectable townspeople. They will not thank you for reminding them of their pirate ancestors." She met his eyes with a rueful smile. "There are many minstrel tales about T'Ronynn and his T'En brothers. They were given a Charter to keep the Pellucid Sea free of pirates. It was not long before they were more feared than those they hunted. Most of Northpoint are descended from them, though they're too proud to admit—" She frowned, her gaze going past him. "You, child. Come here."

A scruffy urchin approached, her eyes fixed on the ground. Unlike the mainland towns, where gangs of homeless children roamed the streets, there were few poor in Fair Isle.

Hugging her son to her chest, Imoshen knelt in her fine velvets to feel the child's thin legs. "This girl's broken leg has not been set properly. That's why she limps." Imoshen's eyes glistened with real anger. "Who is responsible for her?"

A tall man, his red hair silvered at the temple, put aside a crate of late-ripening melons. He raised both hands to his heart and then his forehead, giving the deep obeisance reserved for the Empress. The child sidled over to him like a puppy. His head remained bowed. "I fear Almona followed me."

Imoshen straightened. "Why haven't you sought treatment for her leg?"

"It had already knitted poorly when I took her in. It was beyond the skills of all but a T'En healer." He raised wine-dark eyes to Imoshen. Tulkhan stiffened. It always startled him to find half-breeds. "Her parents are dead."

"But families and friends have always taken in orphans," Imoshen said. "Children are valued in Fair Isle."

"Whole villages have been wiped out." The man's large hand cupped the child's face, lifting her chin so that she raised the same garnet eyes to Imoshen. "And no one wanted a half-breed like her. I have taken in seven others."

Suddenly Imoshen grasped his hand, turning it over. Drawn by her pained expression, Tulkhan moved closer. With a jolted he realized the farmer had five fingers on each hand, plus a stump where the sixth finger had been chopped off.

"I have read of these mutilations during the Age of

Consolidation," Imoshen muttered. "But I did not think to see such barbarity in my time. Who did this to you?"

"My parents. Out of love. They witnessed the stoning of the last rogue T'En. Rather than abandon me at birth, they—"

"That was over a hundred years ago!" Tulkhan objected.

"I carried both the T'En traits, too close to a Throwback for comfort. Everyone knows the males are dangerous. So . . ." He shrugged eloquently.

Tulkhan caught Imoshen's eye. Everyone believed the males more powerful and so they were, but only if the females' greater powers weren't triggered by the birth of children. This knowledge had been hidden until it was lost to memory because Imoshen the First had ordered all pure T'En women to take a vow of chastity.

With the General in his power, Reothe had revealed it was only Imoshen's belief that his gifts were greater than hers that made her his captive. The irony of it had delighted Reothe. Now Imoshen stood beside Tulkhan, his bondpartner and mother of his child, powerful enough to cripple a T'En male. Tulkhan looked on her with fresh eyes.

"But to cut off a child's sixth fingers. So cruel!" Imoshen's arms closed over her son protectively. Her shoulder met Tulkhan's chest as she stepped back, and he felt the tension in her. With her ability to skim minds, he guessed she had absorbed the mutilated man's memories, and this was confirmed when her trembling hand sought Tulkhan's. With the T'En gifts came strength but also vulnerability. He squeezed her fingers and she cast him a grateful smile. She turned to the farmer. "Your name?"

"Eksyl Five-fingers."

"Let it be known that all unwanted children are welcome here. Food and bedding will be sent from the Citadel. I will be back tomorrow to begin the healings. Then I will see what I can do for Almona. There is nothing I can do for you. I'm sorry."

"All I ask is your blessing, Empress."

He sank to one knee and Imoshen raised her left hand, the one closest to her heart. She placed the tip of her sixth finger in the center of his forehead. "You have it, Eksyl Malaunje Protector."

Later, as they walked up the rise to the Citadel, Tulkhan remarked, "*Malaunje?* I don't know that word."

"It is an old High T'En word. It means half-breed, but the connotations were different then. Once the T'En were respected and the Malaunje were their closest kin."

Nowadays it was a curse to be born a Throwback, and Malaunje children were unwanted. Tulkhan noticed how Imoshen brushed her lips across Ashmyr's soft head. He did not want his son to be ostracized.

"How long before you leave to confront your half-brother?" Imoshen asked.

"I sail as soon as Commander Peirs gets here with the army and the ships are prepared," he said, and she licked her lips as if she might say something. "What?"

Imoshen smiled sadly. "Nothing. I know you must go. It is just that I—"

"Had a premonition of disaster?"

She laughed. "Nothing so dramatic. Mine is a purely selfish motive. I will miss you, General!"

Two

WITH THE ARRIVAL of his army, General Tulkhan was ready to go to war. Imoshen matched him stride for stride on the Citadel's parapets, but once he set sail her position would be precarious. Though she was co-ruler of Fair Isle, Tulkhan's men feared her.

Behind her, the General's commanders vied for position with his Elite Guard. Not so eager, the dignitaries of the township kept a cautious distance. Like Imoshen, they were trapped by their position. During the General's conquest their port had borne the brunt of the invasion. Now they played host to Tulkhan's army while his half-brother brooded across the straits, threatening a spring invasion.

The last of the sun's setting rays illuminated the top of town's-gate tower, leaving the township shrouded in twilight. The General came to a stop, looking down on his army, a sea of upturned faces illuminated by torches in the square below. Seeing him, his men shouted his name, striking their sheathed swords on their shields. *Tulkhan,* clap, clap... *Tulkhan,* clap, clap.

Imoshen gasped, assaulted by a wave of devotion. She could taste the army's hunger to shed blood in Tulkhan's name. Reeling in her T'En senses before she was overwhelmed by the Ghebites' emotion, she focused on the township that spilled down to the harbor. This had been a wealthy, complacent port. The four-story mansions of the merchant aristocracy were built of the same white stone as the Citadel, and the great families strove to outdo one another so that each building was more ornate than the last.

In spring two years ago, the invading Ghebites had ransacked and looted in a frenzy of greed. The inhabitants had fled, only to return and rebuild when the General took Imoshen as his bond-partner. Now they crowded every available balcony and window. Families even perched on the rooftops to witness this historic occasion.

Tulkhan signaled for silence and raised his voice. "Tomorrow we sail across the T'Ronynn Straits to crush my half-brother once and for all!" The General took his infant son from Imoshen's arms, holding the boy so that all could see him. A wail broke from the startled babe. "In crushing Gharavan I ensure Fair Isle for my heir, for all our sons!"

A cheer and then scattered chanting followed. Tulkhan's men picked up the hungry rhythm, making Imoshen shiver. Retrieving Ashmyr, she soothed the fretful baby. "You seem as eager as your men to shed your half-brother's blood!"

"I must destroy Gharavan. He will not rest until he has avenged the insult."

"What insult? He was the one who arrested you on trumped-up charges of treason, forcing you to claim Fair Isle for yourself." She swallowed, her mouth suddenly dry. "You should have killed him when I urged you to!"

Tulkhan tensed. "If I killed so readily, you would not be alive. I would have had your kinsman smothered before he could recover his sorcerous powers!"

Imoshen's heart faltered. "Reothe is no danger."

"For now...No, our greatest threat is my half-brother." Tulkhan indicated the west, where the mainland lay, then smiled wolfishly. "Gharavan has made a fatal mistake. I've learned he is accompanied only by his courtiers and one company of Ghebite soldiers. The mercenaries he hired outnumber his men ten to one, and paid killers can be bought by the highest bidder."

"Is that what you intend to do, buy their loyalty?"

"I may not need to. In all the years that I led the Ghebite army, I lost a few battles but never a war." Tulkhan spoke simply, stating a fact. "There is no profit for the mercenary who fights on the losing side. They will switch allegiance and leave Gharavan defenseless." He sobered. "No, I don't look forward to shedding my half-brother's blood. But tonight we celebrate because, as my old tutor used to say, a battle is fought in the field but a war is won in the hearts and minds of men!"

Something stirred deep within Imoshen. She had to admire Tulkhan's head for strategy, even if it had been the downfall of the T'En.

The General held her gaze, his black eyes impenetrable. "I have no illusions, Imoshen. I leave Fair Isle seething with revolt. My spies tell me the remains of Reothe's rebels are hiding in the hills outside Northpoint. I must ensure my hold on Fair Isle while I am away." He faced his commanders and Elite Guard, drawing his sword and planting it between his feet. "Wharrd?"

The grizzled veteran approached, going down on one knee.

"Until I return victorious, I name you leader of the capital's garrison, answerable only to me."

Wharrd accepted this position, renewing his fealty by kissing the naked blade, as was the Ghebite custom.

"Jarholfe?"

Imoshen recognized the man as one of Tulkhan's Elite Guard, fond of good clothes but deadly with a sword.

"Jarholfe, I name you leader of the Elite Guard who will remain on Fair Isle, sworn to protect me and mine."

Jarholfe accepted the honor and stepped back.

Tulkhan's arm slid around Imoshen's shoulders, drawing her close in what appeared to be a fond embrace. His lips brushed her ear as he whispered, "Kneel and swear fealty before my men."

Anger constricted her throat. "Do you doubt me?"

"Should I?" His eyes narrowed. "Imoshen, I ask my men to risk death. What guarantee do they have you will not reclaim the throne while my back is turned? Swear fealty before them and you will be my Voice while I am gone."

Though she understood the necessity of this oath, it did not make it any easier. She beckoned Kalleen, passing her son into the little woman's arms. "He's tired. Take him to my chamber."

Silence fell as Imoshen knelt before Tulkhan and looked up at him. The General was dressed in full Ghebite armor. His helmet hooded his eyes, his cloak billowed in the stiff sea breeze. The last of the sun's rays had left the tower, and flickering torch flames illuminated the narrow blade of his nose, the line of his jaw. His wide cheekbones were hidden by the helmet guards. Imoshen marveled that she had once thought Tulkhan's Ghebite features harsh.

"T'Imoshen, Lady Protector." He combined her old title with her new. "I name you my Voice. Until I return, your words will be obeyed as mine."

The joy of vindication filled her, for this publicly acknowledged not only Tulkhan's trust in her loyalty but his belief in her statesmanship.

"Protector General." Imoshen pitched her voice to carry. "On behalf of the people of Fair Isle, I thank you for defending our shores." She did not kiss the blade but came to her feet, offering her left hand to Tulkhan, palm out, forearm toward him. He copied the gesture, threading his fingers through hers. Their wrists met, arms joined to the elbow, mimicking the T'En bonding ceremony. "I vow to keep your trust and pray that one day soon our people will sit by their hearths in peace and plenty."

Her words were greeted with a cheer from the Ghebites and polite finger-clicking from the townspeople.

Tulkhan smiled ruefully. Imoshen had worded the oath so that his men heard her vow of fealty but the people of Fair Isle heard their empress thank her war general. "Then let us break open the Vorsch and drink to victory!"

"Yes, but first the people of Fair Isle wish to give your army due honor." She cast him a cat-with-the-cream smile and beckoned a little townswoman. Birdlike, the woman scurried forward with a bundle over her arm. "To you goes the honor of releasing the first star-bird, my general."

The woman's gloved hands produced a cylinder, and she blew on the embers in her coal pouch to bring them to flame.

"The Pyrolate Guild?" Tulkhan recognized this procedure from their coronation celebration on Midwinter's Day, when fountains of light had poured from the palace towers to celebrate the joining of the old royal line to the new. He lit the star-bird's tail and it leapt, rising high to burst, a bright flower of light against the night sky. Sparks of gold rained down upon the Citadel.

On this signal a series of star-birds left the highest tower, lighting up the night sky over and over. His men gave their piercing war cry, and the townspeople murmured in awe.

With a smile of delight, Imoshen linked her arm through his and gestured to the mainland. "I've heard that on a clear day the people of Port Sumair can see the white stone of the Citadel's towers. Tonight your half-brother will see the sky above Fair Isle light up and it will be remembered as an omen of his fall. Let him quake in his bed, for his days are numbered!"

Imoshen inspired him. With her at his side Tulkhan felt anything was possible. Pulling her close, he claimed her lips, savoring her sudden intake of breath. He sensed the moment her quicksilver passion ignited and gloried in the knowledge that the last princess of the T'En was his.

Tulkhan pulled back to gaze down on Imoshen's upturned face. Patterns of sparkling light played across her features. He was not blind to her T'En beauty, but it was her mind and spirit he valued. "Truly, I am a lucky man. If you had been the Empress, I would never have conquered Fair Isle!"

Imoshen stiffened. "Please excuse me, General. I sent Kalleen to put our son to bed. I must see if he has settled."

She would have left him but Tulkhan caught her hand. "Imoshen, I did not mean—"

"In winning Fair Isle you lost your half-brother and your homeland, while I . . ." She could not finish, managing only a sad smile. "Neither of us has won, Tulkhan. But we may yet."

Imoshen paused at the tower door to let her eyes adjust. Then she sped down the steps and entered a passage to the great hall. This part of the Citadel dated from the early Age of Consolidation, but later owners had added gleaming mosaics, mirrors, and gilt. She smiled grimly. Four hundred years of prosperity had done much to hide the gracious lines of the original building.

No servants or guards were present in the public hall. She suspected they had climbed to the parapets and balconies to watch the display. Tables were piled high with food, and crystal glittered in the candlelight awaiting the revelers.

Suddenly, Imoshen's vision was overlaid with laughter and people. She saw herself as a child sitting at the high table, looking lonely and lost. Only she had never been here before.

The T'En girl, probably some distant ancestor, stiffened and looked straight across the room of phantom feasters into Imoshen's eyes. With a shudder, Imoshen slammed a mental door on the vision.

Nausea threatened as she fought for control. She needed Reothe's advice, but all along he had held his knowledge to ransom. Anger curled through her, turning her hands into fists. When she had heard that Reothe had woken weak but clearheaded, she had not been to see him, using the valid excuse that she was needed in the hospice.

Moving on soft, indoor slippers, she entered the passage to the central courtyard, where T'Ronynn's Tower stood and Reothe lay, still too weak to rise.

Light flashed above, illuminating every stone of the courtyard. Little gold sparks fell like rain. Delighted by the beauty, Imoshen held out her hand to catch a spark. It faded before her eyes, and in the sudden dark a man grabbed her. His blade pressed between her ribs.

"Keep walking," her captor growled.

She obeyed the familiar voice, her legs stiff with fear.

"Drake!" It was a relief to identify him, even though she knew Drake served Reothe. "What do you want?"

"I have come to free T'Reothe."

"He cannot be moved."

"I'll be the judge of that. Take me to him."

Recalling Drake's reverence for everything T'En, Imoshen did not believe he would kill her. "There is no need to threaten me. I will take you to T'Reothe. He is my honored guest."

"Don't play word games with me. And do not dream of giving me away. I will slide this knife between your ribs quicker than you can say my name." Hatred laced his words. "I know you for what you are, a traitor to your T'En blood."

Her mouth went dry and a familiar taste settled on her tongue. She fought the urge to use her gifts. Drake was but one man; she had to win the support of all rebels if she was to hold Fair Isle.

"I've been searching for a way to get into the Citadel since you captured Reothe. Unlike you, I would willingly die for him, so do not think to call the guards. Move."

Imoshen walked toward the tower that rose before them solid and windowless on the ground floor. She climbed the steps to the door, positioned so that defenders could resist exposed attackers. This caution did not help her now, not with a knife at her back. "If you serve Reothe, then you serve me, because he is in my service now," she bluffed.

Drake gave no answer.

As they climbed the steps Imoshen considered calling for help from Reothe's guards, but she didn't want Drake to have to prove his loyalty by killing her.

At last they stood outside Reothe's chamber. Every nerve in Imoshen's body screamed in protest. The guards sat opposite, speaking with two of their brothers-at-arms, who were urging them to take a look at the Pyrolate display. The men hardly spared Imoshen and Drake a glance.

"Open the door," Drake hissed.

Before Imoshen could take her door-comb and run its teeth across the door's metal groove to announce herself, the door swung inward, revealing a corner of the canopied bed. But confronting them was Kalleen, possibly the only person in the whole of the Citadel who could identify Drake and knew him for the rebel he was.

Imoshen froze, cursing the trick of fate that had brought Kalleen to Reothe's room. Would she recognize this hardened Drake as the youth who had briefly been her lover a year ago?

"My lady?" Kalleen's smile faltered as she looked past Imoshen to the man behind her. "D-Drake?"

He cursed.

"What are you doing here? I heard—"

He lunged. Imoshen saw the knife flash. Kalleen's cry was cut short by the impact of his strike. Too late to save Kalleen, a useless scream of protest tore from Imoshen's throat.

Drake darted into the room. The guards exclaimed and their chairs scraped on the floor. Kalleen's small body hit the doorjamb. She slid to the floor, her skirt belling around her, the rich brocade stiffer than her limbs.

Imoshen dropped to her knees, horrified to see pink bubbles dripping from Kalleen's chin. A knee thumped into Imoshen's back as men charged through the doorway, but she felt no pain. From the angle, it appeared the knife had plunged between Kalleen's ribs, carrying with it all Drake's anger and frustration. Guilt lanced Imoshen.

"I'm dying." Kalleen's words frothed on her lips.

"No." Imoshen's denial was instinctive. She used the hem of her gown to wipe the blood from Kalleen's face. Once, when Reothe had dealt Tulkhan a mortal wound, she had saved him by drawing on the General's own willpower. "Think of the child you carry. That life depends on you!"

Beyond Kalleen, Imoshen was aware of struggling men, smashing crockery, grunts of pain, and hoarse shouts. She ignored the turmoil.

Bending over Kalleen, she willed her to believe. "You are stronger than you think. Trust me."

Kalleen's eyes fixed on Imoshen's face. She nodded, but

when she coughed her fingers tightened, the nails biting into Imoshen's flesh.

A man's death scream made Imoshen flinch.

Shutting everything out, she sought the familiar source of her healing gift. Somehow she must stem Kalleen's blood loss, repair the torn tissue, and ward off festering. But anger swamped her senses. Its source was the life-and-death struggle unfolding across the room. Imoshen felt that energy's primal force pool within her. It rose, flooding through the pores of her skin, almost beyond her control to channel. The origin of this power was a death struggle, but she would turn its purpose, using it to save Kalleen's life.

Desperation lent Imoshen the strength to focus the power and channel it into healing. Kalleen's hazel eyes widened.

"We have him, my lady," a man bellowed.

Imoshen ignored him.

"He killed—"

"Silence!" Imoshen concentrated on willing the knife to slide from its resting place between Kalleen's ribs. The effort required to knit the tissues behind the withdrawing blade caused beads of perspiration to gather on her forehead, stinging her eyes.

Dimly, she heard the man call on his warrior god to protect them from sorcery. Imoshen clenched her teeth. Kalleen's eyes never left her face, her fingers never eased their clawlike grip. When the knife fell onto the stiff brocade of the gown, Imoshen grabbed the blade and slit the bodice of Kalleen's gown, dragging it apart to reveal her small golden breasts and the bloodied flesh where the knife had penetrated.

Imoshen leaned forward, only just stopping herself from licking the wound clean. Instead, she tossed the knife aside and slid her fingers over the flesh.

"Bring water." She hardly recognized her own voice.

The man stumbled away and returned with a pitcher.

"Pour a little over the wound." Imoshen used the hem of her gown to wipe the blood away, revealing a fresh scar.

"Great Akha Khan deliver—" The man's curse was cut

short as the pitcher smashed at his feet. Water sprayed them. A pottery fragment stung Imoshen's cheek.

Kalleen's gasp had barely left her lips when Imoshen swept one arm under the little woman's knees and the other under her shoulders. As she stood, the muscles of her thighs flexed, empowered by anger.

"Fool!" She spun to face the man, with Kalleen in her arms. "Take the Lady Kalleen to her bedchamber and send for Wharrd."

The man's features flushed with something that could have been anger or shame. As he extended his arms to accept the burden, Kalleen's mouth opened in a protest.

"Sleep and heal," Imoshen whispered, touching the sixth finger of her left hand to Kalleen's forehead. Her eyes closed and the tight contours of pain eased. "Go now."

The same fury that had enabled Imoshen to rise with Kalleen in her arms drove her into the room. Two men held Drake on his knees, his wrists twisted up behind his shoulders. He glared at her.

The fourth man lay in a puddle of dark blood, unmoving. There was nothing she could do for him.

Disgust filled Imoshen. "Death dealt in the name of honor. Is this what you want for Fair Isle, Drake?"

Winding her fingers through his hair, she hauled him across to the bed, freeing him from the guards. "Here is your rebel leader." She snatched the sword from the nearest man and flung the weapon so that it lay across Reothe's chest. "Rise up and strike down your captors, T'Reothe!"

On reflex, one of Reothe's hands closed on the hilt, but he did not have the strength to lift the blade, let alone rise.

"You are cruel, Imoshen!" Reothe thrust the weapon off the bed in disgust. It clattered on the floor at their feet.

"Are you satisfied, Drake?" Imoshen demanded.

"Order your dogs to kill me, T'En traitor!"

Dismayed that he still courted death, Imoshen faltered. Drake wrenched free. Snatching the sword, he reared up. With dreamlike slowness she watched the sword point arc toward her throat. One clean slice and she would be dead.

Something snapped inside her head. She saw nothing, heard nothing but the rush of blood in her ears. A pole struck between her shoulder blades, driving the air from her chest. Her head hit the upright at the bed's base, jarring her teeth and filling her sight with pinpricks of light.

Chest burning, she fought to drag in a breath. She had sprung backward the length of the bed to escape Drake's strike. He knelt before her, sword hanging from his limp fingers. As she watched, a great gout of blood erupted from his mouth, spraying across her skirt.

One of the men must have stabbed him in the back. But they were too far away and staggering backward.

Imoshen drew a painful breath and stepped around Drake. His back was free of injury.

Reothe hung half off the bed, supporting himself with one trembling arm. "Help . . ."

"What goes on here?" Tulkhan demanded, thrusting his men aside as he strode into the room.

Imoshen could not speak.

Reothe's expression was an odd mixture of wariness and admiration. "Imoshen turned her gift on Drake, just as she turned it on me."

"No!" she protested.

"No?" Reothe mocked. "He has no visible wound."

She shook her head, but even as she denied it, Drake collapsed.

Tulkhan cursed. His expression made her turn and run for the sanctuary of her room, overwhelmed by the discovery that her healing gift was a two-edged sword, as capable of tearing flesh as closing it.

She threw open the door, startling an old woman who was changing the bedding. Imoshen tore at the fastening of her stained gown and flung it into the fire. Ashmyr woke with a cry. She longed for the balm of his touch. "Bring me the baby, Dyta."

Feeling unsteady, Imoshen backed away from the hearth until her thighs met the bed. She sat abruptly, recalling the guard's expression as she put Kalleen in his arms, the way his companions had fled from her. She hadn't meant to cripple Drake. It had been self-defense, but that would not stop the rumors. In a few heartbeats she had undone all the good she had achieved at Tulkhan's side these last few days.

She opened her eyes to find Dyta watching fearfully. "Bring me a damp cloth."

The old woman scurried to obey.

"Help me sponge the blood from my hands." But it remained under her fingernails. A rush of despair flooded Imoshen. In her mind's eye she saw Reothe's expression. Yet unlike Reothe, who coveted her growing powers, General Tulkhan feared her T'En legacy. But the gifts were nothing more than a tool. Tears of determination stung Imoshen's eyes as she silently vowed to use her powers only for good.

Tulkhan stepped aside as, with due solemnity, the guards removed the body of their dead brother-at-arms. Then he faced the man he had been avoiding.

"Why don't you kill me?" Reothe demanded.

"You insult me, Dhamfeer." He made the Ghebite word an insult. "Do you think me some crude barbarian who would kill his sworn enemy as he lay helpless?"

Reothe lifted his head to glare, then winced. His hands spasmed; one clenched in a fist, but the other twitched feebly. So it was true—one half of his body was crippled, as well as his T'En gifts. And Imoshen had done this to the man whose power she had feared.

"She cripples me, despises me, yet she keeps me alive," Reothe whispered. "Cruel love."

"You assume much," Tulkhan said, but Reothe's suffering struck a reluctant chord with him.

"May the Parakletos feast on that Vaygharian's soul," Reothe cursed. His thoughts followed another path. "I should never have trusted him to be Gharavan's go-between!"

Tulkhan shuddered. Reothe's curse was intrinsically T'En. The Parakletos were legendary T'En warriors, bound by a terrible oath to serve beyond death. They answered the priests' summons to escort the dead through death's shadow to the realm of the dead. Yet, like everything else on Fair Isle, the truth was not so simple.

Several moons ago Tulkhan had stood at Imoshen's side as she said the words for the dead, unaware that she risked her own soul if her hold on the Parakletos faltered. She had revealed that the Parakletos were not the benign creatures of legend. No, Reothe was not wishing the Vaygharian's soul a safe journey. "For all I know, the Parakletos have feasted on his soul," said Tulkhan. "No one has claimed responsibility for his death. His charred remains were found in the fire's ashes, as Imoshen foretold."

Reothe gave Tulkhan a sharp look, reminding him that the rebel leader might be physically crippled and his powers destroyed, but he still had his wits.

Imoshen stood over the sleeping baby, exhaustion battling with her need to know how Drake and Kalleen fared. After Dyta left, no one had come near her, but she had heard them whispering in the hall long into the night. Suddenly the door flew open and the General stalked in.

Tulkhan studied Imoshen. Blue shadows haunted her pale skin, and her eyes held a lambent glow as though she was consumed by an inner furnace. He hated seeing her so fragile. "I will order the rebel executed at dawn and his head spiked on town's-gate tower."

"That is sure to convince the rebels to support you."

"You can't be suggesting I let him live?" But she gave no answer, rubbing her temples. Remorse pierced him. He knew how healing exhausted her. "You saved Kalleen's life."

"And terrified your men, I fear."

"You could have helped Drake escape with Reothe. You could have betrayed me."

Startled, she met his eyes, and he knew this had not occurred to her.

"Ah, Imoshen." He opened his arms and she went to

him. Fine trembles ran through her body, reminding him of a highly strung horse.

Her lips moved against his neck as she spoke, her breath hot on his skin. "Drake went for my throat. My reaction was instinctive."

"What else is instinctive for the T'En?"

She pulled away from him, distressed. "Truly, Tulkhan, I don't know. My family forbade my instruction. They tried to deny their Throwback daughter, when all the world could see..." She lifted her hands to her face.

Tulkhan had once found her vivid coloring, high cheekbones, and narrow features strange. Now he thought Imoshen as exquisite as Fair Isle porcelain, which was prized on the mainland and whose manufacture was a closely guarded secret. This island contained too many secrets. He expelled his breath in frustration. "I'm running out of time. Even now my carpenters work by lantern light to fit catapults to the merchant ships. Soon it will be the Harvest Moon Festival and—"

"It will be just over a year since you entered my Stronghold," she whispered. "Since we..." She flushed, and he was reminded of the first joining in the Harvest bower when he had claimed her for his own.

His mouth went dry. "I was going to talk tactics. But why waste my last night before I go into battle?" When he went to pull her close, she resisted. "What is it?"

"You could die confronting Gharavan." She searched his face. "There is a lie between us, and I will not perpetuate it. Each time you've come to me you've been almost"—she quivered—"fierce. I feel no gentleness in your touch. I don't understand. Not once have you mentioned Reothe—"

He released her, prowling away.

Imoshen watched Tulkhan's restless pacing, torn by the need to know and the fear of what she might learn. "I don't understand, General. You have not asked me how it happened."

He spun to face her. "You have already admitted it is true. By taking him to your bed you dishonored us both. At least now if you carry a child there is a good chance it will be mine!"

She gasped, her hand going protectively to her belly.

His eyes narrowed. "I let myself believe . . . But it is different for the women of Fair Isle. You are trained in the arts of lovemaking. You told me the moment you knew my son was conceived." Suddenly he looked drained. "When Reothe boasted that you carried his child, it was already true. Wasn't it?"

She could not deny it.

"By Ghebite law I should strangle you and my half-breed son!"

Tulkhan's explosive anger frightened Imoshen into revealing the truth. "Reothe tricked me! I did not knowingly betray you. He came to me in your form, and I thought it was you I welcomed to my bed." Her voice dropped. "I did not tell you before because I feared your anger would drive you to kill him!"

"I knew it! I knew it had to be trickery." Tulkhan sank into the chair by the fireplace. "It makes no difference. By Ghebite law you are in the wrong—"

"But I thought he was you."

"That is of no consequence."

"What kind of justice makes the injured person guilty?"

He smiled wryly. "Trust you to see it that way."

Fury kindled in Imoshen but she forced it down, placing her left hand over her heart. "I swear I have never knowingly betrayed you, Tulkhan. Do not be hampered by the boundaries of your upbringing."

"Boundaries don't blind my thinking, Imoshen, but my men are simple soldiers. To lead I must have their respect. Do you think if I truly doubted you I would have made Wharrd and Jarholfe answerable to you when I set sail tomorrow?"

She went to him, her bare feet registering the warmth of the carpet before the hearth. Sinking to her knees, she took his hand in hers. He was leaving to go into battle and she longed to join with him. "If you trust me, why do you come to my bed with anger in your heart?"

He made a helpless gesture. In that instant his barriers were down and she sensed his most private of primitive emotions. She had been stolen from him. Every time they made love he was reclaiming what was his.

"Ah, Tulkhan." She smiled. "You say you are free of your Ghebite upbringing, but I fear it runs deeper than you think."

He opened his mouth to argue, then withdrew his hand, eyeing her thoughtfully.

"What?" Imoshen prompted.

"How can you speak to me of being shaped by my upbringing when you are shaped by your blood? You gave your solemn promise not to use your gifts on me. Yet what did you just do?"

"That was not . . . I mean . . ." She felt herself color and saw his knowing look. "It was not intentional. We were touching and it just . . . happened."

"How convenient."

She found anger in his face, but she also caught a glint of humor and realized he was teasing her. Her heart turned over. Slowly she stood up, offering her hand. "No man can take what I do not give, Tulkhan."

His fingers entwined with hers. But he resisted when she would have led him to the bed. He cleared his throat. "I will take you into my arms but not into my mind. That is how it must be, Imoshen."

"Then I must be satisfied with that." But in her heart of hearts she resented his rejection.

Three

IMOSHEN WOKE TO the golden light of late afternoon. She stretched, surprised to discover she had slept through most of the day. But, then, she had fallen asleep only at dawn when Tulkhan left her bed.

Ashmyr stirred. He might as well have been pure T'En; only his sable hair marked him as Tulkhan's son. She smiled fondly as his mouth worked, sucking in his sleep.

A figure detached itself from the shadows near the door. Imoshen tensed, then she recognized Wharrd. The bone-setter stepped into the light, his expression curiously guarded.

"Where's Tulkhan?" Her voice was rusty from lack of use.

"On the wharves. He sent me to bring you."

Her heart sank. She knew Tulkhan must go, but she dreaded their parting. She felt empty, cast adrift. Resolutely, she fought it. "I will get dressed."

"First hear me out. You saved Kalleen's life. Kalleen is my wife, but I love her as I would love my sword-brother. If he were killed, I would avenge his death. If someone saved his life, I would be under a Ghiad until I had repaid them with an equal service." Wharrd gave a Ghebite salute that she did not recognize. "By the Gheeakhan, warrior code of the Ghebites, I am under a Ghiad to you."

Imoshen hid her annoyance. Wharrd claimed he valued Kalleen as highly as he would value his sword-brother, yet he meant no insult. "Then I release you from your Ghiad."

"You can't release me. My honor must be satisfied."

She shrugged, not about to argue further.

"The rebel Drake still lives," Wharrd announced. "When do you want him executed?"

"I don't want him executed. Not everything can be resolved by killing. Fair Isle needs unity. I must win the rebels to our cause."

"But Drake invaded the Stronghold, threatened your life, spilled Kalleen's blood, and killed a Ghebite. You must—"

"I will not kill him. Would you have this go on forever? A life for a life until no one lives?" A thought occurred to her. "Is it this way in Gheeaba? A life for a life?"

He nodded. "A man must seek revenge or be thought weak."

"Sometimes it takes more strength to forgive."

Wharrd did not look convinced. "What will you do with him?"

She didn't know. "See that his hurts are tended. I must go to the General."

Tulkhan paced the docks, impatient to confront his half-brother. Much had been achieved since he turned the tables on Reothe. The mercenaries who would have been exchanged for Tulkhan had been escorted to the army's encampment outside of town, where their leader had been quick to see reason. Dying for profit was one thing—dying without profit was unthinkable.

Every fishing boat and seaworthy skiff within a day's ride had been commandeered. The carpenters had completed the merchant ships' modifications; their main concern had been securing the catapults so they would not come loose in rough weather.

When the little hairs on Tulkhan's neck lifted, he knew that Imoshen approached. She had sworn not to use her gifts on him, and he believed she did not consciously do so, but surely this intensity was not normal. If he was under some kind of T'En compulsion, he hoped it would fade with time and distance. Then he would know how things really stood between them.

Hugging her cloak around Ashmyr, Imoshen stood on the wharf, watching Tulkhan's profile. She knew he was aware of her.

As the Ghebites embarked, she swore she could see the boats sink plank by plank. Torches blazed and firelight danced on the sea's black surface. Filing past, the men sang rousing war songs.

Imoshen studied the sky. The season was about to turn and autumn would be all too brief. Soon winter snows would blanket the ground and make fighting impossible. The General did not have long if he wanted to destroy King Gharavan and incite the repressed countries to revolt against Ghebite domination.

Since he became war general at nineteen, Tulkhan had consolidated the conquests of his father and grandfather, subjugating most of the known world. Imoshen smiled grimly. It would be ironic if Tulkhan was the one to drive the Ghebites back to the far north.

The call of the battle horns startled her. The tide was turning, the wind was right. She turned to Tulkhan.

As he strode toward her, she was reminded of their first meeting, when he had appeared in full battle regalia, alien and unknown. His unusual height was emphasized by the plume of his helmet. His black temple plaits swung as he walked, his long hair lifting around his shoulders.

Once she had thought his barbarian display ostentatious; now longing claimed her. She was bound to him in ways that went deeper than words. "Strike swiftly, return safely."

His hands closed on her shoulders. As he searched her face she wondered what he looked for.

"If I am killed while crushing my half-brother, you will have it all: Fair Isle, your crippled consort, and what's left of my army."

"How can you say that?" It was a cry from her heart. "Besides, the remaining Ghebites are loyal to you, not me."

"Ultimately, self-interest must motivate my men. None

of us can return to Gheeaba. What will you do? Go to the palace?"

"When Reothe is better we will go slowly, stopping along the way so the people can see that Reothe is under my protection. Only strength will unite Fair Isle, we—"

"Since Gharavan declared me a traitor, my life is forfeit on the mainland. Any man may take my head for the bounty."

"I did not know."

He smiled. "I did not want you to know."

"Oh, Tulkhan!" It was on the tip of her tongue to beg him to stay.

"You hold my life in your hands, Imoshen. Fair Isle is the only home I have. Do not betray my trust." He gave her no time to reply. "Reothe's gifts might be crippled, but he still has his wits. Beware his honeyed tongue."

She nodded, unable to speak.

Tulkhan raised an arm to acknowledge the townsfolk. "Smile for your people, Imoshen."

Lifting her chin, she waved, but she could see little through a veil of tears. Then Tulkhan saluted his men, his teeth very white against his skin. Flinging one arm around his neck, she lifted onto her toes to kiss him, felt his surprise and then the heat of his response. A soul-deep stab of need pierced her. "Think of me."

He pressed her hand to his heart and with great reluctance stepped away.

Alone on the wharf, she watched the General stride toward his ship. The gangplank bounced under his weight. The sailors shouted and withdrew the board. Ropes writhed across the growing chasm of roiling black water. Torches diminished, and all she saw was Tulkhan's masklike face, eyes fixed on her as if he was memorizing her features.

As his form grew ever smaller, Imoshen felt as if a long cord connected them, straining to stretch the distance, sucking her soul from her with painful intensity. A part of her was leaving, and she did not know if she would ever be whole again.

As Tulkhan paced the command ship's deck in the predawn chill, mist lay thick on the water.

"There it is, General—the beacon fire. I knew they'd have the tower lit in weather like this." Kornel pointed, then adjusted the belt of his trousers to sit comfortably below his belly. As a merchant ship's captain, he ate well and took few risks.

Tulkhan nodded. His makeshift flotilla of fishing boats and commandeered merchant ships had to negotiate the harbor entrance safely under cover of the mist, yet their signal bells might betray their presence. He cursed softly. He had campaigned on land for eleven years and knew little about coordinating an attack from the sea, but if all went well he would not have to. "Send for the mercenary leader Tourez."

Tulkhan had dealt with Vaygharian mercenaries before, and he was willing to risk the element of surprise to send Tourez ahead with his offer. The lives of his mercenary band back in Fair Isle were held as surety for his cooperation. They waited in tense silence as the ships negotiated the sandbars and floating islands, their bells dulled to cloak their arrival. They entered Port Sumair's harbor unable to see the famous sculpture of the merchant scales for the mist.

As the mercenary approached, Tulkhan slipped the message cylinder from his pouch. "Once we are inside the harbor you'll be rowed to the wharves. Under cover of this fog we will sit near the docks until the rising sun starts to burn off the mists. Then we will strike. If the mercenaries deliver Gharavan, I will reward them; if not, I'll treat them as loyal Ghebite soldiers and slaughter them to a man."

Tourez nodded. A boat was lowered for the mercenary leader, and the soft sound of its oars could be heard. Then that faded and Tulkhan could only wait.

Imoshen stood at the window, watching stars in the western sky grow dim. She wondered if Tulkhan had struck yet and longed to reach out to him, but her skills had never been good enough to pierce his defenses even if they were touching, let alone over the T'Ronynn Straits.

If he had let her touch his mind when their bodies joined, she might have felt closer, might even have been able to sense if he was in danger, perhaps reach him in an emergency, but he had always rejected her gifts. Resentment burned in Imoshen, yet she could not blame Tulkhan when she recalled how Reothe had used his gifts to trick her. She did not need Tulkhan's warning to beware of Reothe.

The General gazed into the east where the peaks of Fair Isle lay hidden by the dawn haze and wondered if Imoshen slept blissfully unaware of him. He had been sure the Vaygharian mercenaries would change allegiance. But Tourez had not returned.

Tulkhan stepped forward to order the attack. Buzzing like an angry bee, an arrow sailed past his ear to thud into the mast. He stared in disbelief at the mercenary who was already notching another arrow, one leg over the ship's rail. The man's sword-brothers appeared, knives between their teeth.

Tulkhan cursed, throwing his dagger. The archer let his second arrow loose prematurely and fell back, clutching his side. His cry and the following splash heralded the attack. Stealth discarded, the mercenaries boarded. Cries of battle came from the other boats. With a jolt, Tulkhan realized Tourez had not only betrayed him but also his own men back in Northpoint.

A man charged. Tulkhan blocked the strike, countering automatically. All about him he heard the screech of metal on metal, grunts of pain, agonized screams. His boots slipped on the blood-slick planks. Furious, he fought his way to the catapult, but the mercenaries had already disabled it.

Dislodging his weapon from a man's spine, Tulkhan looked up and saw the silhouettes of bowmen on Port Sumair's rooftops, ready to strike as soon as the mist cleared. That was all he needed—flaming, tar-dipped arrows.

Tulkhan hauled the ship's captain aside. For a merchant who lived the good life, he wielded a sword efficiently. "Up anchor, Kornel."

Tulkhan sounded the horn, signaling retreat, then fought his way to the mast to free the sails. The ship's oarsmen were too busy fighting for their lives. The sails bellied down and the growing dawn breeze filled the canvas. Imperceptibly at first, the ship gathered momentum. To Tulkhan's relief, the other great merchant ships also spread their sails.

Shouts then screams rent the air as two merchant ships rode dangerously close. Tulkhan ran to the side, watching helplessly as his ships crushed a small skiff.

Anger drove him across the deck into the mercenaries. They fell back, and the tenure of the fighting changed as they realized they were about to be carried from the harbor. On an unseen signal the mercenaries sheathed their weapons and leapt overboard. It was what Tulkhan expected. Only a zealot fought to the death.

But the ships turned ponderously, and there were still the sandbars to negotiate. Burning arrows hit the decks and sails. Men abandoned weapons to drown the flames and throw bodies overboard. Tulkhan saw a fishing boat burning unhindered to the waterline.

When cheering broke from the observers on the docks, fury consumed Tulkhan. Dousing his head in a pitcher of water, he shook the droplets from his skin, shoved the damp hair from his face, and turned to assess their situation.

A sailor threw a bucket of seawater across the deck, sending entrails sliding like foam on a wave's crest. Tulkhan strode to the captain at the helm. "We'll go over the Seawall and come at them across land."

"Can't be done. These ships can't get in close enough."

"We'll lower the boats and row in."

"Can't be done in these numbers. We'd churn up the mud, be stuck like beached whales."

"Then where is the nearest harbor?"

"All the Low-land harbors are defended. But there is another way to get at Port Sumair. A way they wouldn't expect." The captain glanced at Tulkhan, his features defined by cunning.

The General felt a surge of interest. That was the

calculating look of a man who lived by his wits. Perhaps Kornel's ample belly was a recent acquisition. "Go on."

"It is difficult, but not impossible. I did it before I commanded ships this size. You'd have to use the small vessels."

"That's good. The merchant ships could blockade the port, misleading them about our intentions," Tulkhan muttered, thinking aloud. His spirits lifted. He had learned to surround himself with men who had local knowledge, and he knew how to heed advice. "Tell me more."

As the ship left the harbor and took a bearing northeast, Tulkhan saw the sun break over the peaks of Fair Isle. He was not going back to Imoshen until victory was his.

Four

IMOSHEN EXPECTED NEWS of Tulkhan with the following dawn's tide, but the new day brought no news, and when the late tide arrived with no message, Imoshen felt the mood of Northpoint change. From the candle trimmer to the harbormaster, cautious optimism was replaced with growing concern. She hugged Ashmyr closer.

As Imoshen approached T'Ronynn's Tower, a servant's gesture reminded her of Selita, the rebel who had been her maid while Reothe had her imprisoned. On impulse, Imoshen called, "Selita?"

The girl responded instinctively to her name.

Silently, Imoshen beckoned. Selita cast one desperate glance around the bustling courtyard, then followed her up the tower's steps.

"What are you doing here?" Imoshen whispered. After Drake's attempt to free Reothe, Tulkhan's men were eager to avenge their comrade's death.

Selita stiffened. "I am ready to die for Reothe!"

"Dying is easy. It is living that's hard!" Imoshen chewed her bottom lip. She had discussed nothing of importance with Reothe, at first because he was so ill, later because she was careful never to be alone with him. The last she had heard, the nobles of the Keldon Highlands were ready to rise up in rebellion. She came to a snap decision. "As it happens, Reothe does have a task for you. He wants you to carry a message to his supporters."

The girl looked skeptical.

"I haven't called my guards to arrest you, have I?"

"I would hear this from Reothe's own lips."

"Very well. We shall go to him." Imoshen strode up the circular stairs with Selita at her side.

Acknowledging the guards, Imoshen motioned the girl into Reothe's room and closed the heavy door. "I bring you a visitor, kinsman."

As Reothe struggled to lift his head, Selita ran to the bedside and fell to her knees with a sob. "My T'En lord, your beautiful eyes!"

"Selita, you'll get yourself killed," Reothe rebuked.

"I have explained that we decided to call off the Keldon uprising because Fair Isle cannot afford civil war while Tulkhan is on the mainland," Imoshen bluffed desperately. "But Selita wants to hear the orders from your own lips before she carries your message to Woodvine of the Keld." Holding Reothe's gaze, Imoshen prayed he would rise above personal ambition and consider Fair Isle's fate. "I am here to write your message."

A rueful smile tugged at Reothe's lips. "I heard how Woodvine refused to call you Empress because you had not earned that title. She does not know you as I do." He sighed. "You are right, Imoshen, we cannot have civil war."

Relieved, she went to the desk and selected paper, flicking the excess ink off the scriber. After a moment Reothe began to dictate a letter to the iron-haired matriarch of the Keldon nobles. Imoshen wrote swiftly. Finally she sanded the paper, blowing off the excess.

"What if the Lady Woodvine does not believe they are truly your words?" Selita asked, still kneeling by Reothe's bed.

"Tell her to go to my grandfather, Lord Athlyng, and tell him it was Reothe, not his cousin Murgon, who spilled ink on the map of the mainland and, for this, Reothe begs his pardon."

"Satisfied, Selita?" Imoshen asked, thinking it was

strange the paths their lives took. Murgon was now a high-ranking church official, leader of the Tractarians, who were trained to hunt down rogue T'En.

She held the candle over the folded message until a pool of wax formed, then went to Reothe, who pressed the tip of his left hand's sixth finger in the wax.

Imoshen held it to the light. "So it is true—only the T'En have the double spiral."

He laughed. "Ever the scholar. And if you were to compare ours they would differ. When there were more of us we were taught to recognize the patterns at a glance."

A sense of loss overwhelmed Imoshen. The mysteries of the T'En were her heritage, but Reothe had hidden the T'Elegos, the history her namesake, Imoshen the First, had written the autumn before she died.

"From my hand, to yours, to Lady Woodvine's." As Imoshen gave Selita the sealed missive, there was a knock at the door.

"Ghebites!" Selita hid the message.

Imoshen placed a calming hand on her arm. "Yes?"

A guard opened the door. "Lord Commander Wharrd awaits you, Lady Protector."

"Very well," Imoshen said. "Come, Selita."

Imoshen walked the girl from the room, turning to the guard. "Provide a safe escort for my servant. She is returning to her family for the birth of her sister's child." Imoshen saw the man's eyes glaze over and smiled to herself. The Ghebites' lack of interest in anything that belonged to the "female" world made them easy to manipulate.

Imoshen held Selita's eyes. "The fate of one individual, no matter how dear to us, does not compare to the fate of our people."

When Selita had gone, Imoshen went upstairs to her chamber, where she found Wharrd waiting before the fireplace. She crossed the room to place Ashmyr in his basket. "Send a ship to Port Sumair. I must know how it goes with Tulkhan. Defeat I can deal with, but this silence..."

Wharrd nodded, gave the salute he would have given his general, and departed.

Thinking of the T'Elegos had reminded Imoshen of Reothe's bonding gift. She wedged a chair against the door, then opened her chest, taking out the T'Enchiridion. This was her great-aunt's volume, worn by her many years' service to the church. On her hundredth birthday her great-aunt had been given the title of *Aayel* in recognition for that service. When Imoshen was a child, the Aayel had made her memorize the prayers for the dead and the newborn. But this copy of the T'Enchiridion contained more.

Imoshen's heart thudded as she eased her fingers inside the book's back cover, sliding out a slender, scuffed volume.

At risk to his own life, Reothe had come to her on the day they had planned to bond, the anniversary of her eighteenth birthing day. And even though she had broken her vows to him, he had given her this. She should not have accepted it, but...

Imoshen stroked the embossing on the kidskin cover. *T'Endomaz*. The T'En book of Lore. Opening the book to the title page, she read the childlike script. *T'Ashmyr*. Her son, Ashmyr, was named after the greatest Throwback T'En emperor of the Age of Tribulation. During those turbulent years, Fair Isle had needed a warrior emperor. She hoped she had not foretold her son's future.

If this book belonged to T'Ashmyr himself, it was five hundred years old and should have been redolent with great age. But when she flexed her T'En senses there was no trace of time. Someone had wiped the book clean. This convinced Imoshen that she held an artifact dating from the first hundred years of settlement. She closed her eyes and concentrated on what her fingers told her. The book's fine kidskin cover was worn in six places by the fingertips of many T'En hands.

Anger coursed through her. She was heir to the knowledge the T'Endomaz contained, yet she could not read it because the contents were encrypted. The T'Elegos had to contain the key, but Reothe would not reveal where he had hidden it. Tulkhan was right—she could not trust him.

As the General's small skiff pulled away, he looked up at the merchant ship riding tall above the waves. Its sails glowed in the sunset while Tulkhan and his craft were already in twilight. It seemed symbolic of their separate tasks. Peirs was to return and blockade the port with the three merchant ships.

The remaining fishing vessels and small skiffs, heavily laden with men and supplies, were to follow Kornel upriver through the marshes to a village where they would force one of the marsh-dwellers to show them the safe path to the Marsh-wall. Beyond that wall lay the reclaimed Low-lands, ripe and unready for battle. Tulkhan intended to force-march his men across the plain and attack Port Sumair's landward gate while its defenders were watching the sea. But if he couldn't get his men across the marshlands and into position to attack Sumair at the agreed time, Peirs's sea attack would be a slaughter.

The skiff nudged a larger fishing vessel, and eager arms extended to haul up Tulkhan and his crew. Now his flagship was a fishing trawler with no cabin and a shallow keel, which, according to Kornel, would carry them deep into the marshlands before they had to abandon it. Without the captain's local knowledge, Tulkhan could not hope to spearhead an attack through the supposedly impenetrable marshlands. But he had not told Imoshen this. His message to Imoshen merely informed her of his intention to blockade Port Sumair and ordered the mercenary troop's execution.

Ducking the low beam of the sail, Tulkhan strode to the bow to join Kornel. His odd fleet was already moving into the mouth of the river, the sails reflecting the moonlight now that the last of the sun's rays had faded from the sky.

He had been warned there would be times when they would have to carry the boats across sandbanks. Strange— the trees had not looked so tall and menacing when he had stood on the merchant ship's desk. Then the marshlands had spread out before him like a tapestry laced with gold thread as the setting sun gilded the many small pools and waterways. And edging those sinuous river paths were the saltwater trees of the Low-lands. They hung broodingly over the river's banks, marching boldly into the water itself.

"We're making good time," Kornel observed.

A sailor gave them their evening meal: two chunks of salted meat and wine. Gnawing on the tough flesh, Tulkhan noticed something moving on the far bank. "What's that?"

The captain beckoned a man to the rudder and took a lantern to the side of the boat. Tulkhan joined him. It was hard to distinguish anything, just a blur of trunks.

"Look for their eyes. They reflect the light. The narcts are the reason we couldn't risk getting stuck in the mud near the Sea-wall."

"Seagoing predators?"

"They hunt them out of the port. But here . . . watch this." Kornel tossed the remains of his meat over the side. It fell halfway between the ship and the tree line. Before it hit the water, things slithered out from the cover of the trees, plowing through the river, their wakes glowing in the moonlight.

The creatures converged on the meat. Jaws flashed, teeth gleamed. The snap and crunch as they fought was sickening.

Tulkhan grunted. "Greedy beasts, these narcts."

He tossed his bone overboard. A protest died on Kornel's lips. A series of barks sounded up and down the riverbank.

"They sound like dogs and they're just clever enough to hunt in packs. One narct couldn't bring a man down on dry land, but in the water it's another matter, and when you get a hunting pack . . ." Kornel spat.

Tulkhan watched as the frenzy of feeding slipped behind them, disappearing in their wake, but the barking of the narcts echoed up and down the river. Any carrying of boats across sandbanks would be fraught with danger.

Imoshen nursed Ashmyr as she read Tulkhan's message. Four long days had elapsed since the General attacked Port Sumair. Before Wharrd could find a seaworthy craft to make the crossing, a small fishing skiff had arrived with a hasty note scribbled in the General's own hand. After failing to take the port, Tulkhan set up a blockade. This did not surprise Imoshen. She had known that he would not return until he could claim victory. It was his order to execute the mercenaries that worried her. She met Wharrd's eyes. "By now all of Northpoint will know I have heard from the General and they'll have guessed the worst. The mercenaries will be sharpening their weapons."

"They were held as surety. Their lives are forfeit."

Imoshen laughed. "You speak as if they will simply put down their arms and march to their deaths at the hands of my people." She did not want to sacrifice her people in a bloodbath. Perhaps something could be salvaged from this. "Send for the town officials, the merchant leaders, the guild-masters, and the new leader of the mercenaries. I will see them in the public hall."

When Imoshen walked into the Citadel's great hall it was so closely packed she could not see the mosaic floor tiles. With Kalleen at her heels carrying her son, she made her way to the dais, stepping into a growing well of silent expectation.

Imoshen raised her voice. "Sumair did not fall to a frontal attack. The Protector General has blockaded the port. But do not despair; tell your families and friends that in the eleven years General Tulkhan led his army, no fortified town ever withstood him. It is only a matter of time before Sumair falls and King Gharavan is captured."

A wave of comment greeted her words. The harbor-master approached Imoshen, bristling with indignation. "We thought victory was certain. What went wrong?"

"The mercenary leader revealed General Tulkhan's attack to the defenders at Port Sumair." Imoshen beckoned the new leader. "Step forward, Lightfoot."

He wore the serviceable boots, breeches, and jerkin of his mercenary trade, his weapons better cared for than his garments. His sun-lined features reminded Imoshen of the veterans Wharrd and Peirs. Good. If he had survived this long in his profession, he would not be hotheaded. Like many of the mainlanders, he would not meet her eyes, but this time the Dhamfeer tales served her purpose. Let him fear her.

"Tourez betrayed your mercenary troop." As Imoshen spoke, the crowd renewed its angry muttering. "In doing this he forfeited your lives."

Lightfoot's mouth thinned but he did not argue.

"General Tulkhan lays siege to Sumair while Tourez shelters within its walls. By rights I should honor the General's agreement and have you all executed."

A muscle jumped in Lightfoot's jaw.

"But I seek a practical solution that is fair to everyone. I assume Tourez's actions negate the validity of any contract he negotiated on your behalf?" Imoshen asked.

"What?" He was startled by her change of subject.

"This leaves you free to negotiate a new contract of hire. Am I right?" Imoshen asked, watching him closely. Within a heartbeat she saw his leap of understanding. He wanted an honorable, bloodless solution as much as she did, and he wanted revenge on the leader who had betrayed him. "While I could order the execution of your troop, I am sure your men would sell their lives dearly, and I see no point in shedding their blood or that of my own people." She smiled at Lightfoot's expression. He had not expected such plain speaking. "In return for your lives, I ask that your men take up arms against King Gharavan. Will you fight at General Tulkhan's side?"

"We will."

"Bring me ink and paper." Imoshen signaled Wharrd, who was ready with the agreement she had already drawn up. Even so, she felt light-headed with relief. "We will sign a new contract, which you will deliver into the General's hands."

The mercenary was a lettered man, able to read and write.

"Lightfoot is not a Vaygharian name," she remarked.

"It is the name I have gone by for nearly twenty years."

The man was hiding his true identity. Imoshen wondered if he would be as treacherous as Tourez. She did not want to send Tulkhan a faulty tool or, worse, a tool that would turn on him. If only there was some way to ensure that Lightfoot would honor the contract.

After dripping the wax onto the document, Imoshen held up her left hand and curled all but the smallest sixth finger into her palm. "This is my T'En seal."

She pressed the pad of her finger in the hot wax, closing her mind against the small burn. When she removed her finger, the whorls of her skin remained there imprinted on the document. If only she could seal the mercenary's cooperation as easily. "The contract carries my sign. Lightfoot, I look into your eyes and claim you in my service until you fulfill this contract." Without questioning her action, she placed her fingertip, still hot from the wax, on the center of his forehead. Pressure built inside her head and sparks swam before her vision. With an internal rush the pressure snapped, returning her hearing and sight. "You are mine and I will know if you dishonor our contract."

She smelled his fear.

When she pulled back her hand, a red blister appeared on his skin in the shape of an inverted tear. Strange. She had not thought the touch of her finger hot enough to brand him.

Suddenly she remembered Tulkhan's description of a Ghebite soldier's death. The man had been captured by Reothe, who told him to deliver his message to Tulkhan but said that once he did, he would die. The man had been whole and healthy. There had been no reason for him to utter the message then drop dead, no reason except Reothe's touch.

Now she had used a similar trick on Lightfoot. Imoshen did not even know if it would work, but it was clear the mercenary believed her. She smiled slowly, seeing confirmation in Lightfoot's eyes. It was enough that he believed he was her creature. "Go now and remember, T'Imoshen granted your life and the lives of your companions when she could have taken them."

As he backed away, giving her a deep obeisance reminiscent of the Vaygharian merchant aristocracy, she caught Wharrd's eye and lowered her voice. "I will go to Tulkhan."

"You can't. The townspeople fear the mercenaries will murder them in their beds. They won't be happy until they see the back of Lightfoot and his men. The rebels watch the Citadel. They await Drake's execution as a signal to strike. If you left Northpoint the people would panic. I'll go to Tulkhan."

"You are right. Tell Tulkhan the mercenaries have agreed to support him. I'll send them over as soon as he's ready."

Wharred slipped away and Imoshen's head swam. This time last year she had been plotting against General Tulkhan to save her life and secure Fair isle. Now Tulkhan's second-in-command was answering to her, and she was consumed with worry for the General's safety.

Expecting to hear a bark at any moment, the sweat of fear chilled Tulkhan's skin, but Kornel had been right: The marsh-dwellers had hunted the narcts out around the village.

The General and his men had crept forward during the night. Now they crouched behind boggy hillocks, watching the pole-houses as the sky lightened.

Gleaming narct skins were strung from one high veranda to the next, flapping in the dawn breeze. Smoke issued from the central hole in the nearest roof, bringing the smell of cooking fish.

Tulkhan gave the signal. They crept toward the headman's pole-house. Kornel's advice was to take this man and the village would surrender. Avoiding the green patch where a freshwater spring fed into the river, they crept ever closer. Several chickens, housed in a cage built under the base of the platform, squawked, but no one bothered to investigate.

Tulkhan swung up onto the platform and dropped the ladder into place for his men. He slipped past the woven mat hanging in the doorway to find a woman cooking breakfast on a small metal brazier, with a baby at her breast and a child of about four at her side. She stared, too surprised by their sudden arrival to react. The headman stood before a polished plate, plucking the whiskers from his chin with a pair of shells.

He dropped the shells and leapt for a weapon, but Tulkhan grabbed the small boy, holding his sword to the child's throat. The woman moaned. A whimper escaped the lad and he wet himself. The General cursed. "Kornel, tell them the boy will not be harmed if they cooperate. We have captured their village."

When Kornel spoke, Tulkhan caught a lilt to the language that reminded him of the common trading tongue, but he didn't understand individual words.

The headman spoke to his woman, who lifted the mat obscuring the window. When she reported what she saw outside, the man held his hands out, palms up.

"He is yours to command," Kornel told Tulkhan.

But Tulkhan had seen the anger burning in the man's eyes and he knew his service had been earned through fear, not gratitude. "Kornel, tell him to pack enough food to travel to the Marsh-wall. We'll take the child to ensure his cooperation."

When Kornel translated this, Tulkhan noticed the mother's expression, and he didn't like the man he saw reflected in her eyes.

Imoshen laughed as Almona danced across the grass to her. It had taken several intensive sessions, but the child's leg was straight. "I'm sorry. One leg will always be shorter than the other."

"She is lucky," Eksyl said. "We all are."

Just then a Citadel servant hurried into the hospice garden. "A delegation approaches Northpoint flying the pennant of Chalkcliff Abbey."

Imoshen had long suspected the abbey's seculate of supporting Reothe. Tomorrow was the Harvest Moon Festival, a holy day, and a good excuse to visit and see how the rebel leader fared. Smiling to herself, she caught the servant's bewildered expression and recalled her own confusion when she had questioned her great-aunt about the Church's role. This time last year she had not understood the subtle power plays.

Imoshen bid Eksyl and the children good-bye. They

insisted on escorting her up the rise to the Citadel, where she went straight to her bedchamber.

She was determined to put on a good show for the Seculate. "Dyta, it seems we must dip into the stolen treasures to find a garment to impress the Seculate. It is just as well the late Ghebite Lord of Northpoint had an eye for riches."

"And sticky fingers to match," the old woman muttered. "Will I find something for T'Reothe as well?"

Imoshen stopped unfastening her bodice. Dyta was right. The people would expect Reothe to play a part in the ceremony. If she hoped to defuse the situation with the rebels, Reothe must be seen to be raised high, while serving her. "Yes, thank you."

She pulled the gown over her head and draped it on a chair, staring at the mirror. It was silver-backed glass, as fine as any found in the palace. Under her feet, the carpets lay three deep. Dyta was sure to find a garment fit for an empress, which was how she had to appear before the Seculate. She hated power politics, but if she had to play the game, she would play it to win.

When the maid returned, Imoshen selected a red velvet tabard edged with gold brocade. Settling the skull cap of beaten gold on her hair, she adjusted the single large ruby to hang in the center of her forehead and ordered a formal ceremony of welcome.

As High T'En music played, Imoshen completed the warmed-wine pouring ceremony, grateful to her mother for the boring hours of practice. Seven priests sipped their wine, eyes downcast. On her signal to speak, the Seculate explained his plans for the Harvest Festival and the restoration of Northpoint's church.

Imoshen was sure everything the Seculate saw would be reported to the head of the T'En Church. The Beatific had supported Tulkhan, but Imoshen had long suspected this canny power broker was playing a double game. She put her porcelain cup aside, rising. "I'm sure you wish to see T'Reothe, Seculate Donyx."

She did not miss the quickly masked eagerness in the Seculate's beaklike face. Lifting her arm, Imoshen waited for him to join her. As her hand closed over his, she discovered the man was shielded from her gift. This was either innate, or he had experienced the T'En ability to sift the surface of a True-man's mind via touch and had learned how to guard against it.

Not revealing her discovery by so much as a moment's hesitation, Imoshen escorted the Seculate to T'Ronynn's Tower. In silence they climbed the staircase, which spiraled right so that True-man defenders could back up away from attackers while protecting their shielded sides. Once her ancestors had known who their enemies were. Now she was surrounded by smiling threats, Reothe not the least of them.

When they approached the room where he lay, Imoshen saw that her people had prepared for this visit; the guards were absent and the door of their "honored guest" was ajar. Gliding into the room, she smelled freshly crushed herbs and caught the tang of the sea breeze. The windows were open to the bay.

As Imoshen swept Reothe the formal obeisance, lifting both hands to her forehead, she noticed the floor. Scrubbing had removed the blood, leaving a pale patch. Unbidden, the memory of her encounter with Drake returned, and dizzying revelation seized Imoshen. If Seculate Donyx discovered that she had used her gift to strike Drake, he could petition the Beatific to declare her rogue. But Tulkhan's men had sailed, leaving Reothe the only witness. And he would not betray her, would he?

Reothe was watching the Seculate closely, and he did not look like a man about to greet an ally.

Straightening, Imoshen masked her turmoil with old empire formality. "T'Reothe, Seculate Donyx of Chalkcliff Abbey has come to help us stage the Harvest Feast. You will have the honor of leading the festivities."

Though the whites of his eyes had returned to their normal color, Reothe looked thin and pale. He sat upright, propped on pillows, but he lifted only one hand in greeting.

"T'Imoshen." Her name rolled off his tongue with all the cadences of High T'En. He continued in this language, offering the True-people of the Church formal greeting. He appeared to honor the Seculate and his priests, but Imoshen suspected Reothe was subtly reminding them that the Church was supposed to worship the T'En gifts.

As Reothe's hand hung in the air between them, Imoshen saw his fingers tremble. Before the Seculate could notice the weakness, she caught Reothe's hand in hers. It surprised her to discover that she could not reveal Reothe's weakness before these priests. His skin was surprisingly cool and her heart skipped a beat. It was the first time she had touched him since he had recovered from the fever's delirium, and she realized she had missed Reothe, missed him fiercely.

As she fought the urge to initiate the mind-touch, the moment spiraled down until there was no one but Reothe, nothing but her need to rediscover his T'En essence.

Despite the crippling of his gifts, Reothe sensed something, and he searched her face for the subtleties he would have once been privy to. His garnet eyes narrowed in pain.

"T'Reothe?" Seculate Donyx was perceptive.

Reothe sank back, pale against the pillow. "I will host the Harvest Feast with honor, but I am still recovering."

"A carry-chair will be provided. I see we have tired you. We will withdraw," Imoshen said. As she slipped her fingers from Reothe's, she saw raw need in his face and understood that he was powerless, marooned in a hostile world of True-people. It touched her to the quick. Secretly horrified to discover her vulnerability to Reothe, Imoshen escorted the Beatific's spies from the room.

It was just as well the General had the marsh-dweller's son to ensure the man's cooperation, for he would never have picked the path to the Marsh-wall. For two days they had tramped through tussocky hills and bogs that all looked the same. Still water punctuated by needle-sharp grass filled every hollow.

When the dark line first appeared on the horizon, Tulkhan had thought it was mountains, then hills, then finally he understood it was the Marsh-wall of legend. Somehow he had led his army across the festering marshes without losing a single man to the bogs or the beasts.

They camped a little way from the wall because the ground near it was low, made that way to stop the predators, and they burned the bog itself. Just at dusk the narcts began their nightly chorus. Tulkhan knew they would prowl outside the fire circles, fighting among themselves, ready to take down an unwary man.

"Climb the wall, Kornel; see if you can get your bearings. I want to attack Sumair at dawn the day after tomorrow. We'll travel by night."

"With the twin full moons against us?"

"The moons are going to favor us. We attack the dawn after Harvest Feast, when everyone will be sleeping off their revelry. Don't tell me you object on religious grounds?"

Kornel grinned and shook his head.

Tulkhan dug into his traveling bag for sweet nuts and offered some to the child. To show they were harmless he cracked the shell and ate one himself, then cracked another for the boy, who, after catching a nod from his father, tried the crisp white flesh.

Tulkhan grinned at his delighted expression, then casually offered the father a nut. He took it, cracking it as the General had done, indicating he found the flesh good. But it would take more than a nut to win him.

Kornel went to leave but the marsh-dweller stopped him, asking something in a low, intense voice.

"What does he want?" Tulkhan asked.

Kornel snorted. "This fool thinks you'll let him go home now that we've reached the wall."

If Tulkhan let the man go, he could make it home in two days. Two days from now the General would either have Sumair or be staging a siege. On the other hand...

"There's nothing stopping him going over the wall after us, raising the alarm, and warning Sumair. Then your plans would come to nothing," Kornel said, voicing Tulkhan's concerns.

The General nodded. He could exact a vow from the marsh-dweller to return to his home, but what good was a vow given under duress?

Reothe claimed Imoshen's vow to the General had been given under duress. He said that he was Imoshen's first choice. But Tulkhan believed that when she gave her bonding vows to him on Midwinter's Day they had been freely given.

He rose, throwing the shells onto the fire. "Tell—what is his name?"

"Banuld," Kornel said.

"Banuld-Chi," the man corrected.

Tulkhan looked to Kornel.

"The *Chi* is an honorific, because he is the headman," Kornel explained sourly.

"Banuld-Chi," Tulkhan acknowledged the man. "Translate this, Kornel. In two nights from now you will be free to go."

The marsh-dweller understood him even before Kornel translated the words, and Tulkhan saw his despair.

Tulkhan caught his arm. "Kornel, tell him I give my word. He and his son will be free to return home when their release no longer endangers us. And I'll reward him for his service." Tulkhan did not miss the eager light in Kornel's eyes at the mention of a tangible reward.

Restless, Imoshen paced her room with Ashmyr in her arms. When he fell asleep she paced with empty arms. Finally, she slipped on her cloak and climbed to the top of T'Ronynn's Tower.

Imoshen did not take a torch, preferring the glow of the large and small moons as they neared their full glory. But as she left the stairwell, she recognized a small silhouette. "Kalleen, what's wrong?"

The little woman turned, her cloak wrapped high under her chin, her small face cold and imperious. "You sent my bond-partner on a mission of state and he has not returned."

"Wharrd serves Fair Isle."

"He serves *you,* under Ghebite oath that comes between bond-partners!" Kalleen's intensity made her seem larger. Her eyes were luminous in the moonlight. "His Ghebite honor is greater than his love for me."

"I must have news. If anyone can convince Tulkhan to reveal his plans, Wharrd can."

"Then why hasn't he returned? How do you know Peirs hasn't betrayed the General for his true king? How do you know Wharrd isn't swinging from the ship's mast or feeding the fish?"

All these thoughts and more had crossed Imoshen's mind.

"T'Imoshen, I request permission to return to my estates." Kalleen dropped into the formal old empire obeisance that she had seen Cariah perform so elegantly.

The memory stung Imoshen. Of all the Keldon nobles, Lady Cariah had befriended her and helped soothe the transition of power during that first winter under Ghebite domination. When the other nobles would have shunned Kalleen, a farm girl who became Lady of Windhaven, Cariah had welcomed her. But Cariah made the mistake of rejecting her Ghebite lover. Unable to live with the dishonor, he had murdered her before committing suicide. They remained together in death, the stone lovers, a constant reminder to Imoshen. She had failed to anticipate their tragedy because she had not understood the Ghebite mind. Self-doubt racked her. Had she sent Wharrd to his death?

"T'Imoshen?" Kalleen prodded.

"So formal..." Imoshen whispered sadly. "What of Wharrd? Surely you wish to wait for him?"

"My bond-partner has placed someone before me." Kalleen's chin lifted. "I will go where I can be useful. If Wharrd returns, tell him where I am. If he does not come, I will know what to think."

"At least stay for the Harvest Feast," Imoshen said, and Kalleen nodded. As she went to leave, Imoshen caught her arm. "War is coming. Though you return to your estates, events may soon come to you."

"I pray not."

"I too."

Imoshen was surprised by a swift hug, bringing with it the scent of lavender. Kalleen's soft lips brushed her cheek, her breath hot on Imoshen's skin. "I am not suited to this life of leadership. I long for my own hearth, the turn of the seasons, and my family around me. Forgive me, Imoshen."

Then she was gone, taking with her their shared memories. Kalleen had been at the Stronghold with Imoshen when her great-aunt was still alive. Kalleen had helped sustain her through the first winter under Ghebite rule.

A knot of pain swelled to fill Imoshen's chest. Walking blindly to the parapets, she gripped the stone, registering its cold solidity. Tears stung her eyes, blurring her vision as she stared across the T'Ronynn Straits. The night was so clear she could almost see the lights of the blockading ships. She hoped that the reason Wharrd had not returned was because there was no news.

A sound made her turn.

"T'Reothe asks for you," Dyta said.

"I spoke with him this very day." But Imoshen had not been back to answer Reothe's unspoken plea. "How does he fare?"

"The left side of his body is weak, but he forces his fingers to work a little more each day."

This news only gave Imoshen more concern. If Reothe's body was healing, how long before his powers returned? Frustration flooded her. She needed to read the T'Elegos. Reothe might lie in the bed, weak as a kitten, but he still held the cards she needed to play a winning hand.

"Is there some message you would have me carry to him?" the old woman asked. Imoshen studied her closely. Was Reothe already exercising his gift to win people over? All she read in Dyta's face was concern for an injured fellow.

That this person was Reothe, the last T'En warrior, and that he was both beautiful and crippled was only chance.

Or was it? Did True-people find the T'En beautiful? Imoshen did not know. General Tulkhan had looked on her with reluctant lust so many times that she could not trust her own judgment. "Tell T'Reothe I will see him soon."

The old woman left.

Imoshen imagined Reothe, lying in bed, listening to the sounds of the sea. Vulnerable and alone. Having been under the watchful eyes of the Seculate all day, she was sure the man was her enemy. By the T'En heritage they both shared, she owed Reothe her loyalty. It was loyalty of a different kind from that which she had vowed to share with Tulkhan, but she doubted if the General would understand the distinction. She had to go to Reothe.

Five

H ER MIND MADE up, Imoshen padded down the
stairs. Two Ghebite soldiers sat outside Reothe's
room, playing cards.

"Has anyone been to see Reothe?" Imoshen asked.

"Only the old woman." They did not meet her eyes, not
because they lied but because they distrusted what they did
not know.

Opening the door, Imoshen slipped into the room.
Moonlight silvered the floor and the edge of the bed. She
smelled the sea and Reothe's familiar scent. Her heart rate
lifted a notch.

Not bothering to light a candle, she went to the foot of
the bed. When Reothe did not move, she stood with one
hand on the bed's upright, unsure if she should go.

"Come to mock me, Imoshen?"

"They fear us."

"This surprises you?"

"How did you bear it, growing up in the Empress's
court?"

"At least then I could protect myself. Now I am a
husk."

"The General failed to take Port Sumair. His ships
blockade it. Wharrd is missing. The mercenaries sit outside the gates of Northpoint and grow fat while they
sharpen their weapons. Their leader betrayed the General to

Gharavan. Tulkhan ordered their execution, but they've agreed to fight on Tulkhan's side."

"What did you offer them?"

"Their lives and revenge."

His laughter plucked at something deep within her. Imoshen swallowed, senses strained to interpret his sudden silence, but the crippling of his gift acted as a barrier between them. "Your rebels eat at the tables of the townsfolk and plot to rescue you. My every move is watched."

He pulled himself upright with his good arm, using a rope slung from the bed frame. The speed of his movement startled her. "What do you want of me, Imoshen?"

The moonlight sculpted his fine features. With a jolt she recognized him on an intrinsic level. Like a sleepwalker, she stepped closer. Wordlessly, he swung his arms around her waist. She sensed the strength in his good arm and the weakness in the other. Cradling his head, she felt the warmth of his breath.

Tears stung her eyes and she longed to unburden herself. She ran her fingers through the fine strands of his gossamer-soft hair, and long, insubstantial threads clung to her. When she lifted her hand to the twin moons' light, she saw his hair, glistening like spiderwebs on her fingers. The healer in her understood. She had dealt his body such a severe blow that his hair came away in her hands. Would he ever truly recover? The urge to ask his forgiveness was almost overwhelming. Again, she ached to reach out with her T'En senses and greet his familiar essence.

The force of her longing to initiate the mind-touch triggered a flash of insight. When Reothe had come to her in Tulkhan's form, he had revealed himself at the last moment. With her barriers down, his mind had melded with hers, and now she missed him as she would miss a severed limb. Perhaps he had established some sort of link at that moment and she would never feel whole without him. The revelation rocked her.

Dry-mouthed, Imoshen backed away.

"You must beware Seculate Donyx," Reothe warned.

"He claims to be true to the old ways, but he is a churchman first and foremost. Crippled like this, I cannot help you. I need to be whole again."

"I don't know how to heal you." She had begun to think how it might be done.

"Try." Reothe's eyes blazed a challenge.

"No."

"Why? Because it suits you to have me at your mercy? Does it amuse you to keep me as your gelding?"

"No!" Imoshen dragged in a quick breath. She suspected she would have no defenses against Reothe if he was healed. "Even my healing gift can kill. You saw what happened to Drake."

"It was self-defense."

"That would not protect me from the Tractarians."

"I will not accuse you, Imoshen." He studied her intensely. "You were raised to be a True-woman, and you think like one. You don't realize your full potential. Fair Isle could be yours and yours alone. This is my honest advice. Act swiftly. Execute Drake and me, hire the mercenaries to consolidate your power, rout out the remaining Ghebites, and slay everyone who resists."

"No, I will not!"

"I know," he said, and she could hear the smile in his voice. "What will you do?"

"I don't know."

He sighed and sank onto the pillows. "Then I don't know how I can help you, Imoshen. Or even why I should."

"You mock me."

"Then stop pretending to be what you aren't—a True-woman, a Mere-woman—when I know you could be so much more!"

"I see we cannot agree."

"What did you expect?" He caught the rope, pulling himself up to confront her. Moonlight illuminated his face, austere and beautiful. "Heal me and I will guide you to the T'Elegos. With the Keldon nobles at our back, we can unite the island and take the capital before the General can capture Port Sumair. Seize the day, Imoshen!"

Silently, she backed away, and his soft, mocking laughter followed her from the room.

The day of the Harvest Feast dawned fine and cool. Imoshen wrinkled her nose as she held up a pair of velvet breeches and tried to judge the size. Reothe was taller and more slender than the late Lord of Northpoint. But the silk shirt was broad enough for his shoulders and the brocade tabard suitably ornate.

As for herself, she would spend most of the day barefoot with her hair down, dressed in nothing but a thin white shift. She was supposed to feel the earth beneath her feet when she gave the blessing for next year's harvest and catch.

Shivering, she dropped the shift over her shoulders. It made her feel vulnerable. At least Reothe had the dignity of his ornate clothing. Imoshen turned to Dyta. "Take these clothes to Reothe."

The carry-chair would support him during the day's ceremonies and Seculate Donyx would be at his side, giving them the perfect opportunity to plot against her. She was gambling Reothe had not ordered his rebels to attack today. Her people had reported the influx of strangers in the port's taverns. This was to be expected at festival time. As for the mercenaries, they had no reason to complain. They were being treated like royalty.

"The Ghebites are talking of an execution for today's entertainment," Dyta said when she returned. "It won't do to kill the rebel lad on Harvest Feast Day. No crops will grow, no cows will calve if blood is shed."

"I've ordered no execution!" Imoshen snapped.

The old woman shrugged. "You hear things."

"Hear this. I have not ordered Drake's death." Imoshen's bare toes gripped the thick carpet as she stepped closer.

"I just repeat what is being said, T'Imoshen."

"Then repeat what I say to those who would spread false rumor. And send for the custodian of the Citadel."

Dyta hurried to obey.

Imoshen brushed her hair until it crackled, lifting with a life of its own. She must quash these rumors. With a start, she felt the T'En gift stirring within her, empowered by her anger. She thrust the brush aside and took a long deep breath, concentrating until the sensation passed.

Barefoot, Imoshen prowled into the crowded square before the Citadel. Looking resplendent in a purple tabard embroidered with fine gold thread, Reothe sat on the carry-chair with his four porters behind him. But she noticed he raised only his right hand when he was called upon to give his blessing. Every household had brought a portion of their Harvest Feast for Reothe to bless. This far north, the festival's details varied from those of her own Stronghold.

Because Reothe represented the Church's kingdom and she the worldly kingdom, she had to present the Citadel's portion for his blessing. Did it amuse Reothe to see her kneel before him?

Against custom she met his eyes, brilliant as garnets. He looked composed, his face thin but unmarked by his recent illness. Without his gifts, he could not know how vulnerable she had become to him. His advice had been brutal: Kill him, or kill Tulkhan. But Imoshen refused to believe it was weakness to show compassion.

She accepted Reothe's blessing and rose, passing the tray to a servant. Then, instead of stepping away, she placed her hand over Reothe's weak left hand where it lay on the arm of the chair.

"Bring the prisoner." She pitched her voice to carry.

The crowd muttered uneasily and she felt the tension in Reothe. Several Citadel guards appeared, escorting Drake between them. A hush fell. The air grew thick with expectation.

Drake squinted in the sunlight. She saw him flinch and

knew the picture she and Reothe must present. Safe, pampered, secure in their power. How wrong.

Drake stood shivering on the flagstones.

Imoshen had to raise her voice to be heard over the crowd's murmur. "Everyone here knows how this man nearly killed Lady Kalleen of Windhaven and how he attempted to free T'Reothe. But my kinsman is here by my side. It is his honor to host the Harvest Feast." She felt Reothe's hand tense under hers. Imoshen focused on one dark golden head whose features revealed fear, quickly masked. "Lady Kalleen, step forward."

Kalleen picked up her skirts and moved through the small children who jostled for position at the front of the crowd. Crisp sunlight bathed Kalleen's face, gilding her hair and her skin.

Her beauty made Imoshen catch her breath. "The wrong was done to you, Kalleen. You must decide Drake's fate. Death or freedom?"

"Freedom," Kalleen replied without hesitation, just as Imoshen expected.

"So be it." Imoshen turned from Kalleen to the rebel youth. "You are free to go, Drake. You are pardoned of all association with the rebels. Return to your family."

He stared at her in disbelief.

"For the second time in less than two years, Fair Isle faces the threat of invasion from the mainland." Imoshen paused to give the crowd a chance to quiet. "The people of Fair Isle need to be united against the common enemy. We can learn from the Lady of Windhaven. Let it be known that all rebels are pardoned, free to go to their homes, their farms and families."

Her last few words were lost in the happy cries. Imoshen smiled at Kalleen's surprised face. She beckoned the bewildered Drake, who approached, the force of his emotion making his body tremble. He dropped to his knees, hands raised in the obeisance of deep supplication. "I thank you, T'En Empress."

"T'Reothe wants you to have this, in acknowledgment of your faithful service." Imoshen dropped a drawstring purse into Drake's upturned palms. "Go to your family with peace in your heart. Go with the blessing of the last T'En."

Drake snatched Reothe's free hand, kissing it. "My service cannot be bought. It comes from the heart."

"I know." Reothe's reply was thick.

Heat filled Imoshen. It was the first time she had seen Reothe vulnerable before others.

Reothe slipped his weak hand from hers, briefly touching the tip of his sixth finger to Drake's forehead in the T'En blessing. "Ride swiftly, ride safely."

Drake stepped back a pace. He turned to Kalleen, who had been watching their interaction. She glanced over her shoulder as if she might run, but before she could, he knelt at her feet. Clasping her hands in his, he begged her forgiveness.

Kalleen's expression made Imoshen smile, and she glanced down at Reothe. He was furious because she had dismissed his rebel army. Soon she may have to call on the people to defend Fair Isle, and the rebels would stand behind her, believing she and Reothe were united in purpose. She could be as ruthless in her "compassion" as he was in his willingness to kill.

As Seculate Donyx approached, Imoshen tried to slip away, but Reothe caught her arm and tugged so that she lost her balance. With a twist she avoided falling into his lap and found herself on one knee before him. His good hand clasped her chin and he leaned forward, their eyes almost level. She could feel his tension as he inhaled her scent.

"This garment is indecent." His eyes went deep and dark.

Imoshen felt a rush of desire. This time she could not blame it on his T'En tricks. Hanging her head, she let the fall of her long hair hide her face. She felt more than heard Reothe's sharp intake of breath.

"I don't need my gifts to feel your response. Why do you deny me?"

She could give no answer, none that he would want to hear.

"Curse that Ghebite general!" Reothe hissed, then studied her. "It was a master stroke to pardon my rebels, Imoshen. Truly, if you had stood at my side we would have ruled Fair Isle. We still can!"

A buzz of speculation rose from the crowd. To them it must appear that she bowed before Reothe. "You play a dangerous game."

"I play to win!"

"As do I." She came to her feet. "I am expected down at the wharves."

Under Reothe's mocking eyes she strode away, her escort of priests scurrying to keep up. The townspeople lined the road, waiting to shower her with late-blooming flowers and golden leaves, while on the wharves the fisherfolk awaited her blessing in the hope of a plentiful catch. She could not falter, not for a moment.

As the sun set on Harvest Feast Day, impatience consumed Tulkhan. His army needed to be in position to attack the port at dawn; however, they could not start their forced march until dark. March all night, fight all day. He had asked the impossible of his men before, but he asked nothing of them that he did not ask of himself and they knew it.

He knelt behind the Marsh-wall and adjusted the farseer to study the Low-lands toward the coast. Prosperous farmlets dotted the plain. He checked the position of the rising moons. Time to move.

As the moons rose above the T'Ronynn Straits, the Harvest Feast culminated in the selection of the young woman and man who received the corn sheaf and bull's horn. The town's populace followed them outside the gates to celebrate their joining in the Harvest Bower, and the Citadel's public hall became even noisier. Imoshen tried not to recall this moment in last year's festival. She missed Tulkhan fiercely.

Reothe glared at her and she noticed his white knuckles. She did not want him passing out, though the way the others were behaving it would not have been remarkable. Rising, she gave the Seculate a formal bow. "T'Reothe has overextended himself. I will see that he is carried to his room."

It took a while to locate four servants sober enough to be entrusted to carry the chair. Silently, she followed them to T'Ronynn's Tower. When the servants placed the chair in the hall outside Reothe's door, Imoshen dismissed them.

"Ashmyr?" Reothe asked.

"Asleep." Imoshen found Reothe's interest in the child unnerving, considering who the baby's father was. "Can you walk as far as your bed?"

"What would you do if I said no?" he asked sweetly.

"I would help you."

"Ah, Imoshen. Then I fear I am too weak to walk that far."

She felt a smile tug at her lips as she guided his hand to her shoulder. His fingers bit into her flesh but she did not complain, matching him step for step.

When Reothe swung the door shut after them, Imoshen's heart thudded uncomfortably. Within two breaths her eyes had adjusted and she could see the room. The moons' light was so bright that the furniture cast shadows. "Not far to the bed."

"I go to the windows. I want to bathe naked in the moonlight."

Imoshen refused to imagine Reothe's pale, glistening form. "Do you expect me to undress you?"

"Would you deny me the solace of the twin moons' light? It is beneficial to the T'En. I will feast in my own way tonight."

"Really?" She felt more than heard Reothe chuckle, and resentment stung her as once again she was reminded of the knowledge he kept from her.

In the silver light that angled through the open windows, Reothe stood unaided. He raised his good arm to the ornate tabard. "Remove this."

Anticipating his needs, Imoshen helped him. He wore soft indoor slippers, which he eased off while steadying himself on her shoulder, then he let his breeches drop, stepping unconcernedly out of them.

She would not let herself look on his nakedness. Her gaze stayed firmly on his chest. His good hand lifted between them to cup the moonlight as if it were a physical thing.

Imoshen's breath caught in her throat.

"You feel it?" His voice was a forceful caress. "You must. This is our night. Every double full moon belongs to the T'En. It is an ancient custom from the land beyond the dawn sun."

"I've never heard—"

"What of the moondance?"

"But that's performed by villagers on the seasonal cusps," Imoshen objected. "I thought it was one of their customs dating from before our time."

"Many of their customs overlap ours. Imoshen the First deliberately melded our practices with theirs. In the T'Elegos I read of T'En dances performed naked—"

"I must read the T'Elegos!"

He caught her eager hands, placing her palms on his chest, where she felt the steady beating of his heart. "Heal me tonight under the twin moons." His voice resonated through her. Her heart beat in time with his. "Heal me and I will share the knowledge of the T'Elegos with you."

She could hardly breathe. To deny him was to deny an intrinsic part of herself. Only he knew the burden of their shared birthright. He promised beauty and knowledge when her T'En blood had brought her nothing but ostracism. She longed to open to him, but . . . "I am sorry, Reothe."

His hands tightened on hers. She sensed the force of his fierce will and realized he was trying to use his gift. Suddenly he gasped, his legs giving way.

She sank with him, cushioning his fall. As he lay naked and vulnerable in the moonlight, she leaned closer to inhale his scent, letting her hair trail the length of his body.

Something inside her clenched, and she could not deny her desire for him.

It seemed only right to let their bodies join and open herself to the mind-touch. This alone would assuage the hollow ache inside her. Yet she was sure she would not crave him like this if she had not succumbed to his trickery. He must have implanted this need to be triggered by his nearness and the timbre of his voice. Swimming on a sea of sensation, she fought to center herself, for she could not afford to restore his gifts, not when she had no defenses.

Reothe moaned and his eyes flickered open. They were windows to his soul, containing his fierce intelligence and the pain of his loss. "I cannot live a T'En cripple, Imoshen. You must heal me."

Unable to speak, she pressed her face into his throat. As if in benediction he stroked her hair. Tears burned her eyes.

"You cry for me, yet you let me suffer. How cruel is that? You leave me defenseless, surrounded by adversaries. Even I would not be so cruel to my enemy."

A sob escaped her. She sat upright in the moonlight, her hair around her shoulders like a satin cloak.

"I don't understand you, Imoshen. Your tears mock me." A shiver racked him. "Bring the bed fur."

Silently, she dragged the heavy white fur off the bed. It felt luxurious against her skin. She wanted to lie naked in the moonlight with him. Instead, she knelt at his side. It was painful to watch him roll onto the fur with a stifled curse. Unable to stop herself, she stroked his long flanks.

"Lie with me in the moonlight, Imoshen." He gestured to his body. "Surely you do not fear me."

Imoshen kissed his closed eyelids, then she stretched out on the fur beside him. Gradually she felt the tension ease from him. Closing her eyes, she savored this moment. They were like two children, naked in their innocence, but it was an illusion, because she wanted him whole again and she knew she could not risk healing him.

Imoshen stayed only until she felt Reothe's breathing

lengthen into the rhythm of sleep, then she covered him and left him lying there, wrapped in the pale fur, illuminated by the silver moonlight. She'd sworn she had not willingly betrayed Tulkhan, and she would not, but it cost her dearly to deny Reothe and the bond they shared.

Tulkhan eased his shoulders and flexed his hands. This was the ultimate test of his mad gamble. Leaving the marsh-dwellers under guard, he signaled Kornel to come with him. They approached the port, its walls and peaked roofs silhouetted against the stars. The large moon hung low in the western sky, and the smaller moon had already set. The revelry of Harvest Feast had long faded.

His commanders each had their assigned task. He had chosen to lead the assault himself with a band of seven men. Tulkhan hefted the grappling hook and coiled rope over his shoulder, thinking all it would take was one guard not too soused by drink to discover him.

Kornel spat and eyed the gate towers. "The winch is in the base of the left tower."

Tulkhan nodded. He covered the distance to the wall at a run. Here there were signs of hastily destroyed dwellings. The poor had been taken inside the walls. Planting his feet, he swung the grappling hook. It scythed the air with a sound that was loud in the predawn quiet. Then he let it go, watching it sail dark against the star-speckled sky. A soft *chink* told him the grapple had hit stone. He pulled slowly until it caught and held.

Tulkhan hauled himself up, his boots finding purchase on the wall. Any moment he could be discovered and the rope cut. In his mind's eye he saw himself falling backward and fought a wave of vertigo. At last he hauled his weight over the parapets, sinking low.

With a tug, he signaled the others and drew his weapon to stand guard as they made the climb. Tulkhan led his party toward the gate tower and the sound of a man snoring. Entering the tower, he could just make out his army through the narrow window. They lay like the shadows of clouds on the flat land.

Hefting the drunkard upright, Tulkhan pressed his knife to the man's throat. One whispered command and he led them down the narrow circular steps to the winch room, where Tulkhan set his men to raising the outer and inner gates. As soon as the outer gate was waist high, his men darted under it, entering the tunnel designed to bottleneck intruders. Silent except for the scuff of boot on stone, the rest of the attackers poured into the passage, passing through the inner gate.

Tulkhan tightened his hold on the defender, grimacing with distaste as fear made the man sweat, bringing the stench of alcohol through his skin. "Where does King Gharavan sleep?"

His captive grunted, speaking in the common trading tongue. "I'll not get my throat slit for a Ghebite king. You can tell your General Tulkhan he's welcome to use his half-brother's skull for a soup bowl. He commandeered the Elector's Palace."

"Kornel, do you know where that is?" Tulkhan asked. He nodded. The General handed the port defender into the care of his gate-holders. At his signal a group went to attack the merchant quarter as a decoy, and he headed for the Elector's Palace with a party of thirty men. If Gharavan was captured, the mercenaries would lay down their arms, and Tulkhan believed he could reason with the remaining Ghebites, many of whom had served with him on other campaigns.

With Kornel in the lead, they headed down the main thoroughfare, then plunged into a winding lane where the upper stories of the houses almost met overhead.

They had gone several blocks when a mercenary patrol rounded the corner. The light of their torches flickered on the closed faces of the narrow houses. The mercenaries gaped, stunned to discover the enemy within the walls. With a roar, the nearest attacked.

Cursing his luck, the General drew his sword. Behind the

mercenaries Tulkhan saw a man run off, carrying a warning to rouse the port, but there was no chance of catching the messenger when death danced just beyond his sword tip. The clash of metal on metal sounded loud and harsh in the cobbled street. Tulkhan's men fought silently, while the mercenaries bellowed their battle cries, and soon answering calls filtered through the twisting lanes.

Tulkhan cursed again. Forced to fight four abreast, his men could not pass the mercenaries, who fell back, step by grudging step.

"Separate. Cut around behind them," Tulkhan ordered, and grabbed Kornel. "Take me to Gharavan."

Charging down a dark alley on Kornel's heels, Tulkhan soon left his pursuers far behind. When they entered a more prosperous quarter, Kornel bent double to catch his breath.

Only a handful of men remained with Tulkhan. Pealing bells and shouts of "Fire!" came from the merchants' quarter. More cries echoed from the wharfs, heralding Peirs's attack. Above the rooftops, the sky glowed. He had to find his half-brother before the defenders could mount a cohesive defense. "Kornel?"

"I know the wharves and merchants' quarter best." He pointed. "But I think the Elector's Palace is this way."

They cut through several lanes, then entered a square with an ornate central fountain. Kornel spun around to get his bearings. "There, that building with the spires."

Mercenaries poured down the steps. With a shout they bore down on Tulkhan's much smaller party.

"Fall back. We'll go around." Tulkhan ran with his men at his heels. Trust Gharavan to stay safely indoors while hired swords fought his battles.

But when they entered a lane they ran into another band of mercenaries, who held a party of Tulkhan's men at bay. Tulkhan charged, leaping onto the back of the nearest man and cutting him down. Driving through the melee, he forged on to unite his men. Booted feet on the paving stones echoed down the narrow lane.

Before more port defenders could arrive, Tulkhan

forced a path through to the square. They were spotted immediately and, with one frustrated glance at the Elector's Palace, Tulkhan signaled his men to fall back again. "Take us another way, Kornel."

The ship's captain led them down narrow alleyways that all looked the same. Smoke billowed from the merchants' quarter. Tulkhan's breath rasped in his throat. They fought as they ran, leaving the injured where they fell.

Half blind, barely able to breathe, Tulkhan caught Kornel by the arm. "Can you get us to the gate?"

Gray with fatigue, Kornel nodded. "We're nearly there."

Rounding a bend, they found a hastily constructed barricade of household furniture manned by mercenaries. Beyond it the gates had been recaptured and closed.

Tulkhan had no breath to curse. Soon it would be light enough for archers to send down a rain of arrows. His people were armored for speed and stealth, not for defensive battle. Bitterly, he raised the horn to sound the retreat.

"To me!" Tulkhan cried. They had to retake the gate before his men were massacred. Charging the barricade, he grasped a massive oak table. His thighs screamed a protest as he lifted it. Men joined him. They plowed through, smashing all before them. At his side, men tripped over broken furniture; others fell defending their backs, but the way to the gate was cleared.

Leaving others to deal with the barricade defenders, Tulkhan made for the winch room. A single local fled. Tulkhan threw his weight behind the winch mechanism. But the ponderous cogs were slow to move. The heavy gates screeched a protest as they lifted. Three of his men joined him in the winchroom.

Their escape route secured, Tulkhan returned to the barricade. In the growing light he saw more of his men approaching, fighting as they retreated.

The Ghebite battle cry leapt to his lips and he ran out to meet them. For a few moments it was life and death on the cobbles, under the swinging business signs of tailors and hatters. He held the gap to let the others through, then he dug his hands under the oak table.

Seeing what he was about, several men helped him. Together they turned the tabletop and rammed it into position. As they held back the attackers, Tulkhan took stock. If he could keep the gate open long enough, he could get a force inside and make it a fight every step of the way to the Elector's Palace.

At that moment the angry buzz of a flying arrow decided for him. He had missed the opportunity.

He fought a rear-guard action, holding the narrow gate passage to let the last of his men through. Oil poured from the slits above, landing on the stones between him and freedom. A flaming brand followed. Covering his face with his forearm, Tulkhan leapt through the flames.

As the outer gate made its ponderous descent, he ducked under. Then it was a mad scramble to run beyond bow shot. From narrow slits the defenders sent whistling death.

Even though he knew his unprotected thighs were more vulnerable, the space between Tulkhan's shoulder blades ached with the expectation of an arrowhead. Running and dodging, Tulkhan joined Kornel in the ranks. Then he turned, putting his hands on his knees to catch his breath.

The defenders did not make a sortie, contenting themselves with shouting abuse. Tulkhan smiled. Though the surprise attack had failed, by now the defenders would have reported the impossible to Gharavan—Tulkhan's army was camped outside the gates of Port Sumair, ready to lay siege.

His stomach rumbled as he turned to his commanders. "Break out the stores. I want my breakfast!"

They grinned, catching his enthusiasm.

Six

THE DAY AFTER the Harvest Feast, Imoshen bade
farewell to the Seculate. The wind carried a foretaste of the winter to come, and Imoshen shivered.
Fair Isle had seen too much war. The peaceful years of her
childhood now seemed halcyon and unreal. She did not
want her son's childhood shadowed by war.

Her people had reported a great exodus on the roads
south and east as the rebels headed home. There was much to
be done to prepare for the winter with the prospect of war in
the spring. Finally Imoshen turned and, accompanied by the
officials of Northpoint, she retraced her steps to the public
hall. In her heart she dreaded returning to Kalleen's accusing
eyes. For despite having permission to return to her estate,
Kalleen lingered, hoping for her bond-partner's return.

It was mid-afternoon before the port defenders signaled they
were ready to talk. Tulkhan commandeered a draft horse—
the only mount sturdy enough to carry him—and rode out to
meet them. He wished he had his battle-hardened destrier,
but the horse was still on Fair Isle, doubtless growing fat and
sleek on too much grain and not enough exercise.

He dressed in full armor, wearing the purple and black,
the colors of his Ghebite father, the old king, and the red of his
mother's house. He waited as the gates opened, allowing seven

ornately dressed horsemen to ride out. Tulkhan's hands tightened on the reins as he recognized his half-brother. It was all very well to swear Gharavan's death, but it was another thing to meet the youth face to face. He had taught Gharavan to ride, had made his first wooden practice sword, and now he was sworn to kill him. It left a bitter taste in his mouth.

Tulkhan did not recognize a single Vaygharian mercenary among the company. He had been hoping to strike a bargain, for it was clear to him the Low-landers were not behind Gharavan, and if the mercenaries could be persuaded to change allegiance, he might be able to cut the body from the head of the army.

"Protector General of Fair Isle." Tulkhan stood in the stirrups, giving himself his new title.

The party halted and a single horseman rode out. His ornate clothing proclaimed him one of Gheeaba's new military elite, a breed of young men who played at war while never having to bloody their hands.

"I will speak with my half-brother or no one!" Tulkhan roared.

The others conferred and Gharavan, with six men behind him, ventured forward. His horse sidled nervously.

Tulkhan could smell the perfume on him from here. Their father would have risen from his grave. "Gharavan."

"King Gharavan to you, Protector General!" The youth made the title an insult, his thin voice carrying on the still air. "I see you tore yourself away from your Dhamfeer bitch long enough to come to meet me. Or did you bring her along to warm your bed and hold your hand?"

Tulkhan forced his hands to unclench from the reins. "T'Imoshen holds Fair Isle. I have Port Sumair surrounded. Surrender now and I will discuss terms."

"How many men and ships did you lose? It is a wonder they follow you at all!" Gharavan sneered. "It would be better to take your horse and put it to the use it was bred for, plowing a furrow. Or would you rather be back in Fair Isle plowing the Dhamfeer's—"

"You have until dusk to surrender." Tulkhan contained

his rage. "I will take no retaliation against the people of Port Sumair, because I know they want no part in this. As for the mercenaries—"

"They are loyal to me," Gharavan crowed. "What does your traitorous army call themselves now—Fair Weather Men of Fair Isle?"

The laughter of Gharavan's supporters sounded forced, but it was all Tulkhan could do to stop himself leaping off his horse and dragging his half-brother from the saddle.

"Surrender?" Gharavan laughed. "There's food for two years in the granaries, but long before that, your Dhamfeer bitch will be bedding her rebel prince. Long before that, my auxiliary forces will have marched across the Low-lands to crush you. And when you're mine there will be no ax for your neck. No." Spittle flew from Gharavan's lips as he rose in the saddle. "You will die the death of a Ghebite traitor, tied between four galloping horses, your limbs pulled from their sockets while you scream in agony!"

Tulkhan grew cold and still inside. He lifted his eyes from Gharavan's white knuckles to his fanatical features. His half-brother hated him with an irrational intensity Tulkhan recognized but could not comprehend. Silence stretched between them. A gull called, reminding him that the sea was not far away.

When Tulkhan spoke, his even tone held more menace than any roar. "I thank you for telling me your contingency plans. And I thank you for killing the last love I bore the boy I knew. When I banished you from Fair Isle, I said I no longer had a half-brother. But it took until today for you to make this true. Ride away, little king, scurry back inside your gate and hide under your bed, for you have had the last easy night's sleep you will ever know!"

Gharavan jerked on the reins, making his horse dance in a half circle. "I call down a curse on your house and your blood. The bastard child you claim to have sired will never sit on the throne of Fair Isle, because I will take the island and execute all of your traitorous commanders, saving the

Dhamfeer bitch and her half-breed cub for last. When I have finished with her she will beg me for death."

Tulkhan felt a muscle jump in his cheek, but he remained impassive.

Still cursing, Gharavan and his supporters galloped back to the gate. Tulkhan watched him go, his heart hard as stone.

When the General returned to the campsite, he discovered his hands were shaking. But there was much to be done. Teams of men had been sent to scour the farmlands for food and useful tools. They returned laden with cartloads of stores from the farms and reported the land deserted. Hardly a mongrel dog remained. Tulkhan had left orders not to pursue the Low-landers. He wanted an ally, not an enemy on Fair Isle's doorstep.

His men were exhausted, yet despite the failure to take the port, they were in good spirits as Tulkhan planned his defensive earthworks. They needed to be secure from attack from the port and from Gharavan's auxiliary army.

Full dark saw the General's campsite fires dotting the plain like stars. Not having slept in more than two days, he rotated his shoulders wearily, then turned, surprised by the familiar voice. "Wharrd? I thought I left you in Northpoint. What's that stench?"

"Mud. You try crossing the mud flats below the Sea-wall!"

Tulkhan grinned. "What brings you here?"

"It was come myself or watch Imoshen come." He offered the formal salute of a Ghebite to his leader, but Tulkhan grabbed him by the shoulders, hugging him.

Wharrd cleared his throat. "You had us fooled. We thought you blockaded the port by sea."

"That was the idea." He glanced around. Kornel was nearby as always but out of hearing; even so, Tulkhan lowered his voice. "But as you see, my surprise attack failed, so now I lay siege. How did it fare with Peirs?"

"He bombarded the wharves and dockside as planned. Spot fires broke out all over the city. A third of the merchants' quarter burned down, which will make Gharavan very unpopular." Wharrd chuckled, then sobered. "When Peirs heard you sound the retreat, he recalled his men. The port remains sealed by sea."

"And we have her sealed by land. But they have two years' supply of grain, and Gharavan was foolish enough to let me know he has sent for support from the annexed kingdoms. He looks forward to watching me die a traitor's death. He threatened to execute every Ghebite loyal to me."

Wharrd cursed softly. "How much time do we have before Gharavan's auxiliaries arrive?"

Tulkhan squinted into the flames. "If the Low-landers are anything to go by, there's a good chance the annexed countries will delay to see which way the wind blows."

"I'd be happier knowing your army was up to strength."

"So would I. This plain is perfect for cavalry, and I haven't a decent horse to call my own. Have Imoshen send over siege machines and two companies of my best cavalry, in case Gharavan does get his auxiliaries. You'll have to negotiate for their passage with one of the southern kingdoms. Diplomacy," Tulkhan muttered disgustedly. "And I don't have the weight of the Ghebite Empire at my back."

"You would claim Fair Isle for your own!"

"What choice had I?" Tulkhan countered. They grinned, then fell silent. A man brought them local beer, served warm and flat. Tulkhan sipped his, deep in thought.

"I have some good news," Wharrd announced. "Imoshen bargained with the mercenaries. Their lives for revenge. They will serve you. She'll send them over as soon as you are ready."

Tulkhan smiled ruefully. Trust Imoshen: she could not simply follow his orders, she had to go one better. "I hope they prove more loyal than their leader."

Wharrd shrugged and straightened, stretching. "I'm getting too old for this."

"Never say!"

"I want no part in the fate of kingdoms. A warm fireside, Kalleen, and my children—that is all I ask." He hesitated. "You should know I am sworn to T'Imoshen's service."

Tulkhan looked up at his old friend. "A Ghiad?"

"Imoshen saved Kalleen's life. Until I repay that debt, I am under an obligation to her."

"Does she understand what a Ghiad means?"

"I don't think she will ask me to fall on my sword. In fact, she tried to release me. I told her this was impossible, but, no . . . she doesn't understand."

Tulkhan came to his feet, clasping the older man's shoulder. "Then I don't envy you, my friend, for Imoshen is Dhamfeer and almost beyond a True-man's protection. I fear you will be under this Ghiad until death releases you."

"Then so be it. My honor allows nothing less." Wharrd returned the pressure on Tulkhan's shoulder. "There is honor in serving the last T'En Empress."

Tulkhan could not meet his eyes. If Wharrd knew Imoshen carried Reothe's child, he would not use the word *honor* in the same breath as her name. Worse, he would despise his general for not avenging himself. Frustration ate at Tulkhan, but . . . one problem at a time, for now he had to deal with Gharavan.

"Is there some word you would have me carry to Imoshen?" Wharrd asked.

Tulkhan shook his head.

"I must go." Wharrd swung his cloak around his shoulders.

"Tell her . . ." Tulkhan stopped.

Wharrd nodded. Then he was gone, slipping into the shadows while Tulkhan stared into the fire.

Imoshen was up with the sun, seeing to Ashmyr's needs. She could have asked a servant to care for him, but she delighted in the way his eyes lit up when he recognized her. Her maid's door-comb sounded discreetly, identifying her by its tone. "Enter, Dyta."

Imoshen smiled with relief as the woman escorted Wharrd into the room. She placed Ashmyr in his basket before greeting the veteran. "Do you want something to eat?"

Wharrd shook his head and, as the door closed, Imoshen realized it would be rumored that she had taken the General's closest friend for her lover. But Kalleen knew better. She had been put aside not for lust but for honor. How could she fight a concept?

"Kalleen and I feared for your safety when you did not return or send word."

"Secrecy was essential for the General's plans."

"Tulkhan is alive and well?"

"Yes. He took his army across the marsh-lands."

"Impossible!"

Wharrd grinned. "They attacked Port Sumair the dawn after Harvest Feast but the port's defenses held, so now he lays siege."

"War games!"

"This is no game. If Tulkhan fails, Gharavan will have him dismembered. The General is all that stands between Fair Isle and his half-brother's greed for revenge!"

Hiding her dismay, Imoshen walked to the oriel windows.

"Tulkhan needs you to negotiate safe passage for cavalry and siege machines. And he needs men and supplies immediately."

"As soon as I have the ships I will send the mercenaries and more supplies. You look tired, Wharrd. You should see Kalleen."

He agreed, but she could see he did not understand.

Imoshen looked out over the T'Ronynn Straits, blind to the sea's intense blue. Tulkhan's army needed supplies. The merchants of Fair Isle would not be pleased to find their profits taxed yet again. She would have to select an ambassador to negotiate with the Amirate, the kingdom to Sumair's south. With a sigh she returned to her desk and opened her writing case. Imoshen smiled to herself. The old tales did not dwell on the business of war. It was won or lost on supplies and maneuvering, and she was going to make certain the General won this encounter.

Imoshen stood, arching her back. She had been working since she sent Wharrd to the capital, laden with messages.

"Here's your fresh bread and hot spiced milk, my lady." Dyta placed the tray on the chest before the fire. "It's a cold day for traveling. I tried to get the Lady Kalleen to have some warmed wine, but—"

"Kalleen has gone?"

"Her entourage gathers in the forecourt."

Imoshen ran out the door and down the spiral staircase. From the tower's entrance she could see travelers milling in the courtyard below. Recollecting her dignity, Imoshen slowed as she approached Kalleen, taking the horse's bridle. "You are leaving?"

Kalleen nodded, arranging her cape over her legs to keep out the wind.

Imoshen led the horse a little away from the others. "I had hoped with Wharrd's return you would reconsider."

"He has already left in your service."

"At least let me provide you with an escort." Imoshen called Jarholfe and told him to organize this. Then she returned her attention to Kalleen. "They will be ready soon enough."

For a few minutes they stood in stiff silence, Imoshen at the horse's head, Kalleen straight and cold in the saddle. Around them, the men shouted, horses were saddled, and there was the sound of running boots on the stones as guards went to collect their traveling kits.

"I am sorry it has come to this, Kalleen."

"Ask Wharrd what it means for a Ghebite to be under a Ghiad."

But Imoshen was concerned with other things. "If Fair Isle is attacked from the mainland, Windhaven will be one of the first places to fall. Promise me you will head for T'Diemn at the first sign of attack."

Kalleen eyed her solemnly. "Is war so certain?"

"Nothing is certain. Which is why we must be ready."

Tulkhan's farm horse picked its way through his men, who wielded shovels instead of swords. He rose in the saddle to study the layout of his camp. On horseback he was the tallest point. He could see the smudge that was the Sea-wall, and closer still another smudge was the north-wall. The plain was a maze of landlets encircled by walls until you came at last to the Sea-wall, where even the industrious Low-landers had decided the land was not worth reclaiming.

With no high ground where he could mount a defense, he needed trenches, long and deep to protect his army's back and flanks in the event of attack. Earth was being rammed into place to form a thick-based wall within the trenchworks. This faced inland, stretching in a great half circle from the Sea-wall south of Sumair to the north Sea-wall.

Yet it was not enough if the defenders tried to break the siege. So a second defenseworks was also under construction facing the port.

Tulkhan grinned to himself. All this work kept his men busy. And the digging provided good cover for their attempts to mine under the port's walls. Tulkhan didn't intend to let this siege grow dull. It frustrated him that there was so little timber. The houses were made of dried sods that formed hard bricks. He could not build siege machines or watchtowers without decent wood.

On the breeze he heard the laughter of a child and saw the marsh-dweller's son dashing through his men. The father caught him, cast an anxious glance about, and retreated.

Tulkhan hadn't seen anything of the man and his son since he failed to take the port. Banuld was probably afraid Tulkhan's temper would find an outlet in him. It was a matter of honor with the General to treat his men firmly but fairly. Soon he would reward the marsh-dweller and send him home.

Leaving his mount with the horse-handlers, Tulkhan greeted Kornel. "It would be quicker to bring my supplies over the Sea-wall than through the marshes. I want to see this Sea-wall."

As they rode through the abandoned fields, the moons were waning but they were still bright. Tulkhan gave the port a wide berth and before long he was facing the Sea-wall. On the landward side it was a steep hill, twice as tall as Tulkhan on horseback. He dismounted and clambered up the slope.

Heart thudding with the effort, he reached the crest, where it was wide enough for three men to walk abreast. Tulkhan peered over the seaward side. No water lapped at the Sea-wall's base. Mud stretched for a great distance before he made out the glimmer of moonlight on water.

"Why do they build so high?" he called down to Kornel, who had hobbled the horses and was scuttling up to join him.

He paused a moment to mop his face with his shirttail before answering. "Storm surge. This is low tide just after the twin full moons. See how far the mud flats stretch? Even at high tide a deep draft ship would have to send the men in by the boatload. They'd churn up the mud so bad they'd be stuck waist deep, and then the narcts would get them like beached whales."

"We could stand guard. Kill a few and scare them off."

"They're attracted by blood, and out in the channel..." Kornel pointed to a dark smudge in the moonlit sea. "See the islands drifting with the currents and tides? The narcts nest on them."

Tulkhan realized what he had thought were the shadows of clouds on the sea were actually drifting islands. He would have to bring supplies and men through the marsh. The lights of his blockading ships bobbed on the sea. "I need to signal the ships. Have you something to burn?"

Kornel dragged off his grimy coat. Tulkhan opened his coal pouch. Setting fire to Kornel's coat, he swung it in an arc above his head.

It seemed to take an age before a boat rowed across the moonlit sea toward them. Impatient, Tulkhan slid down the Sea-wall's steep incline.

"Wait!" Kornel began, but too late. The General sank knee deep in thick, sticky mud. It gave off foul bubbles as he struggled to pull his legs out. "Stay there, Kornel. No need for you to get filthy too."

No need for Kornel to hear what plans Tulkhan made. The merchant captain had been helpful so far, but Tulkhan suspected Kornel worshiped only one god and it gleamed gold.

Imoshen studied the mainland map, trying to imagine how Tulkhan had marched his army through the marsh-lands.

"Deep in thought?" Reothe's rich voice startled her.

Pushing the books aside so that the map rolled closed, she walked around the desk to face him. After discovering how much she craved Reothe's presence, Imoshen had deliberately avoided him. Now he confronted her, one side of his face lifting in a painful smile while he leaned heavily on his walking stick. It hurt her to see him like this, yet she was relieved to know his menace was contained in the crippled shell of his body. She could have urged his body to mend itself, but they both knew she was not ready for the intimacy needed to heal.

"You pace the floor at night, this night even more so, Imoshen. I hear Wharrd has returned and gone again."

"What excellent spies you have. Did they also tell you the General crossed the marsh-lands but failed to take Port Sumair?"

"Then Fair Isle is a ripe plum waiting to be plucked by the Ghebites, or any mainland power." He made his way to the desk, nudged the chair, and let his weight down carefully. He sat for a moment, fighting dizziness, she suspected.

Imoshen fought the need to stroke the line of pain from his forehead. "The General lays siege to the port even now. I must send more men, siege machines, and cavalry."

"That will take time to organize."

She shrugged. "That's what a siege is, a waiting game. Usually. Unfortunately, Gharavan has called on the allied kingdoms to send auxiliary armies."

"The T'En once had treaties with the triad of southern kingdoms. It would not hurt to remind them of this."

"They did not come to our aid when we asked for help against General Tulkhan," Imoshen remarked bitterly.

"No. They were eager to see us brought low," Reothe agreed. "But now that the Ghebites are on the move again, they will side with the stronger force. You must convince them that the Empress of Fair Isle and her war general are that force. If you do not, you will have trouble securing a safe port to unload your cavalry and siege machines." He cursed softly. "If only I were whole!"

Imoshen studied him. Reothe, her ambassador? What would stop him from playing a double game, ensuring support to usurp Tulkhan? Perhaps it was just as well he was not "helping" her.

"What?" Reothe asked. "I mislike that expression."

"Your counsel is good."

"Does it please you to see me brought low, Imoshen?"

She gasped. "How can you think that?"

"Then why do you avoid me?"

Imoshen looked away. Whenever she closed her eyes, she saw him lying on the fur in the moonlight and she ached to go to him and claim her T'En heritage in every way. "I have been busy with matters of state."

"How convenient."

She hid a smile. Ashmyr made a soft mewing sound in his sleep and she knelt to watch him.

"The Ancients returned his soul, but... You could delve into his mind to see if he is recovered," Reothe suggested.

"It is against my principles to invade an unwilling mind."

"Unwilling?"

"Uninvited, then."

"Seriously, Imoshen, how can you afford such principles?"

She flushed, meeting Reothe's eyes. He was stroking the vellum map. Once he would have been able to discern her thoughts while she pored over the map.

Reothe pushed it aside. "You are shut away from me. Do I disgust you?"

"No."

"Then why do you avoid me?"

His question remained unanswered because of what Imoshen dared not reveal. She stood and poured the wine, offering him a glass, but he shrugged impatiently.

The goblet was exquisite blown glass, more evidence that the Ghebite Lord of Northpoint had not stinted himself. Everyone looked after their own interests, except her. She wanted what was best for Fair Isle. There was no time for doubts.

She wound both her hands around the goblet's stem. "I will speak plainly, Reothe. Tulkhan is the only one who stands between our island and the greedy mainlanders who have long resented our wealth and power. If the General defeats Gharavan, every petty prince will rise up to snatch what they can of the crippled Ghebite Empire. Hopefully, they will be too preoccupied to bother Fair Isle." She swirled the wine around, watching its deep burgundy surface glisten in the candlelight, rich and dark as Reothe's eyes, which gave nothing away. "But if Tulkhan falls, we face invasion. I need your support."

"Fair Isle almost bled to death during the General's invasion," Reothe said. "He must crush his half-brother. Port Sumair's granaries are deep. Can the General wait out the winter?"

"I'm hoping he won't have to. I will send the mercenaries and more supplies. Meanwhile, my ambassadors will negotiate safe passage for cavalry and siege machines. Who knows? With the right rumors the conquered countries may yet rise up and revolt. King Gharavan could find himself king of nothing!"

Reothe smiled. "I will not insult you by saying you think like a man."

Imoshen felt the blood rush to her face, and a sweet pain filled her. Shortly after their first meeting, Tulkhan had accused her of thinking like a man, a typically Ghebite comment. She and Reothe shared a common heritage.

Drawn to him despite her better judgment, she placed

a hand on Reothe's shoulder. When he pressed his lean cheek to the back of her hand, she felt the heat of his skin. Her lips brushed his head. She longed to open her T'En senses, reach out and touch his essence. She felt so empty she ached. The moment stretched impossibly.

With great effort she pulled away and walked around the desk to top up her wine. "Drink to our bargain?"

"What bargain? I have agreed to nothing, Imoshen." His features hardened. "Or did you think to seal my agreement with the offer of your body? Tantalizing as it is, I must decline."

She froze. Seeing his knowing expression, she realized he could read her actions, even if he could no longer sense her thoughts. Shame and fury lashed Imoshen, but she schooled her features, putting her glass aside. "All I ask is your support to hold Fair Isle."

"I called off the Keldon nobles, didn't I? I am loyal to Fair Isle. Can you say the same?"

"All I have done has been for Fair Isle!"

"Perhaps," he conceded, suddenly tired.

He stood stiffly, and Imoshen took a step toward him, her hand extended. He flicked it aside angrily. "Your maid is a terrible gossip, Imoshen. She will know exactly how long I have been alone with you. By tomorrow morning everyone will believe we are lovers."

"We've been discussing matters of state! If I were a man, they would not think otherwise."

He smiled slowly. "But you are not a man. You are a beautiful woman made more desirable by the power you wield. Besides"—Reothe's eyes gleamed with painful self-knowledge—"we both know the only reason we are not lovers in deed, as well as intent, is because this body of mine is—"

"But I have never sought to seduce you!"

"True. Now tell me you've never desired me."

She swallowed. "You must tell them the truth."

"If you wish. I will explain that we were discussing how to hold Fair Isle in the event of the General's death." He cut short her protest with a shrug. "Let them believe what they choose, Imoshen. It is only a matter of time. The General will disown you because you carry my child."

"Is that why you—" She laughed bitterly. "He told me by Ghebite law he should strangle me and our son!"

Reothe's eyes widened in surprise.

"What did you expect? Ghebites think differently."

"Yet you still live," he countered.

"Yes. As do you. And I don't know why."

"It is a simple thing to find out." Reothe frowned when she would not hold his eyes. "Let me guess. He made you promise not to use your gifts on him, and your honor won't let you break a promise. Why do you find it so hard to break a vow to him, when you broke your vows to me?"

"How can you speak of vows and honor?" Tears stung her eyes, making her realize how deeply his betrayal had hurt. "You tricked me!"

He uttered a short bark of laughter. Her hand lashed out, but he caught her wrist and pulled her against his chest. Her heart raced, her breath caught in her throat. Everything else receded but his nearness. She could have freed herself in an instant but, treacherously, she longed for his touch.

"Yes, I tricked you. But your body recognized me just as it does now. We were meant for each other. Only in your company do I feel truly alive, and when our minds touch . . ." He shuddered. For an instant Reothe's features were illuminated by a fey passion. His beauty stole her breath. He was so Other that she feared her instinctive attraction to him.

She sprang away, shaking her head.

"No?" He gestured to himself. "You did this. You could have turned your gifts on me at any time."

But she did not dare unleash the powers he seemed so sure of. At least for the moment they were equal. His abilities were crippled and hers untutored. "How could I suspect my true potential when everyone believes the males are more powerful than the females? You hid the T'Elegos. It is as much my birthright as yours!"

"You have only to ask and I will share *everything* with you."

She fought a heady rush of desire. He promised so much more than the knowledge of their T'En legacy, but her choice was made. "I'm sorry, Reothe. I must stand by my vow to Tulkhan."

"You surrendered to save your life, Imoshen. Your vow to me is of an older making and sprang from your own free will."

"Our betrothal belongs to a lost future."

"I have the Sight. I've glimpsed many futures. I believe we can claim the future we want. Look at your left wrist."

A sharp sting made her gasp and she covered her wrist. But she could not deny that the bonding scar they both shared had split open.

Shortly after General Tulkhan accepted her surrender, Reothe had come to her at Landsend Abbey. He had offered to help her escape but she had already given the General her word, and the people of Fair Isle relied on her to smooth the transition of power. Before she could explain this, Reothe had cut their wrists to begin the bonding ceremony, but she had refused to complete the oath. In Landsend Abbey she had made a decision to follow her head, not her heart; now, just over a year later, she hoped it had been the right decision. Imoshen gritted her teeth as blood welled between her fingers.

"Imoshen?" The tone of Reothe's voice made her look up to see him raise his left arm. A thin trickle of blood seeped from the wound across his wrist. "I once told you it would stop bleeding on the day we were properly joined. We have shared our bodies and our minds, yet you still refuse me. This might not be a perfect future, but it is all we have and I will not give up!"

His vehemence frightened her. She sealed the wound with her tongue, tasting the bitter tang of her blood. "You forget I hold your life in my hands."

"Then kill me and stop this farce, because I find it too painful to bear. You see, compassion is but another name for cruelty, sweet T'Imoshen." His voice vibrated with truth. He turned his wrist to reveal the bleeding wound. "Heal me."

"Never."

"Then I will never reveal the T'Elegos, and you will destroy yourself and everything you love because you cannot control your powers."

Imoshen staggered, reaching blindly for the table.

"Think on it, Imoshen. I am your anchor. You need me!" Torturously slow, but with great dignity, he left her.

Seven

TULKHAN STRODE TO the entrance of his makeshift command shelter. The smoke of many cooking fires rose on the still, dawn air. Men called to one another, their voices carrying. After eleven years of campaigning it was familiar and reassuring.

Tulkhan cleared his throat. "Kornel, where's Banuld?"

"Probably by the kitchen fires, gambling away his beer rations," Kornel muttered, and disappeared. By the time he had returned, Tulkhan was seated under the awning at a table scavenged from some farm kitchen, drinking warm beer and eating honey cakes. Banuld looked wary, if hopeful.

"Tell the marsh-dweller I have good news and bad. I will be sending him to his village but without his son." Tulkhan saw the marsh-dweller's anger quickly masked as Kornel spoke.

"Ban?" Tulkhan lifted his arms. The boy glanced to his father, who signaled that he should obey. Eagerly, the child ran into Tulkhan's arms. He had won the boy with sweet nuts and rides along the earthworks. Absently, Tulkhan stroked Ban's head, feeling the many tiny plaits the marsh-dwellers used to confine their long hair. He met the father's eyes. "Banuld-Chi, you will lead Kornel and his men through the marshes."

Tulkhan watched as Kornel translated. The boy nudged his arm and pointed to the nuts, and Tulkhan obligingly cracked one between his fingers. Ban tried to do the same trick with his small hands. Tulkhan grinned, taking the nut from Ban and cracking it in his teeth as he would have done as a boy.

Kornel ceased his translation and turned back to the General. "He asks why?"

"I have three boatloads of mercenaries coming across the T'Ronynn Straits. I need you, Kornel, to take the shallow draft boats to the river mouth. By the time you get there, all the mercenaries will be waiting. You'll bring them over the Marsh-wall to me. That is why I need Banuld to guide you through the marshes. I will pay him for his services."

Kornel nodded. "Warn the mercenaries to build big fires and post watch when they make their camp at the river mouth. That should keep the narcts at bay."

It was too late to warn them. Tulkhan had sent a message to Imoshen last night while he was aboard Peirs's ship. He poured three mugs of warm beer, offering them to Kornel and Banuld, who accepted his with surprise. "To a swift passage through the marshes and a short siege!"

When the captain translated, Banuld added his own toast with an elaborate hand signal. Tulkhan looked to Kornel, who explained, "That's their blessing. May your feet always find dry ground."

Tulkhan laughed and drained his beer, wiping his mouth. "After crossing the marshes I can appreciate that!"

Kornel grinned and eyed the remaining beer, so Tulkhan obliged. He needed their loyalty, even though he would send his own men with them; if either one betrayed him, he would be left here with the barest minimum of men and supplies.

Tulkhan lifted his mug. "Sumair is a rich port. I hear her merchants live like princes. To the spoils of war!"

"The spoils of war!" Kornel's deep eyes gleamed.

"A blockade ship has arrived with a message." Dyta stepped back to let a young soldier with a gingery mustache and freckled skin enter Imoshen's chamber.

He gave her a Ghebite bow and dug inside his jerkin to remove a sealed missive. "Rawset, on behalf of General Tulkhan. I made the night crossing."

"Bring food and warmed wine for two, Dyta," Imoshen said. The woman departed and Imoshen accepted the message, noting that Rawset was careful not to meet her eyes or let their fingers make contact.

The residue of Tulkhan's personality remained on the paper, making her skin prickle with the memory of his touch. Lifting the missive to her face, she inhaled. What she learned reassured her. Tulkhan had not written this under duress.

Lost in thought, she rocked Ashmyr's basket while she broke the seal and read. As Tulkhan's words formed in her mind, his voice, his scent, and his manner returned to her. She felt dizzy with his presence and the rediscovery of her love for him. Tears of longing swam in her vision, but she blinked them away fiercely. So the General wanted his supplies and men to travel through the marshes. "You know the contents, Rawset?"

He nodded.

The old woman returned with a tray.

"Dyta, tell Lightfoot the first shipload of his mercenaries will sail this morning," Imoshen said. "Eat while I write a reply, Rawset." She took her scriber, dipped it in the ink, then thought long and hard over a reply—so long, in fact, that the ink dried and she had to re-ink the scriber.

Telling the General her plans did not require a great deal of thought. It was how to word her reassurances that troubled Imoshen. She was sure some rumor of how things appeared between herself and Reothe would eventually reach the General. Finally she opted for formal courtesy. When the mercenaries reached Tulkhan, he would not doubt her loyalty.

"I want you to put this in General Tulkhan's hands, Rawset." She placed the message on the table. "And I want all communication that passes between the General and myself to come via you."

Rawset swallowed, his Adam's apple bobbing, and pushed the plate aside. "I will not see the General until all three boatloads of mercenaries have been delivered to the marsh river mouth."

Imoshen nodded and lifted the candle, pointing to her message. "Hold it flat."

She let hot wax drip to form a puddle, then pressed her sixth finger in to seal it. The heat stung. A rush of urgency filled her as she looked down into Rawset's face. She wanted to ensure his loyalty as she had ensured the mercenary's. "Can I trust you, Rawset of the Ghebites?"

He nodded. "But I am no longer a Ghebite. I am General Tulkhan's man."

"Then you are my man," Imoshen whispered. She fought the urge to touch him with her sixth finger. "You are *mine*."

His eyes never left her face. "I am yours."

Imoshen smiled, stepping back. "Good. Go now."

Four nights later, torchlight flickered as the last shipload of mercenaries left for the marsh-lands, and Imoshen stood on the docks to see them off.

"T'Imoshen?" The harbormaster approached.

On this, her final evening in Northpoint, Imoshen had invited the town officials for warmed wine. In a blur of weariness, she led them back to the great hall, where she performed the leave-taking ceremony, serving them with her own hands, her servitude to them a symbol of her servitude to Fair Isle. She said all the right things, but nothing could change the facts. From the lowliest candle trimmer to Imoshen herself, they faced an uncertain future.

At last they departed and Imoshen retreated to T'Ronynn's Tower. She felt Ashmyr's weight as she climbed the stairs. All was quiet; the servants, their preparations completed, were already in bed.

The door to her room had been left ajar, and she saw that the windows were also open. The candles had not been lit and the fire had been allowed to burn down to embers. Imoshen sniffed in annoyance.

Ashmyr slept soundly as she placed him in his basket, tucking the down-filled comforter around him. She straightened, arched her back, and slipped off her boots, wriggling her bare toes on the rug. It was cold, but there was no point in stirring up the flames until she closed the windows.

Padding lightly across the floor, she went to the semicircle and leaned out to pull in each window. The night was so clear she could almost see the lights of the blockading ships across the straits. Tulkhan had entrusted her to keep Fair Isle safe. She missed her great-aunt's advice. If the rebels hadn't tried to assassinate Tulkhan, the Aayel might still be alive. Unarmed, he had fought off three attackers, which hadn't done his reputation any harm. But it was the Aayel's bravery that Imoshen recalled. Her great-aunt had taken the blame on herself, saving Imoshen by committing suicide. That failed assassination attempt had cost Imoshen dearly.

As she crossed to the fireplace, a shape detached itself from the shadows. An assassin?

Light arced across the room, a thousand small comets of fire. Flames roared up in the grate, throwing crazy, leaping shadows, illuminating Reothe's arrested expression as he balanced precariously without his walking stick.

"Imoshen, don't!" Reothe's warning cut through the roaring in her head.

She staggered back several steps, almost tripping over the baby. With a gasp she discovered live coals glowing on his blanket, eating their way through to him. With a soundless cry of horror, she plucked the coals from the cradle and threw them into the roaring fire.

No pain registered.

"Imoshen, the bed curtains."

Hungry yellow flames licked at the thick material that was tied back to the bedposts. Pushing Reothe aside, she snatched the water pitcher and doused the fire.

But the room was still thick with the smell of smoke, and the fire had dropped as suddenly as it rose. All around her on the floor, the chair, and her desk were the winking, glowing eyes of live coals. Cursing under her breath, she snatched up the hot coals, dropping them in the jug. Any on the floor she stamped out while Reothe lit the candles. He rebuilt the fire, coaxing it to burn brightly, and the sweet scent of fresh popping resin filled the room, overlaying the smell of charred material.

Imoshen went to the windows to empty the water jug of its charcoal sludge. When she turned, Reothe was just rising, one hand on the mantelpiece to steady himself.

He met her gaze, a rueful smile lighting his sharp features. "Remind me never to surprise you."

"I was thinking of the assassination attempt on Tulkhan." She put the jug aside.

"Did you get all the live coals?"

"Yes." Only then did she become aware of the pain in her fingers and feet. Gritting her teeth, she confronted Reothe. "Why are you here?"

"I bribed your maid to go to bed early."

"That is how, not why."

"That was quite spectacular. If I had been an assassin, I would have been surprised enough for you to incapacitate me before I could strike. But it was also dangerous. Ashmyr—"

"Don't you think I know!" She inspected the sleeping infant, but he was blissfully unaware.

"You're burned. Where are your herbs?"

Imoshen was so weary, and she found the idea of Reothe taking care of her insidiously sweet. "The herbs are in the small cabinet behind my desk." Sinking into the chair, she watched him limp to the cabinet and study its contents. "You don't need your walking stick?"

"I pace the parapets three times a day."

Imoshen watched as he unstoppered a glass jar and sniffed the contents. "You will find the—"

"I know what I am looking for. Healing might be your gift, but I have a working knowledge of herbal lore."

She smiled at his tone. In pain but perversely happy, she waited as he returned with the soothing ointment. It was odd to find Reothe kneeling at her feet. A little quiver swept through her. His strong hand closed around her ankle, and she turned her face away to hide the pain he was causing her.

"Curse me, if it will help," he urged.

Imoshen had to smile. She stole a look at him. He was watching her fondly. If only ... A stab of loss made her gasp.

"I'm clumsy," he apologized.

Imoshen shook her head, unable to speak. She resented never having the chance to know Reothe without the fate of Fair Isle coming between them. He took her other foot and she looked into the flames to hide her thoughts.

"Now your hands."

"I can do them."

"Show me."

When she did, she realized bending her fingers around a bottle to take out the stopper would be painful.

"Do not weep, Imoshen."

"I am not weeping. My eyes leak."

He laughed. It hurt her far more than the burns, because she wanted to hug that laugh and never relinquish its intimacy.

"My beautiful liar," Reothe whispered. "Don't look at me like that. I swear I will forget my vow."

"What vow?"

But he only shook his head. "You will not be able to hold the reins tomorrow. We will have to share my invalid wagon."

Imoshen wanted to argue, but he was right.

"Now your other hand," he ordered.

Offering him the other hand, palm up, she found the sweep of his long fingers almost hypnotic. She could have sat like this for hours, bearing the pain just to have him near her, unthreatening.

A quick smile illuminated his features. "Now that I know you will be in the wagon with me, I will not insist on riding until you are well enough to do so. That was why I wanted to see you. It did not suit me to ride in a wagon like someone's grandfather."

Imoshen snorted. "I nearly set fire to the room because

it did not suit your dignity to ride in a wagon? It would have been quicker to send a message."

"Quicker, but not nearly as instructive."

She drew a quick breath. "You are an unprincipled creature, Reothe. Is everything and everyone grist for your mill?"

His smile faded, revealing his underlying acute intelligence. "Ask yourself this, Imoshen. What is really important to you, and what would you give up to ensure that outcome? I know my answer."

"There we differ, Reothe, because my question is not what, but who. I will not sacrifice people for ideals—"

He laughed and stood. "That is what you say. Maybe it is even what you believe. But I see you using True-people every day to serve your purpose. In denying your T'En nature you deny what you could be. Look what happened tonight."

"This was an accident because you surprised me."

"But why didn't you sense my presence?"

Imoshen looked away.

"What game are you playing, Imoshen, pretending to be a Mere-woman, when we both know—"

"I will not be lectured by you of all people!"

The baby woke with a shrill cry of panic. Coming to her feet, Imoshen gasped in pain and almost fell. Reothe caught her. The pair of them swayed as he struggled to keep his balance.

"Sit down, I will bring him to you."

When Reothe lowered the baby into her arms, she tried to undo the bodice of her gown but her hands were too sore. Wordlessly, he knelt at her side, his long fingers unplucking the lacings. Her breasts ached with the rush of milk. An equal rush of heat pooled within her.

Reothe tucked the bodice under her swollen breast and helped guide the baby's urgent mouth to her nipple. A gasp of relief escaped Imoshen. She pressed her forearm to her other breast to stem the flow of milk.

Reothe drew in a ragged breath. When he lifted his eyes to her face, she knew that he wanted her with every fiber of his being, and her body responded with an instant tug of recognition that went beyond conscious thought.

She looked down and took a long, deep breath. It was a mistake. His body's scent had changed, triggering a rise in her heart rate. A dangerous, sweet languor stole the strength from her limbs.

"I ..." She had to clear her throat. "I will not compromise my vows."

"I know."

But he drew nearer to inhale her scent, and shame filled her, flooding her cheeks, because she wanted him.

"You intoxicate me, Imoshen."

"Please, don't do this."

"Don't fear me." His tone surprised her and he held her eyes. "I won't trick you again. When you come to me, it will be of your own free will. Nothing less will satisfy me."

Her mouth went dry, and she seemed to feel her heart beating like a great drum, throbbing through her limbs, each beat a tide of desire, ebbing and rising through her flesh.

When the secondary meaning of his words hit her, tears stung her eyes. "I trusted you—"

"I did not ask you to trust me. I asked you to join me. I told you I would win whatever the odds." His voice was sweet and reasonable. Yet ...

"Am I nothing but a tool to you, Reothe?" Imoshen asked sadly.

"Come to me freely. You will be the breath in my body." His eyes flared, the leaping firelight dancing in their dark depths. "As one we would be invincible."

It came to her that T'Reothe was totally ruthless but honorable by his own code, and she realized that to bond with him meant much more than she had anticipated when she had agreed to their betrothal. A single tear, shed for her lost innocence, slipped down her cheek.

Imoshen stared into the fire.

"You deny me," Reothe whispered. "I offer everything I am, and could be, and you turn your face from me. How cruel is that?"

Swaying a little, he came to his feet. Stunned, he slowly turned away. It pained her to see that his limp was more pronounced. He paused by the door as she knew he would.

"I am weary of our battles, Imoshen. Tonight I am weary beyond thought. But my body heals, growing stronger every day."

"What of your gifts?" It was out before she could stop herself.

"My gifts?" His eyes glittered. "The T'En in me is an open wound. Every day I prod it without meaning to. Every touch sends me to my knees. The pain robs me of the power of thought and speech. You did this. You emasculated the last T'En warrior. Now who will save our people?"

"I didn't mean to," Imoshen whispered. "If it hurts you to use your T'En gifts, don't—"

He laughed softly. "It is instinctive, Imoshen. Every day I am reminded of your cruel love. A love that would let me live in pain."

"I am more sorry than you can know."

His angry gaze met hers, frankly skeptical. "Do not mock your gelding, T'Imoshen; the beast may throw you yet."

Fear made Imoshen's heart redouble its pace, but she would not look down. For a long moment she dared not blink, then Reothe winced and felt for the doorjamb to steady himself.

She flinched in sympathy, understanding he had reached for his gift. "Reothe?"

But he shook his head, closing the door on her sympathy.

Ashmyr stopping suckling, squirmed, and gave a little cry. She lifted him to her shoulder, gritting her teeth at the pain in her hands. Though Reothe was gone, Imoshen's body trembled with reaction. Seeing to Ashmyr relaxed her.

"That's what you get for gulping your food," she told the baby. A satisfied burp escaped him. She looked into his face. He was falling asleep again. "No, you don't. You haven't finished."

Her other breast ached. She tilted Ashmyr across her body and he woke up enough to latch onto her nipple and resume his feed. She leaned her head against the back of the chair. Reothe had deliberately startled her. A rueful smile warmed her. She hoped he had enjoyed the show, but it worried her to have so little control.

Reothe believed she could heal him and she suspected he was right, but if she did, he would become the wild card in her deck. Reothe returned to his full capabilities was someone to be feared. Yet how could she live with herself if she let him suffer? Bitter self-knowledge filled her. She would let him suffer because it was safest. But she did not want to ride in the wagon with him. Imoshen cursed softly and sought to heal herself.

Closing her eyes, she was dismayed to find her gift exhausted. Panic flared. This was worse than when she had been training at the Aayel's side. Then she had not always found the little spurt of warmth that hastened healing.

Wearily, Imoshen opened her eyes and her gaze fell on a charred smear of ash, triggering a memory of flying coals, roaring unnatural flames. Comprehension shook her. The defensive burst had exhausted her reserves. Already she could feel a mind-numbing weariness creeping upon her. It seemed there was a price to pay for the use of her gifts. A prickle of fear lifted the little hairs on her arms. What else was Reothe keeping from her? If only she could read the T'Elegos and learn how the T'En trained their young.

Imoshen closed her eyes as waves of pain and weariness swept over her. She could not stop an assassin now.

This jolted her. Was there no way to defend herself? Sifting into her reserves, she found nothing, but a bright flare of external anger drew her questing T'En senses. Somewhere on the floor below, True-men were gambling. Their avaricious intensity called to her. She could taste it on her tongue, sharpening her awareness.

She was reminded of the time she caught the Ghebites betting on their fighting birds. The buildup of their lust for blood and violence had almost overwhelmed her. That day she had only just managed to channel it into destroying the birds. Now she understood the principle involved.

Four men crouched two floors below her. She could sense their eager reaction to the turn of a card. One was a Ghebite, the other three were locals. It was the Ghebite who interested her. He was a mass of impulses—anger because he was losing, brittle fear because he suspected the Citadel guards of cheating him, though he couldn't prove it, and underlying all this was the threat to his honor. He was looking for an excuse to challenge one of them. To lose was one thing; to lose all night to men who had so recently been his enemy was too much.

The flames of his fury licked at his composure. Imoshen realized it would take only one little push to make him draw his weapon and she could siphon off the energy of this confrontation to rebuild her reserves.

She needed it. Her hands and feet cried out to be healed and her vulnerability urged her to arm herself, but... She would not trigger violence and death to supplement her gift. What manner of creature would do such a thing?

Imoshen looked up, suddenly aware of the room, the dying fire, and the sleeping baby. She was not that T'En creature.

Not now, not ever!

Tulkhan savored the productive buzz of his men at work. They'd widened the ditch until it was twice as broad as he was tall and as deep. Normally it would have been filled with sharpened stakes, but there was little timber. What timber there was had been used to support the tunnels. He had two teams digging under the port's walls, but it was hard work in the boggy soil.

The General stamped his feet to get the circulation going and started out, only to be stopped by a cry from little Ban. Since Kornel and the marsh-dweller had left to escort the mercenaries, the boy went everywhere with him. Ban slipped his hand into Tulkhan's large one, a question on his lips. Without Kornel to translate, he could only guess the boy was asking where they were going. Ban pointed eagerly to where the horses were picketed.

"We're not riding that sorry excuse for a horse today," Tulkhan told him, aware that the child was listening to the tone of his voice. Just as his men were watching him for any sign of fear. "Today we will choose the place for our cavalry to practice."

The boy watched as Tulkhan paced out the area within the defenses. "I want this earth dug up to a depth of one hand, turned over, then leveled." It was almost level now, but the soil needed to be soft and evenly turned so that the galloping horses could wheel without injury. It took years of training for man and beast to act as one, and Tulkhan did not intend to waste that with avoidable injuries. "I need hides prepared for target practice and shelters built for the horses. Get moving."

He did not know how long it would be before the cavalry arrived, but the knowledge that he considered it a certainty would cheer his men.

Come dusk, the boy fell asleep and, as Tulkhan tucked the furs around him, the General looked up to see Rawset. "What news?"

Rawset stepped into the shelter, offering two sealed messages. "I dropped the last shipload of mercenaries at the river mouth this morning. Kornel was already waiting there. I bring you word from T'Imoshen and the commander of your Elite Guard."

"Good." Tulkhan hardly heard him. His hands closed on Imoshen's message. "You must be hungry. Go."

As Rawset left, rubbing his forehead, Tulkhan pried up the wax seal and tilted the paper to the candlelight. The words were those of one official to another, Imoshen the statesman to Tulkhan her war general. There was no word from Imoshen the woman to Tulkhan her lover. Imoshen's hasty, flowing script made her come vividly to life. He could almost see her finely chiseled features, and he felt her presence so strongly that for a moment he wondered if she had laid some T'En trick upon the message. When he lifted the finely made paper to his face, he could smell her scent and ached for her touch.

Removing the wax seal, he noted the tear-shaped impression of Imoshen's fingertip. Turning it to the light, he studied the whorls of her fingerprint, memorizing their double loop. The recurring pattern seemed to draw him in.

"General?" Rawset's voice recalled him, and something in the man's tone told him it was not the first time he had spoken.

Tulkhan looked up, surprised and a little unsettled to see the candles guttered in their own wax.

"T'Imoshen will be in T'Diemn soon. She said any message was to go from your hands to mine to hers." Rawset rubbed his forehead as if he had a headache.

Tulkhan understood Imoshen's fears. "You will be my personal emissary. The merchants of T'Diemn can supply a fast ship."

Rawset looked relieved, and when his hand fell to his side Tulkhan noticed the red birthmark where he had been rubbing.

"Stay until the mercenaries arrive and you can take back news of this. Have a seat."

Rawset seemed to have difficulty switching from correct junior officer to companion, so Tulkhan poured him a warm beer. "Why don't I remember you?"

"I was part of King Gharavan's auxiliary army," he answered uneasily. "When you offered us the chance to leave Fair Isle, I decided to stay."

"Why?"

Rawset looked down.

"Answer freely," Tulkhan urged. "I am a fair man."

A relieved smile lit his young face. "That is what I heard and partly why I took my oath of allegiance to you."

"Only partly?" Tulkhan was amused by his ingenious reply.

Rawset's eyes widened and he held Tulkhan's gaze earnestly. "I never wanted to fight, General. I wanted to be a priest, but my village had to supply men for the Ghebite king. Remember the far western desert campaign? I had no choice."

"Tell me, lapsed priest. Why didn't you agree to go with King Gharavan, then desert him and return to your family?"

Rawset wiped the beer's froth from his mustache. "There

would be no honor in desertion. Besides, with the things I have seen these last three years..." He shrugged sadly. "I have lost my faith. It is a terrible thing to believe in nothing."

"Is it?" Tulkhan asked, surprised.

"Of course. I felt adrift until..." He trailed off.

"Until?" But Rawset would not be drawn. The General changed the subject, learning how the Ghebite Empire's never-ending wars were resented by the conquered countries, which had to supply men and arms for the insatiable army.

In his grandfather's day the war had been tribal, as Seerkhan united the Ghebites before leaving the plains. Tulkhan could not remember a time when Gheeaba hadn't been at war. To conquer and expand was the point of Ghebite existence, but now he wondered how long this could go on. How long before Gheeaba splintered into a dozen warring kingdoms?

Would it matter if it did? The thought surprised Tulkhan.

He caught Rawset watching him and realized he had taken out Imoshen's message and was smoothing it between his fingers, over and over. "She gave you no word for me?"

Rawset shook his head and Tulkhan put the message away, but he could feel it lodged against his skin, above his heart. He dismissed Rawset, then remembered to read the note from Jarholfe. The hired merchant scribe had written in the common trading tongue, but Tulkhan could detect Jarholfe's forceful personality in the words. According to his man, Imoshen had taken Reothe for her lover. They had been meeting in her room late at night.

But Tulkhan refused to believe it. There had to be a simple explanation. Resolutely, he held Jarholfe's note to the candle flame and watched it burn. However, he could not erase the seed of doubt the words had planted.

Eight

LYING ON THE farmhouse's best bed, Imoshen waited for Mother Reeve to change her bandages. Their journey had proved more tiring than she expected. Reothe had driven the wagon, playing her servant as though he hadn't threatened to unseat her from the throne only the night before.

They did not cover a great deal of ground, because Imoshen did not plan on meeting the populace of Fair Isle while unable to walk. She could sympathize with Reothe's wish to ride but she did not believe he was ready, for when they were offered the hospitality of the Reeve's prosperous farmhouse, he had retired early.

At last Mother Reeve arrived with warm water, clean cloths, and herbs. While the bandages were being changed, Imoshen heard how the woman's family had rebuilt the shell of their farmhouse when it was burned out during Tulkhan's campaign. Now several bonded sons and daughters and the rest of the younger children all lived under the one roof. But they had plans for two more wings to house their large brood. Doubtless, Imoshen would have been treated to the life histories of every family member if the woman hadn't been called away to serve dinner.

Propped up against the duck-down pillows, Imoshen watched as Ashmyr was bathed by the three youngest daughters. They fussed over him until he fell into an ex-hausted sleep from a surfeit of attention.

Alone at last, Imoshen wriggled, sinking deeper into the pillows, and she set about healing her burns now that her re-serves had been restored. Experience had taught her that the healing never worked well if she was distracted or in pain.

Clearing her mind of all extraneous thought, she con-centrated on the source of her healing gift. It was like walk-ing a familiar path. She no longer had to strain to discern the markers, and when she reached the pool of her power, it had refilled. This time it was pure and clear because it was her own reservoir, not an outside influx of killing passion.

Metaphorically, she dipped her hands into the healing pool, slipped her feet in, and relaxed. A warmth flowed through her body. She sank deeper into her self-induced trance, visualizing all the blistered skin of her hands and feet growing fresh skin. When the process was finished, she felt sleep steal upon her and welcomed it, not stirring until the cock crowed at dawn.

With Ashmyr's first cry the young Reeve girls entered. The middle one picked the baby up, laughing when he smiled.

The older girl placed a bowl on the bedside chest. "Are you ready to have your dressings changed, T'Imoshen?"

Last night the changing of the dressings had elicited hot tears of pain. Today she hoped there would be no more dressings.

"Baby's hungry." The littlest girl announced, and her big sister brought him to the bed.

Imoshen bared her breast, still clumsy with the bandages. She held Ashmyr in the crook of her arms while the eldest girl pulled back the covers and carefully peeled the linen away from the soles of her feet. Her gasp made Imoshen look up.

"What is it?" asked Mother Reeve, entering with a breakfast tray.

The girl pointed wordlessly at Imoshen's feet.

The mother put the tray on the blanket chest and made the sign to ward off evil—lifting her hand to her eyes, then above her head—willing the harm to pass over. "I'll be blessed. Not a sign of blisters."

The others demanded a look. Their mother let them see, then chased the girls out and poured Imoshen a hot spiced milk.

"Thank you," Imoshen said softly. The woman would not meet her eyes. "I did appreciate your care last night."

"It was not my herbs that healed those burns. Why come here and call on my help when you could heal yourself?"

"I needed time to prepare and...this was the first chance I had to heal myself."

"That baby needs a change." Mother Reeve took him before Imoshen could put him to the other breast. When the woman returned Ashmyr to Imoshen, her hands brushed Imoshen's bare skin. Imoshen caught a clear impression of a small boy of about three. He had the same red-golden hair as the youngest girl, but he also had the wine-dark eyes of the T'En. Imoshen sensed sorrow. "What is wrong with your little boy?"

Mother Reeve gasped and made the sign to ward off evil.

Imoshen caught her arm. "You have been kind. Let me help."

"There's nothing you can do. His is no simple affliction that can be set to rights by a few herbs and a little healing." The woman went to the end of the bed.

"At least let me see him," Imoshen urged. "If I cannot help, he will be no worse off than he was before."

The woman's work-worn hands slowed as she unwrapped Imoshen's other foot. "This one is as good as the first. No, T'En Healer. There's nothing that can be done for my boy. I've seen it happen before. I took sick while I was carrying him. He looks perfectly normal but he cannot hear a word we say. It—" Her face worked as she fought her sorrow. "It makes it hard for him. The other children—not ours, you understand—the others tease him because not only can't he hear but he—"

"Has the T'En eyes," Imoshen finished for her.

The woman nodded. "My mother had the T'En eyes. Sometimes it will skip a generation."

"I'm sorry. You are right. There is nothing I can do if his hearing was damaged before he was born. The T'En can aid healing but they cannot replace—"

Suddenly there was a shout of laughter and the door swung open. A small boy darted inside, followed by his sister. He slipped under the bed and there he stayed, crowing delightedly, as both his mother and sister tried vainly to drag him out.

Imoshen laughed and cut short the woman's apology. "He won't bother me."

Mother Reeve looked doubtful. "Have it your way. It's not that I haven't got enough to do, what with the leader of your guards and T'Reothe himself sitting down to eat at my table, not to mention three dozen Ghebite soldiers camped in my fields. I've no time to stay and play games!"

She bustled off with her daughter, leaving Imoshen to eat her breakfast. The boy soon tired of hiding and peered over the bed base at Imoshen. She smiled. He smiled back. She tore off the honeyed crust of the hot roll and used it to lure the child closer.

In no time he was sitting on the bed, spilling crumbs on the covers. He drank all her spiced milk and finished the last of the bread, then looked hopefully for more. He was so bright. It was cruel to think he would always be excluded from conversation because of his hearing loss and then excluded again because he had the T'En eyes.

She placed a tentative hand on his head and probed as the boy looked up at her trustingly. His awareness was bright and untouched by sound, but so sharp with colors, scents, and sensations that it flooded her like a fresh awakening. She opened herself to it, searching for something she could trip or trigger.

Then she felt a snap inside his small being. With a leap of understanding, he recognized what she was doing and rushed to meet her. His laughter filled her with joy. A physical embrace followed a heartbeat after the mental touch.

"What's going on here?"

Imoshen pulled back, terribly tired. She had no strength to protest when Mother Reeve snatched the boy.

"Even the T'En healers of old could not restore a severed limb. You reach too high, T'Imoshen!"

Mother Reeve's words stung Imoshen. She had been arrogant to invade the boy's privacy without his mother's approval. "Forgive me. I should have asked."

"What's wrong?" asked the teenage daughter.

Imoshen opened her mouth to speak, but the girl suddenly laughed and turned to her little brother. "No, you cannot have another honey bun. You had two already."

"Three," Imoshen said. "He ate mine as well."

Then the three of them fell silent, staring at the boy, who wriggled until his mother put him down. He ran over to the window where a bird had landed on the sill and was pecking at the glass, framed by one of the little wooden squares.

"How did you know he wanted another bun?" Imoshen asked.

The girl shrugged. "I . . . I saw a bun and—"

"Now he wants me to open the window so he can touch the bird," Mother Reeve whispered, awed.

Understanding came to Imoshen. "I tried to help him communicate. I felt something open up inside him."

"You've awakened his T'En gift!" his mother moaned.

She went so pale her daughter guided her to the blanket chest, where she collapsed, leaning against the wall. The girl fanned her mother with her apron until the woman pushed her aside. "T'En Healer, what have you done to my boy? I loved him when he could not hear; now you've taken him from us."

Imoshen was appalled. "At least now he can let you know when he wants things. He won't be so lonely."

"Lonely?" The mother fixed Imoshen with bright, angry eyes. "How can you say that when everyone he meets will shy away from him? T'En eyes were bad enough, but a gift as well? Eh, T'En touched!" She burst into tears.

Imoshen's heart contracted. Had she condemned the boy to even worse ostracism? "I'm sorry. I only tried to help."

The child wandered over to his mother. Climbing up into her lap, he put his arms around her neck. Abruptly, her tears stopped, and she stared at him in wonder.

"By the Aayel," she whispered. "I can feel his love for me!"

Imoshen's eyes stung.

Mother Reeve looked at Imoshen, her sun-worn face serious. "I'll admit you meant no harm, T'Imoshen. But a T'En gift?"

Imoshen shrugged. "I will not lie to you. The gifts are a two-edged sword. Bad luck took his hearing. I have awakened something that was in him. It might have slept all his life or it might have wakened when he reached puberty and became frustrated by the need to communicate. I only hope you and he can live with his gift."

"Why shouldn't we?" The girl smiled, but the mother's expression told Imoshen she could foresee difficulties.

A deep voice yelled up the stairs.

"The others are ready to go," the girl said. "Come, T'Imoshen, we'd best get you packed."

"I can manage." Imoshen tugged at the bandages on her hands. The young woman came over to help her. "At least today I can walk down the steps."

But she discovered when she stood that her new skin was too tender to walk on. By the time Imoshen had been carried down the steps and out to the wagon by two healthy farm lads, the daughters had brought down Ashmyr and the rest of their things.

Imoshen looked up to see Mother Reeve at the open window with the boy in her arms. They were not smiling, but he waved and she had a feeling of sudden happiness and the visual picture of a bird taking flight. It was a lovely sensation. But what if the child was angry? What images might a fierce temper tantrum produce?

Normally the T'En gifts did not arise until puberty, when the young person was mature enough to cope with them. Perhaps it would have been better to leave well enough alone. From now on she would confine herself to simple healings.

"You have overextended yourself with these healings," Reothe said reprovingly.

Imoshen gripped the back of the chair, her head spinning. She reached blindly for the wine jug, but it was empty. "Would you have me turn away those in need?"

"What about your needs? You will do them no good if you burn down like a candle."

Imoshen sank into the chair. It was only natural that she minister to the townsfolk of Lakeside, but the sheer number of people needing her healing gift overwhelmed her. The effort made her ravenously hungry. "I will be fine." The baby gave a cry from the back room. "See to Ashmyr and ask the Tea-house keeper to send in more food."

"Your servant." Reothe gave her a mock obeisance.

Imoshen peered through the windows to the square outside, where people waited patiently under delicate umbrellas of painted silk. Music and singing came to her through the many glass panels of the Tea-house entrance. A troupe of entertainers was performing for its captive audience.

She had stopped in Lakeside to gauge the townspeople's mood. They had suffered twice during the Ghebite campaign—once under Tulkhan's initial attack and the second time when King Gharavan entered. He had burned the outlying houses on the lake's banks, but the older stone buildings, linked by their intricate arched bridges above the lake's shallows, had escaped the brunt of Gharavan's anger. He had saved that for T'Diemn.

This was her first visit to Lakeside, and it was every bit as beautiful as the minstrels claimed. Originally, the inhabitants had built fortified houses on the lake's scattered islands, only to link them as time passed. This square was the largest area of open land in old Lakeside, faced by three-story houses dating from before the Age of Consolidation four hundred years ago.

Imoshen had feared the townsfolk of Lakeside would resent her since the Empress had failed to protect them. But when she arrived with Ashmyr in her arms, Lakeside officials had turned out to greet her. The mayor had cast Reothe a quick, nervous glance, saying, "We heard news that the rebels had been pardoned and sent home, that T'Reothe himself stood at your side."

"And now you see it is true and here I am, ready to heal the sickest of your people," Imoshen had replied quickly. Rumor had it that Lakeside was loyal to the rebels. She needed to win over the townsfolk.

But she had been healing since noon, and now the shadows lengthened. Jarholfe's men stood outside the shop, where normally people would be drinking and eating. The little outdoor tables had been pushed to one side and people waited, the weakest on carry-beds under the shade of the awning.

The Tea-house keeper delivered a tray of fresh food herself, and Imoshen thanked the woman who had turned her premises over to them at a moment's notice. "I am sorry to have lost you your afternoon's custom."

"You did at that. But come tomorrow they'll all be here, sitting in the very chair where you sat, telling of how their cousin's youngest was healed by you. So don't you worry."

Imoshen had to smile. "Did Reothe say the baby needed me?"

The woman shook her head. "He's in the private room back there, singing to the babe."

"Reothe's singing?"

The woman nodded.

Unable to stop herself, Imoshen crept to the far door to find Reothe sitting in a chair slung from the ceiling with Ashmyr in his arms. He faced a courtyard, its ornamental garden designed to promote peace and harmony, and he was unaware of her as he swayed gently. Once she could never have crept up on him like this. She felt as if she was intruding.

His voice was a deep murmur, inherently musical. Though she did not recognize the song, she knew the words were High T'En. Imoshen felt drawn to him. She wanted to go to Reothe and cup his face in her hands. She contented herself with approaching and stroking Ashmyr's soft cheek.

Reothe looked up. Imoshen leaned closer. She wanted to kiss him, not with desire but—

"T'Imoshen?" The woman spoke from the doorway with the empty tray in her hands. "They are asking for you."

"Thank you." Imoshen met Reothe's eyes. "I must go."

"Do not overwork your gift, for unless you heal me, I cannot walk death's shadow to bring you back," he warned.

He was speaking of the day she transformed the fallen bodies of Cariah and her lover into stone. The effort had drained her to the point of death. Only Reothe's willingness to risk his soul in death's shadow had saved her. "I never thanked you—"

"I never wanted thanks!"

She heard voices in the front room. "Nevertheless—"

"Just go, Imoshen. Do not insult me."

Stung, she left him.

Six people waited. Imoshen's heart sank. One man lay on a stretcher that had been placed on a long table, his body covered by a blanket, his face turned away from her. Four of them turned to face her. The fifth lifted his head, his eyes milked over with the blindness that came on some people in old age, though his body was still vigorous. The woman who led him placed a hand on his shoulder.

Imoshen had never attempted to heal blindness before, because her gift was a weak thing, good only for aiding healing. She suspected the blindness could be reversed. But if she healed this man it would exhaust her. Who was she to decide who lived and died?

Imoshen crossed to the table where the Tea-house keeper had laid out food and spiced wine. She poured herself a drink, draining it quickly. Then she tore into the pastry with its tasty filling, licking her fingers before dusting the crumbs from her lips. The food stopped her limbs trembling, but she knew she could not go on much longer.

Imoshen was aware of them waiting expectantly. "One moment." She beckoned Jarholfe from his post at the door. "Please tell the people this will be my last healing for today."

The man nodded, and objections greeted his announcement. Imoshen steeled herself. For now she would do her best for these people. Stepping closer to the sick man on the table, she took his hand in both of hers, addressing the others. "Tell me what is wrong with him."

A surge of awareness shot up her arms. Too late!

A sword leapt up from under the blanket, its point aimed at the V under her ribs. From behind his bandages, fierce T'En eyes fixed on her. "We want to see T'Reothe!"

Imoshen schooled her features. "You had but to ask."

Taking the blade, she turned the point gently away from her body, her eyes never leaving the rebel's. But if she had turned away this man's immediate threat, she had not deflected his purpose. Two of his companions stepped behind her, their desperation palpable. One arm snaked around her neck, and she felt the sharp edge of a blade nudge her exposed throat.

Urgently, she tried to touch Reothe's awareness to warn him, but he was blind to her questing senses. She had made them both vulnerable by refusing to heal him. Regret and frustration raged through her. She swallowed. "You do not need to threaten me. All rebels have been given amnesty. Why not go home?"

"My home no longer stands, and what is a home without the ones you love?" a woman said harshly.

Imoshen sensed stark desolation. She licked her lips. "A home without love is a shell. Yet what is violence but a—"

"Don't listen to her T'En tricks," the one with the hard garnet eyes warned, swinging his feet to the floor.

The blind man's head lifted like a dog who had caught an interesting scent. He pointed. "Someone is in there!"

Imoshen's heart faltered. Anxious to divert them, she raised her voice. "T'Reothe, put your plaything away. You have visitors."

Her son must not be used as a lever.

While the half-breed rebel unwound the bandages from his head, the two who held Imoshen shuffled around to face the back of the room.

If Reothe was surprised to see Imoshen held at knifepoint, he did not betray it. He lifted his arms. "My people, why have you come to me with violence in your hearts?"

"We had to see for ourselves," the half-breed said.

"See what, Obazim? That I am unharmed? No one holds *me* at knifepoint." Reothe glided toward them. Only

Imoshen knew how much it cost him to move so smoothly. "Release T'Imoshen."

The woman relaxed her grip, but the knifepoint stayed at Imoshen's throat.

Reothe's eyes narrowed. "Please forgive my people, Imoshen. They are foolish but sincere."

She felt the wariness of her captors, smelled the change in their body scent.

"All rebels have been granted amnesty. I have no quarrel with these people." Imoshen noticed the blind man whisper something to his guide, who darted into the back room. Praying the woman would not find Ashmyr, Imoshen almost missed Reothe's subtle signal. He beckoned her.

Imoshen took a deep breath and raised her hand to meet Reothe's. His fingers closed on hers. She stepped forward, and the knife blade slipped harmlessly past her throat as the woman lowered her arm. Relief flooded Imoshen, but only for a heartbeat; then she heard furniture being moved in the back room.

Every nerve in Imoshen's body screamed a warning, but she remained outwardly composed. Reothe's hand squeezed hers and he pulled her toward him, turning her so that she stood on his weak left side. She could feel the trembling of his muscles.

Imoshen faced the hardened veterans, all armed with weapons that had been concealed from Jarholfe's men. The Ghebites would come in answer to her cry, but by then she and Reothe could be dead. She did not believe the rebels intended to kill them, but the tension in Reothe's body was not reassuring. And what would she do if the woman found her child?

Imoshen trawled her awareness for that first stirring of the gifts, but she was drained by the afternoon's healing and unfocused with her fear for Ashmyr.

Reothe slung his arm over Imoshen's shoulder, letting her take some of his weight. "We are the last two T'En—"

"Look what I found—the Ghebite General's brat!" crowed the woman. She ran into the room with Ashmyr held out in front of her, his little legs kicking in distress. A mewl of protest escaped Imoshen.

"That child is mine!" Reothe said, his arm tightening on Imoshen's shoulders.

The woman hesitated. "But he has the Ghebite's hair."

"I touched his mind before he was born. He will be my tool when he grows up. Return him—"

"To me." Imoshen stepped forward and held out her arms, trembling with fury. She wanted every last one of them dead.

The air seemed to vibrate between them as Imoshen took Ashmyr from the woman's unresisting hands. At the first touch of her son, a rush of heat flooded Imoshen's body, bringing with it that familiar metallic taste on her tongue.

Every nuance became heightened. She sensed the rebels' pounding hearts and their strained minds opened to her. Fever-pitch tension sang on the air, swamping her senses.

"Go quietly now, and quickly," Reothe urged. "You do not know how close you have come to death. Just as T'Imoshen can heal with a touch, she can kill."

Had Reothe regained enough of his gift to sense her state? She tried to search his perception, but he was a blind spot. No, not blind. She saw his eyes widen and knew if he was bluffing before, now he was aware of the gifts moving in her.

"Go," Reothe ordered.

The woman backed away from her, hands raised in a defensive gesture.

"There are Ghebite guards outside!" Obazim growled, his voice thick with hate. Imoshen could taste it, rich as gravy on her tongue.

"Those Ghebites obey my orders!" Reothe hissed.

In the edge of her vision, Imoshen saw Reothe beckon her to his side. Choosing not to move, she remained between him and the rebels. Like Imoshen, Reothe carried a knife, but two short blades would be poor protection against swords in the hands of killers. Worse, Reothe was crippled and she was holding Ashmyr.

The rebels made no move to leave. Tension rose another notch, wooing her with its sweet, cruel hunger for violence.

Imoshen felt empowered by the rebels' fear and excitement. A laugh escaped her. Why was she thinking like a True-woman when she could turn their own violence back upon them? It was so tempting. Tension trickled from the pores of her body. Not one of them would meet her eyes.

"My people," Reothe whispered. "Have you forgotten? I said the day would come when Imoshen and I would unite to lead Fair Isle."

"But the Ghebite General isn't dead!" the bitter woman objected.

The blind man had gravitated to his guide's side, and Imoshen could see his six-fingered hands opening and closing. His senses were sharpened by the lack of sight. She could tell he was reacting to the buildup of her T'En gifts. Beads of sweat clung to his sun-bronzed forehead. The tang of his fear assailed her nostrils, exotic as any perfume.

"Yes, the General still lives," Obazim said, his hatred making him impervious to the danger.

Imoshen focused on him. Bringing him to his knees would be sweet.

"For now," Reothe conceded. "Because it suits me."

Imoshen sensed the path Reothe wove between lies and half-truths. It made her wonder how many lies he had told her to gain her trust.

Obazim frowned. "General Tulkhan—"

"Serves me!" Reothe snapped. "He serves me by capturing Port Sumair and killing Gharavan. Do you think I want Fair Isle swarming with mainland soldiers again this summer?"

Imoshen's vision faded as everything fell into place and she understood why Reothe was cooperating with her. She could feel him at her back, her beautiful betrayer. Her tension had to be expelled. She wanted to strike out. Their suffering and deaths would empower her further. Exultation filled her.

"T'Imoshen, the people will not leave." Jarholfe opened the door, then stiffened as he took in the drawn weapons. He looked to Imoshen for orders. He was her tool. He would kill at her command. Death and bloodshed. It was hers to call down.

A savage joy flooded Imoshen. It both frightened and

exhilarated her to discover that the T'En part of her would thrive on their deaths. No. The power was only a source; the outcome was hers to choose. Death or life.

"Not death. Hold your sword, Jarholfe." It was a denial that sprang bone-deep. Imoshen moved before she could give in to the urge for violence. Her free hand covered the blind man's face, fingertips spanning his closed lids.

His scream cut the air. As he dropped to his knees, she sank with him. The blind man plucked weakly at her arm, and a keening moan issued from his throat with each ragged breath. Imoshen was only vaguely aware of the others, of chairs turning over, of Reothe's raised voice, and of fierce Ghebite accents. She focused on searing this man's eyes clear of their milky film. It took three long breaths, and it was not gentle.

When she felt no more obstructions, she let her hand drop and he pitched face-first to the floor. His guide caught him. Cradling his head, she cast Imoshen a look of pure hatred.

Reothe pulled Imoshen to her feet. She found the room still and silent. Furniture had been broken, but no one had died while she was occupied. Instead, the rebels looked confused, as if they had forgotten the reason for their anger.

A sob escaped the woman on the floor. Everyone turned. She hugged the injured man to her breast. "How could you do this? You are a healer!"

"It was not gentle. I am sorry," Imoshen whispered.

"Sorry?" Obazim demanded, but even he fought to recall his anger. "She reveals her true nature. Now do you see what she is, T'Reothe?"

"T'Imoshen?" Jarholfe prompted uneasily. He was still ready to kill at her command, but it relieved Imoshen to discover she did not crave their deaths.

She had averted bloodshed, yet the knowledge that it had come so close sat heavily on her. "Obazim, you and your companions are free to go. I will have no lives spent on this day. Go!"

Obazim shuddered and sheathed his sword.

Jarholfe held the door open as the rebels left. The blind

man's guide dragged him to his feet. He staggered, pressing his hands to his eyes.

"The dying man walks!" The crowd cried as Obazim appeared.

Fighting a hysterical urge to giggle, Imoshen joined Jarholfe.

"Do you want them followed and killed?" he asked.

She flinched. Was murder so easy for some people? "No. Let them go."

Imoshen became aware of the growing silence as the entertainers turned their painted faces to her. The crowd would consume her with their need.

Hugging Ashmyr, Imoshen lifted her left arm. She swept an arc, giving the Empress's formal blessing, then let her hand fall, secretly dismayed to have laid claim to the Empress's role. "Your T'En Healer tires. I can do no more this day."

"Tomorrow?" one voice called, echoed by others.

Imoshen nodded. "Tomorrow, but then I must go to the capital if I am to avert war in the spring."

They accepted this and Imoshen reached for Jarholfe's arm. The physical contact told her that he was confused and angry but feared her too much to speak out. Blind with the gray mist of weariness, she leaned on him. "Take me inside."

With Jarholfe's aid, Imoshen entered the Tea-house and waited for her vision to clear. "Help me to the table, and then see to your men."

Imoshen heard the mutter fade as the crowd moved off, heard the men moving tables outside, their voices tense.

"Wine?" Reothe asked.

"Reothe!" The baby gave a cry, startled by her tone. "How can you stand there and offer me wine when you will betray me first chance you get? I have it from your own lips!"

"You mistake me, Imoshen." Reothe took one step back. "I told them only what they needed to hear. I had to buy time."

"Time for what? Time for you to betray General Tulkhan?"

He backed into a table, steadying himself. "They were ready to kill, and so were you. I saw it in your eyes. You are the one who talks of compassion. Today I averted bloodshed. You could have taken one or two of them down with you, but what of Ashmyr and me? Do you think I could stand by and let them kill you? What possessed you to take vengeance on the blind one?"

A bitter laugh escaped her. "You are the one who is blind. And don't talk to me of Ashmyr. I have often wondered why you treat him as if he were your own child. What did you do to my child before he was born?"

"T'En Healer must see me!" a familiar voice cried.

Imoshen went to rise, but before she could, the door was thrown open. A man broke free of Jarholfe's men. He stumbled into the room, stopped, and glared around, blinking fiercely. When he saw Imoshen, he ran to her, dropping to his knees. "Why did you do it? I would have killed you."

Smiling, Imoshen lifted his face so she could study his eyes. They were the clear golden-hazel of the farmer folk. "I am sorry it hurt you."

"T'Imoshen," he whispered, and tears ran freely down his cheeks. Clasping her free hand in his, he kissed her sixth finger. "I have done terrible things in the name of the T'En, but today I have seen what that name means."

Imoshen shook her head, for today she had seen what she could become. The frenzy of their last few heartbeats as they fought for survival would have been incredibly sweet.

"Let me serve you, T'En Healer."

"Serve me?" Imoshen shook her head. "All I ask is that you and your friends hold yourselves ready should I call for help. You owe me nothing. It is I who owe you."

As he gave her the deep obeisance, lifting both hands to his forehead and backing out, Reothe muttered softly, "Do you win them over intentionally, Imoshen, or is it instinctive?"

She saw him with new eyes. When Reothe was whole, did the T'En side of him grow drunk on the suffering of others? She could tell he was trying to Read her. Pushing too far, he reopened the old wound and collapsed in a chair.

She should heal him. It was wrong to leave him vulnerable. It weakened her as well. Her first instinct was to go to him, but she did not. She sat there, listening to his ragged gasps, battling the urge to heal his gifts.

"Look what you have done to me," he demanded, voice vibrating with anguish. "Cruelly crippled, I cannot help you. All I have left is my tongue. But when I use it to save us, you accuse me of betraying you!"

"I don't know what to believe anymore," Imoshen whispered. "Everything you say is plausible." Guilt assailed her. He spoke with such sincerity, and his suffering was real. Imoshen poured wine, her hand trembling.

Ashmyr bobbed against her breast, hopeful for a feed. Absently, she changed his position. He drank greedily.

His sucking slowed and he looked up, as if to check that she was still there. Imoshen could not help smiling. His little six-fingered hand grasped her bodice, as if he would not let her escape. He was so precious. How could she protect him when her own life hung in the balance?

Like a physical sensation, she could feel Reothe watching them, and his claims about the baby returned. But she was terribly tired. Already she could feel the mind-numbing weariness she associated with an overextension of her gifts creeping up on her.

"Imoshen?" Reothe's breath dusted her cheek. Startled, she looked up to find him kneeling at her side. "You must heal me, Imoshen. You need me at your back."

He was right: His weakness made her vulnerable. But her eyes wouldn't focus. "I must sleep."

She heard him call the Tea-house keeper. They urged her to stand, to walk through a mist of nothingness, then to climb steps, so many steps. Then she felt a bed and welcoming cool sheets. When hands tried to take Ashmyr from her, she tightened her grip.

"Let him go. I'll look after him," Reothe urged.

No. Reothe would steal his soul. But the Ancients had already done that and returned it—for a price.

"Very well. Rest easy, Imoshen. I will watch over you."

Strangely enough, she knew in this she could trust him.

Nine

WHEN THE LOOKOUTS signaled the mercenaries' arrival, Tulkhan climbed the earthworks and held little Ban so that he could see his father's return. Then Tulkhan sent orders to the cook to break out the beer and not stint on the evening meal.

But before they could celebrate, he had to meet the new mercenary leader and see this contract that Imoshen had signed on his behalf. In Gheeaba a woman would never sign a contract on her own behalf, let alone her husband's. He smiled fondly. Typical of Imoshen—she had no idea how deeply she had insulted him.

It was just on dusk when Tulkhan met Lightfoot. After reading the contract, he had to admit he could not find fault with the terms. He pointed to the scrawl. "This is your name?"

The man nodded. "Lightfoot. Leader of the mercenaries. When I told the men the news..." He looked up at Tulkhan, his expression hard. "Tourez betrayed us. The men want his blood."

"Get in line. I'll add my signature and you can sign again," Tulkhan said. "You made good time through the marshes."

"I wouldn't have said it was possible."

"That's twice we've done the impossible marsh trek. Your leader betrayed his men, Lightfoot. Why?"

The man spat. "He was outvoted by the other mercenary leaders."

"But my offer was generous. My reputation as a commander outstrips my half-brother's. Why would the mercenaries choose to fight on the losing side?"

"You wish me to speak frankly?"

"Always."

"They don't believe they fight on the losing side."

Tulkhan accepted this without bluster. "Why not?"

"Vestaid," Lightfoot said. The name was vaguely familiar to Tulkhan. "In the last year he has united three troops. His battle strategy is brilliant. The men are happy to follow him for profit and, who knows..."

"Glory?" Tulkhan suggested. It was not unknown for a mercenary leader to gain so much power he unseated the lord who had hired him. But surely this Vestaid did not think he could supplant the King of the Ghebites? If he did, he was playing for high stakes indeed, and he would not consider the loss of one mercenary troop too great a price to pay. Of course, he would not succeed. Tulkhan had yet to meet a man who could outwit him on the battlefield. "What do you know of this Vestaid?"

"There are two types of leaders—those who lead by example and those who lead by fear. Vestaid lets no strong man rise under him."

"My half-brother should look to his back," Tulkhan muttered. The dinner horn sounded. "Come, meet my men."

As they stepped out of the shelter their way was blocked by Rawset. He gave the Ghebite version of a bow to a foreigner whom he considered of lesser rank and, as he straightened, the flickering torchlight fell on his face. The mercenary muttered a surprised oath.

"Do you know each other?" Tulkhan asked.

"No." Rawset frowned.

"I was mistaken," said Lightfoot. "Your men are waiting."

At the table Tulkhan opened a bottle of Gheeaban Vorsch and made the introductions as the drinks were poured. His men jokingly disparaged the locals' warm, flat beer. If Tulkhan hadn't seen Lightfoot's reaction to Rawset, he would have said the man was at ease, but he knew the mercenary leader was hiding something.

Tulkhan studied the men around his table. Kornel took a seat, though it was clear some of Tulkhan's men did not believe he deserved it. The marsh-dweller had retreated to the cooking fires with his son. The General almost missed little Ban.

The talk was of the journey, the trouble with the narcts, and the problems of getting even the relatively light supplies through the marshes.

"A toast." Tulkhan stood. The men followed suit. "To our new allies, Lightfoot's mercenaries."

They drank, slamming their empty mugs on the table.

Tulkhan would have sat down, but the mercenary touched his goblet to his chest as was the Vaygharian custom. "To T'Imoshen and all who serve her."

Tulkhan could understand impressionable young Rawset being overwhelmed by Imoshen. The youth probably half fancied himself in love with her. But Lightfoot was a hardened veteran who killed for profit. Tulkhan heard the question in his men's voices as they repeated Lightfoot's toast. They looked to Tulkhan for explanation. He shrugged it off, but he felt uneasy. Did the mercenary suspect Tulkhan was Imoshen's tool?

"To my woman." He raised his Vorsch. "May we all soon be back between the thighs of our women!"

Tulkhan detected a note of relief as his men roared their agreement.

"To General Tulkhan, Destroyer of the Spar!" one of his men announced. "Leveler of Port Sumair!"

Tulkhan acknowledged their support as he resumed his seat. In his nineteenth year his father had taken a serious wound. At the same time a band of hardy rebels had retreated to an outcropping of rocks known as the Spar. He had not thought of that campaign in years. But it had been similar—a siege.

Lying at the end of a range of hills, with a full day's walk up steep ravines, single file, the fortified outcropping was believed impregnable. His father had told him to take it. All resistance had to be crushed, especially when the king lay deathly ill. So Tulkhan had force-marched his men up the treacherous paths in the dark, carrying their full weapon kits. The engineers had carried their disassembled siege machines. At dawn, when they reached the Spar's defenses, their appearance had astounded the defenders.

Once the walls fell, Tulkhan had ordered his men to kill every last person. This victory had won him his father's respect and the generalship of the army, which led him to Sumair and this siege.

Tulkhan grinned as conversation grew steadily more ribald. Kornel was telling a long story in extremely bad taste about a camp follower and a soldier. The others laughed and egged him on.

When the food arrived, the men greeted this with good humor. They had fresh supplies with chickens, eggs, and rabbits. Tulkhan snorted—next thing he knew they'd bring in cows and goats. If the siege lasted long enough, they'd end up farmers.

The men's laughter and jests flowed past Tulkhan into the night. Within hearing distance were many campfires. This jovial meal would reassure the common soldiers.

Once again the talk had turned to women as the men bemoaned the lack of camp followers. Just then Tulkhan looked up and caught the mercenary watching him. Imoshen had seemed certain of the man's loyalty. The General's hand went to his chest where he felt Imoshen's message pressed against his skin, its creases as familiar as the words.

In salute, Lightfoot lifted one hand to his forehead, touching the first two fingers of his hand to the place where some cultures believed the third eye lay dormant in all but the greatest of Seers. Tulkhan found the gesture oddly familiar, though he did not recognize it as Vaygharian.

For two days now Imoshen had fought a silent mental battle. If she left Reothe's gifts crippled, it made them both vulnerable to True-men. But if she healed him, Reothe would use his gifts to achieve his goals, and these were not hers.

Pausing before the polished mirror, Imoshen wondered what to wear. Tonight she needed her wits about her, for they stayed in Chalkcliff Abbey and she was to dine with Seculate Donyx and Reothe, both enemies, under the guise of friendship.

She selected a skull cap of finely beaten electrum, setting it on her head. Tiny pearl beads hung on small chains in an arc across her forehead, linked to a central ruby that caught the light with the same inner fire as her eyes. To complement this she chose a mulberry gown of richest velvet, laced tight under her bodice. Lastly, she wore a choker of pearls with a central ruby.

Taking Ashmyr in his basket, she stepped out of her room to find Reothe waiting across the hall from her. He wore mulberry velvet with deep brocade cuffs. These were embroidered in the finest silver thread so that they flashed when he straightened and prowled toward her, making her heart thud. She had noticed that his limp was more pronounced in the evening, but tonight there was no sign of it. He had ridden in the wagon today, and now she knew why: He wanted to be alert and physically capable. Her skin prickled with a presentiment of danger.

"T'Imoshen." Only he could roll her name off his tongue with full High T'En intonation. He offered his strong right arm.

"T'Reothe. You appear to be well," she said, letting him know she understood his tricks.

"And you appear to be everything the T'En should be."

"Should I take that as a compliment or an insult?" she asked softly as they walked down the hall toward the abbey's refractory, where the Seculate and his priests awaited them.

Her arm lay along his, her fingers closed over his hand. Through this touch she could feel the slight roll to his step as he compensated for, and hid, the weakness in his left side.

"I merely made an observation on your appearance. You must know you are beautiful." His voice caressed her senses, deep and intimate. "Whether you have the strength of purpose to match that beauty, only time will tell."

"And I suppose you have the strength of purpose?"

They entered a courtyard illuminated by small lanterns under the arches. The air was cool, perfumed with the heady scent of night-blooming roses. Imoshen could hear exquisite singing drifting from the chapel, carried on the evening breeze.

He held her eyes. "I do not doubt myself. Can you say the same?"

She gasped at his arrogance, then chose to reply with a High T'En saying. "The wise know in life, only death is certain."

He laughed. "How can you say that when you cheated death of your own son? What price did the Ancients ask of you, Imoshen?"

But she would not answer, and they traversed the courtyard in silence. Stepping through an arch, they entered the refractory. A stillness settled on the hall's inhabitants. Even the Seculate stopped in mid-step.

Balancing the baby's basket on her hip, Imoshen gave them the Empress's blessing. "Chalkcliff Abbey honors the last of the T'En with its hospitality." Imoshen smiled but she felt heavier, weighed down by the knowledge that she was slipping deeper and deeper into a role she had never wanted.

Seculate Donyx hurried forward, as fast as his dignity would allow. The formal words of greeting tripped from his lips, but all the while he watched them. Imoshen returned his gaze, careful to reveal nothing.

When the Seculate introduced them to the elders of the abbey, Imoshen sensed Reothe's strength fading. She should heal him, speak with him later tonight, and extract some kind of promise.

The Seculate led them into his private chamber, where a low table awaited them, bounded on three sides by cushioned couches. Apparently Seculate Donyx held with the old high-court practice of eating while reclining, something the Emperor and Empress had retained for intimate dinners.

Imoshen placed Ashmyr's basket beside her and began the elaborate wine pouring ceremony. A pot of sweetened, spiced wine sat on the brass burner to maintain the right temperature. Aware of the Seculate and Reothe watching her, Imoshen's hands moved in the formal patterns of preparation, pouring then presenting the fragile porcelain cups.

The ceremony over, she stretched out on the couch while the meal was served. Imoshen nibbled a little of this and that, one hand absently stroking Ashmyr's back as Reothe and the Seculate discussed a theological argument that had been going on for two generations. The finer points were debatable, but the basic question was impossible to resolve. She had never found it interesting, since the whole point of the argument seemed to be outdoing the opponent by quoting tracts from obscure T'En tomes.

It amused her to learn that Reothe had written a book on the subject, and a copy was delivered from the abbey library so that passages could be quoted.

The remains of their food were cleared from the table, and palate-cleansing sweets arrived. Then these too were removed, and still the Seculate and Reothe showed no signs of quitting the table. The evening stretched out like a long tunnel before Imoshen. Sounds became thick and disjointed. Waves of weariness washed over her as her eyelids grew heavy. Though she tried to stay awake, she caught herself slipping lower and lower on the couch. She must not fall asleep at the Seculate's private banquet.

Struggling to lift herself onto one elbow, she swung her legs over the edge of the couch and felt the floor heave beneath her feet. This was not right. She'd been drugged. Panic made her fight it. "Reothe?"

Suddenly he was kneeling before her, though no time seemed to have elapsed since he had been reclining opposite. Focusing on his face with great difficulty, she lifted heavy arms to his shoulders to hold herself upright.

"The food was drugged." Her words were slurred.

"I know."

"I cannot stay awake."

"That you can still talk is an achievement."

She blinked, trying to focus on his face. Suddenly it hit her. He was not drugged. "You . . . you—"

"Go to sleep, Imoshen. No harm will come to you, and what you do not know, you cannot reveal."

This seemed to make sense. Reothe had asked Seculate Donyx to drug her so that they could talk treason. She caught Reothe's arm as he went to rise. "Why now? Why not talk later when I would have been sleeping?"

"Jarholfe watches me like a dog with a bone. He cannot carry back word of this meeting if he believes you are present and no treasonous talk passed between us."

Imoshen nodded; already she was slipping away. "One thing. Ashmyr—"

"Is safe. Sleep, Imoshen."

And then she was lost, drifting down through layers of consciousness. What had they given her? Her herbal training prompted her to analyze the sensations, but all too soon she lost the thread, lost all sense of time and place.

Imoshen was wakened by Reothe's insistent voice and an abominable scent. "Phew!"

"I'm afraid you will have a headache. I cannot let you sleep off the drug. You must walk to your chamber," Reothe said.

She struggled to focus on his face. The room was empty, and the candles had all burned out, except the one Reothe held. Her head thumped.

"I will carry Ashmyr. Can you walk?"

"Of course I can walk!" she snapped, but had to bend double when she stood too quickly. "I hope your treasonous talk went well!"

He laughed softly, offering her his free arm. "Put away your claws. The mouse has gone."

He urged her through the door. She blinked several times to clear her vision. But the walk to her bedchamber was strangely disjointed. At one point they were in the deserted refractory, then the next in the courtyard with the cool night air sighing over the bare skin of her shoulders, and then she was in her room with no memory of walking down the hall. Fear replaced anger.

"... my lady?" It was Jarholfe speaking.

Imoshen wondered how she appeared to him. Stunned and drugged, or tired and aloof? He did not look suspicious.

"Will there be anything else, my lady?" he asked, glancing at Reothe, who was placing the baby's basket beside the bed. He was reluctant to leave her alone with Reothe, but she did not want Jarholfe to realize she had been drugged.

She could not betray Reothe to a True-man, a Ghebite at that. "Leave me."

Jarholfe gave a cold, furious bow and walked out.

"And you can go too, Reothe." Imoshen was mortified. She had come close to healing him, only to discover that her judgment was wrong. "I do not like being drugged. Why must you flaunt your treason before me?"

"Only those who write Fair Isle's history will know who worked treason. Was it T'Imoshen who joined with the invader of Fair Isle, or T'Reothe who sought to restore—"

"You twist everything!" Imoshen muttered. But he had made his point. Suddenly the fight went out of her. "Damn you."

Reothe stroked her cheek. She looked up at him, feeling a kinship that went beyond the blood they shared. If only...

"You want me to absolve you of all other vows so that you can give yourself to me without guilt. But I can't do that, Imoshen. You must renounce your vow to General Tulkhan. Only then can we know the full potential of our T'En gifts. Renounce him, heal me. It is that simple."

She froze. "You sensed my thoughts."

"I read your face."

But she did not know what to believe. If he was regaining his gifts, if he realized how deeply he had penetrated her defenses... "You would have me believing black was white. Leave me. My head is thumping fit to burst!"

He mocked her with the old-empire obeisance reserved for the Empress, then left.

Tulkhan rode along on the newly constructed rampart. Below him the mercenaries' campfires were already alight, their thin plumes of smoke rising on the still, dawn air. The troop's standard lay limp against the pole. Every mercenary would follow it to their death. He needed his own standard to lead his men into battle. Gharavan's slur on his parentage and right to rule still stung.

The night had been very cold and now the sun rose over Fair Isle, which was cloaked by cloud, full of mystery. His heart swelled. For him Fair Isle represented beauty and promise, and Imoshen was Fair Isle.

Imoshen had once begged him, in his haste to claim the island, not to destroy what was good in T'En culture. He had already taken steps to fashion a new society, one after his own heart. He would invite the greatest minds of the mainland to T'Diemn. It would be the dawn of a new era.

Tulkhan's vision glazed over. The sun's rays pierced the low cloud, breaking through in golden shafts, and he knew that the symbol of his reign would be the dawn sun.

He smiled ruefully. The dawn sun was most appropriate; the royal T'En symbol was the twin moons on a midnight-blue sky. As the moons set on the house of T'En, he and Imoshen would create a royal house that was both old and new. Ashmyr was their dawn. At that moment Tulkhan realized the Ancients had returned Ashmyr's life because the boy had a destiny to fulfill. He must unite Fair Isle. Tulkhan left his horse with the handlers, returning to his shelter, eager to set ink to paper.

A short while later Kornel backed through the flap with a tray. He placed the fresh bread cakes on the table. The scent of warm beer and hot bread made Tulkhan's mouth water. "Take a seat. Have something to eat." He put his drawings away and lifted a leather thong strung with triangular gold beads. "What do you think? This much for Banuld-Chi?"

The merchant captain eyed the yellow metal with carefully concealed avarice. "What use is gold to a marsh-dweller? It won't keep his feet dry."

Tulkhan laughed. "True. But I promised him payment."

Kornel's comment was crude.

Tulkhan acknowledged this. Banuld and his son were lucky to be alive. Most commanders would have killed them once their usefulness was passed. But if Tulkhan wanted to see his vision for Fair Isle come to fruition, he had to be at peace with his neighbors, even if they were lowly marsh-dwellers.

Thoughtfully, he watched the triangular gold beads catch the light. Funny. Gold meant nothing to him. It was only a means to an end. He felt the weight of the neck thong compared to the weight of the rod and remaining beads. The rumors of Fair Isle's wealth had not been exaggerated. These easily stacked rods with their triangular beads were a common sight in any prosperous merchant's counting room.

What better use for gold than paving the path of peace? With a smile, he took off two more beads and added them to the leather thong.

"I reward those who are loyal to me," Tulkhan told Kornel. The merchant captain would be more helpful if he thought he would be well-rewarded. "Tell me, Kornel, could you find the way back through the marshes to the village?"

The man's mouth opened and closed once. "Yes."

"You're sure? I will have need of that route to bring in more supplies." Kornel nodded. "Then send in Banuld-Chi."

He left, and Tulkhan placed the rod with its remaining gold beads in the chest under his table.

While waiting for the men to return, Tulkhan wrote to Imoshen, telling her of the marsh-dweller and little Ban. He wrote of Lightfoot and his mercenaries, and of providing Rawset with a fast ship and appointing him their emissary. But he did not write of the way he ached to hold her and how he missed her concise mind and acute humor. If anything, distance had sharpened his need for her.

Rawset pushed the flap open. "I heard you were about to dismiss the marsh-dweller."

Tulkhan let the letter roll shut. "Yes. Why?"

"You may need to use the marsh path again."

"I intend to. Kornel will be the guide."

"I came back here by ship, so I was not with Lightfoot and Kornel, but . . ."

Tulkhan had noticed an unlikely friendship developing between the failed priest and the grizzled mercenary. "What?"

"Lightfoot told me Kornel insisted on leading their way, and twice he would have taken the wrong path but the marsh-dweller stopped him, scouted ahead, and came back to report the way had closed. Lightfoot likened the marsh paths to the floating islands, which are carried by tides and winds."

Tulkhan sank his chin onto his cupped hand.

"I thought you should know," Rawset offered, then glanced through the shelter's flap. "Here they come."

Rawset stepped aside as Kornel entered with the marsh-dweller and his son. Tulkhan realized that he should have learned more than the marsh-dweller's words for food and sleep, but he had thought their association was going to be brief. "Have you told Banuld-Chi I am about to send him home, Kornel?" The man's eager expression was his answer. "Translate this for me. Do the marsh paths move?"

Kornel's mouth opened and closed. He cast Rawset a swift glance, his eyes narrowing. "They move, but I can find my way."

"You might be willing to risk your life, but I will not risk the lives of my men." Tulkhan overrode him quietly but firmly. "I want the truth, Kornel."

The marsh-dweller asked something, his concern evident. Kornel's answer was swift and brutal. The man's expression darkened. The boy clutched his father's hand.

On impulse Tulkhan beckoned. "Come, Ban."

The father stiffened as his son went to Tulkhan without hesitation. The General stroked the boy's head, feeling his braided hair. "Kornel, tell Banuld-Chi he can take his son home to his mother. I ask him to return to serve me." Tulkhan held up the necklace of gold. "Pretty, Ban?" The boy nodded, understanding the meaning if not the words. Tulkhan slid the necklace over his head. "This is a present for his mother."

Kornel's translation faltered, and a spasm of anger colored his face.

"Tell Banuld-Chi"—Tulkhan emphasized the honorific—"that there will be more if he returns to serve me of his own free will."

The words had barely left Kornel's mouth when the marsh-dweller stepped forward and dropped to one knee. Grasping Tulkhan's free hand, he raised it to his lips and uttered the Ghebite word for thanks.

Tulkhan noted that when Banuld-Chi's hands went to the boy it was to hug him, not to paw the necklace, and he knew his assessment of the man's character was correct. Still speaking his words of thanks, the marsh-dweller backed out.

"Why did you give him the gold?" Kornel demanded. "It would have been enough to tell him it was to be his after he served you. Now you'll never see him again!"

"We will see which of us has judged the man correctly. Meanwhile, go with him. Take the boats back to the river's entrance and await the supplies."

Realizing he had overstepped his position, Kornel gave a stiff bow and backed out.

"Do you think I have thrown away my guide?" Tulkhan asked Rawset.

The young emissary shook his head. "I can see why T'Imoshen believes in you."

Tulkhan thought it was a strange thing for a Ghebite soldier to say, but he was eager to get Rawset's reaction to the new standard. "Take a look at this. It will be the dawn of a new royal house. The sun and its rays will be golden. The lower section will be sea-blue. I want you to take this design to Imoshen. Her seamsters can make up the banners. They will fly from every ship and from every tower of T'Diemn. I want them gleaming on the battlefield." He indicated his cloak, which was flung over a chair. "If Gharavan were to lead a sortie from the port tomorrow, my men would be wearing the same colors as his. I need cloaks of sea-blue for all my men and plumes of gold."

Display was vital. Tulkhan knew from experience that if a man looked the part, he felt part of a greater whole. He wanted his new banner flying on the field so that when Gharavan looked down he did not see the banished concubine's son of a dead Ghebite king, but the ruler of Fair Isle. "Leave me now."

Rawset departed, and Tulkhan felt the fire of his vision stir in his belly. This was not the fire of conquering for its own sake. The riches he saw in Fair Isle's future were not the kind you could measure on a jeweler's scale. He was imbued with a sense of purpose greater than himself and he longed to share this with Imoshen, sure she would be as inspired as he was. With this in mind he sat down to finish the letter.

At last he stretched his cramped hand and read back what he had written, adding one last sentence. *I know you see this future too, because you spoke of it the day we stood overlooking Landsend.* He wanted to write of how he had taken her in his arms that day and how he longed to do so now, but it was not the Ghebite way to speak of these things.

Dropping melted wax on the folded message, he stared at the growing wax blob. He needed his own official seal. So far he had used his father's ring seal. But he had no right to that seal, to anything Gheeaban.

With the tip of his knife he drew a rising sun in the wax puddle before it could dry. Would Imoshen notice? Would she make the connection? He smiled to himself. It was a little test.

Rawset returned and Tulkhan gave him the sealed message. "Deliver this into her own hands and see that she breaks the seal herself."

"So be it. I sail tonight for T'Diemn."

"Kornel will take the skiffs back to the mouth of the marsh river to await the supplies. Unless there is a message for me, stay with T'Imoshen." Tulkhan wondered how he could tell this idealistic young man that he wanted him to report on what was happening in T'Diemn. He needed to know if there was any truth behind Jarholfe's message. "Be aware of what goes on around her. There are many enemies who would do harm to our cause, and not all of them live on the mainland."

"I understand," Rawset said, but Tulkhan doubted.

As Rawset left, Lightfoot entered the shelter, saying, "You sent the marsh-dweller and his son home?"

"If he returns, it will be because he chooses to serve me."

"Choice!" Lightfoot muttered, rubbing his forehead, and Tulkhan wondered if he was missing something. Lightfoot looked up at the sky; no stars were visible tonight. "Looks like rain."

Tulkhan nodded. His miners would not welcome rain. Already one of the shafts had collapsed and had to be dug out and reinforced.

That evening Imoshen and Reothe ate in Windhaven Hall, where the farm girl Kalleen was now the mistress.

"My ambassadors should be on the mainland by now," Imoshen said as the servants took away the last of the plates, leaving Kalleen, Imoshen, and Reothe alone. Jarholfe had opted to eat in the courtyard with his men. The hall was not big enough to seat over thirty people. Windhaven was not a large estate, and the home was little more than a fortified farmhouse.

Imoshen pushed her plate aside. The meal had been uncomfortably formal. "So, tell me, Kalleen, what do you think of Windhaven? The soil is good and the people friendly."

"My lady?" A tentative voice spoke.

Kalleen signaled for the woman to approach.

"Some people want to see the T'En Healer. One has the bone ache, another coughs blood, two more—"

"Send them in." Imoshen came to her feet. "Have someone bring the herbs from my baggage." She put the sleeping baby in his basket on the floor before the fire and leaned closer to Kalleen. "I would speak with you later."

She turned to Reothe. "You might as well go. This could take hours."

Ashmyr stirred and Reothe soothed him. At that moment the woman returned with the first of the locals, a farmer whose body was twisted with the bone ache. As Imoshen dealt with the old man, he cast Reothe a speculative glance. She realized that while the rebel leader rocked the conqueror's son, the locals would assume Ashmyr was Reothe's child. Was this his intention or simply chance?

A constant stream of locals shuffled across the ancient flagstones. Some needed only a few herbs and words of encouragement. With others Imoshen had to call on her gift. When Ashmyr fell asleep, Reothe placed the basket on the floor by his chair and observed her. She tried to ignore his presence. But even if she had been able to disregard the tension in her body, she would have been reminded by the way the villagers glanced shyly at him, offering their thanks to both the T'En as though she and Reothe were two sides of a coin.

At last there were no more True-people to be healed and Imoshen packed away her depleted herbs, weary yet satisfied. Reothe rose, stretching like a great cat, flexing and tensing the muscles on the weak side of his body.

"I'm sorry if you were bored," Imoshen snapped, unsettled.

"Bored? Never. Besides, it is good for them to see me with you when you heal." He saw she did not understand. "When you use your gifts, I am included in your nimbus of power."

Imoshen gasped, annoyed because she had not anticipated this.

He shrugged, amused.

She slung the herb satchel across one shoulder, then knelt to pick up Ashmyr's basket. "I thank you for reminding me what you are, Reothe!"

"No one can forget what we are, Imoshen. We wear our heritage on our faces."

"I must go."

"Yes. Kalleen will be waiting, no doubt."

Imoshen felt the heat rise in her face. "She is my friend."

"Kalleen is a True-woman who fears you."

"You don't understand. You see betrayal everywhere, and because of it you cannot trust or be trusted." She felt sick at heart. "I won't become like you, Reothe."

"You didn't grow up in the court of the old empire!"

But she refused to acknowledge this and climbed the stairs to her room, where she found Kalleen dozing in a chair by the fire. At the soft click of the latch, Kalleen gave a little start. For a heartbeat her unguarded face betrayed her wariness, and Imoshen cloaked her dismay. She knelt to place Ashmyr in front of the fire, then looked past his sleeping form to Kalleen. "Thank you for waiting."

"You have had word from Wharrd?"

Imoshen bit her lip and Kalleen looked away to hide her disappointment. "I am here to place a special trust upon you."

Kalleen's features revealed caution and curiosity.

Imoshen stroked Ashmyr's cheek, tears blurring her vision. "He is so small and defenseless. If anything were to happen—"

Kalleen anticipated her. "Please don't ask this of me!"

"These are desperate times. Unless Tulkhan defeats King Gharavan, we face war in the spring. Fair Isle is rife with dissension. The Ghebite commanders, Reothe's rebels, and the Keldon nobles are ready to take up arms against one another. I ask this of you. If something happens to me, look after Ashmyr."

Kalleen's eyes widened. "Have you seen your deaths?"

Imoshen shook her head and brushed tears from her cheeks. "Swear you will take care of my son if I die."

"I swear," Kalleen whispered. "But I don't see how I can save him if you can't. If the worst comes to pass, I will be fleeing Fair Isle with nothing but the clothes I wear and two children. Or did you forget I am with child?"

Imoshen had not forgotten. Kalleen could expect to carry her child around six small moons. Imoshen knew her own pure T'En babe would be carried eight small moons, one year from conception to birth. It would be nearly the cusp of autumn before her child would be born. Then, if Tulkhan denied her, he would drive her into allegiance with Reothe. No wonder she found it hard to take joy in the pregnancy, but the babe itself was innocent. Her hand settled protectively over her flat belly.

"What is it?" Kalleen covered Imoshen's hand. "Are you ill?"

"No." Imoshen smiled. "I want to leave a message in your mind for the day you may need it." She saw Kalleen's imminent refusal and hurried on. "I promise that is all, and the message will not surface if you never need it."

"How..." Kalleen swallowed. "How will you do it?"

Relief flooded Imoshen. "It won't hurt. I promise."

"Very well. Let's get it over with."

Imoshen stood. "Come to the bed. Is your wound healed?"

"Yes. Only the proud flesh of the scar remains." Kalleen climbed up onto the bed and lay back. She undid the drawstring of her nightgown, turning her face away as Imoshen pulled the material apart to reveal her breasts, now swollen because she was in the first stage of her pregnancy. Below her left breast was a puckered scar, evidence of Drake's attack.

"Do you trust me, Kalleen?"

Their eyes met. "I want to."

"Then listen to me." Imoshen began to sing a T'En lullaby that her great-aunt used to croon to her, tracing a circle on Kalleen's abdomen in time to the rhythm. When she felt the familiar metallic taste on her tongue and the ache in her teeth, she knew her gifts were moving. Kalleen's breathing slowed as her body relaxed.

Imoshen focused on the scar. She ran her finger over its puckered surface. The skin stirred like soft white sand. Still humming, Imoshen drew a map of her family's Stronghold on Kalleen's abdomen, stretching and elongating the thin, silver scar tissue to define the shape. When this was done she touched the tip of her sixth finger to the spot where she and the Aayel had hidden the family's wealth.

It was a king's ransom, because that was what they'd thought it would be for. They had feared the Ghebite General would capture their family and demand gold for their safe return. But he hadn't. He had simply slaughtered them. She must not forget what kind of man Tulkhan was. Strange, the man she knew did not mesh with his past actions.

The treasure cache contained more than enough gold and precious jewels for Kalleen to flee Fair Isle a wealthy woman. Imoshen placed this knowledge in the deep cavern of Kalleen's mind, safely hidden until the day she might need it.

Sealing it with a little spurt of her will, Imoshen discovered she was weary beyond thought. Kalleen slept deeply. It was all Imoshen could do to lie down beside her before she lost all sense of self.

Imoshen woke at dawn with Kalleen's warm body tucked around hers and the girl's soft cheek on her shoulder. If the baby hadn't been working up a cry, Imoshen would not have moved. She nudged Kalleen, who pushed the hair from her face, blinking owlishly. Imoshen went to the baby, and Kalleen sat up, then noticed her nightgown was still undone.

"I tried to smooth your scar, but—"

"It does not matter." Kalleen pulled the drawstring closed as Imoshen undid her bodice. "So, you left your message?"

Imoshen nodded. "To thank you seems inadequate."

"Then don't." Kalleen laughed, but it was almost a shudder. "I pray the day never comes."

"So do I."

Ten

IMOSHEN'S HEART LIFTED as she approached Fair Isle's capital. Truly, T'Diem lived up to its fabled beauty. Bathed in gentle afternoon light, the sandstone buildings glowed. The old city was built on hills, bounded by defensive walls constructed during the Age of Consolidation. New T'Diemn lay around the outskirts, twice as large again. Riding down the broad road to the new city's north gate, Imoshen was relieved to see that Tulkhan's fortifications were progressing well. The ditches and towers were almost completed.

She had intended to slip quietly into the capital, but from the moment she identified herself to the gate guards, news of her arrival preceded her. People came out in droves to see Imoshen with T'Reothe riding proud beside her. They pointed and whispered, and she knew every conceivable rumor was taking life.

Was T'Reothe reconciled, or was he playing a double game? Their Protector General was on the mainland laying siege to Port Sumair. What if he failed to defeat his half-brother? The people of T'Diemn had experienced King Gharavan's cruelty firsthand, and Imoshen felt the weight of their expectation.

A crowd gathered in the square before the palace of a thousand rooms. Once Imoshen had dreaded entering the palace, overwhelmed by its myriad passages, army of ser-

vants, and seething court factions. Now she saw it as a beautiful, flawed pearl, an aggregate of buildings added to and
literally overlaid by her ancestors during six hundred years
of T'En rule. The original building, which had been rebuilt
after the fire of sixty-four, lay deep within, enfolded by later
additions.

Of all the towers, Sard's was the tallest, built by Empress
T'Abularassa. Together with the first Beatific, she had cre-
ated the Tractarians to contain Sardonyx when he went rogue
and led the revolt that saw the palace burned. Imoshen
looked up at the Grieving Towers erected by the families of
rogue T'En, and her throat grew tight with emotion.

Reothe claimed the Church had betrayed the T'En, yet
the Tractarians had given their lives many times to protect
Fair Isle from dangerous T'En. Until now she had always
seen this as a noble sacrifice; however, their history had
been written by the survivors. But, as Reothe said, who decided what was treason?

The most recent stoning was T'Obazim's. Imoshen's
great-aunt had witnessed his death as a young girl and lived
in fear for the rest of her life. With a shiver, Imoshen turned
her attention to the church's center of power.

Directly opposite the palace, the basilica's great golden
dome gleamed in the afternoon sun. This building rivaled the
palace in complexity and beauty. Careful to accord
the Church's leader due honor, Imoshen led their party to the
basilica's steps, where the Beatific stood flanked by high-
ranking officials. While offering formal greetings to the
Beatific, Imoshen wondered what report Seculate Donyx had
sent by fast horse.

She deliberately turned away so that she did not have to
watch the meeting between the Beatific and Reothe. Did the
woman within the Beatific still love Reothe?

Imoshen sensed an intensity that equaled hers and
searched the ranks of the church hierarchy until she found
Murgon, leader of the Tractarians. His unguarded expression was a window to his mind. He not only feared Reothe,
he envied him. It was a dangerous combination.

With a sigh, she urged her horse across the square to greet the palace staff, who had assembled on the steps. It wasn't until she had formally been welcomed by all those persons who thought it necessary to receive direct instructions that Imoshen could retire to a small study. She enjoyed the simple lines of this room, with its desk of inlaid polished wood and tripod chairs. It had been decorated in the Age of Discernment, when elegance was valued above opulence.

Taking over the candle lighter's job, she instructed him to send for Wharrd, but he reported that the commander was in the south, conferring with the Keldon nobles. Imoshen sighed; she had hoped to hear Wharrd's report. "Then please send food."

Servants soon arrived. Soundlessly, they placed the food trays on the desk before leaving. Spreading out paper and tapping the ink from her scriber, Imoshen prepared to work, only to be interrupted by Jarholfe.

"Yes?" She looked up.

"The Elite Guard is greatly depleted. Do you want me to assign men from the general army to be trained?"

Imoshen frowned. Unlike her own Stronghold Guard, she did not trust the Elite Guard. She wished she could dismiss Jarholfe, wished there were no need to fear treachery and assassination. "Provide me with a list of the Elite Guard who remain in T'Diemn and their skills." Even as she spoke, she recalled that he could not write. Someone knocked. "Enter."

Imoshen's heart sank as the Ghebite priest strode in, his ornate surplice swinging with each step. Since arriving in T'Diemn, the Cadre had been as contemptuous of other beliefs as he had been vocal in preaching his warrior god's path. Jarholfe met his eyes, then looked quickly away.

The Cadre gave an abbreviated Ghebite bow. "I am here to offer my services, Lady Protector. In his haste to defeat his half-brother's army, General Tulkhan has been remiss. He cannot expect a woman to rule Fair Isle in his absence."

Imoshen came to her feet. "On the contrary, in the presence of his commanders and Elite Guard the General said I was to be his Voice."

But the Cadre continued. "Fortunately, Lord Commander Wharrd remains in Fair Isle; together with myself and Jarholfe, we will be able to guide you."

"What would you advise, Cadre?" Imoshen asked silkily.

"Make an example of this rebel leader. Execute him and outlaw all those who would support him," he urged. "I had reports that the Keldon nobles were massing on the plains. They have since dispersed, but their threat must be contained. Confiscate the estates of the troublemakers. As for the rest, take their eldest sons hostage—"

A door-comb scratched on the door's tang. By the comb's tone Imoshen knew it was a noble from the old empire and guessed it to be Reothe. He entered before she could think of a way of dismissing him. Reothe's gaze swept the room's inhabitants, and when his eyes met hers they held a question.

"The Cadre was offering me much the same advice you offered in T'Ronynn's Tower," Imoshen explained. The priest's confusion made her smile.

"Palace intrigue is not for the fainthearted," Reothe said.

A spasm of hatred, quickly masked, traveled across Jarholfe's features, and the Cadre would have spoken but Imoshen forestalled him. "I thank you for your offer of assistance, Cadre. If I am in need of your advice I will send for you." She included them both in a gesture. "You are dismissed."

They backed out, seething.

"A pair of snakes," Reothe remarked. "The Cadre hates you. It's not surprising, when minstrels from one end of Fair Isle to the other sing of how you shamed him."

"I caught him smashing our hothouses. I could not let him destroy the herbs that control fertility. He would reduce women to breeding cows." Imoshen sat wearily. "Every day I battle to educate these barbarians, but I fear the Ghebites are blinded by their culture."

"That, and fear. I don't need my gifts to smell Jarholfe's

fear of us." Reothe lopped off a wedge of cheese, eating it
from the knife like a farmer. "Watch him."

"I have plans for Jarholfe, and the security of the palace
will not be his responsibility."

"And what is my responsibility? Or am I to be your lapdog?" Reothe gestured with the knife. "Give me something
to do, Imoshen!"

His barely contained tension made her gift flare. She
forced it down and poured a glass of wine. Since Chalkcliff
Abbey, she had decided caution was the safest path with
Reothe. She dare not heal him. "I need you to inspect the
city's new defenses. I want to know how close they are to
completion. Tell me if you can spot any weaknesses."

A servant's door-comb sounded. "Emissary Rawset
wishes to speak with you."

Imoshen rose, pushing her untouched wine aside. She
could not bring herself to read Tulkhan's message under
Reothe's mocking gaze. She picked up the baby's basket.
"Send Rawset to my bedchamber."

Reothe stabbed another piece of cheese. "Entertaining
yet another man in your bedchamber, Imoshen?"

"I work for the good of Fair Isle. Be grateful I do not
drug you while I discuss matters of state!" She headed for
the door.

"Do not be so sure of your high moral ground. Remember, the historians decide who works treason!"

The sound of his laughter followed her out of the
room, echoing in her head as she strode the long gallery. She
doubted if the palace would ever be big enough to share
with Reothe.

Her chambers had been warmed and lit and her clothes
unpacked. She was used to the opulence now and barely noticed the walls' inlaid amber panels, other than to appreciate
the glow reflected from the candles.

Imoshen placed Ashmyr's basket near the fire and
tucked the blanket under his chin. There was barely time to
straighten before a servant scratched discreetly at the door,
announcing Rawset.

He gave her the Ghebite obeisance, following this with the T'En court greeting, taking her hand and kissing her sixth finger. "You are safely returned to us."

"Why would I not be safe?" Imoshen asked.

"There is talk of rebel bands roaming the countryside. I'd heard stories and feared—"

"We took our time and we had no trouble on the road." This was strictly true. "What word from the General?"

Rawset removed a message from inside his cloak. "From his hands to yours."

Imoshen smiled. She felt much older than Rawset, yet she suspected he was at least five years her senior. Taking the message to her desk, she wished him gone so that she could pore over every word alone with the General's memory.

The seal was odd. It looked as if someone had drawn in the hot wax. Why hadn't Tulkhan used his usual seal, the rearing stallion, the Ghebite god's symbol? Perhaps this new seal was visible evidence of a shift in the General's thinking.

Carefully, Imoshen pried the wax away from the paper and spread the sheets. It was all as she expected until she came to his plans for a new standard. Blue and gold—the dawn sun rising over a new era for Fair Isle. Her throat tightened and tears of loss stung her eyes. She had witnessed the old empire's death throes, but General Tulkhan's plans reopened the wound.

The T'En twin moons had set and Tulkhan's house was in ascendancy. So be it. Wiping her eyes, Imoshen focused on the design for Fair Isle's new standard. "I will inspect the cloth merchants for appropriate materials and speak with the seamsters on the morrow, Rawset."

"General Tulkhan said I was to return with the finished banners and cloaks."

"Cloaks for a whole army? I will have to see what the cloth merchants have in stock." Imoshen felt a familiar fire ignite her. She loved a challenge. In her mind's eye she was already illuminating the standard, imagining finely spun thread of gold on the purest azure blue.

She glanced down at the General's letter. There was no

private word for her, nothing but a fleeting mention of the
time they had stood on the lookout above Landsend and
shared a vision for Fair Isle's future. Imoshen closed her
eyes, recalling the sharp sea breeze and the way Tulkhan
had taken her in his arms and kissed her. She wondered if
this was what he had intended.

She wanted, needed, to believe that Tulkhan, with the
limitations of a True-man, had deliberately written of that
moment to reach out to her across time and distance.

Imoshen cleared her throat. "When everything is ready,
I will write to the General. I will have a sleek, seagoing ship
assigned to you in case we need to contact him quickly. I'm
hoping to have good news from my ambassadors in the
Amirate. Until then, take your pleasure about town."

Alone at last, Imoshen considered how she would handle Jarholfe and his men. Though it was entirely logical to
combine the Elite Guard and the Stronghold Guard, she
knew the Ghebites would resist. They did not respect a
fighting force that accepted women.

Tired of confined spaces, Imoshen opened her door to
find one of her Stronghold Guard on duty. "Ashmyr sleeps.
I'm going for a walk. Let no one in."

Imoshen walked, deep in thought, until she found herself
in the portrait gallery, which dated from the Age of Tribulation. She paused before the panel to the secret passage that
she had ordered sealed. It led to the catacombs, and no one
must venture down there for fear of rousing the Parakletos.

The bodies of the Paragian Guard might be entombed,
but those who had died while under oath to Imoshen the
First knew no rest. They had given more than their lives to
subdue Fair Isle—they had given their deaths as well, becoming the Parakletos, death's guardians.

Imoshen pressed her cheek to the dusty wood grain;
though she longed to explore those ancient catacombs, her
fear of the Parakletos was greater. Reothe had said they had
no power in this world, but she had sensed their animosity.

Resuming her pacing, she found herself in a narrow
connecting gallery that led to the ball court. The alcoves in

this gallery were painted with lifelike renderings of mythical and historical scenes.

In the alcove facing her, the Parakletos escorted the soul of Imoshen the First from this world to the next. The artist had chosen to illustrate not the darkness of death's shadow but Imoshen the First's destination. The dawn sun blazed behind the Parakletos, who were depicted as fierce creatures with great white wings. In this representation they were stern beings of beauty and majesty escorting the soul of one who had devoted her life to the service of others.

Imoshen frowned. How different the beliefs of Fair Isle were from Ghebite beliefs. For a bonding gift Tulkhan had presented her with a torque of pure gold, embellished with exquisite filigree work picked out in niello. It was a work of art, yet the scene it illustrated was the great Akha Khan trampling his enemies beneath his hooves. All the Ghebites knew was violence, and their god reflected this. He appeared in the form of the black stallion, a half-man–half-stallion, or a giant of a man like Tulkhan.

His Elite Guard would not take kindly to being amalgamated with her Stronghold Guard, but she needed a palace force loyal to her. Suddenly, Imoshen's vision swam and she saw the half-man–half-stallion as it appeared on Tulkhan's torque, overlaid on the painting before her. Pure light glowed through the stallion, making it a white-winged protector.

When Wharrd returned to T'Diemn, Imoshen ordered a meal laid in her favorite dining room. The Jade Room dated from the early Age of Consolidation. Jade deities, gifted from a mainland king long dead, stood in niches around the room. A central low table was bounded by three couches suitable for intimate dining.

At this knock she told Wharrd to enter, but it was Reothe.

"Were you expecting someone else?"

"You know I was expecting Lord Commander Wharrd, else why did you knock?"

He smiled disarmingly. "Wharrd reports on matters of state. The fate of Fair Isle concerns me. I know the General has designed a new standard for Fair Isle. I know Rawset will get a ship of his own. Why bother to hide things from me, Imoshen? I gave you my report on the defenses, and you agreed the wharfs were the city's weakest point."

"Yes, but your plans to make the wharfs safe would drive the merchants mad, obstructing the unloading and loading of stores. Besides, an invader would have to take every lock, killing each of the lockkeepers between T'Diemn and the sea before they could give their alarm. Only then could they attack the wharves. Impossible."

"They said taking an army across the marsh-land was impossible but your General did it, and forget the merchants. They are interested only in profit. You will get nothing but complaints from them until they are under threat. Then see how quick they are to blame you for not taking adequate precautions. I know where I would attack if I wanted to take T'Diemn."

His threat hung on the air. Imoshen felt her body and gifts quicken to his challenge. Reothe stood across the room from her, his eyes glittering with febrile brilliance. A T'En warrior in the full capacity of his gifts was a terrible thing to contemplate. Thank the Aayel, she had not healed him.

"What?" he pressed.

He was too perceptive. Imoshen opened her mouth to put him off, but there was a knock at the door. "Enter."

As Wharrd let the door swing shut behind him, Imoshen caught the veteran's uneasy glance in Reothe's direction.

"Wine?" Imoshen offered. "Have you eaten?"

"No, nothing." He did not sit down.

"You can speak before T'Reothe. He does not want a spring invasion any more than we do. We have called a truce, haven't we, kinsman?" She held Reothe's eyes.

"Yes, kinswoman. As you say, we are allies, Empress."

Imoshen wondered what Wharrd would make of the use of that title. Reothe's antagonism was clear enough. But

Wharrd ignored Reothe, explaining that ambassadors had been sent to all three southern kingdoms, though the Amirate capital was the preferred port. Following her advice, he had selected bond-partners, Ghebite lord commanders and Fair Isle noblewomen. No word had returned as yet.

"As for the siege machines, I checked them personally," Wharrd continued. "They are safely stowed in the ships' holds, ready to sail at a moment's notice."

"The merchants will not like that. While their ships sit idle in dock they are losing money!" Reothe observed.

"They'd like it less if Gharavan sacked the wharves and burned their ships to the waterline," Wharrd muttered.

"Enough." Imoshen was tired. She'd seen the way Reothe and the Beatific greeted each other during the formal dinner on their second evening in T'Diemn. The interchange between the rebel leader and the Beatific had been too correct, and Imoshen despised herself for caring. Her only amusement had been surreptitiously watching Murgon seethe behind his polite facade.

"The cavalry drill every day. It is good exercise for the men and their horses. They have grown fat with too much easy living," Wharrd said.

"I would like to see this Ghebite cavalry," Reothe announced.

Yes, Imoshen thought. Study your enemy, Reothe. One day you may be facing the cavalry; much better to know their strengths and weaknesses. The look Wharrd cast her told her he had the same idea. She gave Wharrd a nod. "Arrange a display." Ashmyr stirred and she rocked the cradle gently. "That will give me a chance to invite the Beatific and the guild-masters and let the townspeople know. It would not hurt to make a display of strength. Let the news of our battle-readiness filter back through the mainland spies to the Amir and his allied kings. Let them think twice about dishonoring their old alliances." She smiled with relish.

Reothe silently lifted his wineglass to her, the echo of her smile in his eyes. She felt that familiar tug of like to like.

"You rock the cradle with one hand while you rule Fair

Isle with the other. You think like a man; I don't—" Wharrd seemed to realize he had spoken aloud. The bone-setter-turned-diplomat rose stiffly, his coppery skin growing darker. "Forgive this old campaigner, T'Imoshen. I have been in the saddle since dawn. I bid you good night."

With a soldier's bow he left the room.

Reothe's gaze met hers. "These Ghebites do not know what to make of you, Imoshen. They are not used to a woman who can reason with the best of them. I raise my glass to Imoshen the Statesman."

She flushed. As a compliment it touched her far more than any flowery phrase. "I wish only for peace and the chance to sit by my own fireside."

He laughed. "So you say, but you would be bored within a small moon!"

Imoshen shook her head.

He studied her, frankly skeptical.

"Give me peace and quiet any day!"

"I think you honestly believe that. But I fear it will not be our fate, Imoshen. We are the last of the T'En. Death will not come to claim us in our dotage by our firesides."

She knew at a visceral level that Reothe was right, and she longed to ask him if he'd seen their deaths. He claimed to have the Sight. Perhaps he fought so feverishly because he tried to wrench the path of destiny into one of his own making. She looked over at him.

"Ask," he prompted.

But she would not reveal her thoughts. Reothe was a law unto himself, and for all his apparent compliance, she did not trust him.

Imoshen looked up as a servant announced Lord Athlyng. Athlyng was one of the three Keldon nobles who had approached Imoshen about reopening the Causare Council, which had been closed since Tulkhan conquered the island. Though the Council had reopened to traders, its other function—to debate Fair Isle's policy—remained unfulfilled.

Tulkhan had agreed to establish a new council, but only if an equal number of his commanders had a vote. Naturally, the Keld had objected to this. But it was immaterial, for while they were at war they could debate but not formalize decisions.

"Have warmed wine prepared in the greeting room," Imoshen ordered, and the servant departed. She sorted the notes on her desk. The cloth merchants' guild had been quietly ecstatic at the thought of so much business. The most gifted designers of the seamsters' guild were inspired to refine Tulkhan's design.

Since Wharrd's return, Imoshen had left Reothe to oversee the completion of T'Diemn's defenses. He had resumed the wing of rooms that had always been his, and she suspected, though he rode the defensive earthworks every morning, that Reothe was also contacting old friends and calling in old favors.

The Beatific had paid a courtesy call and offered support in the war against King Gharavan. General Tulkhan had formally recognized the T'En Church's laws. If Gharavan took T'Diemn, he would loot the basilica and encourage his soldiers to rape the priests. Imoshen had the support of Reothe and the Beatific, albeit motivated by self-interest. Now she needed the support of the Keldon nobles.

She opened the connecting door. "Lord Athlyng."

"T'Imoshen." He gave her the formal obeisance.

Imoshen took her seat and performed the warmed-wine pouring ceremony. Only when the porcelain cups were steaming before both of them did she meet his T'En eyes. "Have the Keldon nobles selected their six representatives for the Causare Council?"

"You toy with me, T'Imoshen. In times of war the Council has no power." He met her eyes frankly. "No, I am here unofficially. We—"

Athlyng broke off as Reothe entered the room.

His spies were most efficient, Imoshen thought wryly.

Reothe smiled as he met her eyes, then greeted the old lord. "Grandfather."

Casting back through their shared family tree, Imoshen realized she was speaking with the man who had bonded with her great-aunt's sister. Even though Athlyng's relationship with Reothe was through the lesser, paternal line, it explained the support Reothe had received from the Keld. They saw him as one of their own.

Reothe sank gracefully into the seat on Imoshen's left. His hand settled on her forearm.

Athlyng's wine-dark eyes rested briefly on Reothe's hand. "They said the last of the T'En were reconciled. I came to see for myself."

"Fair Isle cannot afford division," Imoshen said. "I want confirmation that the Keldon nobles will stand at the General's side if Gharavan invades. Tell Lady Woodvine and the others that the Causare Council will be reopened when Gharavan is dead and the six places on that council will be filled by those who have proven their loyalty."

Reothe chuckled. "Imoshen believes in speaking plainly."

"Imoshen can speak for herself," she snapped.

Lord Athlyng smiled as he came to his feet, an old man grown whip-thin with age. "I will return to the highlands this very day. All along I have argued for temperance." He gave Reothe a hard look. "My greatest ambition is to die of old age in my bed, surrounded by my family. How many of us have died in our sleep in six hundred years, Reothe?"

"Not enough, Grandfather." Reothe embraced him.

When Athlyng gave Imoshen the obeisance for the Empress and departed, she realized with a start that she was T'Imoshen the Empress to almost everyone. She was not yet nineteen, but few people saw past the power to the girl–woman who had risen to meet the challenge of her position.

Impatience seized Tulkhan as he shaded his eyes against the midday sun, watching his ships on the brilliant sea. If only he had the siege machines. It was a litany that never ceased. He could not attack by land without the machines, and the ships alone were not strong enough to break the siege.

Suddenly he swore softly under his breath, for he had been thinking like a landsman. He could erect the siege machines on the ship's decks. The more pressure he placed on the people of Port Sumair, the more likely they were to turn on Gharavan.

Skidding down the landward side of the Sea-wall, he caught his mount's reins, already planning his message to Imoshen. Unfortunately, Rawset was in T'Diemn. How could the General convince Imoshen his message was genuine?

"The Elite Guard are waiting in the sword-practice courtyard, along with your Stronghold Guard," Wharrd reported.

"Thank you." When Imoshen had first told him her intention to unite the two guards, Wharrd had advised against it. He had talked of the Gheeakhan code of honor, and of a Ghebite soldier's military ambition. This had given Imoshen the insight she needed to devise a strategy to win the Ghebites over.

Followed by two servants who carried a hastily painted banner, Imoshen approached the courtyard with some trepidation. Stepping into the sunshine, she sensed the Elite Guards' resentment. Her own Stronghold Guard—what remained of the twenty men and women who had accompanied her to T'Diemn—waited uneasily.

"Crawen and Jarholfe." Imoshen acknowledged the guard leaders. "I have called your people here today because Fair Isle faces her hour of greatest need. King Gharavan threatens a spring invasion—"

"General Tulkhan will trim his wick!" a Ghebite called. Someone added a ribald comment, and the men laughed too loudly.

Imoshen let the laughter die down. "But Fair Isle faces internal threats. In the southern highlands there are stiff-necked Keld who whisper treason, and bands of leaderless rebels wander the countryside terrorizing decent folk, while in the palace of T'Diemn the people who should be protecting the royal family are watching each other, ready to take insult at the slightest provocation. I speak of my Stronghold Guard and the Elite Guard."

Jarholfe muttered under his breath. Imoshen signaled Wharrd, who stepped forward. Without his support she could not have hoped to carry this off. He outranked Jarholfe in seniority.

"As you know, the General gave me the protection of T'Diemn," Wharrd said. "But I find myself under a Ghiad to T'Imoshen and unable to fulfill this role. Jarholfe, I call on you to take over the role entrusted to me by General Tulkhan. I name you leader of T'Diemn's garrison."

No ambitious career soldier could resist this promotion, and Jarholfe was quick to give the Ghebite salute, arm across his chest, fist clenched. "I am honored. By the great Akha Khan I will not fail this charge."

The Elite Guard were now leaderless. Wharrd stepped back and caught Imoshen's eye. She raised her voice. "My faithful Stronghold Guard, you left your homes and families at an hour's notice and have not returned for over a year. I release you from your oath. You are free to return home. As for the Elite Guard, they are free to return to the regular army or follow Jarholfe into T'Diemn's garrison."

This was greeted with uneasy muttering.

Imoshen signaled for silence. "General Tulkhan has claimed the dawn sun as his house symbol. Behold the symbol of the new palace guard." Imoshen undid the banner's ribbons so that it unfurled to reveal the white horse, half-man–half-beast, wings outstretched as he leapt over the dawn sun. Her own people would understand the reference to Imoshen the First's Paragian Guard. The Ghebites would believe she honored Tulkhan and the Akha Khan.

"Anyone who can meet the high standard of the Parakhan Guard is free to join." She caught Crawen's eye and smiled. "They will be trained in unarmed combat under Crawen, and in the use of the Ghebite sword by Edovan."

Imoshen beckoned him. Traveling with Jarholfe's men had given her a chance to study them, and she believed Edovan, though he appeared startled now, would adapt quickly. "Jarholfe has recommended your skill with the sword, Edovan. Will you accept this honor and become Sword-master of the Parakhan Guard?"

To refuse would be disloyal to Jarholfe. He gave the Ghebite salute. "I would be honored to serve General Tulkhan as Swordmaster of the Parakhan Guard."

Imoshen indicated that Crawen and Edovan were to turn and face their fellows. "We of Fair Isle believe that, like the small and large moon, men and women are different. Each has their strengths and weaknesses, but like the moons they shine strongest when they shine together." She wanted to say more but held her tongue. This was one small step toward her ultimate goal of uniting Fair Isle.

Imoshen's heart leapt in anticipation of the unveiling of Tulkhan's new royal standard. She signaled the servants to release the ties, and the heavy material unrolled, revealing its rich blue and gold, brilliant even in the dull light of the autumn day. The huge banner hung across the rear wall of the palace's great public hall. She had to step back to take in its magnificence.

The seamsters used finely spun gold thread to highlight the rising sun and its shafts of light. The sea was a deep, royal blue, the sky an intense azure, and in the top left-hand corner she had instructed the embroiderers to illuminate the twin moons of the T'En in silver thread. All about her the seamsters and guild-masters congratulated each other.

The house of Tulkhan rose with the dawn, watched over by the T'En. The people of Fair Isle would understand the significance.

A familiar voice made Imoshen turn. "Wharrd?" She gestured to the banner. "What do you think? We will have new flags on all the towers of T'Diemn. Tulkhan's cloaks and the battlefield banners are loading even as we speak. And, by the by, the Parakhan Guard are looking fine in their new uniforms."

"Fine fittings do not make a lame horse whole."

She lowered her voice. "You think the Parakhan Guard a lame horse, Wharrd?"

"No." He grimaced. "Merely unused to the bridle."

"That can be remedied. In time we—"

"Time is what we don't have. Can we speak?"

Imoshen's stomach clenched. "A moment." Raising her voice, she thanked everyone, but even as they beamed at her she was trying to anticipate Wharrd's bad news.

When they returned to her private chambers, she turned to him. "Speak."

"We've had a reply from the Amirate." He handed her a message scroll.

Imoshen frowned, reading quickly. "They regret they cannot honor alliances drawn up with the old empire... General Tulkhan, bastard son of the Ghebite invaders, has no authority..." Imoshen lifted her head. "They are refusing to give us port access. But it is only one kingdom of the triad. One of the other kingdoms may yet agree. They constantly vie for an advantage—"

"Keep reading."

Imoshen returned her attention to the message. "Treason? Our ambassadors are imprisoned, accused of treason against the Amir himself?"

Wharrd nodded. "It gets worse. They expect us to pay an enormous sum in compensation before they will consider releasing our people."

"What happened?" Imoshen sat down heavily.

"Our ambassadors arrived in the middle of a feud between the maternal and paternal relatives of the infant Amir. By Amirate law the boy cannot be crowned until he reaches sixteen, so the paternal grandfather was declared Amiregent. The maternal uncle arranged for the old man's assassination and seized the chance to lay the blame on our people."

Imoshen cursed softly.

"If we don't reply, it will be seen as an admission of guilt and our people will be executed. If we don't pay the compensation, it will be seen as an admission of guilt and our ambassadors will be executed. We have until Large New Moon to deliver the compensation."

"Ten days," Imoshen whispered. She had not expected such treachery.

"Can we find the gold?" Wharrd asked.

"We won't pay."

The veteran opened his mouth to speak, then stopped.

"What haven't you told me?" Imoshen prompted.

"The ambassadors are Lord Commander Shacolm and Lady Miryma, Lord Fairban's youngest daughter."

Imoshen fought a wave of nausea. Already that family had paid for her misjudgment with Cariah's death. Now this. . . .

Wharrd cleared his throat. "I thought sending bond-partners would—"

"It was what I recommended," Imoshen agreed. "We could not know the political situation was so volatile. We. . . I have been concentrating on Fair Isle, without giving thought to the intrigues on the mainland." She frowned. "The new Amiregent and his confederates probably hope King Gharavan and Tulkhan will worry over Fair Isle like two dogs over a bone and forget their miserable kingdoms. While the Ghebite army expends itself on internal warfare, the triad is safe from expansion. It appears Fair Isle will not get help from the mainland unless we prove we are stronger than Gharavan with all of Gheeaba behind him." She could feel a tension headache building. "What will I tell Tulk-han?"

"The truth. The ambassadors' servant is waiting, if you want to speak with him."

Imoshen nodded. "In time. You may go."

As Wharrd left, she realized she could expect a visit from Lord Fairban. For a moment she wondered why Miryma had accepted a Ghebite for her bond-partner.

After Cariah was murdered, both of her sisters had broken off all involvement with their Ghebite admirers.

Imoshen dipped her scriber into the ink, then hesitated. Not wanting to reveal her failure, she told the General only that negotiations with the Amirate were continuing. Then she wrote of the new Parakhan Guard and enclosed their banner, closing with the news that his army's new cloaks and standards were on their way.

She sent for Rawset and was ready when he arrived just at dusk, dressed for sailing.

"For the General's own hands." She gave Rawset the message. "And this is to be placed around Tulkhan's neck." She held up a thin chain. The large brass seal swung heavily. "It is the General's new seal."

She dropped it over Rawset's head and tucked it inside his shirt. Her hand rested for a moment over his heart, which she could feel thudding under her palm. "This must not fall into enemy hands. If your ship is lost, throw the seal overboard."

"I understand. What's this?" He pointed to a large traveling satchel.

"The General's own clothes, standard, and a banner. Be sure to take this to him along with my message."

"What will you do about the ambassadors?"

Imoshen groaned. "Does all of T'Diemn know?"

"I heard it from my ship's captain."

"Very well." Imoshen sat down to tell Tulkhan that she would deal with the Amiregent. As she waited for the ink to dry she asked, "And what does T'Diemn think of this?"

"They are outraged. They want you to save our people but they don't think you should pay the gold. What will you do?"

Imoshen sealed the message. She did not know how she was going to save Miryma, but she owed Cariah this. "You can tell General Tulkhan that I will not let our people down."

Eleven

WHEN A SERVANT announced the General's emissary, Imoshen frowned, for Rawset had set sail
only the evening before. Her frown deepened
when the mercenary leader entered.

"Lightfoot," she greeted him, wondering if he had
proven as untrustworthy as his former leader. "When did
you become the General's emissary?"

He reached under his cloak to unbuckle the sword he
wore. "The General said I was to show you this weapon."

"I know it." Imoshen formally accepted the massive
sword, palms up, head bowed. This sword had belonged to
Tulkhan's grandfather, Seerkhan, who united the Ghebite
tribes. The General's father had honored him with the
weapon. It was thought to be imbued with the character of
the men who wielded it.

The day before their bonding, Tulkhan had drawn this
sword to reveal how her breath made the metal's snakeskin
pattern dance up the blade. Then he had spilled a little of
his blood, explaining that Akha Khan demanded a tribute
every time the sword was drawn. Imoshen treasured the
memory of that shared moment.

She wrapped her hands around the hilt. It was a hand-
and-a-half grip for a giant of a man. Even so, Gharavan
could have found a similar sword and trusted she would not

recognize the difference. Ignoring Tulkhan's edict not to use her gifts, she opened her T'En senses to the weapon.

Many life forces had been dissipated by this blade, but she ignored the pain and quested for the identity of the person who had held this weapon before Lightfoot. A sense of Tulkhan enveloped her. It was as unmistakable as it was intimate, and she missed him fiercely.

Turning away from Lightfoot, she pressed the hilt to her lips. Imoshen returned the sword with the formal salute the T'En reserved for weapons of great antiquity. "You speak truly."

Lightfoot gave her Tulkhan's message. The General's plans for ships armed with siege-breaking weapons sounded good. "Tell Tulkhan I will speak with the engineers."

But when Lightfoot departed, Imoshen went straight to Reothe in the library. "Those siege machines—" she began, then stopped as the absurdity of asking advice from Tulkhan's sworn enemy struck her. But they shared a common enemy in Gharavan, and Reothe was Fair Isle's greatest sea captain.

"What about the siege machines?"

"Could they be mounted on ships?"

"The giant scaffolds with their protective shields could be mounted. Planks could be thrown across from the top of the scaffolds to the port's wall. But the whole thing is academic. Such heavy machines would make the ship unseaworthy."

"What if the machines were assembled while lying off the port and taken apart when the ship was at sea?"

"That's a possibility...." He frowned. "Why do you ask?"

Imoshen hesitated.

Reothe's eyes widened. "The General learns quickly. Send him his siege machines, but hold some in reserve. He still needs to build up his land forces." He frowned. "If you send Tulkhan the means to take Port Sumair, what becomes of Fair Isle's people held hostage in the Amirate?"

"What can I do?" Imoshen leaned on the table. Old maps of the city were held in place by statuettes made for this purpose. Everything of the old empire was designed for beauty, even these paperweights. The one before her portrayed a couple locked in an amorous embrace of exquisite sensuality. She picked it up, admiring the lines, then put it aside. Distress made her abrupt. "I cannot let Cariah's sister die!"

"You cannot pay the compensation."

"No." Imoshen paced. "I need to break the siege of Port Sumair. The longer it goes on, the weaker it makes Fair Isle appear. The Amirate will side with the winner. We must *crush* Gharavan."

"We must free our people. If the pretty princelings of the mainland believe they can flout the old alliances with impunity, they will soon be vying to divide our island between them."

"Exactly! But how can I save them?"

"I know how hard it is to negotiate from a position without power," he said.

But Imoshen would not be diverted. "The Amiregent sees only the fate of the regency. Who knows if the infant Amir will live to be crowned?" She paused. This could be her son's fate. If she were killed and the General fell in battle, both Tulkhan's loyal commanders and the Keldon nobles would try to seize Fair Isle in Ashmyr's name.

"What will you do?" Reothe asked.

"Send Tulkhan his siege machines for now."

Tulkhan entered his shelter to find that Lightfoot and Rawset had returned. The mercenary presented him with Seerkhan's sword, saying, "I think she used some Dhamfeer trick to be sure I was not lying. T'Imoshen said she would speak with the engineers."

As Tulkhan strapped the weapon around his hips, his hand caressed the hilt, but he could draw no sense of Imoshen from the gleaming surface.

Rawset placed two bundles on the table. "I left more food and men with Kornel at the marsh river mouth yesterday evening."

"What news?" Tulkhan asked.

He dug into his jerkin to pull out three messages, then

felt around his neck to remove the seal. Tulkhan accepted the chain, catching the seal to hold it to the light. It was his new standard repeated in miniature. He smiled. Little escaped Imoshen.

Dismissing them, he lit the candles, sure that the small, hasty-looking message from Imoshen was something private. But as he read the note he cursed. The Amiregent's insult called for immediate action. Digesting the bad news, Tulkhan slowly broke the seal of the larger letter. This was all good news about the delivery of his standards, banners, flags, and cloaks. Imoshen wrote in glowing terms of the Parakhan Guard, bidding him to view their banner.

When Tulkhan unrolled the banner he had to admire Imoshen's daring. She had adapted the symbol of the great Akha Khan himself, combining it with figures he recognized from palace paintings. Yet he had to admit the image made his heart race with reluctant recognition.

Putting the banner aside, he unpacked his new standard. The sun's surface flickered in the candlelight. Unable to resist, Tulkhan ran his hand over the embroidery, marveling at the golden thread, spun so fine it could be sewn.

Eagerly, he stood the banner upright. The dawn sun blazed forth against an azure sky. In the candlelight something flashed silver. His fingertips brushed the material at the top left-hand corner. Raising the candle, he identified twin moons sewn in silver thread. A rueful smile tugged at his lips. Ever the diplomat, Imoshen had found a way to include the T'En symbols.

Tulkhan unwrapped the last bundle, revealing his cloak, helmet, and crest. Never again would he wear the red, purple, and black of Gheeaba, colors of violence and death. His new colors promised life and hope. When the rest of the cloaks and banners arrived, he would have a symbolic burning before the gates of Port Sumair. The colors of Gheeaba would turn to ashes while his half-brother watched.

He heard Lightfoot's voice outside and lifted the flap, beckoning him. "Come see my new standard. Your men will wear my blue cloaks. In the heat of battle we don't want soldiers forgetting whose side your men are on."

Lightfoot rubbed the material between his fingers. "Fair Isle cloth. Finest there is. Why the newly risen sun?"

"Because Fair Isle will see a new dawn. I will build on all that was good in the T'En Empire to create an island of culture and learning, an island where a man is valued for his worth, not his birth." He paused, hearing Imoshen's mocking voice in his head. What was this vision worth if it excluded half of Fair Isle? Tulkhan amended his words. "A person will be valued for their worth, not birth. Everyone will have a voice. From the landless to the titled, all will be heard and all will be held accountable, even the rulers."

Lightfoot stood, rubbing his forehead thoughtfully. He let his hand drop. "She should have trusted me to keep my word. She shouldn't have done this!"

"Done what?"

"This, the T'En stigmata!" He gestured to his forehead. "I would have served out my contract. And now, knowing you, I..." He knelt. "I offer my services beyond this contract."

"I accept your service," Tulkhan said, and pulled Lightfoot to his feet.

"Can you get her to remove the stigmata?"

He stared at Lightfoot. "Remove what?"

"You mock me. It is there for all to see. The T'En sign!" Lightfoot touched his forehead, indicating an inverted teardrop scar. "T'Imoshen touched me with the tip of her sixth finger. It burned my skin like a brand. She looked into my eyes and left me naked in her sight. She said if I betrayed you, she would know."

Imoshen's interference angered Tulkhan. "I will tell her in my next letter. Rawset will put it in her own hands." Lightfoot's expression hardened. "What now?"

"You do not see what is before you, General Tulkhan. Next time you speak with Rawset, look for the T'En stigmata on him too."

Was it possible that, in his absence, Imoshen had become the dreaded Dhamfeer of legend, manipulative and cunning? Tulkhan opened the message from Jarholfe, but he boasted of his new commission and made unprovable accusations against Reothe.

"Ask your emissary who he truly serves, and why."

"Call Rawset. Say nothing of this to him."

When Lightfoot left, Tulkhan reread both of Imoshen's letters, looking for anything that might reveal her hidden plans. Soon Lightfoot returned with Rawset, who was wiping his wispy mustache.

"Is there some message for me to take back to T'Imoshen?" he asked. "I thought you would want to tell her how to handle the Amiregent. He can't be allowed to execute our ambassadors. Large New Moon is only—"

Tulkhan cursed, for Imoshen had not revealed this detail. "Tell me all you know."

"The Amiregent arrested our people on trumped-up charges of treason. He demanded a massive payment in gold or he will execute them. If we do not reply, he will execute them anyway."

"I see." Tulkhan selected a sheet of fresh paper. The Amiregent had overstepped himself. He laid down his terms decisively, then waved the paper in the air to dry. "I've demanded the release of my ambassadors. I also insist that the Amiregent honor the old alliance and allow the passage of my cavalry and siege machines. I will regard anything less as an act of war." Tulkhan caught Lightfoot's nod of approval. "I have asked for an immediate reply."

"But... but that would mean a war on two fronts," Rawset whispered.

"If need be."

Rawset swallowed. "What if the Amiregent doesn't agree? He threw the others in prison!"

Tulkhan understood. "I won't be sending you, Rawset. You are too inexperienced for this."

"I'll take your demands," Lightfoot said. "I insist, the honor is mine!"

Tulkhan folded the message and used his new seal. "Take my fastest horses, Lightfoot. How many men will you need?"

"A dozen soldiers will not protect me if the Amiregent takes offense. I ride alone," Lightfoot announced.

"But . . ." Rawset croaked. "But you could be executed!"

Lightfoot smiled. "Then the General will have his answer. I serve the General. *Who* do you serve?"

"Yes, who do you serve, Rawset?" Tulkhan raised the candles. Flickering light fell across the young man's freckled face, illuminating his sensitive features and the T'En sign that Tulkhan had mistaken for a birthmark. "You were right, Lightfoot. It is there."

"What is? Why do you look at me like that?"

"No time for lies," Tulkhan snapped. "There is no dishonor in admitting you bear the T'En stigmata. What Trueman can stand against a Dhamfeer? Why did you not tell me that Imoshen forced this service on you?"

"You appointed me to this position. I am your emissary."

"So you say. But who do you really serve?" Lightfoot countered.

Rawset dropped to one knee. "I serve the T'En Empress who serves Fair Isle. You are her bond-partner and her war general, so I serve you."

"No double-talk," Tulkhan insisted. "She forced this service upon you with the touch of her sixth finger and held you with threats."

But Rawset rose, shaking his head. He glanced to Lightfoot, then back to Tulkhan. "No, my general. I serve because I choose to."

"But the T'En stigmata?" Tulkhan indicated the blemish on Rawset's forehead.

"This?" Rawset shrugged. "It itches. As the conviction came upon me that I must serve T'Imoshen, so did the itching and this blemish."

Tulkhan frowned. "There is no coercion involved in your service?"

Rawset straightened his shoulders. "Since I failed in my priestly studies I have been cast adrift. In Lady Protector T'Imoshen I have found my purpose."

Tulkhan shook his head. Itching stigmata—what next?

Just when he thought he understood the T'En, some new facet arose to confound him.

"Was it not thus with you, Lightfoot?" Rawset asked.

"No, it was not! I had already signed my agreement to serve the General when she forced her sign on me and with it my compliance. But I will be free of it soon. The General has promised."

Tulkhan felt both men look to him. He had promised to free Lightfoot, but as for Rawset, how could he free a man who wanted to serve?

"I must pack my traveling kit and select a horse," Lightfoot announced. "I ride at dawn."

When Lightfoot had gone, Rawset turned to Tulkhan. "The Amiregent will have him killed. Why did you let him go?"

"He claimed the honor."

Rawset looked as if he might argue, but he observed the General's expression, made a quick obeisance, and left.

Tulkhan sat down stiffly. He had sent men to their deaths before in the full knowledge of what he did, but it did not get any easier. Perhaps he should be grateful for this.

Imoshen found Reothe reading the journal of his namesake, Reothe the Builder, on the fortification of T'Diemn.

"You may go, Karmel." Imoshen dismissed the Keeper of the Knowledge, who retreated, her birdlike eyes bright with curiosity.

Reothe closed the book with a snap. "I must thank you for my new assistant."

"The Keeper?" Imoshen was lost.

"No, Jarholfe. As leader of T'Diemn's garrison, he has asked me to prepare a report on the city's readiness to repel attack."

Imoshen smiled. "I trust you will be very helpful. By the way, I've implemented your suggestion. In time of war no one will be able to get past the lockkeepers without the passwords." Her smile faded. "I've spoken with the engineers and the ship's captains. General Tulkhan will have three ships with siege machines as soon as they are ready to sail. And I have decided to go to the Amirate to free my people."

"Why would the Amiregent listen to you?"

Imoshen hesitated. He would have to listen because she would use her gifts. "The Amiregent will listen to me."

Reothe's eyes kindled like twin flames. "I will come with you."

"No."

"Yes. I can sail across the Inner Sea by the stars. None of this coast-crawling. I can have you there in three days, less if the winds are good. But I have my price."

She had foreseen this and had her response ready. "I will not attempt to heal you. I might do more damage, and you need to be able-bodied to captain my ship."

"You mistake me. I want to see you work your gifts!"

"Why?" Imoshen felt drawn to him.

"It excites me."

Her heart skipped a beat and she fought the irrational urge to unburden herself to Reothe, to admit how she missed the intimacy of the mind-touch, how she longed to trust him. She walked to the window, watching the sunlight glint on the beveled glass. "I shall take you as my captain, nothing more."

"I am yours to command," he said, but he mocked her, and she knew it.

"You must not risk your life," Wharrd insisted. "I will go. I am your Ghiad."

"I have my reasons for going," Imoshen temporized. She was not about to reveal that she meant to use her gifts on the Amir. "Your task is to maintain order while I am gone. Have the cavalry and remaining siege machines readied. I intend to free our people and negotiate safe passage for Tulkhan's supplies."

"What will I say to the General if you are killed? At least leave his son here."

Imoshen repressed a surge of anger. In Ghebite eyes she

was no more than a vessel for the bearing of sons. "Ashmyr comes with me."

"What will the people of Fair Isle think?" Wharrd asked.

"I am not deserting my island. The mainland kingdoms need to see that Fair Isle cannot be bullied!"

"I understand, but heed me at least in this: Don't go with the rebel leader."

"Enough! Before Reothe was the rebel leader he was Fair Isle's greatest sea captain. He mapped half the mysterious southern land. I think he can sail cross the Pellucid Sea."

Wharrd closed his mouth, but he remained unconvinced. Imoshen dismissed him. She had her own reasons for keeping Reothe with her. While he was by her side, he could not be working treason with the Beatific. Fair Isle faced threats on too many fronts for her to contemplate a threat within the capital.

"I wish you luck, T'Imoshen," Wharrd said formally.

"I believe in making my own luck!"

As Tulkhan rode up to Port Sumair's gates, the golden crest of his helmet gleamed in the sunlight. His brilliant blue cloak lifted in the dawn breeze, and behind him his army stood rank upon rank, cloaked in his new colors. He grinned, aware that the defenders would be madly sending for Gharavan.

Escorted by Kornel and the marsh-dweller, the supplies had arrived late the previous evening. He had ordered the new uniforms passed out and an extra ration of food and wine distributed. With Banuld's voluntary return, the General's judgment had been proved correct.

Tulkhan was about to strike a blow at the hearts and minds of the defenders. He wanted Gharavan to see how his army had grown and to despair. The thickest walls in the world could not protect a city if the men did not fight with fire in their bellies. All Ghebite colors had been collected and were stacked high before the gates of Port Sumair, ready to be torched. His trumpeter rode up and down, playing the Ghebite battle signal, reminding Tulkhan that he did not have a call of his own.

But using the Ghebite signal would irritate Gharavan, just as burning the Ghebite colors would incense him. Hopefully it would drive the little king to lead a sortie. This could be the opening Tulkhan needed to crack the shell of Sumair's defenses. The second tunnel had collapsed, killing two men, and he had temporarily halted any attempt to mine under Sumair's walls.

Soon heads clustered thick as flies on a corpse along the defending walls and gate towers. Tulkhan galloped toward the Ghebite standard. He caught it on the end of his spear and carried it to the heaped Ghebite cloaks and banners. Dropping the banner, he took a flaming torch. His horse sidled, snorting nervously.

"When I am finished there will be nothing left of Gheeaba but ashes and memories!" he roared. "They'll say that King Gharavan was the man who lost the Ghebite Empire. Every kingdom that bowed to our father will spit on your memory. Watch your standard burn, Gharavan, King of the Ghebites. King of Nothing!"

As Tulkhan tossed the burning torch, he felt a savage surge of painful joy. Hungry flames licked over the oil-doused material. The fire roared into life and his men gave a spontaneous cheer.

Tulkhan hoped his half-brother was spitting with rage. He hoped the useless arrows, which even now fell short of their targets, were an indication of a sortie to come.

He rode back and forth before his men as they cheered. The flames leaped high on the air. The smell of burning cloth stung his nostrils. He was reminded of the Aayel's funeral pyre, how Imoshen had let no one but herself touch her great-aunt's corpse. It had come full circle. He had lost his family and his home to gain Fair Isle.

His thoughts turned not to the lifeless land itself but to Imoshen, her quick mind, her wry sense of humor. She would understand the value of this display. He longed to have her at his side, sharing the moment with him.

"How they yell! I'll lay odds the Ghebite King launches an attack!" Rawset crowed at the General's side.

"Gharavan was ever one to act and think later," Tulkhan said. But this time wiser counsel prevailed, and the defenders of Port Sumair did not retaliate.

On Reothe's advice Imoshen had taken two ships and half the Parakhan Guard, led by Crawen. While making the crossing she had interviewed the ambassadors' servant, a one-armed Ghebite veteran who was not eager to confront the Amiregent again.

Just at dusk their ship had crept into the deep river estuary that housed the Amiregent's capital and taken shelter in one of the many secluded inlets. Now the pulleys creaked as the sailors lowered a dinghy.

Reothe caught her arm, leading her away from the others, his voice low and intense. "If you don't take me with you, how will I know if you are in danger? If only my gifts were healed!"

"Tonight I will observe the Amiregent and find his weakness. Rest easy, I will not take any unnecessary risks. Trust me, as I trust you to care for Ashmyr."

Before he could protest, she left him, swinging her weight over the side of the ship and scrambling down the rope ladder to the waiting boat. Taking the oars, she threw her back into rowing, pulling away into the darkness as Reothe glowered over the side, holding the lamp high.

Imoshen soon rounded the bluff, glancing over her shoulder to the Amiregent's city. Many lights winked from windows, just as the ambassadors' servant remembered it. She had used every opportunity to skim the surface of his mind, absorbing his description of the Amiregent's court and the tower where his master and mistress were imprisoned. Her greatest danger was the overuse of her gift. If she overextended herself, she would drift into a vulnerable stupor of exhaustion.

Overlooking the port a tower stood silhouetted against the large moon. The tower was thick at the base and at least four stories high. Built within the city walls and situated on the cliff-edged bluff, Tulkhan would have described it as a good last line of defense. She winced, aware that he would not have agreed with her plans.

Soon she heard the cries of the night seabirds scavenging in the waste from the fish markets. The smell was enough to tell her she was near. This was the greatest city of the Amirate. Many ships were berthed at the wharves.

Imoshen pulled into a deserted pier and tied up the boat. She climbed the steps of the wharf, dressed in the garments of an Amirate palace servant, with her head covered by the cowl and her face masked from the nose down. As long as she kept her six-fingered hands hidden and her eyes lowered, she could pass unremarked. The place was strangely deserted.

Even the dockside taverns were closed, their light and laughter hidden behind shutters. Several sailors and their women came out of a bawdy house. Though they passed within touching distance, they deliberately ignored Imoshen. Following the servant's memory, Imoshen climbed steadily, past the prosperous merchant quarters, which reminded her of the merchant town houses in Northpoint, to the palace itself. With a start she recognized the tower where Cariah's sister and her bond-partner were imprisoned. Because she had touched the servant's mind, however briefly, she experienced the man's fear. Her mouth went dry.

Imoshen entered the palace through the kitchens. It had been her experience that, with the many comings and goings of a great household, the kitchen's entrances were the least carefully observed. She made her way through the storerooms and preparation rooms, just another servant, ignored by everyone—including the over-servants, who thought her someone else's responsibility.

Stepping into the quiet passages, Imoshen followed the Ghebite servant's memory to the wing where the Amiregent entertained. It was in these interconnecting rooms that Miryma and her bond-partner had been arrested. Their servant's memories were vividly laced with dread.

Imoshen slipped through the servants' door and joined the others behind an ornately carved screen at the end of a mirrored gallery. The room was all subtle shadows and wavering candlelight, reflected in the highly polished floor, which glistened like water. On their left, behind another screen, musicians accompanied the mimers who performed for the Amiregent and his courtiers.

At the sight of one particular ornately dressed man, Imoshen felt a jolt of terror and recognized the Amiregent from the servant's emotion-laden memory. From his painted face to the tips of his elaborately dressed hair, he was a strange creature. He might look like a court jester, but the man had not hesitated to assassinate the last Amiregent, then blame this murder on Fair Isle's own ambassadors.

Imoshen was familiar with the written form of the Amirate's language, so she was able to understand the Amiregent when the mummery ended and he dismissed the performers, calling for servants to remove their meal.

Imoshen waited until all but the last of the performers had filed past, then caught the man's arm. "Where is the boy Amir?"

Her words triggered the man's recent memory. He stood on a busy street in late afternoon amid a crowd who were watching an old woman and a boy pass by in a gilded carriage. Only Imoshen could see the intangible bars that held them prisoner. She had a strong impression of a tall, thick-based tower, broodingly dark. The tower on the bluff.

"Didn't you hear? He's with his grandmother. They were sent to the tower after the assassination for their safety!" The man looked as if he might add something but shook his head disgustedly.

She let him go. What had kept him quiet was another memory of a cage suspended from the palace's walls. Carrion birds whirled around, fighting over its grisly human remains.

Imoshen's head reeled with the implications. Opening her T'En senses, she discovered the court of the Amiregent was thick was fear. Its taste was so rich it hit the back of her throat, making her gag. She reined in her awareness.

So much for taking the boy hostage to ensure the Amiregent's cooperation. It was more likely the boy and his grandmother would not leave that tower alive.

"Send for the Dreamspinner," the Amiregent called. "I will have a foretelling. Dim the candles."

After a few minutes a woman entered, carrying a delicate cage. Imoshen could just make out something flashing through the bars. The woman wore a simple gown compared to the courtiers, but she carried herself with pride.

"Dreamwasps!" gasped a servant.

"They say it hurts," another muttered, her eyes and lower face veil illuminated by patterns of light that came through the screen. "But only at first. Then it feels exquisite."

"My mistress built up a tolerance to their poison until she could bear the first sting," the other whispered. "She rewards us with lesser stings."

"What visions do you have for us tonight, Dreamspinner?" the Amiregent asked. "I want to know what the General of Fair Isle plans."

"My Amiregent, the wasps' dreams cannot always be spun into cloth of our choosing," she warned. "But I will see."

The courtiers sat forward eagerly, their eyes glittering as the Dreamspinner raised the delicate cage. With a smile she unclasped her gown, letting it fall from her shoulders to bare her breasts. From her pocket she withdrew a small jar. She offered it to the Amiregent, who uncapped it eagerly. Dipping an applicator in the contents, he rubbed a little on the pulse that beat at the base of her throat.

"I will have the second sting," he said eagerly. Voices rose, claiming the privilege of the lesser stings. "Quiet, you will have your turn. This must be done properly."

When they were sufficiently composed, the Dreamspinner crooned a soft, seductive song. Opening the cage, she coaxed the Dreamwasp out onto her finger. It sat there, large as a small bird. The nobles gasped in envious admiration. It was an exquisite creature, all iridescent wings.

Imoshen could sense their anticipation. Her heart pounded in sympathy. She had heard rumors of this practice. It was frowned upon in other mainland countries, but the Dreamspinners of the Amirate were trained from childhood to endure the stings and weave a vision from the dreams. It was said many were called but only a few survived the training.

Was it a true seeing, or wish fulfillment? Imoshen flexed her T'En gifts, questing... The Dreamspinner stiffened. Her eyes widened and her gaze went to Imoshen's screen.

Startled, Imoshen reeled in her T'En senses.

"Why do you delay?" the Amiregent snapped.

"It moves!" a noble whispered.

Enticed by the sweet scent of the ointment, the Dreamwasp climbed up the woman's arm. All eyes focused on its progress.

The Dreamspinner's croon changed tone to a higher pitch, almost an insectlike hum. Imoshen realized the Dreamwasp was singing in reply to her, its tone just on the edge of hearing. She wanted to extend her senses to discover what was passing between the Dreamspinner and her wasp but dared not.

Everyone, servant and noble alike, held their breath as the Dreamwasp's body pulsed. A buildup of inner light flashed through its dark abdomen in rhythmic patterns. Suddenly, in a flash of radiance, the wasp struck. The Dreamspinner gasped and swayed.

The Amiregent snatched the wasp, carefully holding the stinger away from him. "The ointment. Quickly. I am next."

Someone applied it to his inner wrist and he held the wasp against his flesh. The wasp's body pulsed and flashed again, then it was passed on. Nobles swarmed around the Dreamwasp, each begging for a lesser sting.

Imoshen grimaced disgustedly. Perhaps she should leave the Amiregent to his visions. The snap of boots on the stone made her hesitate. Soldiers entered, escorting a captive.

The Dreamspinner swayed, lifting one hand to point to the captive. "Death's messenger has come."

"Step forward." The Amiregent's voice was high and breathless.

The soldiers moved aside to let through the mercenary leader, Lightfoot. Imoshen bit back a gasp.

Twelve

"**H**ONORABLE AMIREGENT." LIGHTFOOT gave the mercenary bow and tossed his sea-blue cloak over his shoulder. "I carry a message from General Tulkhan."

A servant scurried forward to pass it to the Amiregent, bending low. Imoshen shifted impatiently as he read it.

The Amiregent tossed the message to the Dreamspinner with a curse. "And how does this figure in your spinning?"

The Dreamspinner caught the scroll, her cheeks flushed, eyes ablaze with inner visions. She did not read it. "I see a kingdom in flux. I see a great leader rise."

"I am that leader!" the Amiregent claimed. "Arrest this man. I'll have his hands—no, his head. That will be my answer to the Ghebite upstart. Protector General of Fair Isle? Let him see how he protects his men now." The Amiregent paced the floor. "I see visions too. I see the Amirate more powerful than Gheeaba!"

Lightfoot strode forward. "If you harm me or the ambassadors, General Tulkhan will regard it as an act of war."

"War?" the Amiregent snarled. "Your general can't even put down his half-brother, that snapping pup Gharavan." He smiled cruelly at Lightfoot. "Put him in with the ambassadors. He can tell them they will die at midday tomorrow and their heads will be sent to General Tulkhan as a token of my esteem!" The Amiregent turned.

"Well, Dreamspinner, see how I make my dreams come true? What do your dreams tell you?"

He and his nobles gathered close, but Imoshen had no time for dreams. Slipping out of the room, she went to the servants' corridor, which led to the tower room where the ambassadors were being held. On the way she passed a long table where trays of half-eaten food had been stacked. Hastily, she selected the best of several meals so that it looked like she had a fresh tray. Even condemned prisoners would expect a meal.

Waiting in the shadows, she joined the end of Lightfoot's escort. The soldiers met up with the tower guards, where there was much cruel jesting at Lightfoot's expense. He endured it in silence. When they could get no entertainment from him, they unlocked the doors and marched into the chamber beyond. Imoshen followed, carrying the tray.

Miryma and Shacolm stood hand in hand, fear written large on their faces. Theirs was a gilded cage, complete with thick carpets and scented sandalwood screens.

"We have a friend of yours," the soldier announced. "He brings you news!"

They stared at Lightfoot in confusion. When Lightfoot did not speak, the soldier pushed him forward and he fell to his knees. He was slow to move after the bruising they'd given him removing his weapons. Miryma and Shacolm helped him to his feet.

"That's right," the man jeered. "Treat his hurts. Make him well for tomorrow's execution. Oh, didn't he tell you his news? The General demanded your safe return. Tomorrow we'll send your heads as a token of the Amiregent's regard."

Shacolm lunged, but the nearest guard struck him with the flat of his sword, sending him staggering into Miryma's arms.

"Enjoy your meal," the soldier said, shoving Imoshen as they left. She recovered her balance and the door closed behind the guards.

"He can't execute us. Fair Isle will not allow it," Miryma insisted.

"Fair Isle's anger does us no good after our execution," Shacolm told her, then turned to Lightfoot. "You are Vaygharian by your accent, but I don't know your colors. How do you come to be carrying my general's message?"

"Lightfoot." He gave the Vaygharian bow. "I am the General's man, and I wear his new colors."

"I fear General Tulkhan's message will be the death of us, Lightfoot," Miryma whispered.

Imoshen put the tray aside. She had meant to find the Amiregent's weakness, then bargain for their release, but events had forced her hand. "How many men guard your door?"

They turned in surprise.

"How many?" Imoshen pushed back her servant's headdress, letting the veil fall.

"Dhamfeer!" Shacolm hissed, and Lightfoot made the Vaygharian sign to ward off evil.

Miryma ran to hug her. "Imoshen! You have come for us."

"It is pure chance that I am here tonight. Lucky chance for you and for Fair Isle. I did not know the General had moved to confront the Amiregent." Anger tightened Imoshen's voice. Suddenly ravenous, she devoured the sweet flesh of a roasted bird. "And nothing more marvelous than a sleek merchant ship brings me to you. It lies off the port, awaiting our return. Now, the guards?"

"Two, no more," Shacolm said. "But there is the palace and the town to get through."

Tossing the bone aside, she wiped her fingers. "The townspeople dare not peep outside their doors. The servants go about, eyes downcast in fear. The nobles are drunk on Dreamwasp visions, and we can deal with the guards. There is an old T'En saying that translates, *Why use force when deceit will do?*" She smiled at their confusion. "Miryma, last winter you took a part in the entertainments."

"Yes, but—"

"I want you to pretend you are furious with Lightfoot. Try to scratch his eyes out. Shacolm, you call for help. Here, take this." She handed the young Ghebite her own knife. "We will lure the guards in, attack them, then slip away."

"How will we get out of the palace?" Lightfoot asked.

"Trust me." Imoshen resumed her headdress.

She met their eyes one by one. Their fear and faith mixed oddly, sitting on her tongue with a bittersweet tang. She no longer felt hungry and shaky. The tension they exuded was enough to sustain her. "Now, Miryma. Scream!"

The young woman opened her mouth, but no sound came out. Imoshen slapped her. Shacolm shouted and started toward them. Imoshen thrust Miryma into Lightfoot's arms so that he stumbled.

The girl sprang to life, uttering a bloodcurdling scream. "You've killed us. You and your arrogant Ghebite general!"

Lightfoot stood stunned by the attack, then her nails raked his cheek, drawing blood. He caught her wrists and bellowed with rage as her teeth sank into his hand. "Get her off me! I swear I'll strangle her!"

Shacolm glanced to Imoshen, who had moved to one side of the door.

"Help, guards," Imoshen cried. "They're going to kill each other!"

The soldiers opened the door. They laughed as Miryma, whose head came no higher than Lightfoot's shoulder, kicked him in the shin. He cursed her. The guards plowed in. One grabbed Miryma and threw her across the room. She careened into the table, sending crockery and food onto the carpet.

Imoshen swung the door shut and darted over to help Miryma to her feet. Miryma bit back a scream and pointed. Imoshen spun in time to see Shacolm dodge the guard's lunge. The man's own momentum carried him onto Shacolm's knife. The guard plucked futilely at the blade's hilt as he staggered and fell. Suddenly Imoshen felt a rush of heady warmth as the life force left him. She reeled in her T'En perception, unwilling to partake in death.

Businesslike, Lightfoot broke the neck of his guard and let him drop. Silently, he went over the body, removing all weapons. He straightened. "Let's go."

Imoshen fixed on his sun-lined face. He did not kill for pleasure, yet he killed without compunction. She went to touch him and discover how he could extinguish life without remorse, then thought better of it.

Miryma ran to Shacolm. "You are unhurt?"

He caught her to him, laughing shakily.

"What's the next step of your plan?" Lightfoot asked.

If she could get them safely down to the docks and out to the boat where Reothe waited, the Amiregent would have no leverage on her, but she still had none on him.

"One thing at a time," Imoshen said. She opened the door to peer out. The anteroom was empty. The cards lay facedown, the game never to be resumed. "Bring the bodies."

Imoshen arranged the dead guards in the chairs with their backs to the entrance so that they appeared to be dozing. A casually thrown cloak obscured the worst of the blood. At a quick glance it seemed they would spring to attention and apologize for sleeping at their posts.

Locking the prison door after them, Imoshen turned to the others. "Into the hall, and keep to the shadows."

"This way," Shacolm urged. He was headed toward the public rooms of the palace.

"No. We want to pass unnoticed. We go through the servants' passages." Now she wished she had thought to take three of the household tabards. "Hold hands. I will lead us down only the empty passages."

Miryma grasped her hand, fingers trembling. Shacolm was next and Lightfoot last. Even now Imoshen could feel the need of these three people sustaining her. She called on that T'En part of herself that had wanted to feast on the death of those guards. Tension built in her. The corridor as far as the steps was empty.

"My head hurts," Miryma whispered. "Am I supposed to feel like this?"

"Come," Imoshen urged. She guessed Miryma was more susceptible to the gifts than most.

Relying on her senses to tell her if a corridor was empty, she led them back to the storerooms just off the kitchens and from there into the deserted courtyard. When Imoshen had entered the palace, the larger gates had been open for delivery wagons; now these were closed and only a small gate stood open, manned by a single sentry.

Lightfoot reached for his knife. "I'll—"

"No. You deal too freely in death. We'll do it my way. Hold hands."

"I think I'm going to be sick," Miryma warned.

"Just a little longer."

The guard grimaced, then strode off around a corner. In a moment they could hear him relieving himself.

"Quickly." Imoshen darted through the gate.

They hurried after her, keeping to the shadows of the narrow street, until at last they reached the wharves and the boat. It looked inviting. Imoshen was weary, but she would achieve nothing if she did not have a lever on the Amiregent.

"Go quickly now. Once you round the bluff, you will see the lights of my ships. Tell Reothe to send the boat back for me. I'll look for it here."

"You're not coming with us?" asked Lightfoot.

"No." Imoshen moved into the shadows as the boat slipped quickly away on the dark water.

The sky was lit only by starlight and the large moon. The small moon had already set. Silhouetted against the stars was Imoshen's destination: the tower. She picked her way through the quiet streets.

Away from the town, a path wound toward the bluff. There was not enough light to cast a shadow on the grass. Imoshen slipped off her shoes to walk over the bare earth of the wheel ruts and opened her T'En senses. The grandmother and the boy Amir had passed this way. The old woman did not expect to leave the tower alive.

When Imoshen heard horses approaching, she stepped into a hollow and watched as two riders passed. They roused the guard and he opened the gate. Torchlight fell on the men's faces. Foreboding gripped her as she recognized the Amiregent without his court finery.

He swung down from the saddle, saying, "I have not

been here this night, guard. Whatever you hear, do not climb the stairs."

The man nodded and took the horses aside. Imoshen slipped inside the courtyard.

The light of a single flaming torch danced on the stonework as the Amiregent climbed the tower stairs, followed by his companion, who carried something under a silken cover. Imoshen clung to the shadows just beyond the curve of the steps.

"If we are to have war with Fair Isle, I want no civil unrest. No one will use this brat to unite the people against me. He and his grandmother die tonight. And there must be no one to claim this was anything other than suicide. Kill that gate guard before you leave," the Amiregent ordered softly.

"Then it will be war?"

"Oh, yes. Fair Isle is ripe for plunder. And whether Gharavan or Tulkhan wins, the Ghebites are a spent force. Internal strife will consume their empire."

"What of the T'En?"

"Only two of the Throwbacks live, and they are at each other's throats from what my spies tell me."

Imoshen went cold.

"You have my jewels?" the Amiregent asked. "Good, open the door."

There was a soft jingle as his companion selected a key. The mechanism clicked as the tumblers fell inside the lock, and the door creaked open. The light faded as the men entered the room. The keys swayed in the lock. Imoshen listened at the open door.

"Wake, old woman. Your time has come!" the Amiregent said.

A soft scuffle followed, and Imoshen imagined them dragging the Amir's grandmother from her bed.

"Take your hands off me. What manner of man are you?" a querulous voice demanded. "Why do you come at this late hour?"

He laughed. "You should be honored I come in person. General Tulkhan has forced my hand. Wake the boy."

The old woman uttered a sharp cry of denial and a child's frightened whimpers urged Imoshen to act, but she held back.

"Remove the cover." A high-pitched buzz filled the air. "Hush, my jewels," the Amiregent purred.

"Dreamwasps?" the old woman gasped. "You can't—"

"By tomorrow evening all of the Amirate will know how you bribed the guard to bring Dreamwasps. You induced them to give you and the boy a fatal dose of their sweet venom, bringing you eternal sleep instead of brilliant dreams." He laughed softly. "How can I be blamed for your suicide?"

Imoshen felt the old woman's terror and the little boy's fearful confusion. She sensed the bright points of anger that were the enraged Dreamwasps. They knew nothing of their role in the larger world, wanting only to vent their fury.

Imoshen stepped into the doorway. By the light of the single torch, she saw the two men and the old woman with a small boy clinging to her. The Amiregent held a delicate cage, his concentration on the contents: four glistening creatures, their iridescent wings flashing.

The other man noticed her and raised the torch. "Evil eyes!"

"Run." The old woman thrust the boy toward the door. "Run for your life."

"No, you don't!" The Amiregent lunged for him.

Imoshen kicked his grasping hand. The force of her strike drove him around in an arc. His arm struck the flaming torch. He screamed, dropping the Dreamwasps. Their cage fell to the stone with a tinkle of breaking glass.

But Imoshen was still moving. The ball of her foot caught the Amiregent's conspirator in the midsection. He grunted as the torch fell from his hand and rolled under the bed. They were plunged into darkness, except for four whirling points of angry light.

"My jewels!" A flash of light from a passing wasp illuminated the Amiregent's features as he reared back.

Imoshen dragged the old woman toward the door, colliding with the boy, who had stopped to watch. Shoving them out of the room, Imoshen gripped the handle.

"No!" The conspirator lunged across the floor on his knees. A Dreamwasp landed on his face. Its body flashed with rage as it attacked. His roar changed to a high-pitched scream.

Imoshen slammed the door and spun the keys in the lock. Another scream rent the air, muffled only slightly by the thick walls and solid wood.

"I hope he dreams his death a thousand times before it comes!" the old woman whispered with relish.

"Come," Imoshen urged. "The guard was told not to investigate, but this might bring him."

"I doubt it. The Amiregent ruled by fear."

"Still. I want to speak with you." Imoshen felt for the stairs. "Link hands."

Silently, they made their way down the dark steps, while above them sounded guttural male screams and the splintering of furniture.

At the foot of the stairs, they found the guard standing irresolute, a flaming torch in his hand.

"Amir!" He dropped to his knees before the boy and the old woman, then he recognized Imoshen for what she was. With a cry of terror, he drew his sword. "Beware the Accursed!"

"Fool!" the old woman hissed. "Bring me a branch of candles, then saddle some horses. The Usurper is dead. I am Amiregent."

He lit the candles, then hurried away.

"Will he betray you?" Imoshen asked.

The old woman smiled. "Not if he wants to live. Now, what do you want of me? Are you really T'Imoshen of Fair Isle?"

"I came to seek the lives of my ambassadors."

"They will be freed. That fool let greed make his decisions. I am not so certain the Ghebites are a spent force." The child pulled on her hand, whispering that he was hungry. "Hush, boy. Listen and learn. One day you will have to lead your people. We will gather my loyal followers, then enter the palace. By dawn we will have the city. My first official act will be to release your people."

"They are already free," Imoshen said.

The old woman's sharp eyes fixed on her. "Then why are you here?"

"I came to strike a bargain. I need safe passage for my army's cavalry and siege machines to the borders of the Low-lands."

"Done."

Imoshen laughed.

"I've no time for anything but straight talking tonight," the old woman said. "The balance of power shifts, and it must shift in our direction. Tomorrow my grandson will be restored to his rightful place as Amir of the Amirate!"

"I must go. Tomorrow we will renew the old alliance," Imoshen said. She was weary and she ached to hold Ashmyr and feast on his innocence. Tonight four men had died. She did not have to strike the killing blow for her to be the cause of their deaths.

Across the room, the boy Amir was playing with wood chips, fighting imaginary battles on the cold stone flags. Were they all tools of their destiny?

"Till tomorrow, then," the new Amiregent said.

When Imoshen returned to the wharves, all was quiet, misleadingly so. Soon the new regent would begin her night of bloodletting to consolidate her power. Imoshen knew that before dawn the streets would ring with the sounds of soldiers loyal to the dead regent making their last stand. She wanted to be gone long before that. The sight of the empty rowboat at its mooring was welcome. Imoshen ran the last steps down to the pier, then hesitated. Where was the sailor who had rowed the boat? Someone grabbed her from behind.

She knew that scent. "Reothe!"

"This time! But it could have been a trap. Have care, Imoshen." He shook her. "Into the boat."

Knowing that he was right, she took the bow seat. Reothe bent his back to the oars, his silence oppressive. Imoshen watched his shadowed face.

After they rounded the bluff but before they neared his vessels, he shipped oars. "You lied to me, Imoshen. You said you were only going to discover the Amiregent's weakness!"

"My ambassadors are safe, and tomorrow when we—"

"Meet the Amiregent we bargain from a better position. I know. But this wasn't what we agreed!"

Beyond his shoulders, the dark silhouettes of their vessels rose up and down with the swell. Imoshen licked her lips. "General Tulkhan forced my hand. He demanded the release of Fair Isle's ambassadors; the Amiregent's response was to order their deaths."

"So Lightfoot said."

"There's more. The Amiregent is dead, and by the time we dock tomorrow, the child Amir's grandmother will be regent. She has promised to honor the old alliance."

"Imoshen!"

She waited, but he said nothing more. There was nothing but the sound of the night birds calling over the sea. Weariness overcame her. "They said Fair Isle was ripe for the taking, Reothe. They did not fear us, because the last two T'En were at each other's throats!" She forced herself to think ahead. "Tomorrow I will renew the old alliance with the Amiregent and then return to T'Diemn. I must get word to the General. The Amiregent can send her fastest rider as a sign of good faith. We'll be back in T'Diemn by then. But I want to send support sooner. If the people of Sumair know the siege machines are coming, they might try to break the siege. How long will it take to send the ships from T'Diemn, then drive the wagons across the Amirate to the Low-lands?"

"These things always take longer than you expect," Reothe answered at last. "Why not send Lightfoot with my second ship straight up the coast to the blockade at Port Sumair?"

"Good. With luck Tulkhan will be planning Gharavan's execution a few days from now!"

Suddenly Reothe dropped to his knees and gripped her shoulders. The boat rocked. "You're lucky it isn't your execution."

Imoshen clutched the sides of the boat and said nothing.

"You could have been killed!" Reothe's cruel grasp softened as he pulled her closer. He pressed his lips to her forehead, then pulled back. "If you face death again, I want to be by your side."

Imoshen's breath caught in her throat. "You have no right to make that demand, and I make no promises."

He released her. "No, you promise me nothing."

"I did what needed to be done."

"You cripple my gifts. Then you leave me to mind your child while you risk your life. You have a hard head and a hard heart, Imoshen."

She looked away. Let Reothe believe her heartless.

He resumed the seat, taking the oars but not dipping them into the sea. "I wish I had been there to see you exercise your powers!"

She thought of the screaming men, the angry Dreamwasps, and she shuddered. "Luck was with me. I hardly used my gifts at all." Her voice caught. "Take me to the ship. I killed four men tonight."

"You did not kill; death's shadow walked by your side. Our ambassadors' lives for theirs. It is a fair bargain."

But she shook her head and would not speak again.

Imoshen sealed the message with the print of her sixth finger and handed it to Lightfoot, who was about to sail up the coast to join the blockade of Port Sumair. "For General Tulkhan."

Lightfoot tucked it inside his jerkin, then hesitated. "I owe you my life."

"There is no obligation." Imoshen read his face. "Speak your mind."

"We mercenaries have a saying that service given freely is more enduring than service bought by fear or wealth."

"The T'En have a similar saying," Imoshen replied. The rhythmic chant of Amirate wharf workers unloading cargo came through the open cabin window.

"Would you have me beg?" Lightfoot ground out.

Imoshen stared blankly at him.

"I cannot live enslaved by your stigmata!" He gestured to his forehead.

Then she recalled touching him with her sixth finger. She had not known Lightfoot would prove loyal beyond his mercenary contract. She was not even sure if her touch had done more than mark his skin.

"Forgive me. I was not mocking you. Much has happened since that night." She called on her healing gift and brushed the pad of her thumb across the mark on his forehead. The inverted teardrop scar was gone, as was the frown line that had marked his forehead. "There, you are your own man."

With evident relief he gave the mercenary salute. "I swear to serve you and your war general, T'En Empress."

"I accept," Imoshen said, thinking it was strange: Removing her sign had made him more her servant.

Tulkhan recognized neither the horse nor the rider who wore the colors of the Amirate. He expected bad news, but the man offered obeisance and presented him with a message sealed with the imprint of Imoshen's sixth finger.

Curious, Tulkhan broke the seal. He gave a bark of laughter. By luck Imoshen had been in the Amirate ready to negotiate a new alliance when his messenger arrived. "The Amiregent grants our cavalry and siege machines safe passage. Port Sumair is ours!"

The men nearest him cheered, and the cry went up through the encampment.

"Send in Banuld," Tulkhan told Kornel.

By the time the marsh-dweller arrived, every man in the camp knew the Amirate had agreed to honor the old alliance with Fair Isle.

Tulkhan threaded several gold beads onto a leather thong. "Kornel, tell Banuld-Chi that I have valued his service. And that he is free to go."

"You've already paid him," Kornel muttered.

"He has proved his loyalty. Tell him what I said." Tulkhan came to his feet and grasped the marsh-dweller's arm.

Kornel translated with bad grace.

When they had gone, Tulkhan looked up to see Rawset. "Do you wish me to carry a message to T'Imoshen?"

Tulkhan shook his head. "Not until Port Sumair is mine. Share a mug of Vorsch. We'll drink to Lightfoot's safe return!"

On her return to T'Diemn, Imoshen had not expected to be greeted with pomp and display, but neither had she expected silence, shuttered doors and windows. It reminded her of the climate of fear that hung over the Amirate, and she grew more uneasy with every passing moment.

Anxious to give Wharrd the good news, Imoshen did not bother to send servants on ahead but set off in the growing dusk with Reothe, Miryma, and Shacolm.

Changing Ashmyr's basket to the other hip, she left the lower city behind and crossed the fortified bridge to enter the old T'Diemn. Beyond the lanes, the formal square was empty. No servants clustered on the steps of the palace awaiting instructions, but, then, they were not expecting her.

Imoshen entered the palace and rang for a servant. "I want to see Lord Fairban and Lord Commander Wharrd. Have the kitchen send up a festive meal. I will await them in the Jade Room." The man hurried off and Imoshen turned to the others. "Dine with me. Your safe return and the honoring of the old alliance will be celebrated throughout Fair Isle, but for tonight let us have an intimate celebration."

Once inside the room, Imoshen placed the sleeping baby's basket in a quiet corner and lit the candles, while Miryma and Shacolm moved the low couches for an intimate old-empire meal.

"Something feels wrong, Imoshen," Reothe said softly.

"Your gifts?"

"I don't need the gifts to sense the tension. Don't you feel it?"

Imoshen pinched out the taper. "Wharrd will know what's going on."

Suddenly the door flew open. Kalleen stood there, grief distorting her features. "Wharrd died this morning!"

Imoshen reached for Reothe. "How can this be?"

"You would follow the Empress's example. You would flaunt your lover!" Kalleen pointed to Reothe. "The Ghebites don't understand. They think you've dishonored their general. Wharrd died bound by his warrior code! A curse on the Gheeakhan! This very morning I held him in my arms and begged him to live long enough for you to return, but—"

"Miryma?" Lord Fairban thrust the door open. He had aged since Cariah's death, but his face lit up at the sight of his youngest daughter. "When they told me of your plight, I lost all hope!"

"Father!" She laughed and ran across the room to throw her arms around him. "Imoshen saved us."

"Blessed be the Empress," Lord Fairban whispered in High T'En, then put his daughter aside, turning to Imoshen. "But evil has been at work in T'Diemn. The—"

Shuddering on its hinges, the door was flung open a third time. Imoshen froze as a dozen fully armed Ghebites entered the room, Jarholfe as their lead. "Arrest the woman and her Dhamfeer lover!"

Thirteen

JARHOLFE GESTURED TO Reothe contemptuously. "Don't hesitate to take the male. His gifts are crippled and he has no strength in his left side."

The T'Diemn garrison guards spread out, circling Reothe, who moved to keep the wall at his back.

"Stop this!" Lord Fairban ordered, but they ignored him.

Sick disbelief filled Imoshen. She turned to Kalleen. This was what she had come to warn them about but had been too bound up in her grief to explain.

"Betrayer, get out of my sight!" Imoshen grabbed Kalleen and shook her, but in the instant before she pushed the young woman aside, she whispered, "Take Ashmyr. He's by the door. If you bear me any love, get him to safety."

Off balance from Imoshen's push, Kalleen tripped, falling between two low couches. Ghebites stepped over her.

Imoshen spun to see Reothe strike out, a slender jade statuette his weapon. One man's sword went flying, another fell with a broken wrist. As Reothe ducked to grab the fallen sword, Jarholfe pounced, brutally pinning his arms behind his back.

From behind the strands of disheveled silver hair, the last T'En warrior glared up at his captors. One of them struck the back of Reothe's head and he collapsed. The impact made Imoshen's head ache in sympathy. Nausea threatened to swamp her.

"Now the Dhamfeer bitch!" Jarholfe ordered. As they

turned on Imoshen, she recognized the Ghebite priest at Jarholfe's side. The Cadre's eyes gleamed with malevolent satisfaction, and she realized he was putting words in Jarholfe's mouth.

"Not T'Imoshen!" Miryma's cry pierced Imoshen's abstraction. "She saved us. She has organized safe passage for siege machines. She—"

Jarholfe's slap sent her flying. "Get your woman out of here, Shacolm, or I must question your loyalty too!"

Miryma's bond-partner swept up her limp body and, casting Imoshen one swift glance, slipped away quietly.

"You call this loyalty, Jarholfe?" Imoshen demanded icily. "Who appointed you leader of T'Diemn's garrison?"

"Don't listen to her, she twists everything with her Dhamfeer cunning!" the Cadre hissed.

Imoshen faced the circle of men. They had served her on the road from Northpoint, and now they hesitated. Respect for authority was deeply ingrained.

"I forgive your actions so far because you have been misled," Imoshen said. "But from this moment forward, I will forgive nothing. Step aside. I must speak with your commander."

They glanced at one another. They had seen her restore a blind man's sight. Respect, or perhaps self-preservation, overcame the conflict of orders.

Untouched, Imoshen stepped through the men to confront Jarholfe and the Cadre. "By what right do you take this action?"

"Gheeakhan!" The Cadre was exultant.

"The Ghebite warrior code? I don't see the connection." Imoshen focused on Jarholfe, believing him more reasonable. "You served me well on the journey south. I would hear this from your lips. Why do you betray my trust?"

"As your Ghiad, Lord Commander Wharrd defended your honor against the charges of dishonoring General Tulkhan. Two days ago he took a mortal wound and died this morning, confirming your guilt."

"Only your death and the death of your half-breed brat can restore the General's honor," the Cadre intoned.

Imoshen forced herself not to search the room to see if Kalleen had escaped with her son. A rush of potent anger made her vision swim with a thousand fireflies of fury. Desperately, she sought to influence the men, but without physical contact both were impervious to her gift.

As she went to touch Jarholfe's hand, he pulled away and she changed the gesture into a plea. "This brings me great sorrow. You have assumed the role of judge and executioner, murdering Wharrd, a good True-man. This is Fair Isle, not Gheeaba. By General Tulkhan's signed agreement, the laws of the T'En Church govern our society. In Fair Isle *Might is not Right.*"

Her head spun with the implications. If the Ghebite priest could overturn the Beatific's ruling, how many other basic rights could he overturn? Would she live to see Fair Isle go the way of the mainland, where, except for a few aristocratic women, no female could own property or speak for herself?

"The General has been bewitched by your black sorcery. We must act to save his soul," the Cadre said piously.

Imoshen snorted. If the priest had his way, she would not live long enough to see the women of Fair Isle brought low.

Behind the Cadre, she was aware of movement as Kalleen scuttled out the door with Ashmyr's basket in her arms. Praying the baby would not choose this moment to wake, Imoshen glared at the men. "You have overstepped your authority, Jarholfe. General Tulkhan ordered you to serve me. It brings me no joy to place you under arrest for the murder of Lord Commander Wharrd."

Jarholfe would have protested but Imoshen overrode him, gesturing to one of his men. "Send for the Beatific. Tell her to prepare a hearing. She must bring representatives for both the Lady of Windhaven, on behalf of her dead bond-partner, and Jarholfe, who stands accused of Wharrd's murder."

Reothe groaned as he regained consciousness. Imoshen blocked out the sound. She must not think of him restrained and vulnerable. Returning her attention to Jarholfe, she spoke to him, but her words were for the Cadre. "The Beatific will be your judge, by the laws of Fair Isle."

"The Ghebite priesthood does not recognize those laws," the Cadre said.

Lord Fairban bristled. "The Empress's word is *law*!"

"This is all the law I need!" Jarholfe grabbed him, bringing his knife to the old nobleman's throat. "I won't take orders from a stinking Dhamfeer!"

Imoshen's heart faltered. She had failed Cariah; she must not fail her father. "Let Lord Fairban go. I will not resist."

"No. You won't resist. You'll be too busy with this!" Jarholfe shifted the blade lower and drove it into Fairban's abdomen in a cruel, gouging movement.

The old man screamed. Jarholfe shoved him into Imoshen's arms. His blood stained her traveling tabard.

Jarholfe strode past them to kick Reothe in the face. "Take the rebel leader away. He's nothing but a powerless cripple. It's the woman we have to be wary of, and she has her limits."

While Imoshen fought to stem Fairban's blood, the men dragged Reothe away. She had not trusted him enough to restore his gifts, and the knowledge turned like a knife in her.

Jarholfe crouched beside her. His malignant expression was a revelation. "I have seen you wear yourself out healing worthless peasants. Heal this old man if you can, Dhamfeer." He sprang to his feet. "Lock him in with her."

"You can't move Lord Fairban. It might kill him." Imoshen pressed the wound closed, her hands warm and slick with blood. The old man was barely conscious.

"Then you'll have to make sure he lives!"

Without apology, the Ghebites swung Fairban off the floor. Half tripping in her attempts to keep up with the men, Imoshen hurried at their side. They carried the old nobleman along the hall, down the steps, and into the storage rooms near the upper servants' quarters. A door opened on darkness and they threw the injured man inside, pushing her after him.

"Wait. Search her. She carries a knife!" Jarholfe ordered.

When none of his men moved, he strode into the storeroom to confront Imoshen. Before he could lay hands on her, she pulled the knife free and held it out hilt first.

He hesitated as if he expected a knife thrust.

"Fool!" she hissed. "Unlike you, I value life."

Cursing, he took the weapon and shoved her. She fell onto the cold stone and the door swung shut. The bolt shot home. Imoshen knew that she could urge the bolt to do her bidding, but not yet, not until she was certain she could escape with Lord Fairban.

His soft panting came to her. Every few heartbeats it would stop as a moan escaped him, then start up again. Despairing, she strove to stanch the bleeding.

Lord Fairban caught her hands. "You mustn't waste your gifts on me. Save yourself. The Cadre means to wipe out the last of the T'En."

She shook her head and prayed that Kalleen had escaped with her son. But she must not let fear for Ashmyr shatter her concentration. For now, his fate, like Reothe's, was beyond her control. Imoshen fought the one battle she knew she had a chance of winning.

A single shout alerted Tulkhan. By the time he stepped out of the shelter, a dozen or so of his men had arrived, dragging a prisoner. Torchlight fell on Kornel's bruised face.

"We caught him trying to sneak out of the camp."

Unless he was contacting spies from the port, Kornel had no reason to leave the camp. Tulkhan frowned. "Turn out his pockets. The penalty for treason is death."

"I'm no spy," Kornel insisted. "Haven't I proved my worth? Without me, you would never have taken your army through the marsh-lands."

Rawset joined them as one of the men handed Tulkhan something wrapped in a rag. A heavy gold necklace unrolled and fell into his hand. Tulkhan recognized it as belonging to Banuld-Chi. "Where is the marsh-dweller, Kornel?"

"How should I know? He lost the necklace on the fall of a dice. I haven't seen him since he left yesterday."

"Why were you leaving the camp?" Tulkhan asked.

"I wasn't. I couldn't sleep. Went for a walk. Needed to

take a leak so I went to the outer ditch rather than the latrines. They don't half stink."

It was true. The logistics of providing fresh water and latrines for an army this size was staggering.

"If the smell offends you, we'll move the latrines. You can be on digging duty." Tulkhan laughed at Kornel's expression. He nodded to his men. "Let him go."

Kornel straightened his clothes and left.

Rawset lowered his voice. "Answers spring too easily to that man's tongue."

Tulkhan weighed the gold in his hands.

"You two." He gestured to the men who had brought Kornel in. "Take the three fastest horses and return with Banuld. I will have verification of Kornel's words from the marsh-dweller's own lips."

At least he had good news. That very evening three ships had arrived from T'Diemn and were in the process of erecting siege towers. The pressure on Port Sumair was growing.

Much later, Imoshen woke to blazing light and shouting voices. Blood had dried, leaving her hands and her tabard crusty. Lord Fairban slept with his head on her lap.

Squinting into the glare, she identified Jarholfe, his men, and the Cadre. A spurt of fear washed away her weariness but did not restore her drained gifts. Her vulnerability was terrifying.

"Not so proud now," Jarholfe sneered, fingering his sword hilt. Surely they did not mean to kill her like this? They needed the sanctity of a trial to change her death from murder to execution. "Stand up."

Careful not to reopen the tender new skin that covered Fairban's wound, Imoshen slipped his head from her lap. His hand sought hers. She squeezed his fingers briefly.

Jarholfe waited at the door, his branch of candles bright after the darkness. He waved a sheet of paper covered with fine Ghebite writing. "The Cadre has drawn up your confession, Dhamfeer bitch. Sign it and save yourself the grief of torture."

Mouth dry, Imoshen met his eyes. No spark of empathy stirred in their depths. "I will sign nothing."

"You will sign. Be sure of that. Everyone signs eventually. I see the old man still lives."

Imoshen heard the implied threat and her heart sank.

"You think you're so clever," Jarholfe snarled. "But we have your lover, and he will break soon. He will sign his confession and implicate you! As for the half-breed brat, he will not get out of T'Diemn alive!"

Triumph flared in Imoshen. Kalleen had escaped with her son. But they were torturing Reothe. She must divert them. "I am innocent of the charges, and I can prove it. The Orb of Truth will vindicate me before all of Fair Isle. Call on the Beatific to bring the Orb of Truth!"

"The Beatific has no authority here," the Cadre said. "Besides, your own actions have condemned you. Only one who deals in the black arts of sorcery could have healed this man."

"The only blackness is in your hearts and minds. It clouds your vision. When General Tulkhan hears of this, he will have your heads on pikes over the gates. He made me his Voice."

"We act to save him from himself!" the Cadre shouted. "Lock her away before she poisons your minds."

Jarholfe slammed the door.

Only a sliver of illumination came under the gap between the door and the floor. Imoshen could hear them walking away. In the darkness she sank to her knees. If only she could contact Tulkhan. But he had refused the intimacy of the mind-touch and now, in an emergency, she could not reach him. The irony of it hit her. She had not trusted Reothe enough to heal him, and Tulkhan had not trusted her enough to let down his defenses.

"I am sorry," Lord Fairban whispered.

"We are not dead yet."

"Hope is the province of the young." He quoted an old T'En saying.

But Imoshen had no time for philosophy. If the Cadre and Jarholfe did not take the Orb as bait, she would have to move swiftly. She must free Reothe before they could force a confession from him, but first she needed rest to restore her gifts. Her greatest consolation was knowing that Kalleen and Ashmyr were safely hidden somewhere in the old city.

The dawn before Large New Moon found Tulkhan preparing to ride the camp's defensive perimeter. He pulled his hood up against the fine drizzle. A shout drew his attention just as he put his foot in the stirrup.

Rawset ran up to him. "Lightfoot's returned!"

Tulkhan walked his mount back to the horse handlers and went to meet Lightfoot, who was waiting under the awning of the shelter.

Tulkhan clasped his shoulder and caught Rawset's eye. "Send in some Vorsch."

Lightfoot turned his face to the dim sun peeping beyond the clouds. "Do you see the T'En stigmata?"

Tulkhan searched the man's forehead. "Not a sign."

"She removed it. I . . ." He shook his head.

Rawset returned with the drink and food.

"Pour a drink and raise your glass," Tulkhan said. "To the fall of Port Sumair."

He grinned as the men echoed him. It might be raining and the camp ankle-deep in mud, but the siege was about to turn in their favor.

Imoshen woke with the bitter taste of fear on her tongue. The storeroom was dank and dark, yet her inner senses told her it was late morning. When she touched Lord Fairban, his skin was hot with fever and she knew that despite her best efforts the wound was festering. Another day in this place and he would be dead. She stood, arching her back, and wished for warm water, food, and a change of clothes.

Searching her T'En senses, she found her gifts restored—

at least for now. She was ravenously hungry, and if she eased the old lord's fever she would further deplete herself.

Imoshen concentrated, sifting through the minds of those nearest for something that might help her. Not surprisingly, the palace servants went about their tasks in terror. Of the two Ghebites at her door, one had gone to relieve himself and the other was asleep, snoring loudly. Imoshen concentrated on the door's bolt. It slid without a sound and the door swung inward at her touch.

Heart thumping, she glanced up and down the hall. The stench of alcohol was strong on the sleeping man's breath. Returning to the storeroom, she lifted the lord onto her shoulders; her leg muscles ached as she straightened. It was the work of a moment to close the door and send the bolt home.

Carrying the old man, she went up the passage. At the entrance to the servants' quarters, she paused to ease Fairban's weight, then entered Keeper Karmel's room.

Leaving Lord Fairban on the bed, she stripped off her bloodstained clothes and refreshed herself, bathing in a basin of water still lukewarm from the servant's use. Then she cleaned the old man, sponging him down to cool his heated flesh.

She had not fed Ashmyr since the evening before. Her breasts ached with the buildup of milk and the onset of the milk fever, which could be fatal. Huddling in the chair, she sought to heal herself. The effort left her so weary she slept.

"T'Imoshen?"

She woke with a start, momentarily disoriented, then everything came back to her in a rush. The Keeper looked startled. "Shut the door, Karmel. Have you any news of my son?"

"They look everywhere for him. All gates out of the old city are closed and soldiers search the houses, but they rob and drink as much as they search."

"Good! And Reothe?"

"They have him in the ball court. None of the servants is allowed near."

"What of the Beatific?"

"She is under arrest in the basilica."

"My Parakhan Guard?"

"Some died in the initial confrontation. The rest have gone into hiding."

"Murgon and his Tractarians?"

"I have heard nothing of them."

Relief swept Imoshen. Her greatest fear was that the Cadre would use Fair Isle's own weapons against her.

"Lady Miryma and her bond-partner have retreated to their chambers," the Keeper said. "I spoke with their servant during noon meal. No one knows what to do. With Jarholfe's men roaming the palace, I thought it safest to return to my room."

Imoshen's stomach rumbled. "I fear I must ask you to bring me food, my formal clothes, and healing herbs. And see if you can bring Miryma here."

Keeper Karmel slipped away. She was an old woman, worthless in Ghebite eyes. Imoshen hoped her comings and goings would not be remarked upon.

As Imoshen bathed Lord Fairban's forehead, she considered her position. It would take only a small trigger to tip the balance of power. Did she want the townsfolk to pick up kitchen knives and tools of trade and turn on the Ghebites? If only Woodvine and the other southern nobles had not returned to the highlands. She could have used Reothe's Keldon supporters now.

An image of Reothe as they dragged him away returned to her. Resolutely, she turned her mind from him and the fate of her son. She had to think like a statesman—not a mother, not a woman. But a wave of weariness rolled over her. Anxiously, she felt her forehead, fearing the fever would burn up her gift's reserves.

For once she had to place her trust in another. She sat in the chair beside the cot and dozed, waking every now and then to bathe Fairban's head. The afternoon passed in a haze of gray exhaustion and feverish dreams.

Imoshen's stomach told her it was late afternoon when the Keeper returned with Miryma and Shacolm.

"I'm sorry I took so long," the old woman whispered.

"You are safe, that is all that matters," Imoshen said, aware of Miryma and Shacolm watching anxiously. If she failed, their lives were forfeit. She accepted salted meat and wine, draining half a cup in one gulp. Chewing the meat, she mixed an herbal drink for the old man and something very similar for herself. She handed Fairban's drink to Miryma to administer and drank her own, ignoring the taste.

With the Keeper's help she dressed in an elaborate formal tabard with a shimmering undergown. If she was to unite the people against their oppressors, she must look the part. Her pregnancy did not show and would not for a while. She was glad no one knew. If the Cadre suspected who the father of this child was, he would have killed her himself!

"I must free Reothe before I make a move against Jarholfe and the Cadre. And we must hide Lord Fairban." Imoshen remembered Reothe's unexpected arrival in the library. She turned to the old woman. "You were close to the last Keeper of the Knowledge. Do you know the secret passages?"

The woman smiled.

Imoshen felt an answering smile on her lips.

Cold anger consumed Tulkhan as he crouched over Banuld's lifeless, mud-stained body. "Where did you find him?"

"Less than halfway to the Marsh-wall. One of the dogs led us to him."

Tulkhan nodded and came to his feet. They were under the awning of his shelter. A stinging sleet fell, its icy needles piercing all but the thickest clothes. "Bring Kornel."

The man was not a spy. He was something much simpler: a greedy murderer. Tulkhan heard Rawset and Lightfoot behind him, conferring. As he looked down at the corpse at his feet, it came to him that he had failed Banuld.

"What will you do with him?" Rawset asked.

"Send his body back to the marsh village with his gold and my apologies. It is the least I can do," Tulkhan muttered.

Rawset cleared his throat. "I meant Kornel."

"Execute him."

"General?" A soldier approached. Water dripped down the man's haggard face and plastered his hair to his head. "Kornel is gone."

Tulkhan cursed. "Search the camp." But he suspected Kornel had already escaped. The man was too cunning. The clouds to the west parted and the sinking sun's golden light bathed their camp, slanting through the icy rain. It was nearly dusk.

The Keeper led the way while Shacolm carried Lord Fairban to the safety of the secret passages. Imoshen was grateful for his assistance. Weak from the milk fever, she could not have carried Lord Fairban far.

Leaving the wounded man in the care of his relatives, Imoshen took the old woman aside. "Why haven't they noticed my escape?"

"The Cadre and his acolytes are ransacking the basilica. Jarholfe's men dice for the largest treasures in the square even now." Keeper Karmel pulled out a knife. "This was all I could get away with."

"You have done well." Imoshen hid the knife. The Ghebites were playing into her hands. It would only take a leader among the townspeople to unite them, someone familiar with weapons and tactics. "Reothe has followers in the city. Find them. Tell them to unite with the remaining Parakhan Guard and lead the people against Jarholfe and the Cadre's supporters. Can you do that while I free Reothe?"

The old woman repeated the message, her memory trained by years of study.

Imoshen slipped out of the secret passage and concentrated on cloaking her presence from the few servants who scurried nervously about the palace. Reothe was being held in the very ball court where only a few moons ago the Ghebites and Keldon nobles had gathered to watch a display match.

It was nearly dusk. Imoshen realized she hadn't heard the basilica's bells all day. Once the bells had rung the hour and the half hour; now nothing marked the passage of this black day. This struck her as a symbol of the destruction of T'Diemn society.

Avoiding the usual entrance to the ball court, Imoshen climbed the steps and slipped through the door that opened onto the highest row of seats. She looked down into the court, empty except for Reothe, who was tied to the far post. His arms were pulled above his head, the bonds slung through the ring that usually supported the net. He was naked, and blood seeped from vivid welts on his back. His long hair had been roughly hacked off, revealing bloodied scalp in places.

She had failed him. She should have restored his gifts.

Reothe leaned against the pole as though his will was broken. Her heart went out to him. What had they done to crush Reothe? The thought brought her heightened T'En senses a visible answer—Jarholfe laughing as his men abused their prisoner. Sickened, she shut down her gift, unwilling to witness the Ghebite's calculated cruelty.

Heart hammering with anger, Imoshen ran lightly down the tiered seats. She leapt over the balustrade, dropping a body length to the court below. Even though she hugged her swollen breasts, the jolt made her lurch with pain, and nausea threatened.

She paused to gather her strength. The court appeared empty but she could not be sure without using her T'En senses, and that would open her to Reothe's pain. He would not welcome her sympathy. He was opposite her now, his back to her. She saw his shoulder muscles tense, though he gave no other sign that he was aware of her presence.

Imoshen darted across the polished floor to slip under Reothe's outstretched arms. One eye was swollen shut, the other widened at the sight of her.

"Imoshen?" The word cracked his bruised lips.

"Did you think I would abandon you?" Her voice was thick. She brushed the bruise over his temple, willing it to heal so he would be able to open his eye. "Where are your captors?"

"They went to dice for the riches of the basilica."

"We are in luck. Jarholfe's men run amok."

"Luck!" He turned away from her.

Imoshen longed to beg his forgiveness, but nothing would undo events. Rising on her toes, she hacked at the leather thongs that bound him so tightly his fingers were blue. One arm swung free and he gasped, flexing his shoulder before raising his free hand to his mouth to catch the leather thong in his sharp white teeth and tear at it.

A buzzing sliced the air. Reothe hissed with pain, swinging by his left arm, which was still bound to the pole. An arrow shaft impaled him through the other shoulder.

Heart in her throat, Imoshen spun to confront their attacker. "Jarholfe!"

Fourteen

"**T**HROW DOWN THE knife. The next arrow goes through his heart," Jarholfe ordered from the safety of the watcher's gallery opposite. He had another arrow notched. Imoshen tossed the knife aside. "I knew you would come for your lover. Now, where is the brat? I will wipe out this nest of Dhamfeer!"

Imoshen flinched, placing her body between Jarholfe and Reothe. "Truly, I don't know. And even if I did, I'd die before I told you!"

"That's what I thought. I'm an excellent shot. At this distance I could put an arrow through his eye before you could get anywhere near me. My men claim you escaped from a bolted room while they were both on guard, but I don't believe it. I know you have limits. I should have come back and gutted the old man a second time to keep you busy. I won't make that mistake again. I should have set Murgon on you. He was eager enough."

"Jarholfe, I—"

A messenger ran into the gallery. "Commander. The square is full; the town officials are demanding to see the Empress. They say we dishonor their basilica and call on us to release the Beatific."

"The townspeople outnumber you a thousand to one, Jarholfe," Imoshen said. "Kill me and they will rise up."

"But if you convict yourself with your own words, they

will have to sanction your execution!" he said, and told the messenger, "The Cadre must bring the Beatific and that Orb he finds so fascinating. Send in the town officials. We will give them their Empress, convicted by their own laws!"

The messenger scurried off and Jarholfe remained, his arrow notched. Imoshen stood before Reothe, unwilling to take her eyes from the Ghebite.

"The Cadre has been studying this Orb of Truth. They say it can tell if a man speaks the truth and that it exacts punishment from those who lie. Are you prepared to place your palm upon the Orb and swear you have never taken this Dhamfeer for your lover?" Jarholfe sneered.

According to the records, the Orb would glow with the pure light of truth if she spoke truly. The Cadre and Jarholfe would not be able to deny the evidence of their own eyes. But she *had* taken Reothe as her lover, even if it was only the once and only because he had deceived her by coming to her in Tulkhan's form. Imoshen felt trapped. When she had defied them to bring forth the Orb, it was to buy time. She had never meant it to come to this.

Seeing her expression, Jarholfe smiled.

The passages beyond the ball court echoed with the clamor of approaching town officials. As they took their seats, they radiated an air of fear and a desperate dignity.

"Imoshen?" Reothe whispered at her back. "Heal me!"

"If I heal you, he will hurt you again. You heard him."

"No. I mean really heal me!" Reothe pleaded. "He cannot see my T'En gifts. It is only because they do not fear me that they dare to abuse me."

He was right, but . . . "It could hurt you!"

"I am willing to take that risk." His voice told her he would risk anything for revenge.

Imoshen shook her head. "If I am to make my move, I want you physically able."

"Imoshen!" His despair tore at her.

But already events were moving, dragging her with them like debris on a flood tide. The Cadre and his acolytes entered, escorting the Beatific and Murgon, who carried the Orb in its caged chalice. Warm, velvety anger flushed through Imoshen, for Murgon's expression told her he reveled in Reothe's downfall. When the Beatific caught sight of Reothe, she glared at Imoshen, fury kindling the woman's mature beauty.

Tulkhan lifted his head at the cry of *To Arms!* A soldier charged into the shelter. "Sumair's gates are open and mercenaries pour out."

"Saddle my horse." He sent a servant to bring his armor. Had the auxiliary army arrived and somehow gotten word to the defenders of the port? His men had not reported any movement during their scouting forays. "Watch for a secondary attack."

When he stepped out of the shelter, several youths waited, ready to carry his orders. Other runners would bring him reports. Striding across the soggy soil, Tulkhan approached the man who led his horse. As he swung into the saddle, he felt the familiar welcoming rush as his men prepared for pitched battle. Beyond the defensive earthworks he heard the mercenaries' drummers playing.

Forcing the horse to tackle the incline of the earthworks' inside slope, Tulkhan made the crest and surveyed the plain before Port Sumair's city walls. Mercenaries swarmed across the flat ground, but they were not a rabble. They were wellprepared, with defensive hides made of wood and straw, and they carried ladders to throw across the ramparts' outer ditch.

He glared into the twilight. The sleet had stopped, but it was a strange time to attack. Death whistled overhead and a man screamed. Protected by their hides, mercenary archers were firing in high arcs, trusting their arrows would find a mark inside the camp.

Tulkhan saw no Ghebite foot soldiers. It appeared Gharavan did not trust his own men.

Riding down the mound's incline, the General walked his horse through the bustling camp, pausing to speak with his men preparing for the first strike. All the while arrows fell about them. Some landed harmlessly on the ground, others carried his soldiers to their knees. A man did not know when random death would claim him. But this was what they had been waiting for—the breach in the port's defenses.

Why had they attacked now? Perhaps Kornel had taken word that the siege machines and cavalry were on the way. Grimly, Tulkhan thanked the merchant captain, for now all he had to do was sit tight, let the defenders wear themselves down on his defenses, and then, when the moment was right, send his men out. How he wished for cavalry to pummel the foot soldiers and spearhead the counterattack. With the mud the way it was, the cavalry would have had to go out lightly armed, but even so, foot soldiers could not withstand a mounted attack.

He glanced at the sky again. By the look of those clouds, they might have the first snow of the season tonight. There was little daylight left, but a battle could be won or lost in an hour.

"General Tulkhan?" Rawset rode up to join him. "King Gharavan's mercenaries are trying to force the north entrance."

The defensive ditch was knee-deep in water. Tulkhan threw back his head and laughed, and his men took heart as he meant them to. "Pour oil in the ditch and set it alight. Then go to the Sea-wall and signal Peirs to mount a counterattack."

Imoshen blinked as torch bearers filed into the ball court, now a court of trial. Heavy, snow-laden clouds dulled the light that filtered through the high windows, and with the torches came an early night. None of the Ghebites thought to light the lamps, which were designed to be raised and lowered by pulleys. Imoshen realized these Ghebites were blind to the marvels of the old empire.

The murmuring of the crowd ceased as, on the Cadre's signal, Murgon stepped into the center of the polished wood floor, carrying the Orb's chalice. Imoshen caught her breath. Older even than Imoshen the First, this Orb had come from the land beyond the dawn sun. It was revered, and the mystery of its making was lost.

The Cadre raised his voice, turning to confront the town officials. "By Ghebite law the Lady Protector is already guilty of dishonoring her husband, the Protector General Tulkhan." He raised his hands to stem their angry muttering. "But we are fair men. We understand you wish to see her guilt for yourselves. What is the sentence for a rogue T'En, Murgon?"

"Death by stoning."

"Death!" the Cadre repeated.

But the Beatific would not see her authority undermined. She raised her voice. "Only the Beatific can declare one of the T'En rogue, and then only if it can be proven that the accused has used their T'En gifts to take a Trueperson's life or to overthrow Fair Isle's rulers."

"Then if we can prove that this Dhamfeer dishonored Fair Isle's ruler by taking a lover, you would sign the decree?" the Cadre pressed.

The Beatific glared at him. "Declaring one of the T'En rogue is not something to be done lightly. Over the centuries, many have given their lives to bring in the rogues. Many Tractarians are required to contain them so that the sentence can be carried out."

The crowd whispered uneasily.

The Cadre spoke to Murgon. "And this Orb senses the truth?"

"It glows with the pure light of truth," the Beatific answered for him.

Murgon was quick to qualify this. "But if the accused lies, the Orb will glow dull and dark."

Imoshen saw the Cadre exchange a look with Jarholfe, who was flanked by six of his men. More waited up in the seats. They stood by the entrances, hands on weapon hilts. Imoshen suspected Jarholfe planned treachery, whatever the Orb's response.

The Cadre beckoned. "Bring me the Orb!"

A collective gasp came from the crowd. Once in a century the Orb might be called upon. Those who failed to prove their innocence had been known to lose their minds, for the Orb not only exonerated the innocent, it punished the guilty.

Imoshen shivered. In her heart she knew the truth. She loved two men, and there would be no peace for her. But she had not dishonored Tulkhan, not by choice. She felt Reothe touch the small of her back where no one would see.

"Remember how I tricked you," he whispered. "Your words of love were for him, not me."

"Give me the Orb." The Cadre held his hand out, palm up.

"Only one of T'En blood may unleash the power of the Orb by asking the question and holding it against their skin," the Beatific announced, stepping between him and Murgon. When the Cadre looked perplexed she explained, "In the hand of a True-man or woman the Orb remains impervious."

"I claim the honor of holding the Orb," Murgon said.

"No!" Reothe protested. "Only one without bias can hold the Orb."

While the people in the gallery whispered their agreement, Jarholfe turned to the Cadre, but the Beatific spoke up. "By tradition it is the Empress herself who holds the Orb. Always the Empress has carried T'En blood."

"You can't give it to that Dhamfeer bitch!" Jarholfe objected.

The town officials muttered.

"I will hold the Orb." Murgon was eager to see her convicted.

"Is there no one among the townsfolk of T'En blood?" Imoshen cried. "Someone who is without bias?"

The crowd shifted in their seats; one stood and pointed. "The silversmiths' guild-master."

"Where? Step down," the Cadre ordered.

Imoshen heard the whispers grow as a woman was escorted onto the court floor by Jarholfe's men.

"You have the Dhamfeer's accursed eyes. Who are you?" the Cadre asked.

"Maigeth, guild-master of the silversmiths." It was Drake's mother. She met Imoshen's gaze briefly, revealing the fear behind her composure. "But I relinquish this honor. I am unworthy."

"Will this woman do, Murgon?" the Cadre asked. Before

Murgon could open his mouth, the Beatific gave her approval. The Cadre ignored her. "Murgon?" He nodded. "Then proceed."

"Bring the Orb," the Beatific ordered. She unlocked the cage and turned toward the silversmith. But before Maigeth could move, the Cadre stepped between them, taking the Orb in his bare hands. The townsfolk of T'Diemn gasped in dismay, and the Beatific's mouth tightened in annoyance.

"Sacrilege!" Murgon hissed.

"Take this Orb and reveal the truth, silversmith," the Cadre ordered.

Maigeth hesitated.

"Take it," he urged.

"I can't. I have the T'En eyes, but I have no gifts." She cast Imoshen a trapped glance.

"What is she talking about, Murgon?" Jarholfe demanded.

"Well?" the Cadre pressed.

"Not all we half-breeds are cursed with the lesser T'En gifts," Murgon said at last. "I have harnessed and trained mine. Give me the Orb."

"No!" Imoshen fixed her gaze on the silversmith. "Take the Orb, Maigeth."

The woman shook her head. If she touched the Orb and it flared into life, it meant she had been hiding her gift from her family and her friends. They would never trust her again. If she did not, Imoshen feared Murgon would ensnare her.

"Maigeth. I have stood by you. Stand by me." Imoshen had not revealed how Maigeth's son joined the rebels. She had never intended to use it against the woman. Only desperation drove her now. "Do this for me. I am ready to swear that I have taken no man but General Tulkhan into my bed and into my arms."

"Do it!" the Cadre hissed.

The silversmith's wine-dark eyes centered on the Orb as, almost against her will, she took it from the Cadre. At her touch it flared once in recognition.

The watchers gasped and murmured.

Imoshen knew that from this moment forward, Maigeth would be regarded with suspicion by the True-people she had counted as friends.

"I've read that in rare cases the gifts could lie dormant for years until some crisis triggered them," Murgon whispered.

The Beatific shook her head. "I thought if the gifts did not come on at puberty, they—"

"Enough!" the Cadre snapped. "You people could debate while T'Diemn burned!" He turned to Maigeth. "You, silversmith, ask the Dhamfeer bitch if this male is her lover."

Maigeth licked her lips.

Imoshen locked eyes with Maigeth. The fingers of Imoshen's left hand hovered over the Orb. The brief glow had faded but she sensed its awareness, almost as if it were a living thing. Its surface was alive with palpable tension.

Imoshen heard her own words falling from the silver-smith's lips: "... taken no man but General Tulkhan to your bed and into your arms?"

"I have never taken any man but General Tulkhan into my bed and into my arms," Imoshen repeated, her mouth so dry she could hardly speak. Her fingers splayed over the Orb, expecting to feel a cold slick surface or heat, but instead she felt resistance. It flared, illuminating her hand so brightly she could see the bones inside her six fingers.

The townspeople exclaimed her innocence as the after-image of the light danced on Imoshen's vision, blinding her.

"The Dhamfeer manipulated the Orb. She escaped from a bolted room without disturbing the guards!" Jarholfe roared.

The townspeople of T'Diemn surged to the bal-ustrades, protesting.

"The Orb is false!" the Cadre screamed. "Murgon. Tell me the Dhamfeer manipulated the Orb."

The Tractarian opened his mouth. Imoshen tensed. Would he lie for the Ghebites?

"The Orb cannot lie," the Beatific insisted. "To manipulate the Orb brings on madness. Others have tried and failed." Her words were echoed by the townsfolk.

"Jarholfe, have your men get them out of here before

they riot," the Cadre ordered. Then he spun and snatched the Orb from the silversmith, knocking her aside.

Imoshen broke Maigeth's fall, asking under cover of the noise and confusion, "Is Drake with you?"

"He was all for attack, but I wanted to seek justice."

"Tell him to move against the Cadre and Jarholfe. Their supporters must be found and—"

The Cadre dragged Maigeth away from Imoshen. "Get out, woman. Or do you want to suffer the same fate as a full-blood Dhamfeer?"

Maigeth fled.

Imoshen held Murgon's eyes. "Look deep into your heart. To hate us you must hate yourself, Malaunje." She deliberately used the High T'En word for half-breed, dating from a time when the T'En were honored and the Malaunje only slightly less so.

Murgon lifted his left hand to his mouth and mimed biting off the sixth finger he did not have, spitting it aside.

Imoshen was stunned by his hatred.

Cries of outrage rent the air as Jarholfe's men drew swords on unarmed townsfolk, who had come expecting to see a fair trial conducted by the laws of the old empire. Instead, they faced naked steel and overzealous soldiers. Even as Imoshen watched, some were slain and the rest fled. She had failed her people.

"Imoshen, free me," Reothe hissed.

She retrieved her knife and ran to his side, sawing at the bonds that held his left arm.

"No you don't." The Cadre snatched a handful of her hair, dragging her away.

Tears of pain stung Imoshen's eyes. She clamped one hand over his, pressing his fingers to her skull. Then she dropped and twisted inside his hold, wrenching his wrist. Bringing the knife up, she aimed for his heart. The Orb, which was pressed to his chest, flared eagerly.

Jarholfe's boot took her in the ribs. The force of it sent her flying into the near wall. The knife spun from her fingers and the breath was driven from her body as she sank to the floor.

"I warned you not to go near her, Cadre!" Jarholfe growled.

Imoshen fought for air. Specks of light flecked her vision. Each breath seared. She saw the last of the townspeople escape, pursued by Jarholfe's supporters. Only Murgon and the Beatific remained along with Jarholfe, the Cadre, and his acolytes.

Jarholfe cursed and advanced on Imoshen with his naked sword.

Fingers splayed, she reached for the knife hilt. Jarholfe's heel came down on her hand, crushing the fine bones. Her cry was drowned by the Beatific. "Cadre, you must return the Orb. Murgon, tell him!"

Hugging her injured hand to her chest, Imoshen looked up to see the Cadre backing away with the Orb held above his head.

"It played us false, Murgon. You told me it would convict the Dhamfeer. Accursed relic!" The Cadre cast it down.

The Beatific's mouth opened in a silent scream as the Orb shattered at her feet.

Imoshen was reminded of the smashing glass of the Dreamwasps' cage, and an ominous foreboding swamped her. "Run!"

Before the Beatific could take a step, something intangible was released from the Orb. It had no shape or color, yet Imoshen could see its essence distorting the terrified features of the Cadre's acolytes beyond. Murgon made the sign to ward off evil.

"Engarad!" Reothe used the Beatific's private name.

Her form wavered. As Imoshen watched the unknown presence invade her, the Beatific crumpled.

The Cadre and his men backed away.

"Imoshen, help her!" Reothe urged, trying to lift his injured arm to undo the bonds that held him.

She had no idea how to help. Even so, her healing instincts drove her to the Beatific's side.

Imoshen rolled the woman over with her good hand. Already the Beatific's skin was waxen, her features lifeless.

Imoshen leaned down to listen for her heartbeat. That was when she sensed the vengeful presence of a force long caged.

Calling on her gift, Imoshen placed her good hand over the Beatific's still heart and pressed, willing that heart to beat. The woman's mouth opened in a silent gasp. Imoshen leaned close and expelled her breath into the Beatific's open mouth, propelling her gift.

The dead woman jerked with the impact of the life force. The Beatific exhaled, and Imoshen inadvertently inhaled the vengeful presence. Frightful cold filled her chest.

As if she were looking through imperfect glass, Imoshen saw Murgon drag the Beatific away, his features contorted with piteous fear. From a great distance she heard Reothe calling her name. Jarholfe's harsh voice demanded to know what was going on, and she felt his hand on her arm as he pulled her upright. The Orb's presence was going to kill her; already she could feel it overcoming her resistance. She must pass it on or die.

In her mind's eye Imoshen saw Jarholfe gutting Lord Fairban, saw him laughing as his men abused Reothe. With the last of her strength, she swung her free arm around Jarholfe's neck and planted her lips on his. Exhaling, she drove the vengeful presence from her body into his. It went eagerly, sensing his defenseless life force.

As she pulled away from Jarholfe, his eyes met hers, revealing dreadful comprehension. Imoshen imagined the cold embrace closing around his desperate heart, leaching the life from him. His mouth opened. Before he could speak, Jarholfe dropped to the floor, dead at her feet.

Imoshen stared at his still body.

The Cadre's acolytes tried to flee but were hindered by the return of Jarholfe's men.

Imoshen noticed the Beatific and Murgon exchanging glances. By using her gift to take the life of a True-man with them as her witnesses, she had signed her own death warrant.

"Fiend!" the Cadre shrieked. "The Dhamfeer must be killed." He gestured to the frightened acolytes. "Take Murgon and the woman back to the basilica and hold them."

Imoshen marveled. Even in his extremity, the Cadre insulted the Beatific.

Eagerly, the acolytes drove Murgon and the Beatific ahead of them, stepping aside for Jarholfe's returning soldiers, who reeked of sweat, blood, and death. They were dismayed to discover their commander dead. Several would have lifted Jarholfe's body, but Imoshen stopped them. "Don't touch him if you value your lives. The Orb's presence is still dissipating."

They glared at her. Imoshen knew her life hung in the balance. How many could she take with her—one, maybe two? She felt drained of her gift, but who knew what she could do in an emergency? She might escape, but she would not leave Reothe.

Four of Jarholfe's men advanced on Imoshen, their swords raised. A boot caught the remains of the Orb's crystal, sending it skittering across the polished wooden floor to the wall. The sound scraped Imoshen's raw senses.

"Hold your weapons," the Cadre ordered, his voice rich with malignant triumph. "The Dhamfeer has played into our hands. Tomorrow, if I am not mistaken, we will have a double stoning, with the full approval of the Church's lawgivers."

Imoshen straightened, aware that she had a reprieve for now. "What did you promise Murgon to betray Fair Isle, Cadre?"

He laughed, then shuddered. "Fair Isle? Rather Fell Isle, filled with feral creatures."

Imoshen realized he was lumping her with the thing that had been imprisoned within the Orb. "You were the one who smashed the Orb. You are responsible for Jarholfe's death, not I!"

"Silence!" the Cadre roared. "I will not listen to your poisoned words. You are convicted by your own actions, Dhamfeer bitch. Tomorrow you die. But first you must be safely secured for the night."

He glanced around, as if considering where she and Reothe would be imprisoned. Then he retrieved her knife and went to Reothe. Imoshen expected him to slit the bonds that held Reothe's wrist. Instead, he pressed Reothe's fingers against the pole and hacked them off.

A cry left her lips; its twin came from Reothe.

With satisfaction, the Cadre tossed the severed fingers aside and slit the bonds that held Reothe. Reothe fell to his knees, clasping his hand as blood pumped from the finger stumps. Imoshen tore the hem of her underdress to stem the bleeding. She urged the wound to seal.

The Cadre watched in satisfaction. "I've heard you two can climb like mountain goats. Let's see you try it now. Take them to the top of the tallest tower and shut them outside."

Soldiers pulled Imoshen away from Reothe. She twisted free of their grasp. "He'll die from blood loss if I don't pack the wounds."

"Then you'd better heal him, bitch," the Cadre urged. "According to Jarholfe, each time you heal it reduces your powers. So heal him and yourself if you can. And we'll see how much T'En trouble you give Murgon's Tractarians after you have spent a night exposed on the tower."

Tulkhan frowned. In the gathering gloom he could just make out the ebb and flow of battle. The ditch still burned, topped up with oil. All about him, men fought amid the roar of commands, the clash of metal, and the stench of burned flesh. The camp's north entrance had held despite repeated attempts to breach it. Each time Gharavan's mercenaries threatened, Tulkhan sent reinforcements. There had been no secondary attack, and now he detected a slowing in the pace of the onslaught.

"Look, over by the port gates." A man pointed.

Squinting past the glow of the ditch fires, Tulkhan strained to make out what was happening. "They've closed the gate on their own men!"

"But why?"

"The Low-landers wanted nothing of this war. It would not surprise me if..." Tulkhan headed down the embankment, letting his momentum carry him far into the camp. It was the perfect opportunity to catch Gharavan's mercenaries in the open. "Form a column!"

Tulkhan grinned as his men fell into formation. Now that the Low-landers had cut off the mercenaries' retreat, it wouldn't surprise him if the port officials handed his half-brother over, trussed like a pig for the slaughter. His good mood infected the men, and soon he had the mounted attack force ready to form a pincer.

"The gates have been shut and the mercenaries fall back in dismay," a runner reported.

"This is the night we take Port Sumair," Tulkhan roared.

His men took up the cry. Tulkhan rode out with a small contingent of mounted men to spearhead the attack. Their horses' hooves sounded over the hastily lowered bridge.

With the burning ditch behind him, he faced the darker plain, littered with scattered fires caused by the burning hides. He heard the furious shouts of the betrayed mercenaries, and signaled the attack while his men cheered from the ramparts.

Gharavan's mercenaries formed a hasty square to meet their onslaught, but the force of the heavy farm horses broke their ranks. Tulkhan found himself in the midst of struggling bodies, fighting in the dim twilight, where it was hard to tell friend from foe. He stood in the stirrups as the battle raged around him and raised the victory horn to his lips, believing the sounding of the horn would be enough to prompt the cornered men to lay down their weapons.

At the horn's call, the tone of the fighting slowed and Tulkhan wheeled his horse, pulling back to assess their position. A strange sight greeted him. Several burning wagons dotted the plain between him and the Sea-wall. One by one these winked out, as if a black veil of darkness rolled toward him. The sound of fighting was overcome by a dull, hungry roar. Suddenly, the men between him and the blackness rose up, screaming. As they were carried toward him, Tulkhan realized the darkness was a wall of raging water engulfing friend and foe alike.

Too late, men cast down their weapons to flee.

Tulkhan's horse screamed and reared up against the boiling wave. Now that it was close he could see the froth and limbs of men trapped in it. Suddenly it was upon him. He was swept off his horse, carried away, turned over and over so that he didn't know which way was up or down.

His helmet was torn from his head, his sword from his fingers. Dragged under by the force of the water, held down by the weight of his armor, he struggled against ignominious, impartial death. His head broke the surface and he barely had time to snatch a breath before he went under again. Spinning in cold blackness, he tried to undo his chest-plate clasps. He felt ground under his feet and broke free of his armor, surfacing for a breath, only to lose his balance as something collided with him.

The breath rushed from his body. Frantic for air, he drove his legs down but the ground slid out from under him. Then hands clasped his arms and hauled him up. He discovered he had been pinned halfway up the steep embankment of the defensive earthworks. His rescuer helped him to his feet.

Dragging in a deep breath, he looked about. By the light of scattered patches of burning oil and the few stars that pierced the cloud cover, he watched the water pour through the camp's northern entrance, tearing down sections of the ramparts. A great frothing flood engulfed the camp. The screams of his men left him seething with impotence.

"The Sea-wall must be down," his companion muttered.

Tulkhan realized that, to rid themselves of both the invaders and Gharavan's mercenaries, the townspeople of Port Sumair had locked the port's gates, then breached the Sea-wall, deliberately flooding their land.

Most of Tulkhan's men could not swim, but they would survive if they could make it to the embankments that bounded the camp on two sides.

"What's that?" The man pointed. "A boat?"

Tulkhan spun to see a dark shape sail past. The outline was too irregular to be a boat. Then he heard the hunting bark of the narcts, and fear curdled in his belly. The sea swirled around the embankment, rising steadily. He spotted another of the floating islands swept in from the channel. It was carried past them with its deadly cargo.

"Are you armed?" Tulkhan demanded.

"Just my knife; I lost my bow."

"Draw your blade and put your back to mine. The water is full of narcts."

The man muttered an invocation to Akha Khan. Tulkhan had nothing but his ceremonial dagger. He wished for a sword or a spear. To his left the water frothed and roiled. A man's screams were silenced as the narcts tore him apart.

Cries of despair rose from the men along the ramparts.

"We must band together!" Tulkhan roared.

"Something swims toward me!" his companion warned.

Tulkhan swung to face the threat.

"Akha Khan, help me," a man cried, thrashing through the water in his desperation to reach safety.

When Tulkhan stepped forward to take the man's arm, his leg went straight down. Only his companion's quick actions stopped him from going under. Bracing himself against the man's weight, the General grabbed the soldier's outstretched hand.

Tulkhan found his feet. "Beware, Vaygharian. The top of the earthworks is wide enough for only two men."

He had not been fooled by the man's choice of god. The mercenary tensed and would have thrust off their helping hands.

"Truce, man. We have a common enemy," Tulkhan said, and as if to confirm this, they heard another chorus of barking.

"We were betrayed."

"Doubly so," Tulkhan agreed. "The gates were locked, then the Sea-wall opened to the ocean. I think you can consider your contract with Gharavan canceled."

The mercenary cursed.

"Take heart, men," Tulkhan yelled. "It could be worse. It could be snowing!"

Fifteen

"IT'S SNOWING," IMOSHEN whispered. Wearing only her underdress, she could not repress a shiver as the first flake caressed her cheek. "Now, don't argue, Reothe; put this on."

He pushed her helping hands away, but she could tell it was an effort for him to dress himself in her brocade tabard.

They had been driven at sword-point up the ladder to the top of Sard's Tower. Before the trapdoor was bolted, the Cadre had crowed, "If you can force that bolt with your gifts, these men will be waiting. I give them leave to hack off any limb that comes through this trapdoor. You'll bleed to death as quick as any True-man!"

Recalling the fearful, glittering eyes of the guards, Imoshen knew they would be only too eager to follow the Cadre's command.

Imoshen went to the tower's crenelated edge to peer down. It was a sheer drop to the steeply sloping roof below. Even if she were to risk the jump, the icy roof slates would give her no traction. She imagined sliding off to plunge four floors to the ground below and shuddered.

"How far down is it?" Reothe asked.

"Too far to climb."

But he had to study the drop for himself. "It could be done if the roof were not covered in a thin layer of ice."

"I doubt if I would attempt it even then. Now I must

heal your wound and bind it properly." Imoshen's reserves were pitifully low, for she had had little to eat and, worse, her body still burned with the milk fever.

Reothe hugged his wounded hand to his chest. "Why should I be whole in body if my powers are crippled? You must heal my gifts!"

Seeing him at Jarholfe's mercy, she had decided to heal his gifts, but the moment he confronted her with it, her instinct was to deny him. In her heart of hearts, his trickery still hurt and she feared she could not trust him.

"Imoshen?" His face was a pale oval and his features ill-defined, yet she did not need to see him to know his expression. His bitter, desperate tone conveyed it all. Knowing how Jarholfe's men had abused him, she understood his rage, but she did not make the mistake of offering pity.

"I cannot return your lost fingers, but I can promise to heal your wounds. To be frank, I am too exhausted to attempt more."

He pushed her entreating hand aside and she gasped in pain. "Why haven't you healed yourself, Imoshen?"

"Your need is greater." At best, she could only hasten her own healing. "Show me your hand."

"So that you can exhaust yourself healing me? Would you leave me a useless T'En cripple but physically healed to witness your stoning?"

"What would you have me do? There are so many Ghebites, and I am almost exhausted." She looked across at the basilica, blinking fiercely to clear her vision. Everything was covered with a layer of snow. Tomorrow the Ghebites would come for them, strip them naked, and lead them into the square. "They will have to send wagons to the quarries outside of town to bring in cartloads of stones. The snow will make that difficult. How many stones does it take to kill? I suppose it depends how well they are aimed."

"Stop it!" He pulled her to him. "How could you hold the Orb and deny me before everyone?"

"But it was you who showed me how I could word it so it would not be a lie."

"You always let your head rule your heart."

"And you don't?" She waited, but he said nothing. At last, she kissed his cracked lips. "Let me heal your body."

"What good is that if we are to die?" Reothe's breath dusted her face with his despair.

"I have sent word to your rebels."

Reothe cursed. "I'm afraid you'll get no help from my people until the Ghebites open the old-city gates."

"I sent the guild-master of the silversmiths to Drake. He can organize the townspeople—"

"To do what? You saw them today. They came expecting justice and they came unarmed. The people of T'Diemn are sheep to the slaughter."

Imoshen had to admit the truth of this. "After today they will know better."

"Much good that will do us!" The moment stretched between them. "Why did you come back for me, Imoshen? Why didn't you escape when you had the chance?"

Wordlessly, she slid her good hand inside his tabard. As her fingers traveled over his back, she willed the lacerated skin to seal, felt the warmth flow from her into him.

He gasped. "Your touch is sweet, T'Imoshen."

"You used your T'En tricks on me from the first, Reothe." Anger thinned her voice. "You tried to manipulate me into your arms."

"A little," he admitted, resting his forehead on hers. "But my gifts have been crippled these past weeks, and you can't deny what we share."

"You dishonored me by your trickery. I would have come to love you, given time."

"We had no time. It has been against us from the first. Remember when I came to you on the day of our betrothal? If I had told you that the Church was our enemy, you would have thought I was mad."

She hesitated, remembering how she had not understood her great-aunt's reluctance to call on the Church for help.

"You see," he whispered. "If only you had been older and known something of the world. But you didn't, so—"

"So you sought to manipulate me. It was wrong, Reothe!"

"I was desperate."

"Still wrong."

"A small wrong for a greater good."

She shook her head, surprised to discover that, despite her pain and weariness, her anger was raw and immediate.

He straightened, but before he could speak, she indicated the arrow. "Now I must break this with my good hand."

"Do it quickly." He leaned against the tower's stonework, bracing himself. She caught the shaft in her teeth, took the feathered end in her good hand, and snapped the shaft. Even so, she felt him shake with the shock of it. With the arrow broken, she felt behind him for the barbed head that protruded from his flesh and pulled it through, using her gift to knit the flesh behind it. The heat of her anger faded with the effort it took to seal the wound.

Dropping the arrowhead from numb fingers, she nearly lost consciousness. Reothe caught her before she could collapse. "Heal yourself, Imoshen. We must be gone from here before dawn."

"No. Your hand next."

"Why did you save the hardest for last?"

"Because you never know what you can do until you must."

A soft laugh escaped him, and he kissed her forehead. "Can you wonder that my love for you made me careless of honor?"

It was the closest he had ever come to an apology. She stared into his pale face, pierced by the twin pools of his dark eyes. "I thought love made a person strong, not devious."

He flinched.

She took his injured hand to study the wound. His first two fingers had been sheared off at the base; the third was severed at the knuckle. "So cruel."

"They threatened worse."

Behind the bitter humor in Reothe's voice, she heard fear. Guilt assailed her. "Not once have you reproached me for leaving you vulnerable."

"Heal my hand, Imoshen."

She understood he would not reproach her. "Relax and open yourself to me."

He tilted his head back, his face turned up to greet the falling flakes. She sensed him growing receptive. Concentrating on his injury, she called on her reserves to knit and seal the stumps of his fingers. It was surprisingly easy to work her healing on Reothe. Suddenly she understood the dual nature of their bond. With the most intimate of the mind-touches, she had grown to need him. But he had also become vulnerable to her. This was why she had been able to injure his gift when she had lashed out. The revelation left her trembling.

"Ah, to be without pain! Bless you, T'En Healer." He used the High T'En invocation then, pulling the tabard around his body and sinking down with his back to the wall. "Come close. Your skin is wondrously warm."

She was burning up with fever and her maimed hand throbbed with every beat of her heart, but if she expended any of her gift to heal herself, she would have no reserves to maintain their body heat during the long night. "You must not sleep." Her teeth chattered, breaking up her words. There would come a point when they no longer felt cold and a curious warmth would spread over them. But she would not let it come to that. "To sleep in the snow is fatal."

"Sweet death, they say. It would cheat those Ghebites of their stoning."

Imoshen flinched. The abuse Reothe had received at the hands of his Ghebite captors was designed to destroy his pride. Imoshen knew it was possible to die of this kind of injury. Her ears buzzed in the absolute silence of the snow-bound night. At least there was no wind, only the ever-falling snow seductively luring her to sleep in its deadly embrace. Though her fever raged, she shook with cold.

"Look down into the square," Reothe urged. "Are the townspeople gathering? They must come to us soon, for I doubt we will last the night."

She could distinguish nothing moving. The old city of T'Diemn slept peacefully under its blanket of fresh, crisp snow.

"What do you see?"

"Nothing. The snow falls too thickly," she lied.

"Let us hope it aids our supporters. Come to me, Imoshen." He took her hand, and again she could not conceal the pain. "You haven't healed yourself?"

"I'll use what's left of my gift to keep us warm."

"So that we may be stoned in the morning?"

She smiled. "By then Drake will have organized a revolt."

"Now that I can think without pain, I don't want to remain here. If Drake does lead an uprising, the first thing the Cadre will do is have us killed. We must make our move before then." Reothe's voice dropped. "There is something you could try. Sometimes it is possible for one of the T'En to draw on the True-people around them."

Imoshen went very still as the horror of the confrontation in Lakeside returned. Was Reothe asking her to drive someone to murder, to renew her flagging gifts?

"Just as people have distinctive physical features, they give off distinctive emanations," Reothe whispered. "I can taste it on my tongue, sense it lingering on the air after they leave the room. Some of them are much easier to tap into than others. Engarad can close me out at will. She's always been able to. That was how I found her."

Imoshen heard the smile on his voice. And though she didn't want to know, she experienced Reothe's memory—he was an arrogant, lonely youth in a city of alien creatures, discovering a closed creature, one that fascinated him.

"What is it?" Reothe prodded.

"I said nothing."

"Don't shut me out, Imoshen, there is so much I could share with you. The first time you crossed my path, I—"

"What were you going to tell me about the T'En gifts?"

She did not want to hear how she had first appeared to him, raw and gauche in the court of the Empress. Knowing about the Beatific was painful enough.

After a heartbeat Reothe continued. "Open your senses. Trawl the minds of those in the building below. Find someone engaged in an intense moment and open yourself to them. Use them to sustain us."

Perhaps this skill was mentioned in Imoshen the First's memoirs. "The T'Elegos—"

"Will be ours to explore when all this is over, when you stand at my side and Fair Isle is ours."

"How can you put a price on knowledge?"

"Everything has a price, especially knowledge. That much is very clear to me. There is so much I must achieve. This Ghebite general destroyed my plans and forced a terrible choice upon you, and you have been regretting it ever since."

"I love Tulkhan."

"I know. But this isn't about him, or you and me. It is about the fate of the T'En."

"The Golden Age of the T'En?"

"Don't mock me, Shenna."

Imoshen ducked her head. No one else used her pet name.

"Open your senses," he urged. "I will hold you safe until you find a source."

She settled in Reothe's arms, cradled against his chest. The cold was fierce. Uncontrollable shivers racked them both. But when she tried to open her mind, she could not. "Don't watch me."

"I can see very little!"

She could hear the smile on his voice. "Turn your face away."

"If that is what you want."

With the pain in her hand and the milk fever, it was hard to find that peaceful place where she could leave her body. Would she be able to return to it?

"Trust me," Reothe whispered.

She wanted to ask why she should when he had lied and

manipulated her from the moment they met, yet somehow she believed she could trust him in this.

At last she was able to relax and her awareness drifted. Individual True-people called to her like beacons. As Reothe said, each one had a particular flavor. The palace servants radiated enticing fear. She paused as she came in contact with each one to draw off a little, leaving them more peaceful and herself stronger. The Ghebites were easy to identify by their rampant hostility, but strangely enough they, too, radiated fear. It was the motivating force behind their aggression.

In this state there was no up and down, yet Imoshen found she was able to orientate herself by relating back to her point of origin. Far below Sard's Tower, she found a Ghebite terrorizing one of the serving girls. The man was drunk but not drunk enough to stop him from raping her. Before he did, he wanted the girl to beg.

Revulsion filled Imoshen and she knew she had found her source. She disciplined herself to siphon off a little at a time as she milked the man's anger. Its rich and heady force urged her to drive him further but she restrained the impulse, recognizing it for her own weak craving, which she must keep secret even from Reothe.

Using this Ghebite as a source, she let one part of her awareness return to her body, consciously increasing her heart rate, lifting her temperature, until her flesh radiated heat. She used this to burn the last of the milk fever from her body.

"I could warm myself in your fires forever, Imoshen," Reothe whispered, and she understood that she was his lodestone.

Then she concentrated on maintaining body heat with the Ghebite as the source. His fires were fed by the serving girl, who suffered so that Imoshen and Reothe might live.

Revulsion roiled in Imoshen. She could not condone this. Better to release the girl from her torment. The idea was the deed. Drawing on the Ghebite's life force, she let him fall into a stupor.

As Imoshen sensed him collapse, she wondered if she had

enough in reserve to last the night. The girl gave off anger, bright as a flame. It seemed a waste not to absorb her fury.

Imoshen concentrated on opening herself to the girl, only vaguely aware of the servant's grasp on a knife. Triumph flashed through them both as the knife plunged into the unconscious Ghebite's heart. His death was rich beyond measure, for with it came the rush of his fleeing life force.

Mentally reeling with the impact, Imoshen lost all sense of self. In a leap of understanding she thought she saw the relationship between the Parakletos and the souls of the dead, and almost grasped how Imoshen the First bound them under oath. Suddenly she was aware of the Parakletos waiting in death's shadow, each curious, eager, or vengeful, according to their nature. They had been drawn to her like predators to an injured beast. They would consume her with their need. Terror engulfed Imoshen and she fled, retreating to her physical self.

"You're back!" Reothe exclaimed. "I feared your soul lost and your body consumed by fever."

Numbly, she shook her head. Pressing her fingers into her closed eyes, she rediscovered her injured hand. At least she could heal it now. "Wake me near dawn and I will try to shield us while we escape."

"Imoshen?"

But she would not answer.

The sea stopped rising when it reached Tulkhan's thighs, and the tide turned. It retreated, leaving them shivering on the embankment in ankle-deep water. The surviving men had formed a long snakelike column along the inner ramparts. Tulkhan knew that there were men on the outer ramparts, because he'd heard their cries as they fought the narcts, which even now circled, too wary to approach.

When the sea began rising again, his men became concerned.

"It will rise no further than it did before," Tulkhan assured them. "Be ready for the return of the narcts."

"I can't feel my fingers to hold my knife," the man next to Tulkhan muttered. "The narcts will have us for breakfast."

It was the coldest part of the night, when despair was closest to a man's heart. If only there was higher ground. Then it struck Tulkhan that the highest ground was the Sea-wall. Surely it was not all demolished.

"This way. We'll outwit those narcts yet!" he called. Tulkhan moved through the ranks to take the lead. Men lost their footing but their companions pulled them up. Meanwhile the narcts waited, ready to snatch the stragglers.

As Tulkhan slogged through the rising water, he prayed that the Sea-wall remained standing where it joined the ramparts. It was hard to judge distance in this watery world. The clouds had cleared and starlight revealed a flat expanse of sea, with the occasional floating island.

In the gray light of dawn, Tulkhan spotted the dark band that was the Sea-wall, rising like a causeway above the water. The incline was steep and muddy.

Tulkhan struggled up the slope onto the top of the Sea-wall, then turned to help the next man. Port Sumair rose out of the ocean surrounded by its stout walls, an island fortress. There was no sign of fire or cries of battle coming from the port. He feared for Rawset's life.

When he came to the place where the Sea-wall had been eaten away by the in-rushing ocean, he could see the silhouettes of his blockading ships. Tearing off his undershirt, he waved it above his head.

He had survived and the remnants of his army had regrouped. On this high tide, his ships, armed with their new siege machines, could come right up to the port's walls and demand its surrender. When the defenders closed the gates on Gharavan's mercenaries, they must have turned on him. Sumair would surrender his half-brother and he would return to T'Diemn triumphant.

With great reluctance, Imoshen let Reothe drag her back to awareness of her cold, miserable state. So cold...

"They will come for us soon, Imoshen. We must move."

Fear settled in the pit of her belly, and she discovered she did care if she lived or died. "When it's done, I will have nothing left." Her voice was a croak. "I'm going to cloak us."

He nodded.

Imoshen sought the most susceptible of the two minds below. She was familiar with them because of her earlier wanderings. In the guard's mind she planted the idea that the prisoners had escaped.

"They're coming. Join me, Reothe." She drew him down beside her and gripped his good hand, willing them both as white as snow. She had to hold this for only a few heartbeats. Through a veil, she saw the trapdoor swing up, sending powdered snow flying. Snow dusted the man's head.

"I tell you they can't have escaped," he was saying. Cursing, he searched the tower top.

A second head appeared. "I knew it. They flew away."

"Impossible!"

"Where are they, then?"

"More to the point, what's the Cadre going to say?"

The younger man went pale.

"Come on. We must report their escape."

They retreated, leaving the trapdoor open, and Imoshen let the illusion fall away. Already, waves of nausea washed over her.

Reothe darted across to the trapdoor. "Come, Imoshen."

Holding her tender, newly healed hand to her chest, she crawled toward him. Her whole focus was to find a warm place to lie down and sleep. She was beyond hungry.

"You can't give up now, Imoshen."

"I never give up!"

He smiled, and she realized he was deliberately baiting her.

Waiting at the base of the ladder, he looked up. "I'll steady you."

A neutral gray mist settled on her vision, so it was by feel alone that she made her way down. Reothe caught her around the waist, turning her to face him. His features swam before her. He cursed softly, then swung her over his shoulder.

She gasped indignantly. "Put me down."

He did not bother to answer. As he strode off, she gave a moan of discomfort. The floor passed under her, dimly lit, then deeply shadowed. After several twists and turns, Reothe stopped and did something to open a concealed door, then stepped inside a musty passage. He lowered her and Imoshen leaned against a cold stone wall.

"Just leave me here in the secret passage to sleep." Her words were as slurred as a drunkard's.

"I need you at my side to unite the people against the Cadre."

A wave of despair swamped Imoshen. "I used my gifts to kill Jarholfe in front of the Beatific. She will have me stoned!"

"Engarad's a pragmatist. We'll go to her now."

He went to lift her again, but Imoshen refused. She did not want to arrive at the Beatific's door carried like a sack of potatoes.

Reothe led her on a short trip through the secret passages to his own rooms. "If we are to defeat the Cadre we must look like conquerors." He turned her toward the bathing room. "Go wash. I'll get dressed."

She would have loved a warm bath, but there was no time. Her skin looked thin and there were dark circles under her eyes. So much had happened since she stepped off the ship. At least Kalleen and Ashmyr were safe. The Cadre would have boasted if they'd found her son.

"Ready?" Reothe scratched at the door.

Imoshen came out to find clothes laid on the bed.

"My boots will be too big. Try the indoor slippers."

He went into the bathing room and she heard him curse. "They've butchered my hair!"

Imoshen smiled. Reothe had been raised in the high court of the old empire, where a person dressed and spoke with elegance. Spots floated in her vision. It was an effort to remember to breathe.

"Ready?" Reothe asked when he returned. She had not even started to change her clothes. "Dreamer!"

Despite her protests, he tore off the damp underdress and helped her into trousers, shirt, and tabard, all slightly too big. Then he knelt at her feet to draw the laces of the indoor slippers tightly about her ankles. Reothe's lowered head revealed raw scalp. Imoshen touched his head, longing to heal him completely.

He looked up, smiling. "There. Bit loose but better than nothing."

"Reothe," Imoshen whispered. "I am not worthy of you."

He gave an odd laugh. "Come."

It was imperative that they seize the moment. The trip through the secret passages filtered in and out of her awareness as she fought the encroaching fog of exhaustion. She found herself watching Reothe's back, willing her body to keep moving.

He paused at an intersection. "This leads straight to the basilica. How do you think I used to meet Engarad?"

Imoshen wished she had her wits about her to memorize the way. After what seemed an interminable walk, Reothe led her up several narrow flights of stairs, then stopped.

"I must leave you here to find the Beatific."

Imoshen nodded, noting how he opened the hidden door. She waited. When she judged he had gone far enough, she tripped the door's mechanism and followed him. Imoshen did not want the Beatific and Reothe making bargains without her.

Though she felt flat and stale without her gift, she had no trouble following Reothe discreetly. She saw him hesitate at a door where a sentry waited, too interested in what was going on inside the room to notice Reothe until it was too late.

Reothe caught the man around the neck and pulled him backward into an anteroom. When Reothe reappeared, he was holding the man's sword in his maimed left hand. With a curse, he transferred it to his right hand. He felt its weight and balance thoughtfully before stepping into the Beatific's room.

Even from the end of the hall, Imoshen could hear the

raised voices. Eager to miss nothing, she hurried after
Reothe. There was an untouched food tray on the chair by
the door. Ravenous, Imoshen drained the wine, then
grabbed the bowl of stew and a freshly baked bun.

Hugging the bowl to her chest with her tender left
hand, she peered through the open door. The room was lit
by a branch of candles, which sat on a desk. A roaring fire
was built up in the hearth. It was the Beatific's private sanc-
tum, richly decorated with thick carpets and intricately
carved wood panels picked out in gold leaf, yet it looked
lived in, with papers strewn on the desk and a discarded
overgown draped across a chair.

Imoshen longed to lie down before the fire and sleep,
but Reothe held the sword at the Cadre's throat. The man
backed up until he came to the far wall. They did not notice
Imoshen, who hid in the shadows, devouring the stew.

"You can't kill him here!" the Beatific protested.

"Where do you want me to kill him?" Reothe asked.

The Cadre squeaked.

"He's the head of the Ghebite Church and must be
dealt with according to the laws of Fair Isle."

"Law and order did not help us when the Orb declared
Imoshen innocent."

The Beatific stepped from behind her desk. "I was
working on freeing you."

"And Imoshen?"

The leader of the T'En Church hesitated.

Reothe spared her a hard glance. "She saved your life,
Engarad."

"Imoshen killed a True-man with her gift, Reothe."

"It was self-defense. And she saved you from the Orb's
power!" His tone scalded. "Hurry, Beatific. My arm grows
weary!"

"I have not signed the decree. In the eyes of the Church,
you aren't rogue and neither is Imoshen—yet."

"Don't threaten me, Engarad. When I entered this
room you were the Cadre's prisoner and he was bullying
you into signing away the rights of the Church." Reothe

lifted the sword point until the Cadre strained on tiptoes to avoid it. "We must rid ourselves of this malignant fool. At least the General is a statesman, not a fanatic!"

"I am ready to die for my beliefs!" the Cadre insisted.

"Then let me oblige you," Reothe growled.

"No, Reothe!" Imoshen crossed the room. She felt the Cadre's angry glare as she put the empty bowl on the Beatific's desk. "Tulkhan must be the one who orders the Cadre's death. Only that will legitimize our position."

The Beatific and Reothe exchanged glances.

"What of the Cadre's supporters? Jarholfe's men fought pitched battles in the palace corridors," the Beatific said. "They displayed the bodies of your Parakhan Guard in the square."

Anger boiled through Imoshen, but she would not think of her people's pointless slaughter.

The Beatific tilted her head as the basilica's bells heralded the hour. "Dawn. Our people will strike now. Without a leader, the Ghebites will not stand long."

But Imoshen was fast losing track of the conversation. The fire's heat combined with the food swamped her senses, and the room swayed about her.

"Where will we imprison the Cadre? On Sard's Tower?" Reothe asked.

"No, in the basilica," Imoshen mumbled. "The Cadre's greatest crime is against the laws of Fair Isle. He threatened the right of every individual to a fair trial. The Beatific must lay charges against him on behalf of the Church."

"True," the Beatific agreed. "I—"

But Imoshen heard no more. The carpet met her face with a suddenness that should have hurt but didn't.

The General strode the deck of Peirs's ship, impatient to be moving. His worst fears were confirmed when he learned that Rawset had never delivered his message.

Tulkhan gripped the seasoned wood of the ship's sides. Before him, Sumair rose from the ocean. Its church spires and pointed roofs reflected in the sea, which was as smooth as glass on this cold, still morning.

He had dressed in borrowed armor and eaten a hot breakfast. But the horrors of the night so narrowly escaped still pressed on him.

"Everything is ready, General," Peirs announced.

"Sound the attack."

With no wind to fill the sails, the men had to row. As he watched, the other ships turned their prows toward the island port. Cumbersome with their new siege machinery, the ships bore down on Port Sumair like great beasts of prey, slow but inexorable.

Tulkhan imagined the feelings of the port's defenders and relished this moment. All night he had listened to his men's screams as they fought the narcts. The townsfolk had broken the Sea-wall knowing the beasts would finish what the flood began.

While they approached the walls, Tulkhan studied the port's defenses through the farseer, watching the hurried consultations of gathered heads on the parapets and the frantic signaling from tower to tower. Tulkhan closed the farseer with a snap and looked up at the siege machine's hide, which was made of beaten metal wrapped around braced wood. With this protection they could come abreast of the walls, attack the defenses directly, and throw ladders across to the parapets.

"They're surrendering!" Peirs pointed.

Fierce elation filled Tulkhan. He felt the same rush of conquest as he had known when the Spar fell to him. Then he had shown no mercy, putting everyone to the sword, and his father's war advisers had respected him for it. In his mind's eye he saw himself kneeling before his father to receive Generalship over all the Ghebite army. But it wasn't his father he imagined turning to him from the royal dais this time—it was Imoshen. Disgustedly, she pointed to his hands, covered in the blood of the defenseless women and children he had ordered slain. "Murderer!"

The people of the Spar had been fighting for their freedom.

He had quashed their rebellion in his father's name, but it had been his choice to do murder. Revulsion filled Tulkhan.

His vision cleared to see Port Sumair glistening in the early-morning sun. A slight breeze had sprung up, rippling the lucid, mirrorlike surface of the water, flapping the pennants on the spires, and drawing his gaze to the flag of surrender.

"I'll take the ship alongside," Peirs announced. "You can accept their surrender on the ramparts."

Only a few heartbeats had elapsed from the first sighting of the surrender. Tulkhan's shattering revelation had taken no time at all. He felt cold and hollow. He was a murderer tens of thousands of times over. While he could not bring back those innocent lives, he could deal differently with the people of Port Sumair.

The walls drew nearer as the sailors on the siege tower prepared to throw lines across. The gentlest of swells made the ship's deck lift and fall.

"How many men do you want at your back?" Peirs asked.

Tulkhan cast his gaze over the assembled soldiers and indicated a dozen men. "Come with me."

Their low, eager voices sounded as they followed him up the ladder. Stepping out into the sunshine, he walked across the plank onto the walls of Port Sumair, victorious once again, but he was a very different man from the brash, hubris-filled youth who had ordered the slaughter of the defenders of the Spar. Tulkhan had looked into the dark night of the soul and discovered he did not like what he found.

Half a dozen port dignitaries dressed in the heavy brocaded collars and half skirts of Low-land merchants waited anxiously.

Behind him, Tulkhan heard the chink of the soldiers' armor and weapons as they took up position. He leapt down onto the walkway. "Where is Gharavan?" Only when he asked this did he realize how much he dreaded confronting his half-brother. He had no choice but to order his death. One death, no more.

A man stepped forward, gray with fear. He bowed low,

as was the Low-land custom. "General Protector of Fair Isle. As Elector of Port Sumair, I want you to know that we did not choose to side with the Ghebite King. He arrived with his mercenaries and took up residence in our town."

"Where is he?"

The man exchanged looks with his companions and lifted his arms in a very Low-land gesture of helplessness. "He escaped sometime last night after the Sea-wall went down."

Tulkhan cursed. He should have expected his cowardly half-brother would ensure his own survival. "What of the Ghebite soldiers who were with him?"

"Those who did not escape with their king are safely locked away, awaiting your pleasure." The Elector looked relieved to report this. "Execution by drowning is the Lowland way."

"I'll make that decision."

"We do have one prisoner you will want to see," another merchant volunteered eagerly. "Captain Kornel."

"Take me to him."

But when they escorted him to Kornel's cell, Tulkhan found the captain had escaped his revenge. Kornel had hung himself by his belt from the cell bars.

The port officials apologized profusely. They took Kornel's body down, tied his corpse to a chair in the Elector's square, and had Tulkhan pronounce sentence. Then, as though the traitor still lived, they suspended Kornel's body over the wall and lowered it into the sea until he was pronounced drowned.

Tulkhan went along with all of this, understanding intuitively that it served the purpose of expiating the man's sins. It was evident his own men took comfort from the procedure. Tulkhan's hand went to his chest, where the messages from Imoshen had lain, but they had been lost in the flood, along with his grandfather's sword. He felt the loss keenly.

Kornel's bizarre trial and execution over, Tulkhan turned to the Elector. "Now, about the terms of surrender."

Sixteen

WHEN IMOSHEN AWOKE she knew by the pattern of sunlight on the polished wooden floor that it was mid-afternoon. Ashmyr's soft crow of laughter struck her as significant. Then it all came back to her and she sat up to find herself in her own chamber. Reothe leaned against the far bedpost, watching Kalleen play with Ashmyr. A wave of relief rolled over Imoshen.

"You wake at last." Reothe greeted her with a smile.

It was so normal, as if the Cadre's attempted coup had been nothing but a bad dream; then she noticed Reothe's maimed left hand and she knew they had all barely escaped death. "Kalleen, bring Ashmyr. What's been happening in T'Diemn?"

Reothe stepped aside as Kalleen came to the bed. But when Imoshen took her son in her arms and bared her breast, she discovered her milk was gone, burned up by the fever. Ashmyr gave an indignant yell.

"Never fear," Kalleen said. "I will feed him."

Imoshen blinked back tears. Her arms ached to hold her son. Had she been alone, she would have wept with gratitude to have Ashmyr safely returned. "Where did you hide, Kalleen?"

"With the guild-master of the silversmiths." Kalleen tested the warmth of the milk and settled the baby. "Don't rush, you'll get wind, my greedy boy."

Reothe laughed softly.

Imoshen had to remind herself that he was still the enemy, but he did not feel like an enemy. "What has happened since I feel asleep this morning?"

"That was yesterday morning," Reothe said. "I appointed Drake Shujen of the Parakhan Guard. They scoured the palace and the old city, searching for the Ghebites who had turned against us. I fear many a Ghebite soldier is still in hiding."

"It will not serve us if those loyal to Tulkhan are killed, Reothe. And Shujen? I don't know that term."

He gave her a secretive smile. "In Imoshen the First's time a Shujen led Paragian Guard."

"I don't remember that part," Kalleen remarked absently.

Reothe was quoting from T'Elegos, teasing Imoshen with glimpses of their hidden heritage. "Shujen is an old High T'En word for commander. As for these Ghebites, the Beatific has been trying them by the laws of Fair Isle, which is probably more of a hearing than they would have given us."

Imoshen bowed her head in the knowledge that he was right.

"This morning the Beatific declared the trials over and the gates were opened. The people of T'Diemn poured into the old city by the thousands. The square is packed. They want to see you for themselves."

"Let me bathe and eat," she said, and Reothe gave her the old-empire obeisance reserved for the Empress, then left them. "How is Lord Fairban?"

Kalleen's face fell.

"When?"

"This morning. He was old. You did all you could. May the Parakletos guide his soul."

Imoshen kept her silence. The old saying no longer offered her comfort. She padded across the room to kneel at Kalleen's side and gaze on her son.

Tentatively, she stroked the baby's fine, dark hair. It hurt to see Ashmyr feeding peacefully in Kalleen's arms, oblivious to her. He stopped sucking long enough to regard her seriously, deigned to smile, then returned to the teat.

"He is a charmer," Kalleen remarked.

Pain twisted inside Imoshen. He was *her* son. She would die for him, had nearly died protecting him from Jarholfe. She forced herself to banish the resentment.

Imoshen met Kalleen's eyes. "You saved my son. I am forever in your debt. I will watch over you and yours all the days of my life."

It was a deliberate reversal of the usual custom of assuming responsibility for the life saved.

Kalleen's face grew solemn as she took in the significance of this pledge. Tears of sorrow filled her eyes. "I could not let them kill Ashmyr too!"

Suddenly Imoshen remembered that Wharrd had died protecting her honor. Helplessly, she opened her mouth, but no words came.

"The man of my heart died in the service of the Empress. I wanted to hate her," Kalleen whispered. "But I cannot."

A sob escaped Kalleen, and Imoshen embraced her. They both wept freely. Finally, Imoshen smoothed the tear-damp hair from Kalleen's face, kissing her. "Bless the day you fell at my feet. I'm proud to call you friend."

"It is hard to be a friend of the T'En."

Imoshen managed a rueful smile. "It is hard to be the last of the T'En."

Kalleen gave a short laugh and held up the baby. "Take him while I run your bath and lay out your clothes."

Imoshen cradled Ashmyr, delighting in his soft skin and the smell of him. "You don't have to be my maid, Kalleen."

"I do what I do because I choose to," she replied, and Imoshen understood it would always be this way with her.

Kalleen went into the room beyond and Imoshen heard the water running. Alone at last, she held her son and gave thanks that they had both survived the Ghebites' treachery.

Tulkhan watched the Low-land dancers perform for the assembled port officials and his commanders. Lightfoot, back from the dead, sat opposite. Only this morning the townspeople of Port Sumair had gone out in their boats to scour the drowned land for survivors. Lightfoot had been found clinging to a church spire.

Upon reporting to Tulkhan, he said that even though he had abandoned religion long ago, it had not abandoned him, then he had fainted from cold and lack of food.

Silently, Tulkhan now raised his wineglass to the grizzled mercenary, who returned the gesture. Tulkhan saw a word leave his lips. *Rawset*.

The youth had not been found, and now it was unlikely he would be discovered alive. Tulkhan scowled. A high price had been paid for this victory. He was impatient to return to Fair Isle, but the signing of the terms of surrender had to be celebrated. He tried to show an interest in the performance, as several dancers wearing long blue-green gowns swirled around others, engulfing them.

"Those dancers represent the sea?" Tulkhan asked.

The old man next to him nodded. "We Low-landers do not worship the sea, nor do we fear it, but we do respect it. The dancers in white symbolize the moons, which govern the tides."

Tulkhan nodded. He had been speaking with Sumair's engineers about the enormous job of draining the flooded land. It had been made clear to him that the breaking of the Sea-wall had been deliberately delayed until it would do the most damage. That it happened to coincide with Kornel's betrayal was all the better from the Low-landers' point of view.

"Before spring we will have the Sea-wall rebuilt and the land ready for planting," the old man said.

"So much work."

Faded eyes studied him. "I will speak plainly. You have been generous in your terms of surrender, General Tulkhan, offering the service of your men to rebuild. But we do not regret flooding our land. It is the price we pay for freedom.

We wrest our land from the sea, and if we choose to return it to the sea, that is our business."

Holding Ashmyr, Imoshen stepped onto the balcony over-looking the square. As she raised her left arm and gave the Empress's blessing, a sibilant sigh of relief swept the crowd. A minstrel struck up an old-empire song of praise and the crowd joined in. Tears stung Imoshen's eyes. This was her home, her people, and they had not deserted her.

When the song came to an end, she raised her voice, willing it to carry across the square, aware that the words would be carried across Fair Isle. "People of T'Diemn, I thank the Beatific for upholding the laws of the T'En Church. And I thank Drake and the Parakhan Guard for standing true. Though the Cadre and the Ghebite usurpers are vanquished, we are not safe. Fair Isle faces a time of tra-vail as dangerous as the Age of Tribulation. This is why I am reviving an old branch of the Church. Today I recreate the T'Enplar warriors. And I appoint T'Reothe, Sword of Justice, leader of the T'Enplars."

She smiled at the crowd's joyous reaction. Reothe's tan-talizing mention of the T'Elegos had made Imoshen think. Recreating the T'Enplars appealed to her sense of history. When Imoshen the First's death released the survivors of the Paragian Guard from their oath of service, they had sought service with her daughter, the pure T'En woman who became Fair Isle's first Beatific. She had formed the original T'Enplar warriors.

Imoshen turned to the Beatific and Reothe. She was protecting him with the mantle of the Church's power. "When General Tulkhan returns, I don't want him to find you in the palace, Reothe."

His face was a mask. Imoshen held her left hand out to the Beatific. Though Engarad inclined her head and kissed the sixth finger, her mind remained closed to Imoshen. By the glint of triumph in her golden True-woman's eyes, Imoshen knew that the Beatific believed she had made a wrong move in the game of power. The Beatific supported her only so long as it suited her own goals.

In a way she was grateful to the Cadre and Jarholfe for weeding out those Ghebites most loyal to the old way of thinking. She would tell Wharrd to—Imoshen almost staggered as his loss hit her. She had not realized how much she had come to depend on the veteran bone-setter.

In a daze of grief, she left the balcony to find the palace over-servants awaiting her. She spoke to each one, thanking them for their loyalty. When she came to the woman who ruled the kitchen, she paused to order food and drink to be distributed in the square. At last she came to Keeper Karmel, and Imoshen led the old woman into the library. "You risked your life in my service. Is there anything you want or need?"

The woman pondered, then a cunning look came over her face. "I want access to the basilica's archives. For years the Master-archivist has jealously guarded them."

Imoshen laughed. "T'Reothe will see that you have it."

She returned to her room to write to Tulkhan. Her message would leave with the evening tide, and she had to trust a new emissary. She missed Rawset.

Without anything being said, Kalleen moved into her old room next to Imoshen's, and the days passed in a rush of activity. The families of the murdered Parakhan Guard had to be notified and provision made for their future. Imoshen rewarded Drake's initiative and loyalty by giving him the official title of Shujen. The Parakhan Guard's numbers were greatly depleted. Townspeople wanted to be compensated for the destruction of property.

Imoshen's head spun with the complications. Frightened Ghebites kept coming out of hiding, and she had to consult with the Beatific on how they should be treated. Simply returning the men to the community was dangerous for their own safety. A hundred times a day Wharrd's loss returned to her with renewed pain. Kalleen mourned privately, spending most of her time with Ashmyr.

Someone knocked at the door. Imoshen looked up from her desk with a sigh. "Enter."

"General Tulkhan!" Kalleen gasped, and Imoshen nearly upset the inkwell.

The General strode into the room, making it seem small. She longed to feel his arms around her and the sight of him made her heart race with joy, but when she spoke her throaty voice did not reveal this. "You are returned sooner than expected, General."

"Port Sumair has fallen."

"When?"

"These five days past."

Imoshen blinked. The port must have fallen around the time she and Reothe regained the capital. It appeared her messenger had missed the General and he was not aware of Jarholfe and the Cadre's treachery.

"I bring you victory and you grow pale as milk. What is it?"

Imoshen signaled Kalleen to take Ashmyr into the far room. But before she could do this, Tulkhan strode past both women. He picked up his son, who gnawed anxiously on his fist.

"He's teething," Imoshen explained.

"He looks just like any other baby."

"You mean apart from his T'En eyes and his six fingers?" she asked, then wished the words unsaid.

Tulkhan was not amused. "Kalleen, take my son for now."

Imoshen's mouth went dry. A charged silence filled the room as Kalleen took the boy from the General and retreated. She held Imoshen's eyes just before she closed the door, and Imoshen knew if help was needed, Kalleen would come. That was typical of her, loyal and outspoken. Loyal, like . . .

"Wharrd is dead," Imoshen confessed. Tulkhan looked stunned. She knew how he treasured the veteran's friendship. Tears burned her eyes as she sought to comfort him. "It happened while I was returning from the Amirate. There was nothing I could do."

A great rushing filled Tulkhan's head. He could hardly think. "H-how did it happen?"

"Jarholfe and the Cadre forced Wharrd to defend my honor."

"As your Ghiad he could not do otherwise," Tulkhan muttered. "What possessed them?"

"They wanted a legal excuse to have me executed."

Jarholfe had acted on his suspicions even though Tulkhan had ignored the man's messages. He pulled away from Imoshen, suddenly aware that her hand rested on his arm; who knew what she might be gleaning from the contact?

"The Cadre and Jarholfe tried to force the Beatific to sign a declaration to have Reothe and me stoned," Imoshen revealed.

Her words drummed in his head, the import too much to absorb. He paced to the fireplace, gripping the mantelpiece in both hands. One thing was clear to him: The Cadre and Jarholfe had caused Wharrd's death. He spun to face Imoshen. "Where are they now?"

"Jarholfe is dead, but the Cadre is being held by the Beatific for crimes against Fair Isle. Where do you go?"

He thrust past her, heading for the door, and Imoshen fell into step at his side. Despite her height, she had to take extra skipping steps to keep up with him. He found the man he wanted waiting in the hall outside.

"Lightfoot, send a message to the Beatific. She is to escort the Cadre into the square. I want twenty of my Elite Guard in full uniform and I want them in the square in half an hour. Tell them to bring the dueling swords."

"Lightfoot," Imoshen caught his sleeve. "Drake is leader of the Parakhan Guard. Convey the General's message to him."

In the heat of the moment Tulkhan had forgotten that Imoshen had disbanded his Elite Guard.

"Jarholfe's Ghebites hunted down our people, Tulkhan. They displayed their bodies in the square."

He was eager to translate anger into action.

She hurried after him. "General, wait. Do you intend to fight a duel with the Cadre?"

"If he has the stomach for it." He headed down the steps with Imoshen at his heels.

"But, General, the Cadre has broken the laws of Fair Isle. As leader of the T'En Church, the Beatific must preside over his trial. Your role should be to advise on punishment. You are the wronged party. Not only you but Kalleen and her un-born child have been wronged. Slow down and listen, Tulkhan!" She caught his arm before he could throw open the small door to the square. "Think of your position. As Protector General of Fair Isle, you set the tone for the whole island. If you resort to violence, you are no better than the Cadre and Jarholfe, who ignored the letter of the law when the Orb of Truth proclaimed my innocence!"

"My men expect me to act swiftly and decisively against any threat to my leadership." He thrust the door open, then stopped, surprised to see the square full of townspeople, gathered in the early-morning sunshine. The season's first snow had melted, but the air was cold and crisp. The smell of roasting nuts and cinnamon-apples came to him, and he realized some quick-thinking merchants had set up stalls.

"They expect a celebration, General. Your men will have spread the good news by now. They want to honor your victory over your half-brother."

"He escaped. The merchant fathers of the port dropped the Sea-wall and nearly drowned my entire army. Do you call that victory?"

Imoshen's mouth opened, but someone recognized them standing on the steps and the shout went up.

Reacting to the cheers, Imoshen threaded her arm through his, drawing him down into the square. "Smile, General. In their eyes you are victorious. Let appearance become substance."

He found himself walking through a crowd of well-wishers. They came from every strata of T'Diemn society, from street sweepers to rich merchants, from blue-fingered cloth dyers to gray-haired masters from the Halls of Learning. And all of them wanted to touch him. This time he was as sought after as Imoshen. He felt an unexpected sense of homecoming.

The rush and surge of the crowd carried them across the square. The clamor of voices drowned out individual comments, but the tone was one of welcome, and still they pressed. Was every citizen of T'Diemn here today?

Imoshen sensed intense scrutiny and lifted her gaze above the throng to find Reothe watching her. Only the thin line of his mouth revealed his fury. His eyes were hooded by shadowy sockets of a half-face helmet. The ceremonial T'Enplar weaponry looked as if it was made for him. Imoshen felt Reothe's silent accusation of betrayal like a physical assault. Her heart contracted as the dual tug of loyalties tore her apart.

Reothe marched through the crowd toward them, followed by his T'Enplar warriors. The townsfolk reacted with instinctive awe to the sight of the last T'En warrior and his supporters resplendent in ornate chest plates, embroidered cloaks, and half-face helmets complete with dyed horsehair crest. The armor dated from the middle of the Age of Consolidation, when Fair Isle's ceremonial weaponry was designed for display.

Imoshen felt the jolt of recognition run through Tulkhan's body when he saw Reothe. People kept moving back so that suddenly the three of them stood alone in a sea of watchers.

Knobs of fury moved under the skin of Reothe's jaw. The moment stretched impossibly. Imoshen willed him not to antagonize the General, who was primed for violence.

"Protector General Tulkhan, Lady Protector." The Beatific stepped into the silence, sweeping them a regal obeisance that claimed as much honor for herself as it accorded to them. She was dressed in full regalia. Her mantle of rich velvet brushed the cobbles as she bowed, and the tassels of her ornate headdress dipped and swayed as she straightened.

"All of T'Diemn speaks of your munificence, General. When you could have ordered death, you showed mercy. The people of Port Sumair will remember your restraint." A priest approached and the Beatific inclined her head to listen to his report. They had arrived with chairs and a large, portable dais. "My people are ready. I must prepare for the trial."

Imoshen was relieved. With her usual acumen, the Beatific had stepped in to prevent General Tulkhan's execution of the Cadre by trial of combat.

"Protector General Tulkhan." Reothe delivered the old-empire military salute, lifting his sword hilt to his forehead then resheathing the weapon. "I stand before you, the Church's Sword of Justice, leader of the T'Enplar warriors, to deliver the prisoner, the Ghebite Cadre." Behind Reothe, a dozen T'Enplars in matching armor repeated his salute.

Imoshen thought she recognized some of them and doubted very much if their loyalty was to the Beatific. It seemed Reothe's rebels had found redemption in service to the Church. As for the Cadre, he stood unrestrained in their midst, his hate-filled eyes fixed on Imoshen.

A flash of mulberry robe in the crowd reminded Imoshen of Murgon and his Tractarians. As Sword of Justice, Reothe was on the same level of the Church hierarchy as Murgon. While he had been leading the rebels, Reothe had received covert support from the Church. She wondered how those canny brokers of power would react to finding him in their midst. Imoshen did not envy Reothe his position. But, then, she did not covet her own position either.

"Sword of Justice?" Tulkhan muttered.

"I recreated the T'Enplar warriors and appointed Reothe to this position. They serve the Beatific to uphold the laws of Fair Isle—your laws, General."

But Tulkhan knew they weren't his laws. Most of the laws of Fair Isle were unknown to him—this production, for instance. It appeared the Beatific was preparing to stage a trial when he had intended a quick, lethal duel.

The crowd parted as Lightfoot arrived with the Parakhan Guard. The mercenary moved to stand behind Tulkhan. Drake approached Imoshen and Tulkhan, offering his salute to both of them before opening a case in which rested two swords on a bed of black velvet.

"Violence was ever the Ghebite way." Reothe's voice dripped scorn.

"We Ghebites may not be as civilized as the T'En, but we protect what is our own." Tulkhan held Reothe's eyes across the dueling swords.

Reothe's features revealed his understanding but they held no deference. Tulkhan seethed. Didn't Reothe know he lived on sufferance?

A muscle jumped in Tulkhan's cheek. He could not order Reothe's execution. His army was scattered from Fair Isle to Port Sumair. He was surrounded by townsfolk who could just as easily turn on him if the hereditary heirs of Fair Isle tried to reclaim the throne.

"General?" Imoshen held his eyes. "There is more than Wharrd's death at stake here. What the people witness today will travel all over Fair Isle on the lips of the minstrels. Do you want them to sing of barbaric bloodshed or of the justice shown by the Protector General of Fair Isle?"

Even though Imoshen was right, he was annoyed that she dared to counsel him before others. But, then, she was not a Ghebite female. She was T'En, more royal than the Empress herself.

"Here comes Kalleen with the Empress's heir!" a voice cried, and the crowd parted to let Kalleen through.

"I see you brought T'Ashmyr, Lady Kalleen. Good," the Beatific said as she rejoined them. "His life was also threatened. Come, everyone, take your places on the dais. We are ready to proceed."

A church servant waited with a silk shade cunningly stretched over supple wood. He held it above the Beatific to keep off the sun as she took her seat. Tulkhan glared at the man who would have held a similar piece of nonsense over him, but Imoshen did not remonstrate. She and Kalleen sat in the shade of the Church's beneficence as the trial began with Reothe reading the charges. His words fell in absolute silence. The people of T'Diemn seemed to find this real-life drama better than any Thespers' Guild performance.

"How do you plead?" the Beatific asked when Reothe had finished.

"Yes, speak up, Cadre," Tulkhan urged.

The T'Enplar warriors had stepped back to form a semi-circle behind the Cadre. Behind them the Parakhan Guard formed a larger semicircle, and beyond them was the crowd. People stood on wagons, clustered on balconies surrounding the square, and filled the air with their expectancy.

The Cadre was dressed in his stained surplice, but his stance was not one of defeat. Raising his hand, he gestured to the Beatific, his eyes alight with the fervor of fanaticism. "I do not acknowledge this female. It has been proven that women's weak souls are channels for evil. I appeal to you, General Tulkhan." He stepped closer to the edge of the dais, which was thigh-high. "Do not forget the ways of your father's people. It was your honor I was defending, and your dishonor that I sought to erase. This..." His voice grew scathing as he pointed to Imoshen. "This Dhamfeer killed Jarholfe with her vile sorcery. She should be stoned. She, her half-breed brat, and her lover should all be—"

"Enough!" Tulkhan roared. He ached to choke the poison from the priest's tongue.

Imoshen's voice cut through Tulkhan's fury like cold water on hot coals. "I call on Maigeth, guild-master of the silversmiths, to speak for me. It was her honor to hold the Orb."

In that instant Tulkhan understood that to kill the Cadre would not remove the accusations. Imoshen had to be *seen* to be cleared of these crimes.

"Come here, Silversmith Maigeth," the Beatific ordered.

"Yes. Step forward," Tulkhan urged, determined to wrest control of the proceedings from the Beatific.

The spectators parted to let the woman approach the dais.

"Can you vouch for Imoshen's innocence?" Tulkhan asked.

"I can, and so can everyone else who was there that day. We all saw the Orb glow bright with the light of truth." The words fell from the woman's tongue as though she was speaking an ancient formula, making Tulkhan recall the Orb of Truth, which Imoshen had acknowledged as part of the crowning ceremony.

The crowd sighed and whispered in agreement.

"I say the Orb lied!" the Cadre cried.

People gasped. Sacrilege!

"Can the Orb lie?" Tulkhan asked the Beatific.

"All those who tried to use it to further their own ends died horrible deaths, in fear for their immortal souls."

Again the crowd voiced its agreement.

"Then bring forth this Orb and let everyone see if the Cadre will venture his soul on the truth!" Tulkhan ordered.

The townspeople went strangely silent. Even the Cadre looked down. Tulkhan turned to the Beatific for an explanation.

She glared at the Ghebite priest. "The Cadre smashed our holy relic!"

"It was the Cadre who released the Orb's essence," Reothe said. "He is responsible for freeing the ancient power that killed Jarholfe, not Imoshen."

"She killed a True-man with her vile T'En gifts," the Cadre crowed. "And by the Church's own law she must die. Deny me that, Beatific!"

Silence hung heavy on the air.

Suddenly Imoshen sprang to her feet. "I call on Murgon, leader of the Tractarians."

Reothe sent Imoshen a charged look that Tulkhan found hard to interpret, but the Beatific was already calling for Murgon.

When Murgon stepped from the throng, Tulkhan tried to place the man. He had the T'En eyes and wore deep-purple robes. Suddenly he recalled Murgon's malevolent gaze as Imoshen knelt on their coronation day to give her oath of Expiation.

"I ask only that you speak the truth, Murgon," Imoshen told him.

The man's mouth worked as if he chewed on something

bitter. "I saw T'Imoshen breathe death into Jarholfe's body. She killed him as surely as—"

"She killed in self-defense after saving the Beatific," Reothe insisted.

But the crowd stirred, unable to deny the ancient law. Tulkhan saw it all slipping away from him. He met Imoshen's eyes and knew it was true. She had killed Jarholfe. The *why* of it did not matter. It was the *how* that would be her death.

"No! Not Empress T'Imoshen!" a new voice cried.

Tulkhan spun to see a weatherworn member of the Parakhan Guard push through the T'Enplars. Sibilant whispers echoed. *Empress T'Imoshen, Empress T'Imoshen...*

"I am the blind man who sees, and I will be heard!" the Parakhan Guard announced.

"Speak," Tulkhan directed.

The man looked at each of them in turn, meeting Tulkhan's eyes last.

"I am the blind man who sees," he repeated, gesturing to his eyes. "And these eyes of mine see beyond the Ghebite priest's lies, beyond the Tractarian's half truths. I see our Empress, who has served Fair Isle in honor. I also acknowledge the old laws of Fair Isle. A True-man died by the T'Imoshen's gift." As he unsheathed his sword, the shrill sound rang on the silence. "I assume the guilt for the death of the Ghebite, and through my own death absolve the Empress of all—"

"No!" Thursting Ashmyr into Kalleen's arms, Imoshen ran to the edge of the dais. "I won't let you die in my place!"

The crowd moaned like a wounded beast.

Imoshen lifted her hands, pleading for their understanding. "People of T'Diemn, I used my gift to pass on the Orb's essence and it killed Jarholfe, but this was self-defense. And the Beatific knows this. I call on the Beatific to look into her heart and ask herself if she is not here today because I saved her life. Am I to be condemned because I saved our lives in exchange for the Ghebite's?"

As the Beatific reluctantly joined Imoshen on the edge of the dais, her servant kept pace with her so that she remained under the silken shade's protection. Imoshen went down on both knees, lifting her hands palms up in the deep-supplication obeisance. "You have the power to absolve me, Engarad. Look into your heart."

The Beatific flinched. Her lips parted. Tulkhan could tell she was going to pardon Imoshen.

"No!" The Cadre snatched the blind man's sword.

Tulkhan drew his knife but could not risk a throw. Imoshen was between him and the Cadre.

Time slowed.

Helplessly, Tulkhan watched Imoshen hurl herself backward as the Cadre leapt onto the dais. He stood over her. His sword blade flashed in the autumn sun. Tulkhan threw his knife. Even as it left his hand, the tip of a ceremonial sword sprouted from the Cadre's chest, slender blade quivering. Tulkhan's knife struck home. The Cadre collapsed on Imoshen's thighs.

Tulkhan hauled Imoshen upright, spinning her to face him. For a heartbeat her eyes were windows to her soul. Tulkhan had seen that look before on the faces of men who had survived death against all odds.

"Death stalks me," she whispered, "claiming others when I escape."

Dimly, Tulkhan heard the exclamations of the crowd.

Reothe crossed the dais and knelt at the Cadre's side to retrieve his sword, which he had thrown like a spear.

"Good throw," Tulkhan said.

"Surprising, considering." Reothe flexed the fingers of his left hand. Tulkhan was struck by its malformation.

"Dead?" The Beatific did not deign to examine the Cadre.

"Dead," Reothe confirmed as he cleaned his sword.

"What happened?" Tulkhan flexed his own hand.

"The Cadre envied me my six fingers, so he removed a few," Reothe said, then leapt down from the dais, gesturing to his T'Enplars. "Take the traitor's body away."

"Wait!" Tulkhan ordered. "Say the words, Beatific."

She looked confused.

"Say the words. Condemn the Cadre!" The effect of Kornel's trial and execution after his death had not escaped Tulkhan. He wanted Imoshen absolved of all guilt so these events could not be used against her in the future. "Speak loudly, Beatific. I want all of Fair Isle to know that Imoshen is absolved of guilt."

The Beatific made this declaration and the crowd looked on as justice was seen to be done. Then the T'Enplar warriors carried the Cadre's body away.

Imoshen beckoned Kalleen. Retrieving her son, she turned to Tulkhan. "Protector General, Kalleen's quick thinking saved our son. Wharrd's widow carries his unborn child. All of his estates are now hers in accordance with the laws of the T'En Church. Wharrd died in our service. Such loyalty deserves reward."

"I want no reward," Kalleen protested, her eyes glittering with unshed tears. She bit back an angry sob. "I held Wharrd in my arms as he died. Nothing can restore him to me. Nothing!"

Imoshen shifted her son to one hip and hugged Kalleen. Seeing the two women embrace, Tulkhan was struck anew by the loss of his old friend. When he looked away, he noticed that the Beatific was watching him closely.

Imoshen pressed her cheek to Kalleen's and whispered urgently, "Every woman in Fair Isle depends on us. The Cadre is dead, but his thinking lives on. General Tulkhan must acknowledge your rights of ownership and your right to Wharrd's estates. We cannot let Ghebite thinking disinherit the women of Fair Isle. Do you understand why I do this?"

Kalleen met Imoshen's eyes, hers glowing with fury. "You use me for your own ends!"

"The higher we rise, the more we serve," Imoshen reprimanded. When she slid her arm through the General's, she felt the tension in his body. "As the Beatific is our witness, General, we must reward Kalleen. In Fair Isle the punishment for treason is death and forfeiture of lands and titles."

"It is the same in Gheeaba," Tulkhan conceded.

"Then it is only fitting you reward Kalleen with the estates and titles Jarholfe held. The Beatific can have the new deeds and titles drawn up."

"It will be done." The Beatific signaled to one of her people, who ran back to the basilica. The news spread through the crowd, which broke into spontaneous singing.

Imoshen held the General's obsidian eyes. "The traitors have been vanquished and your army is victorious. Let us call upon the thespers' guild-master to organize entertainments in the square while the palace kitchen prepares food for a celebration."

Tulkhan returned Imoshen's gaze, thinking that with this morning's trial she had not only vanquished her Ghebite accusers, she had also consolidated her position as co-ruler of Fair Isle. Yet when he looked past Imoshen's shoulder to Kalleen's miserable face, he had to agree. Kalleen should be rewarded and the future of Wharrd's unborn child secured.

How had the reins of power slipped so easily from his fingers into Imoshen's?

Seventeen

LATE THAT EVENING, when Imoshen and Kalleen retired to the Empress's chambers, Kalleen looked blankly at the estate deeds. Imoshen joined her. "How does it feel, farm girl, to be one of the richest women in Fair Isle?"

"My child's father is dead. Yet I feel nothing. Am I heartless?"

"No." Imoshen took her hand. "You are weary, my friend. One day, all too soon, you will feel again."

"I will never love again. Not like I loved Wharrd."

"No," Imoshen agreed, and squeezed her hand. When she looked down she saw not her own hand holding Kalleen's but Tulkhan's battle-scarred coppery hands. What did it mean?

"Imoshen?" Kalleen asked. "What troubles you?"

"Nothing. Can you watch Ashmyr?"

Going down the main stair, Imoshen glanced up at the ceiling frescoes of the T'En royal line's great deeds and wondered if her ancestors had also longed for peace and quiet.

Since he had returned she had not had a private moment with the General. He was not in the great hall. Opening her senses, Imoshen discovered he was in one of the small private chambers. She slipped down the dim passage and paused outside the door, wrinkling her nose. Tulkhan was with someone who was her enemy.

"Without his T'En gifts, Reothe is no more dangerous than a True-man," the Beatific said. "If you wish, I could give him the title of the Aayel. He would find himself busy from dawn till dusk in the Church's service."

Tulkhan understood what she was offering, but it was not true to say that Reothe was no more dangerous than a True-man simply because his gifts were crippled. "Reothe needs no more honors."

"Very well."

"Go, and thank you for your support, Beatific."

The woman offered him the obeisance between equals, raising only one hand to her forehead before leaving.

Tulkhan strode to the multipaned window, where the candles reflected in the glass. If only there was a way to kill Reothe without endangering Imoshen!

The skin on the back of his neck prickled. He focused on the window, becoming aware of Imoshen's pale face and hair reflected in the square of glass. His heart faltered and he felt as if his thoughts had been exposed. Disguising his disquiet, he turned to greet her. "So now you come and go like a ghost?"

She gave a soft laugh. "The extent of T'En powers is greatly exaggerated, General."

"I wonder...Today the Beatific absolved you of a True-man's death."

She glanced down, then up, candlelight glistening in her pleading eyes. "It was self-defense, and at least I did not suffer like I did with the Vayg—" She gave a guilty start.

"So you did kill the Vaygharian."

"He deserved to die!"

"If I went around killing everyone who deserved to die..."

"Don't mock me. I paid for his death." She hugged herself, suddenly vulnerable. Tulkhan fought the need to take her in his arms. She misinterpreted his silence. "You don't believe me? You thought me ill with a fever, but it was far worse. For the T'En the barriers between this world and the next are much frailer. The Vaygharian's vengeful soul tried to drag me through death's shadow with him, while the Parakletos watched and mocked or turned their faces from me. I barely escaped!"

Tulkhan had to put his back to her to hide his savage surge of triumph. With Imoshen's admission he understood it was only coincidence that she and Reothe had both suffered the night he'd nearly ordered the rebel leader's death. He was free to kill Reothe, and the shock of this revelation ran through his body.

"Tulkhan?" Imoshen whispered. Her hands slid around his waist. He froze. "Don't shut yourself away from me. I feared for your life and, when mine was in danger, I longed to reach out to you. But because you always resisted the mind-touch I could not reach you."

"Never ..." He cleared his throat and turned in the circle of her arms. "I will never open up to your gifts. I must have the privacy of my thoughts."

She tilted her head, eyes reflecting the many candles like the garnets they resembled. "I know your warrior code belittles women, but I live by my own code of honor, General, and I have given my word not to take advantage of your trust. Do not hold yourself aloof from me."

"As if I could!" His hands circled the small of her waist and he pulled her close. Imoshen melded to him, but even as his body responded to hers and he ached to open to her, he held back. If he was to plan Reothe's accidental death, he could not risk discovery.

"The royal line descends through the Empress, so she selects the best males to father her children," the Keeper of the Knowledge explained, her deep-set eyes keen with intelligence. "It is not so different from what you were telling me of your Ghebite customs. Only instead of quantity, with many wives and children, the ruler of Fair Isle looks for quality."

"Enough," Tulkhan said. "Leave me."

He stared at the complicated family tree. Imoshen had

shown him this chart once before, pointing to her own name. She had even said something about the royal line following the women, but he had not understood. Imoshen might claim he thought like a Ghebite, but she thought like a woman of Fair Isle.

"General?"

Tulkhan looked up. "Lightfoot."

"The town officials are ready to view the city's outer defenses." The mercenary had assumed command of T'Diemn's garrison.

Tulkhan thrust the book aside. To fund the massive defensive works, he had called for a levy from all businesses and households. The defenses he was constructing would surpass those designed by Emperor T'Reothe four hundred years ago.

Though the townspeople of T'Diemn were incredibly wealthy by the standards of the mainland, this did not make them eager to part with their gold. Imoshen had suggested that a tour of the new defenses might make the townspeople realize where their money was going.

His men now believed her innocent because the Orb proclaimed her so, yet when her pregnancy began to show he would have to acknowledge another man's child as his own or else admit Reothe had cuckolded him. He felt like a bear in a trap. There had to be a way out of this dishonor.

Imoshen met Kalleen's eyes as a servant announced that General Tulkhan wanted to speak with her. She glanced down at her notes. New standards, flags, and cloaks had been ordered to replace the ones lost in the flood. But the cloth merchants' stocks were depleted. Imoshen had decided to send a message to the Regent of the Amirate for supplies. Better to let it be known that Fair Isle was preparing for war than to pretend it would not happen.

"I will watch over Ashmyr," Kalleen said.

Imoshen nodded and came to her feet. In the long gallery she passed servants busily trimming the wicks and lighting the candles. Just lighting the palace of a thousand rooms was a huge expense. If they faced another season of war, Fair Isle would have to tighten her belt to finance her defenses.

Imoshen opened the door to Tulkhan's map room, where she found him lighting a branch of candles. "If your half-brother mounts a spring campaign, the cost of refitting the army will have to be met somehow. Did your tour of the new defenses loosen the pockets of the town officials, General?"

"Yes. Shut the door." He pinched out the taper, and the smell hung on the air. "I have come to a decision."

"Oh?" Imoshen did not like his strained expression.

"I know the women of Fair Isle control their fertility. I am sure you can rid yourself of an unwanted pregnancy. Get rid of Reothe's child and I—"

Imoshen turned to go.

Tulkhan strode after her, swinging her around to face him. "Don't walk away from me!"

With a flick Imoshen freed her arm and would have pushed past him, but he thrust one hand against the door, holding it shut.

Imoshen's heart raged, one giant drumbeat of denial. Knowing her strength was no match for his, she made no further attempt to leave. The familiar metallic tang settled on her tongue as her gift roused, sensitizing her, but resorting to her powers would only alienate him further. "I will not even discuss this!"

"Before long all of T'Diemn will know you are with child."

"What of it?"

"When the child is born they will know I am not the father! Think of my position."

"How does that compare to the life of a child?" Outrage made her voice vibrate.

"You would have me accept another man's castoff?"

"I will not kill my own child."

He ground his teeth. *"Look,* they'll say. *There goes Tulkhan. While he was away defending Fair Isle, his wife took the Dhamfeer rebel for her lover. Poor fool. He cannot see past his lust!"*

"Tulkhan!" Imoshen reached out to him. In that moment he was exposed to her. She realized another layer had been added to the General's being. In a flash she understood it was not generosity that had led him to spare the defenders of Port Sumair but guilt. Words spilled from her lips. "Would you add the killing of the unborn to your list of murders?"

Tulkhan's coppery skin went gray. "Is that what you see me as, a murderous barbarian?"

She wanted to deny it. She knew he was so much more, but she remained silent because it gave her power.

"How you must despise me! I marvel that you can bring yourself to stand at my side," he whispered.

Imoshen caught his hands in hers. "Mainland spies watch us. Their masters wait like carrion birds to peck clean the bones of Fair Isle's carcass. I know you find it hard to understand my people, but—" He snatched his hands from hers. "Don't close me out, Tulkhan."

"I must. Is it any wonder, when I can feel power radiating from your skin?"

Imoshen looked up into Tulkhan's features, once so alien, now so dear. "It is true I surrendered my Stronghold to the superior force of your army, but since then I have come to know you. As T'Imoshen, on behalf of the people of Fair Isle, I have tried to make our alliance work. But I ask this of you as your bond-partner. Can you not find it in your heart to mend this breach between us?"

"You don't understand, Imoshen. By the warrior's code a man must have the respect of his peers!"

"Where is the honor in killing an unborn child?"

"You ask the impossible of me!"

Imoshen closed her eyes and recalled that dawn morning when she held her dead son in her arms and faced the blinding presence of the Ancients to restore his life. "Don't talk to me of what is impossible. We can make anything happen if we want it badly enough. Think of Ashmyr."

"But think of the cost," Tulkhan countered. "What price did you agree to pay?" When she wouldn't answer, he went on. "You saved Ashmyr from death's shadow. I have seen you call on the Parakletos, and death's own guardian angels obeyed you. Perhaps that is why you will not admit defeat, but I am only a True-man. My life has boundaries."

"I, too, have boundaries. Tulkhan, I...I fear for us."

He pulled her into his arms, crushing her with the force of his emotion. His words were a deep rumble in his chest, muffled by her hair as he pressed his lips to her head. "Ah, Imoshen, so do I."

She held him with all her strength, as if she could halt the forces that strove to drive them apart. If only they were simply a man and a woman, and not the embodiment of their people. Tears stung her eyes. She pulled away to search his face. "Promise at least to listen to me."

He removed the Ghebite-seal ring. "My father gave me this after my first victory. There are only two, and the other rests on Gharavan's finger. If you are ever in trouble or it seems there is no hope for us, send me this and I will listen, even if it goes against all reason."

Imoshen slid the ring onto the longest finger of her left hand, a symbol of hope. She made a fist to keep it safe.

"Why do you cry now?" he asked, his voice gentle.

Angrily, she brushed at the tears. "Will you take your meal with me, General Tulkhan?"

He smiled. "If that is what you wish."

"I would pretend for this evening that we are simply a man and woman with no greater decisions than which fields to plant in the spring."

He laughed, and Imoshen felt lighter. "We should have a feast."

"Another feast?" he teased.

"When the defenses are finished."

"The first phase will be finished come spring, but I could go on fortifying T'Diemn forever."

"Aayel forbid!" Imoshen grinned. "I was taught a leader should use every opportunity to impress on her people the power and achievements of her rule!"

"If the royal line passes through the women, why did

Imoshen the First marry her nephew, not her daughter, to
the old ruling line of Fair Isle?" Tulkhan asked abruptly.

"Imoshen the First's daughter was pure T'En. It was
decreed that all pure T'En women were to remain chaste, so
she became the first Beatific." Imoshen regarded him
fondly. "You have been reading the old histories in the original High T'En. Your scholarship is to be admired."

"I may be a Ghebite, Imoshen, but I am not stupid."

She held his gaze. "I may be a woman, but..."

"Will you never stop?"

"Never!"

He laughed, and it warmed her to the core.

Tulkhan watched the servants clear away the remains of the
feast. Tonight's celebration was to acknowledge and reward
his faithful lord commanders who had returned from the
mainland.

The high table was set in front of the back wall, under
his huge standard. The dawn sun, embroidered with thread
of finely spun gold, glittered in the candlelight of the public
hall, which was as crowded as the day he had awarded
Wharrd and his men their titles. Again he felt that tug of
loss. The old bone-setter had served in honor, blood, and
death, just as the white, red, and black ribbons of the T'En
investiture signified.

Tulkhan stood aside while the servants removed the
table. The musicians struck up a dance, and the floor became crowded.

"That one bears watching," Lightfoot remarked softly.

Reothe was dancing with Imoshen. Before the whole
hall, he held her hand and looked into her eyes as though
she was the sun to him. It stung Tulkhan to acknowledge
that they formed a perfect pair, stepping to the measured
paces of the old-empire dance with innate T'En grace.

"The rebel's claws have been drawn," Tulkhan replied.
He was only awaiting the opportunity to have Reothe assas-
sinated. Lightfoot would have been an ideal assassin but,

even though Imoshen had removed the T'En stigmata, Tulkhan was not certain she couldn't call on him under the right circumstance. "When Imoshen destroyed Reothe's gifts, he became an empty shell, nothing but a symbol of the old empire."

"The people need symbols. That one gathers about him a brotherhood of fanatical warriors. The T'Enplars swear an oath to the Beatific, and Reothe claims to serve the Church, but I know where their loyalties lie!"

This confirmed Tulkhan's suspicions.

"Here comes another cat that needs declawing," Light-foot muttered.

Tulkhan suppressed a grin as the Beatific joined him. He greeted her and they both sat down. She had taken the seat on his left. Imoshen's seat was on his right—not, as he had once thought, because this acknowledged her importance to him, Protector General of Fair Isle, but because it placed him on her left hand. Since the T'En were left-handed, the left was the position of honor. Tulkhan had had to unlearn much to understand the people of Fair Isle.

The Beatific smiled on him, beautiful, worldly, and . . . malicious?

"You do not dance?" he asked.

"Dancing is for children, not for leaders of state."

Tulkhan winced. The woman was flattering him because he never danced. But the comparison and intended insult to Imoshen only reminded him that the T'En lived so much longer. Here he was over thirty with maybe another twenty years to live, and there was Reothe in his thirties, but if he wasn't killed he could expect to live another seventy or eighty years.

"You were curious as to how Reothe's hand was maimed," the Beatific said. Tulkhan nodded. By tacit agreement he and Imoshen had not discussed her kinsman. "The Cadre sliced off his fingers to prevent him from helping Imoshen to escape from Sard's Tower. They were shut out there, exposed to the first snowfall so they would be weak but alive when they were stoned. Imoshen sealed Reothe's wounds, but even the greatest of T'En healers could not replace a severed limb or a gouged eye. Somehow Reothe escaped from the tower and saved Imoshen."

Twice now Reothe had saved Imoshen's life, once with his T'En gifts and this time with nothing more than bravery. The General frowned. He did not want to admire his enemy.

Feeling herself under observation, Imoshen's cheeks grew warm. She did not have to turn her head to know that Tulkhan watched her with Reothe. She had only danced with him once before, on the celebration of their betrothal. On that day so long ago she had laced her fingers with his and bathed in the glow of his admiration, knowing he wanted her. The memory made her writhe with anguished resentment. She did not want to be reminded that her first, freely given vow had been to Reothe.

She turned on the ball of her foot under his outstretched arm. Her skirts settled around her with a soft sigh. "You should not have asked me to dance."

"It would have been remarked upon if I hadn't." His arms encircled her without actually touching. His breath caressed her ear, intimate, mocking. He spoke as concisely as the steps they performed. *"What are the last T'En hiding?* people would have said. *Why don't they acknowledge each other?"*

Though their bodies did not touch anywhere but at the fingertips, she was aware of tension radiating from him. She stepped back and held his eyes. "Everything you do is marked, Reothe. They tell me more T'Enplar warriors join you every day. Beware or you'll be perceived as a threat."

He laughed bitterly. "How could the Ghebite General perceive me as a threat? You have denied me before everyone." Fury ignited him. "The Orb of Truth lied for you, Imoshen."

"My words were true. You came to me in Tulkhan's form. You even told me how to speak the truth without incriminating myself."

"Yet you carry my child, and it is only a matter of time before *he* denies you!"

Reothe's triumph washed over her, making the little hairs on her skin rise up in protest. Was his gift healing? The heat, the scented candles, the press of the bodies—everything faded. Her vision blurred and narrowed down to an aura of light surrounding Reothe's shorn silver hair. The room spun. Couples moved around them in time to something Imoshen could not hear for the roaring in her ears. She stumbled.

Reothe caught her, then flinched because he had tried to Read her.

Imoshen wondered if he had been aware of that momentary flare. "I have had enough of dancing."

Aware of the Beatific's sharp eyes on her, Imoshen would have dismissed Reothe as soon as she reached her seat, but he made the formal obeisance of supplication, going down on both knees before the General, hands lifted palms up.

Light glinted on Reothe's closely cropped hair. The T'Enplars were all wearing their hair shorn in honor of their leader. "I ask a boon of Protector General Tulkhan."

"Ask."

"As Patron of the Halls of Learning, you can grant me the right to establish a new Hall of Learning."

"A Hall of Learning?"

"I ask only for an old wing of the palace to house the children no one wants. There I will establish a Malaunje Hall of Learning."

Tulkhan noticed Imoshen and the Beatific exchange glances. The word was familiar. "Malaunje?"

The Beatific answered, "Malaunje is the High T'En word for half-breed."

In a flash Tulkhan understood. Reothe meant to build a power base—an army of rebels wearing T'Enplarian colors, and a school of half-breed children all loyal to the last T'En warrior. "These half-breed T'En can study in the Halls of Learning now. What purpose would this new school serve?"

"Across Fair Isle there are many children of part T'En blood who are grudgingly accepted in their own homes and villages. I want to gather them together and restore their self-worth." Reothe started to speak dispassionately, but as he went on his voice grew vibrant. "Even the name Malaunje has faded from our language, as if to deny their very existence. Once there were levels of Malaunje just as once there were ranks within the pure T'En. Now there are only unwanted *half-breeds* and *Throwbacks*. Ask Imoshen what it is like to live as an outcast in your own family."

Tulkhan glanced to Imoshen and saw the naked dismay in her face before she masked her feelings.

"What of your service to the Church?" Tulkhan demanded. Did he want a palace full of Dhamfeer half-breeds? He heard his father's voice. *Keep your enemies close to your heart, the better to see what they plan.*

"I will continue to serve the Beatific, but there is not enough for me to do," Reothe said. "I need more."

Imoshen was sure Tulkhan would refuse Reothe his Malaunje Hall of Learning.

"Very well," Tulkhan said. "You have your school."

Imoshen's gaze flew to Tulkhan. He was watching Reothe, who offered formal thanks then turned to the Beatific. "I ask to be excused from my Church service for as long as it takes to travel Fair Isle and find these children."

"You would leave soon?" the Beatific asked.

Reothe nodded. "It is nearly winter's cusp. I must leave before the snows set in."

"Then go with the Church's blessing."

"Where will you go?" Tulkhan asked.

"The Keldon Highlands before the snows close the passes."

Tulkhan smiled. "Excellent. I was planning to inspect our defenses. I will go with you."

"I was planning on traveling lightly, with only a small band of T'Enplar warriors," Reothe said quickly.

"Good. I also intend to travel swiftly, with a handful of men," Tulkhan announced.

Though the General smiled, Imoshen saw there was no humor in his eyes, only determination. Her teeth ached, and the T'En taste grew strong on her tongue.

"As you wish." Reothe rose with old-empire grace.

Tulkhan stood. Suddenly, a great gash appeared in his thigh and he fell forward into Reothe's arms, crying, *Betrayed!* Imoshen leapt to her feet, with Tulkhan's name on her lips.

Everyone turned to her.

Tulkhan stood before her, uninjured, his long legs planted firmly on the dais. A rushing noise filled her head as normal sounds and sensations returned. She could only stare at him. Was Reothe going to kill Tulkhan the first chance he had?

"What is it?" Tulkhan asked.

To reveal what she had foreseen would condemn Reothe.

"What alarmed you, T'Imoshen?" Tulkhan asked formally.

"I have had too much wine. Please excuse me."

Aware that this was hardly a worthy excuse, she collected Ashmyr's basket and Kalleen. Imoshen did not need her gift to tell her that everyone watched her departure with speculation.

After Kalleen closed the door to the Empress's bedchamber, she turned to Imoshen. "You have the Sight."

"It came on me like this once before, when I foresaw the Vaygharian's death."

"Whose death did you foresee this time?"

Imoshen shook her head and placed the sleeping baby's basket safely on the floor. Again she saw Tulkhan stagger with the force of the blow as he fell into Reothe's arms, injured and vulnerable.

"Imoshen?"

She looked up to find Kalleen crouching at her side.

"If one of them murders the other, it will be on your conscience," Kalleen warned.

"It will be no more than everyone expects!"

"I can guess no good will come of this journey," Kalleen said. "But if I had the Sight, I'd feel duty-bound to warn—"

"Warn him of what? If I say anything, I precipitate the death of someone I love, and if I don't, I let my love go to his death!" Imoshen swallowed a sob. "I can't bear this, Kalleen. I am torn in two."

Firelight danced in Kalleen's hazel eyes, belying her serious expression. "All of Fair Isle is torn, Imoshen. Would it be kinder to send one of them away?"

If only it were that simple. Tulkhan would not relinquish Fair Isle. Since his half-brother had called him traitor he had no other home; and as for Reothe, Fair Isle was his home and she, his once-betrothed. "Which hand will I cut off, Kalleen, my left or right?"

"Don't linger; winter comes early to the Keldon Highlands," Imoshen advised.

Tulkhan checked the saddle's girth for the second time. Fifteen of the Parakhan Guard, selected because they were loyal to Tulkhan, were already mounted. And behind them milled an equal number of Reothe's T'Enplars, dressed for cold weather.

"I want the outlying defenses finished before spring."

"No one attacks in winter. Besides, your half-brother is probably licking his wounds."

"If I know Gharavan, he will be planning revenge, and don't rule out a winter attack. Fair Isle is bleeding from repeated warring."

It was more than he had said to her since the feast. As Tulkhan swung his weight up into the saddle, she caught the reins. "Beware a betrayer." The words escaped Imoshen before she could stop herself.

Tulkhan looked down on her, his Ghebite eyes sharp. "Did your vision tell you who this betrayer is?"

Imoshen shook her head numbly.

"And your scryings are never accurate either." His voice grew gentle, teasing. "What are these marvelous Dhamfeer gifts the old tales speak of? In real life they are nothing but market-day tricks to amuse small children!"

Imoshen's heart turned over. His tone warmed her to the core. But why tease her so lovingly when he was about to leave? She caught his hand in hers, peeling back the leather glove to plant a kiss on the pulse inside his wrist.

"Take care, General Tulkhan." With tears blinding her vision she stepped back, hugging her body to keep out the chill presentiment of death. The horses shuffled past.

Boots appeared on the ground before her and she looked up to find Reothe holding his horse by the reins.

"You cry for him, yet you won't even say good-bye to me. Did you tell him which one of us died in your vision, Imoshen?"

She shook her head. "You take no Parakhan Guards-women?"

"General Tulkhan would see that as a sign of weakness." He surprised her by sinking to one knee, offering the old-empire formal salute of leave-taking. "I ask your blessing, T'En Empress. I go in the service of our people."

Imoshen lifted her left hand, placing the tip of her sixth finger on his forehead. Would she see Reothe alive again? Her heart twisted within her. Reothe or Tulkhan. Why did it have to be this cruel choice? She let her hand drop. "If you return alone, I will kill you myself."

"Those are not the formal words of blessing, Empress."

"That is what my heart tells me."

"And what does your head tell you?"

Imoshen stared into Reothe's wine-dark eyes, then stepped back. "Nothing. My head tells me nothing."

"Perhaps you are not listening." He swung up into the saddle with a little smile on his lips.

But Imoshen would not meet his eyes.

Eighteen

O N THEIR FIRST night out, Tulkhan selected a
campsite just off the main south road. The
weapons of the T'Enplars remained in view, just as
his own men had not disarmed to make camp.

While the men lit their cooking fires, he approached
Reothe. "Walk with me. I would like to know what can be
seen from the top of that rise."

Reothe glanced in the direction he pointed. The rocky
outcropping was a dark silhouette against the setting sun.
"I would say very little that can't be seen from here. But
sight and perception are two different things."

"Another T'En proverb?" Tulkhan asked.

Reothe straightened, stiffly favoring his left side. They
walked in silence through the gloaming twilight to the rise
and climbed it. Standing there with the afterglow of the sun's
rays illuminating Reothe and himself, Tulkhan was aware
that their men would be able to see them as two silhouettes.

"We must call a truce while we travel," he said.

"And why is that?"

"Don't spar with me, Reothe. Your T'Enplar warriors and
my Parakhan Guard are at dagger's point with each other."

Reothe looked back toward the camp.

Tulkhan realized it would be so easy to stab him in the
back or knock him off this rock and spring down to dispatch
him as he lay injured. But Reothe had to die by accident.

"Give me one good reason why I should trust you," Reothe said at last.

That gave Tulkhan pause, and the Dhamfeer laughed softly, goading him into speaking. "I asked Imoshen to order your execution, but she wouldn't do it."

"No? Did it occur to you that if she were to hand over General Tulkhan to his half-brother to prevent a spring war, it would give her time to rebuild Fair Isle's army? But she wouldn't do that either."

Tulkhan scowled. He knew Reothe's assessment was right. It was a personal grudge with Gharavan. His own death would delay another invasion, perhaps indefinitely. It irked him to learn Reothe had been discussing matters of state with Imoshen. "I could kill you myself."

Reothe looked at him, his features barely visible in the fading light. "Why don't you?"

Tulkhan lifted a hand in frustration. "Imoshen—"

"Exactly. Where she leads, the people will follow, and without the support of the people, neither of us can retain Fair Isle. Your army is reduced to a scattered mass of men and a few loyal commanders; my rebel army was never more than that. It all comes back to Imoshen." Reothe rounded on him. "Why can't you move on, General? I have. My goal is to preserve the T'En. If I can restore the people's faith in us, Fair Isle will grow strong again. No one would dare attack an island with an elite band of T'En warriors like Imoshen the First's Paragian Guard."

It would take only a few generations of bonding half-breeds to create a band of Throwbacks loyal to Reothe, who would never have to regain his gifts; he could wield all the power of the T'En through his followers.

Tulkhan reeled at the prospect. "I am but a True-man. I cannot touch you to discover the truth of your words. Imoshen once said you could make the truth sound like a lie. For now, for the sake of Fair Isle, I suggest a truce. Do you agree?"

Reothe lifted his left hand, forearm open to Tulkhan. "A truce."

Tulkhan mimicked the action, and their fingers interlaced. He could feel Reothe's bonding scar. Did this mean Reothe meant to keep the truce?

"Agreed." Tulkhan let his arm drop, secretly relieved that Reothe no longer had his gifts, because if he had, he would know Tulkhan meant to break his word. Even if Reothe were to put short-term gain aside for long term, Tulkhan's son would face the loss of Fair Isle.

The General had put his plan in motion before he left T'Diemn, which was why he had been avoiding Imoshen. His defenses against her were good, but he could not be on his guard every waking moment.

When Imoshen had warned Tulkhan to beware a betrayer, his heart had faltered and he had only just managed to divert her with a jest. He smiled grimly. It was lucky for him her gift was erratic, for somewhere on this journey their group was going to be attacked by bandits. His own man, Commander Haase, would arrange it. In the heat of battle, no one would know where each sword strike came from. He would carry Reothe's body back to T'Diemn in state, accompanied by at least one T'Enplar warrior who would swear the General was blameless of his leader's death.

As for Imoshen, she would mourn Reothe's loss, but if Tulkhan was not to blame, she would accept him. All that remained was the child Imoshen carried. If it was a girl, he might let her live. If it was a son, he would have to have him killed by subterfuge. It was cruel, but young children died all the time. They caught fevers, played dangerous games. What was one more murder to add to his long list of killings? A bleakness enveloped Tulkhan's spirit.

"It grows dark," Reothe said. "Deepdeyne Stronghold lies two days from here."

"I want to inspect Deepdeyne. If my half-brother attacks south of T'Diemn, it could be our first line of defense."

"We must be out of the Keldon Highlands before winter sets in. We can stop at Deepdeyne on the return journey."

"Very well," Tulkhan agreed. This suited his plans. It gave Commander Haase time to prepare an ambush. Reothe's death had to appear to be a random act of violence and would be better happening on the return journey, when everyone would be less vigilant.

Tulkhan turned to climb down from the outcropping, giving Reothe his back and a chance to strike treacherously, but he didn't. Tulkhan smiled as he returned to camp, his smile hidden in the twilight, hidden because Reothe's gift was crippled.

"See," Reothe greeted the camp sentry. "We are returned safely. Neither of us stabbed the other in the back!"

The man laughed uneasily. Tulkhan did not blame him.

Imoshen's heart went out to the two brothers, the most recent Malaunje children to arrive escorted by one of the T'Enplars and one of the Parakhan Guard. Willingly turned over by their parents, the boys found themselves in the palace, where everything was strange. She watched them put their small bundles in the chest at the foot of their beds.

By housing the Malaunje children in T'Reothe's Hall, Imoshen hoped the peace and solidarity of his long reign would be associated with Reothe's venture. Reothe the Builder had been the First Emperor of the Age of Consolidation, but the hall still had the characteristics of the Age of Tribulation—thick walls and narrow windows, as though the T'En did not feel truly secure even in their own palace.

"Now that you know which are your beds, you can go outside to join the others," Imoshen told the boys. "Drake is showing them how to use the T'En sword."

They glanced at each other. Imoshen sighed. The brothers were probably used to being ostracized by their village playmates.

"This way." She walked them down the stairs and into the courtyard, and the boys approached the group warily. Imoshen became aware of Maigeth in the doorway behind her.

She took the silversmith's arm. "I wanted to thank you for hiding my son."

"You shielded my son when he joined the rebels."

Imoshen nodded. Drake was showing the eldest girl

how to hold the sword correctly while the others waited impatiently for their turn. Imoshen picked her words carefully. "Have you noticed your gift growing since the day you touched the Orb?"

A shutter came down, cloaking the woman's expression. Though Imoshen still linked arms with her, she could sense nothing. Maigeth might deny the T'En gift, but she was very good at blocking it.

"I have been replaced as guild-master. I have lost the friendship of my dearest friend, who was like a sister. I have seen everyone but my son turn away from me."

"I am sorry."

Maigeth looked at her. "I believe you are, but that does not give me back my life."

It was a small village like many Tulkhan had passed through in the Keldon Highlands. The rugged countryside was too poor to support large towns. According to the elders of the last village, a family lived here with four half-breed children; some even had both traits—the six fingers and the wine-dark eyes—nearly full Throwbacks.

Smoke drifted from the central holes of the snug dwellings, but they were deserted except for a cat that watched from a windowsill. When Tulkhan had met with his commander of the Greater Pass, the man spoke of roaming rebel bands robbing honest merchants, but this village was not wealthy enough to attract thieves. Tulkhan turned in his saddle to Reothe. "Where is everyone?"

The Dhamfeer dismounted. He stepped carefully over the churned mud and half-melted snow to the entrance of the largest cottage. The door opened at his touch and he disappeared inside.

Tulkhan's horse snorted. The beast did not like the cold. Tulkhan did not like living intimately with someone he planned to murder. It was not easy to break bread and joke with a man, knowing he would soon be dead.

Reothe came out of the house and looked up at the

ridges behind the village, frowning. The trees were coated in a mantle of snow, still and silent.

"Well?" Tulkhan prodded.

"There is bread baking in the oven above the fireplace." Reothe took his horse's reins, put his boot in the stirrup, and swung up into the saddle. "They must have run away."

"Why would the whole village run away? Everyone else has been glad to hand over their half-breeds; why not this family?"

Reothe spoke for Tulkhan's ears only. "Because they think their children will be murdered once you have killed me."

Tulkhan's body tightened. The horse responded to the pressure of his knees, sidling. He brought it under control before speaking. "What nonsense is this?"

Reothe met his eyes. "Each time I have been given a Malaunje child, I have had to promise on my life that no harm would come to them."

Tulkhan digested this in silence. So far he had not detected the Dhamfeer in a single lie. Reothe had been the perfect traveling companion, uncomplaining and ready with a jest when the going got tough. This empty village, however, did not make sense. "But wouldn't the villagers be glad to be rid of a half-breed family in their midst?"

Reothe's expression reminded Tulkhan forcibly of Imoshen—alert, intelligent, and just slightly amused. When he spoke, he pitched his voice to carry as though he suspected there were watchers in the undergrowth. "This far south the people respect the old ways, the ways I wish to restore!" Then he lowered his voice. "You know the saying, *Scrawny sheep and stiff-necked Keld.* Likely everyone in the village is related to the Malaunje family. They may be loved and revered."

A whole village steeped in the old ways? Tulkhan glanced back with a shudder. Already the snow-shrouded trees had closed around them. He doubted if he could find his way back here again.

"I fear there will be no more part-T'En children for us to find if this village is anything to go by," Reothe muttered.

"Good. I'm tired of ravines and snow. The sooner we return to the plains the better!" Tulkhan urged his horse forward. The sooner they were attacked and Reothe killed, the sooner he would rid himself of this taint of betrayal that sat like underripe fruit in his belly.

"Eleven children and the snows have set in," the Beatific remarked as they watched the small figures riding sleds down the hillside overlooking the ornamental lake.

Imoshen tucked the fur around her knees. Ashmyr and Kalleen were sleeping in the warmth of the palace, but Imoshen had greeted the Beatific's invitation with relief. She was already tired of being cooped up and winter had barely begun. Besides, if the Beatific had something to tell her, she would rather speak where no one could overhear. "So what did you wish to talk about?"

"Move on," the Beatific told her sleigh driver. He cracked his whip and the horses responded, surging forward.

They followed the curve of the lake, and Imoshen frowned as she identified the well-worn way to the stone lovers. On the fresh snow she could see the marks of horses, boots, and several sleighs.

"Not that way, driver. Take us to the lookout," the Beatific directed.

The delicate lookout rotunda with its tall columns stood silhouetted against the winter-blue sky. When the sleigh slid to a halt, the Beatific threw back her furs to climb down. Imoshen watched this with misgivings. The only protection she wore was a knife strapped to her upper thigh, accessible under her brocade tabard, but the Beatific would not assassinate her here, not when everyone knew they had ridden off together.

Placing her boots in the indentations left by the Beatific's steps, Imoshen followed the woman to the rotunda. One of the stone seats was cracked. No one bothered to come up here; the old-empire fashion for eating outdoors was not popular with the Ghebites.

Directly below the lookout's cliff was the rock-edged river; beyond the river was old T'Diemn. The air was so clear that she could see individual tiles on the roofs. The spires of the new T'Diemn stood tall beyond the old city's walls, and far beyond that the rolling foothills were dressed in a mantle of pure white snow. Would Gharavan attack in mid-winter?

Enemies surrounded her. "I am listening, Engarad."

The Beatific's golden eyes held resentment. "I know you don't like me, Imoshen, but I am here today as your friend."

"I don't trust you; that is different," Imoshen replied. "I am listening."

The Beatific waved a hand over T'Diemn. "The people don't like change, and so much has changed in the last two years. The people fear Reothe's plans. These children claim the name Malaunje, and Reothe creates a Hall of Learning where half-breeds seek to tap into their nascent gifts!"

"Isn't that what Murgon's Tractarians do?"

"That is different. They serve the Church. Besides, it is impolite to speak of the lesser gifts of the Malaunje," the Beatific corrected primly, then frowned. "People fear what they do not know. They whisper that you and Reothe flew down from Sard's Tower and that you absorbed the power of the Orb into yourself."

"I nearly died, as you well know!"

The Beatific had the grace to flush. "When Reothe comes back, talk him out of this."

Imoshen shook her head. If Reothe did not have his Malaunje Hall of Learning, she dreaded to think where his energies would drive him.

"At least try," the Beatific urged.

"You try. He is your lover!"

The Beatific smiled. "I have known Reothe since he was a youth of seventeen, passionate and ambitious—so ambitious he would stop at nothing to achieve his goal of ruling Fair Isle."

"Maybe that is what he was like, but Reothe is no longer that youth," Imoshen said, regretting her hasty tongue. "He has other goals now."

"If you believe that, you fool yourself. If Reothe could sacrifice his own parents to be near the Empress and the seat of power, what makes you think he will be satisfied with these scraps you throw him?"

Reothe sacrificed his parents? Imoshen shook her head. He had been discovered beside the cold bodies of his mother and father, who'd committed ritual suicide.

"Reothe drove his parents to kill themselves," the Beatific insisted.

"You are mistaken, Engarad. Reothe was only a child."

"Children are totally self-absorbed. Reothe is absorbed in his own goals, he—"

"Reothe is not like that!" Imoshen read pity in the woman's face. It goaded her beyond belief. "You hold a mirror to the world and so attribute your motivations to others!"

The Beatific's hand flew up in an arc. Imoshen could have stopped her, she had time to block and counterattack, but she did nothing. Instead, she absorbed the full force of the slap in the knowledge that she had handled that badly.

Imoshen's face stung and her left eye watered as the Beatific stalked back to the sleigh. Waiting until the tingling in her cheek eased, Imoshen pretended to study the city, but the thought of riding next to the Beatific made her uncomfortable. Yet any sign of a breach between herself and the Beatific would be gleefully noted by the mainland spies. Imoshen glanced over her shoulder to see the Beatific seated in the sleigh and her servant staring stoically ahead.

Taking a deep breath, she picked her way carefully down the slope to the sleigh. Before she could arrange the fur over her knees, the Beatific signaled the driver. With a jolt, the horses strained against their harnesses.

As they began the ride back to the confinement of protocol and thousands of watchful eyes, Imoshen thought of her family's Stronghold. It was more than a year since she had ridden off at an hour's notice. Homesickness welled within her, making her gifts stir. The Beatific glared, shifting away as far as possible.

Imoshen marked this. Most True-men and women were

not so sensitive. Perhaps it was because the Beatific had known Reothe intimately. Imoshen cleared her throat. "I spoke in haste, Engarad."

The Beatific inclined her head in acknowledgment, but her expression did not soften.

Imoshen tried again. "I value your advice. After all, we both want the best for Fair Isle. We both want to protect ourselves and our sisters from Ghebite arrogance."

This time the Beatific met her eyes.

"Although Kalleen has the deeds to seven estates, her hold on these is tenuous. If she were to take a Ghebite for a bond-partner, he would expect the ownership to transfer to him."

Contempt twisted the Beatific's face. "The Church will do all it can to curtail these Ghebites. It is lucky so many of them were killed in the Low-lands. It will be easier to absorb them without their ways influencing our people."

Imoshen nodded, but the Beatific's comment had revealed one of Imoshen's hidden fears. General Tulkhan's army was greatly reduced, making his hold on Fair Isle even more tenuous.

Again she saw him fall wounded into Reothe's arms with the word *Betrayed* on his lips, and her stomach churned with anxiety. Perhaps the Beatific was right and Reothe was a subtle creature of great cunning and cruelty, capable of such deception that he would drive his own parents to suicide. But she could not believe it.

The dual loyalties of her heart tore at her, yet not by so much as a sound did Imoshen betray her fears to the Beatific. They were allies, but only in desperation.

Tulkhan shifted in the saddle, stiff with cold. The eight remaining men—four Parakhan Guards and four T'Enplars—did not complain. They had been riding since before dawn, looking for something Reothe expected to discover in the deserted foothills of the Keldon Highlands.

"There!" Reothe pointed with satisfaction.

Tulkhan could just distinguish the thin plume of blue wood smoke against the ice-blue sky. Distance was hard to judge in these clear conditions, but it appeared that two hills separated them from the cottage. If it was another village there would be more evidence of settlement.

"Wait here." Reothe dismounted.

Tulkhan watched him pick his way soundlessly, wondering if Reothe was planning to circumvent Tulkhan's betrayal with a betrayal of his own. The General waited until he had crossed the crest of the hill before dismounting. "Watch the horses."

Without explanation, he followed Reothe. The air was cold enough to make his chest ache and his nostrils sting. Tulkhan breasted the crest to look down into a little valley. Steam rose from vents in the rocks, reminding him of the last time he had visited a hot pool. Tulkhan's mouth went dry with fear. He had woken the power of the Ancients, drawing Reothe in his insubstantial form. Reothe had laughed, saying, "I am your death. You do not know it, but you are a dead man who walks and talks." Only Reothe's death would prove his prophecy wrong.

Tulkhan frowned as he watched Reothe creep, silent as a snow cat, up the slope to a small crofter's cottage so laden with snow and built into the hillside that it was almost invisible.

A huge shaggy dog lifted its head. In the clear air Tulkhan could see the dog's ears twitch. Reothe straightened. There was no chance to creep up on the inhabitants now. The dog was big enough to fight off wolves, maybe even a bear. The beast charged Reothe, leaping on him. Its paws rested on his shoulders, its head level with his. To Tulkhan's amazement, the dog's tail waved in greeting and it barked joyously.

The cottage door swung open and a small woman or child came out. She froze.

"I told you I would come back," Reothe said.

"Six years!"

Reothe had no answer for that. "I've come for Ysanna."

"You can't have her."

"I told you this day would come. I'm collecting Malaunje children."

"There's nothing of the T'En in her."

"Untrue."

A tiny child stepped out of the cottage, armed with a bow bigger than she was. She already had an arrow notched, aimed at Reothe. "Shall I shoot him, Mam?"

She looked no more than three; Tulkhan was surprised she could speak so clearly.

When the mother did not answer, the girl shifted her feet. "My arms are getting tired. Who is this man?"

Silence.

"Why don't you tell her?" Reothe prodded.

The woman flung up her arms in despair. "It is your father!"

"My father died last spring. Killed by bears."

"That was your stepfather. This is your father."

The girl did not lower the bow.

"I have fifty soldiers waiting over the rise," Reothe said. "I could have ridden in here and taken her, but I didn't. I came to take her with your blessing."

"You came to take her with or without my blessing!" the woman snapped.

"I don't want to go anywhere," Ysanna said.

The little woman turned her back on Reothe and walked over to her daughter. Their two fair heads leaned close together as they spoke. At last the child lowered the bow and unnotched the arrow.

The woman sent her daughter into the cottage, then approached Reothe. Tulkhan could not hear her words, only the intense tone of her voice. She came no higher than mid-chest on Reothe, but she was not intimidated. She seemed to have a lot to say, to which Reothe was agreeing.

When Ysanna reappeared with a bundle, the woman gave her a quick hug, then called the dog and walked into the cottage without looking back. The child stood there, undecided. Reothe beckoned her and she went to him.

Tulkhan waited for Reothe and Ysanna. As they made

the crest the child's golden eyes widened at the sight of him. "So giants are real!"

Reothe laughed. "This one's real enough. It's Protector General Tulkhan come to see for himself, because he does not trust me."

The girl studied Tulkhan frankly, her five-fingered hand holding the bundle to her small chest. She had the deep golden skin of the True-people, but her hair was almost white.

She wrinkled her nose. "Does he always scowl?"

"He scowls because he does not understand."

"If this girl is yours, why does she have none of the signs?" Tulkhan snapped, goaded.

"Often T'En males don't breed true, but she is part T'En, nevertheless." He smiled on Ysanna. "You will like T'Diemn. The Empress is beautiful and clever, and she will be your teacher."

When they rejoined the others, Reothe selected one of his T'Enplar warriors and one of Tulkhan's men to escort the child back to T'Diemn.

She cast the men uneasy glances.

"You will be safe with these men. Be good for the Empress, Ysanna." Reothe stepped back, and the girl's small frame was hidden from sight as she rode in front of the men.

Tulkhan wondered briefly why Reothe would go to so much trouble for a daughter, then he concentrated on what lay ahead. "Commander Haase's estate lies west of here, two days' ride."

Reothe nodded. He glanced back toward the cottage where the woman now lived alone.

Tulkhan swung into the saddle. Was he regretting taking the child? It did not matter. Within two days Reothe would be dead and Tulkhan would be freed of this burden. The children could all be returned to their homes. That little woman would not spend the winter pining for her daughter, and Tulkhan would regain the respect of his men. It all hinged on his willingness to commit one more murder.

Tulkhan looked down at the Stronghold of the estate he had gifted to Haase. It was an odd shape, built on a curve in the river. The river had been diverted to flow around the other two sides of the high walls to create a constantly flowing moat, filled with icy water. The river was spanned by a bridge with a sharp bend in the middle, protected by a small tower.

"Looks sturdy," Tulkhan muttered.

"Deepdeyne dates from the Age of Tribulation, so it was built for defense, not appearance," Reothe said. "Lying west of Imoshen's family holdings, Deepdeyne was the last great Stronghold built to contain the highlands in the early years of T'En rule."

Tulkhan studied the path down the slope. There was nowhere for bandits to hide. His party consisted of Reothe and himself and six men—easy targets. Haase's scouts would have reported their approach, and Tulkhan had expected an ambush by now, but Haase must have decided to set up the bandit attack after their visit.

Tulkhan urged his mount down the slope toward Deepdeyne. When they entered the Keep, Haase did not reveal by so much as a glance that he planned murder. By Ghebite standards, his greeting to the fallen rebel leader was polite.

Tulkhan accepted his commander's formal salute, then clasped his arm. These years in Fair Isle had aged Haase. Tulkhan was reminded that the man was only three years older than himself. Before the year was out, Tulkhan would turn thirty-one. He was middle-aged by Ghebite standards. Haase was thinning on top and growing thicker around the waist. Tulkhan gave Haase a mock punch in his belly. "Too much easy living!"

Haase grinned and gestured to the scaffolding. "The work never stops. At least when you lead the men, there are breaks between battles and the decisions are simple."

Tulkhan understood that dilemma only too well.

"Your men can take their horses through to the stables." Haase indicated the way. "Come share a bottle of Vorsch with me. We're still living in the original Keep while they finish work on the new hall."

"Vorsch? Reothe, come try a real man's drink."
Tulkhan wanted the Dhamfeer where he could see him.

Reothe's lips twisted in a parody of a smile as he relinquished his mount's reins.

After climbing two flights of tower stairs, they entered
the great hall. Even though it was mid-afternoon, little light
filtered through the high narrow windows. As if to compen-
sate, a fire roared in the huge hearth. The scrubbed table
had been laid with fresh food and fine goblets. Sweet-
smelling herbs had been sprinkled on the floor, releasing
their scent when crushed underfoot. True to Haase's word, a
bottle of Vorsch awaited them.

Tulkhan walked to the fireplace, noting how the three ribbons of office Imoshen had awarded Haase hung from the tip
of a spear mounted above the mantelpiece. Tulkhan pulled off
his gloves and dropped his cloak on the high-backed chair, un-
clasping his sword. He caught Reothe's eye, and the Dhamfeer
followed suit. If Haase chose to go unarmed, then so must
they. The man was playing his part of host with consummate
skill. Even knowing that he was party to the plan to have
Reothe killed, Tulkhan could not fault his manner.

Tulkhan turned and stretched, feeling the heat of the fire
warm his travel-weary muscles. The smell of roasting meat
made his mouth water. As Haase uncorked the Vorsch,
Tulkhan repressed a pang of envy for the simple life.
Strange—the higher he rose, the less freedom he had.

When Haase poured three goblets, Tulkhan raised his.
"To Fair Isle and her rich bounty."

It would all be his again as soon as Reothe was dead.
He drained the goblet in one long gulp.

Reothe was more tentative. He seemed unsure of the
flavor. It was not the best Vorsch Tulkhan had ever tasted,
but then, this was not Gheeaba.

"Another drink?" Haase refilled their goblets.

"A toast to peace—a warm hearth, a willing woman, and
a full belly!" Tulkhan drained his goblet. He noticed Reothe
give him a sharp look. "Don't the T'En drink to peace?"

"They do," Reothe acknowledged. "But they don't insult

women by equating them with basic necessities. If you want to see sparks fly, salute Imoshen with that toast."

"What, drink a toast with a woman?" Haase muttered. "You jest!"

Even as Tulkhan laughed, he saw the gulf between himself and his fellow Ghebites widen. He stood with a boot in both worlds. "It's just as well you aren't keen on palace life, Haase."

Reothe grinned.

Tulkhan swilled the Vorsch around in his goblet, watching the liquid glint in the candlelight, thinking it was a cruel thing to discover a kindred spirit in the man he was sworn to kill. He had first suspected this the night Reothe risked his life searching death's shadow to save Imoshen. Tulkhan might fear Reothe and he might not trust him, but he respected him.

Tulkhan drained the last of the Vorsch. The alcohol was bitter on his tongue, bitter with the knowledge that he intended to betray Reothe. At least in war you knew who your enemies were. The silence stretched, growing uncomfortable.

"Reothe of the T'En, would you offer us a salute?" Haase spoke with more diplomacy than Tulkhan would have given him credit for.

When Tulkhan turned to Reothe, his head spun.

Reothe lifted his goblet. "There is a T'En saying that translates something like this: *Better the enemy you can trust than a weak friend.*"

It was an odd toast. Tulkhan drained the Vorsch, then went to put his goblet down on the table but missed. It fell to the floor, hitting the planks with a dull thud.

"I'll ease off on the Vorsch, Haase." Tulkhan was surprised to hear his slurred words. "What's to eat?"

Blearily, he focused on his commander, who was speaking earnestly about his relatives in Gheeaba, something about them being held prisoner. Tulkhan could see the man's mouth opening and closing, but his voice sounded like it was coming down a long tunnel. This was not the effect of the Vorsch on an empty stomach. The Vorsch was drugged!

But he'd seen Haase pour out of the same bottle. The goblets must have been prepared. Perhaps Haase had changed the plan. If he had, he should have drugged only Reothe's Vorsch. Had the Dhamfeer poisoned him? Fear made Tulkhan's heart pound. He glanced to Reothe, expecting to see triumph in those wine-dark eyes. Instead, Reothe was frowning into his own goblet.

Armed men charged into the hall.

Tulkhan lunged for his sword and spun about, intending to grab Haase and hold the blade to his throat, but Haase was already closing in on him, a weapon suddenly in his hand.

Tulkhan blocked. Too slow. Haase's sword traveled down his blade's length, the force of the strike taking it past the tip. Tulkhan saw the sword slice through the material of his breeches, saw the bright plume of blood. He felt nothing, nothing but the ignominy of discovering his own man had betrayed him.

"Betrayed!" Tulkhan lunged for Haase, who darted away. He would have fallen but Reothe stepped in, catching him. The impact took them both to the floor. Where were his men? Probably ambushed in the stables.

"So this was her vision," Reothe muttered.

Light flashed on a blade. Something struck Reothe from behind, and he pitched sideways.

Helpless to save himself, Tulkhan collapsed.

"Three goblets each and they were still standing. I'd have a word with your healer if I were you," a mocking voice remarked with a Vaygharian accent. Tulkhan realized Imoshen had foreseen this and tried to warn him, but he had been too consumed with his own plans of betrayal.

As the General lifted his head, a boot flew at his face, the impact laying him out on the floor. Even though he felt no pain, he knew his nose was broken.

Nineteen

IMOSHEN WOKE, HER cheeks wet with tears, the echo of her cry still ringing in her ears. She spun at a slight noise and found Kalleen peering around the door, holding a candle.

"You called for the General." Kalleen crept over, her face alive with fear and curiosity. "What does it mean?"

"Too much relish on my meat?"

"Imoshen, how can you jest? Has harm come to Tulkhan?"

The baby stirred in his basket beside the bed, reacting to the tension. Imoshen lowered her voice. "I don't know what it means, because I was not trained in my gift!"

"What did the Sight show you?"

"Tulkhan crying *Betrayed* as he fell wounded into Reothe's arms."

Kalleen paled. "Then he is dead?"

"I don't know!"

"Will you do a scrying?"

"It shows only possible paths, and I will not exhaust myself in false trails." She wrung her hands helplessly.

"Oh, Imoshen." Kalleen knelt on the bed, her nightgown billowing over the swelling of her pregnancy. Sympathy made her golden eyes glisten.

"Now do you understand why I must save Reothe? Only he has—knows our heritage." She almost let slip that the

T'Elegos had survived Sardonyx's revolt. "Without Reothe, I am cast adrift. I . . . I am afraid of my T'En powers."

Kalleen's eyes grew wide. Imoshen waited, heart in her mouth. The little True-woman opened her arms and Imoshen went to her. She could feel Kalleen's heart beating against her cheek, reassuring and solid.

"I am Empress in all but name," Imoshen whispered. "But in the dark night of my soul I am only Imoshen. And I am alone."

"We are all alone," Kalleen said. They held each other with a single candle to hold back the night.

When Tulkhan woke, his head felt fragile, as if any movement would split his skull. His nose seemed three sizes bigger than normal and stuffed with snow. It was so cold his limbs were numb. He knew he should be worried, but for the moment he was in too much pain to remember why.

"Can you hear me?" Reothe asked.

Tulkhan opened one eye, but this achieved nothing. Either they were in the windowless prison or it was night.

"They will send us to the coast at dawn," Reothe said. "We must escape now. It will be light soon."

"How . . . how do you know?"

"The drug affected us differently. It paralyzed me but I was still aware."

Tulkhan strained, but all he could see were the dancing patterns produced by his night-blind eyes. "Where are we?"

"In the chapel off the great hall. Ironic, really. It was dedicated by a distant ancestor of mine. Deepdeyne has been in my family for over five hundred years." Reothe's tone was hard and bitter. He fell silent. When he resumed, his voice had regained its usual timbre. "Haase and his Ghebites feasted late, celebrating our capture. You are to be returned to your half-brother for trial and execution."

"And you?" Tulkhan did not know why Reothe still lived.

"The Ghebite king is having trouble with his alliance kingdoms. He wants a chained Dhamfeer to exhibit throughout his empire. He thinks it would restore respect for his rule if he re-captures Fair Isle and subjugates the legendary T'En. He in-tends to keep Imoshen alive too, if he can. But I don't—"

"Why? Why did Haase betray me?"

"Why does any man betray another? Love or wealth. Haase tried to tell you. His family are imprisoned back in Gheeaba. They bound your leg, by the way. They want you alive for your execution."

Of course. "Our men?"

"Dead."

Tulkhan nodded to himself, then winced. He flexed his body and bit back a groan. As sensation returned, he realized he had been tied to a cot bed that was too short for him. His arms were tied behind his head, one to each leg of the bed, and his knees hung over the end of the cot, where his ankles were strapped to the uprights. "Are you tied up?"

"Same as you."

"Can you see?"

Reothe was silent, as though considering what answer to give. "I may be crippled, but I still have the eyes I was born with. Do you feel as if you could walk?"

"I can't even feel my feet." He heard Reothe chuckle. There was a soft crack of splitting wood. "What was that?"

"These banks are old and brittle." More soft cracking and rustling followed.

Tulkhan flexed his arms, welcoming the pain in his hands as sensation returned. Could he crack the cot's legs, and if he did would his head hit the floor to add to his woes?

"Careful, don't start the leg wound bleeding."

By the sound of his voice, Tulkhan could tell Reothe was kneeling beside him and guessed the Dhamfeer could see bet-ter than he would admit. The bonds fell away from Tulkhan's hands and he sat upright, repressing a grunt of pain. His head felt as if it might burst. Nausea threatened.

"Can you stand?" Reothe freed his legs.

Tulkhan wondered if Reothe was helping him because they stood a better chance of escaping together. Perhaps Reothe planned to exchange his life for Tulkhan's if they were recaptured. Should it come down to a fight, he could not be blamed if Reothe was killed attempting to escape. Suddenly, Tulkhan did not like the man he was becoming.

"If I can find it after all these years, there's a secret passage leading from one of the lower storerooms," Reothe said.

"Another secret passage!" Tulkhan felt his bandaged thigh and flexed the muscle carefully. "I can barely walk. Can we lead horses through this passage?"

"No."

Would Reothe leave him to his fate? One thing was certain: Tulkhan was not going back to his half-brother alive.

"We can get horses from the stables," Reothe said at last. "We'll need food and blankets. Winter is a brutal time to be living off the land."

Reothe spoke from experience. Only last winter he and his rebels had been hiding out in the Keldon Highlands. "Come, Tulkhan. The door is not locked."

"Weapons?"

"The wall displays hold effective, if outdated, weaponry. But it would make more sense to slip away quietly."

"To the stables, then."

The door to the main hall opened on silent hinges. Tulkhan could hear the snores of a score of men. He was sure if his nose hadn't been completely blocked, he would have smelled their winy breath and sweaty bodies.

"Walk where I walk," Reothe whispered.

It was all very well for the Dhamfeer—he could see. Tulkhan felt his way, senses strained. They made it across the hall to the stairwell without discovery. In silence and darkness, Tulkhan kept one hand against the stone stairwell. His leg pained him, and the warm dampness told him the wound had broken open.

Two floors below, they unbarred the door and moved out onto the tower's narrow stairs. It was the darkest time before dawn. Nothing stirred as they stepped into the stone-flagged courtyard.

"This way. I can smell the horses," Reothe breathed.

The stables were snug, much warmer than outside.

Tulkhan wished for light. His horse greeted him with a soft whinny as he slipped the bridle over its head. Getting onto the horse's back was not easy. He levered his weight up onto a mounting block and swung his wounded leg over.

Reothe led his horse out into the courtyard. Tulkhan's mount followed after a little urging. The beast was not eager to leave the stable's warmth. Riding high on the creature's back, Tulkhan studied Deepdeyne's defenses. It was a well-designed Stronghold—a pity, because he would have to come back and take it before he could kill Haase.

"The gates are locked. I think our unknown ally cannot help us here," Reothe muttered.

"What ally?"

Reothe looked up at him, his silver cap of shorn hair glinting in the starlight. "The healer who gave Haase a weaker drug than he requested. The people of Deepdeyne are mine, General."

Now Tulkhan understood the ease of their escape, but there was still the gate. He urged his horse into the deep shadows, holding the reins of Reothe's mount while the Dhamfeer unbarred the gate. The heavy wood creaked on its hinges.

It was enough to wake the dozing sentry, who staggered out of his warm nook, drawing his weapon. Reothe struck swiftly, but not before the man gave a strangled cry. A dog barked; more joined it, raising the alarm.

They made it through the first gate onto the short arm of the bridge. But Haase had stationed men on the tower at the bridge's bend and they were alerted. They brandished torches, swords drawn. Tulkhan knew Haase's men would be assembling in the courtyard behind them.

Reothe's horse shied. The reins tore from Tulkhan's fingers. He urged his horse forward, intent on getting past the defenders at the tower.

The narrow bridge had no rails, and as the General's horse barreled into the men, one fell into the water. Tulkhan's boot smashed into another man's face. His mount screamed and went down. Before his wounded leg could be trapped, Tulkhan rolled aside and dodged a strike to his head. He tried to rise, but his bad leg gave way.

Suddenly, Reothe was at his side, hauling him upright. The defenders regrouped, blocking the bridge. Behind them Tulkhan saw the gleam of torches and the crush of figures pouring from Deepdeyne Stronghold.

"The river," Reothe urged.

Tulkhan glanced at the icy black water. "I can't swim. Save yourself."

Instead of diving into the river, Reothe shoved Tulkhan. Off balance with his leg wound, he could only stare up in horror as he fell backward. As his back hit the river, he saw Reothe leap after him. Then the water closed over his face, so shocking, so cruelly cold that he gasped, taking in a mouthful. He was a dead man. His body tumbled over.

The irony of it hit Tulkhan. Reothe had turned the tables by murdering him in such a way that he could not be blamed.

Then Tulkhan collided with someone. Arms grabbed him, legs kicked with a purpose. Their heads broke the surface. Tulkhan gasped and coughed. He tried to grab something but there was nothing. They were in midstream. Torchlight danced crazily back on the bridge. Men shouted, pointing in their direction.

"They've seen us!" Reothe muttered. "Take a deep breath—we're going to drown."

Tulkhan drew breath to protest. Before he could, they were underwater. He had swum only once before, and that was the night he dived into Northpoint harbor to save his son. Only by opening his mind to Imoshen had he been able to swim. She had driven his arms and legs, propelling him to the wharf. Now he tried to recall those actions. The force of the swiftly flowing river drove them along. Reothe was trying to swim across the current. Tulkhan kicked until his chest protested.

Just when he knew he could last no longer, their heads broke the surface. This time the lights of Deepdeyne were far behind and they were much closer to the riverbank.

"Under again, before they spot us," Reothe urged.

Tulkhan took a breath and let himself go. The next time they surfaced, the banks consisted of black trees and pale snow. The cold had him in its clutches; bone-deep, it made his body ache and his teeth chatter uncontrollably. "Have to get out of the river."

"Not yet. They'll search the banks for our tracks." Reothe kept kicking, driving them along with the current. His body shook with cold. "Must let the river carry us further. We're lucky no one jumped in after us."

"Ghebites don't swim."

Reothe snorted. "So how did you learn to swim?"

"I'm not swimming. I'm d-dying of cold!"

They went with the current, keeping near the bank. At last Reothe caught a tree trunk that had collapsed into the river. Shaking uncontrollably, Tulkhan hauled himself onto the steep, snow-laden bank. With despair, he realized his wounded leg was useless. Unable to walk across the snowy fields to find a warm cottage, he was doomed to freeze before Haase and his men could find him. Reothe would be the one to escape, the one to return to Imoshen, guiltless of Tulkhan's death.

Reothe held out his hand.

Tulkhan looked up, seeing him silhouetted against the starlit sky. "Why?"

"Give me your hand. The snow will cover our tracks."

Self-preservation won out. Grunting with the effort, Tulkhan took his weight on his good leg and Reothe wound his arm around Tulkhan's waist. They plowed up the uneven, slippery bank in silence.

On the high ground, they paused to catch their breath. Tulkhan dragged great gulps of air in between bouts of shivering. They faced rolling snowy fields. It was hopeless. If the cold did not kill them, riders on horseback would find them by circling in ever-increasing spirals from the riverbank.

Tulkhan cursed. "Without shelter we will die."

"You forget. I know Deepdeyne. On this side of the river there is a secluded hot spring. If I can find it."

Tulkhan gave a grunt of understanding, then put all his

energy into moving. Snow fell silently about them. For a while
he could not tell if it was getting light or if it was just the snow
filling the air. After that he did not care. Every now and then,
Reothe stopped to get his bearings in the winter landscape.

Moving became an impossible effort, and the snow began
to look inviting. No longer cold, Tulkhan wondered if it would
not be simpler to tell Reothe he was right. Fair Isle belonged to
the T'En and he, Tulkhan, was the usurper.

Then even the reason Reothe was helping him ceased to
plague him. He would not give up. Survival became his imperative. For a long time he concentrated only on lifting one
foot after the other.

Suddenly he sensed a change in Reothe's pace and looked
up to discover it was light enough to see. Hope surged.

They stumbled down a steep embankment, sliding into a
snowdrift. At the base Reothe dropped Tulkhan's arms and
staggered forward to scrape at a dark patch. Snow collapsed to
reveal the entrance to a cave filled with steamy darkness.

Tulkhan crawled toward it.

With her secret fear hidden deep within her, Imoshen entered
T'Reothe's Hall. No word had come from Tulkhan and
Reothe's party except for this girl who had arrived last night,
and no one had thought to tell her until now. The child's escort
knew only that Tulkhan and Reothe were going on to
Deepdeyne. The men had reported the curious fact that this
latest child showed no sign of T'En blood.

Imoshen climbed the stair and stopped at the door. "I
greet you, Ysanna."

The little girl was a striking creature with white hair and
golden skin. She stood beside the bed and met Imoshen's eyes
with unblinking concentration. When she spoke it was with a
maturity that belied her size. "I want to go home."

Imoshen joined her. Dropping to her knees, she took the
child's small hand in her own. "Everyone will be kind to you.
You must not be afraid."

"I am not afraid."

"Of course not." Imoshen used the contact to probe, but she met a blank wall—an impressive wall. Few adults could resist her so thoroughly. Imoshen studied Ysanna's sweet face. The child's chin might tremble, but her mouth remained closed in an obstinate line. Imoshen's heart contracted in sympathy. "Wouldn't you like to live in the palace, wear fine clothes, and study with the other Malaunje children?"

"No. I only came with the T'En lord because my mother said I must. He said he had fifty men, but when I got over the hill, he had only a handful!"

Imoshen almost smiled. "If you don't like it here, you can go home. But will you stay just for a little while to see if you like it?"

"How long must I stay before I can go?"

This time Imoshen did smile. "Just till T'Reothe comes back."

"Very well."

Imoshen left her with Maigeth, who had become a fixture of the palace. Five girls, nine boys, all with T'En traits except for the last child. Now, there was a mystery. It was said the T'En males did not breed true. Unless she was mistaken, the girl was Reothe's daughter, which made her half-sister to the child Imoshen carried. By Fair Isle custom, Imoshen was duty-bound to care for her unborn child's blood relative, even though the girl was not hers.

No lessons had begun, because Reothe had left instructions only for the children's comforts. Imoshen hoped he would return with the T'Elegos. Excitement surged within her, followed by a stab of anger. How dare Reothe return if he betrayed Tulkhan? She would not be able to look him in the eye knowing he was a murderer. But she could not believe it of Reothe, *would* not believe it. Yet in her vision it had been Tulkhan who took the wound.

Imoshen massaged her temples. Why was she tormented with these gifts if they obscured more than they revealed?

"T'Imoshen? There is a man with a message."

She turned to Lightfoot. "Where is he?"

"I will escort you."

She fell into step beside him. "Do you know this man?"

"No. He is Lord Commander Haase's man from Deepdeyne."

Imoshen increased her pace, sure it was a message from Tulkhan. Eagerly, she entered the room, then stopped. "I thought you said he was waiting."

"He was." Lightfoot strode to the single table where food had been served. "And here's the message."

He glanced uneasily around the room, as though the man might be standing behind one of the hangings with a knife at the ready. But Imoshen knew he wasn't. The room was empty, yet it held the tang of something she did not recognize.

She removed a single sheet of paper from the brass cylinder and broke the plain seal. Imoshen frowned, then sniffed the paper. "Strange, it is written in the speech of Fair Isle but by a mainland scriber." She scanned the words, taking in the first three lines before she had to go back to the beginning because she could not believe what she was reading. The brass message cylinder fell from her nerveless fingers, clattering on the tiles.

"What is it?"

Silently, she handed the paper to Lightfoot. Imoshen's trembling fingers smoothed the front of her gown, where there was no sign of the life she carried. The child's father, if this message could be believed, was as good as dead.

"General Tulkhan is to be tried for treason by King Gharavan?" Lightfoot muttered. "I swear this is fell news."

"And must not go beyond this room. Haase did not write this." Imoshen indicated the paper. "He can barely make the letters of his own name. Gharavan ordered this written on the mainland, to be delivered to me on the event of their capture."

"How many days to Deepdeyne?"

"Three by fast rider. I fear Reothe and Tulkhan are already out of Fair Isle and sailing for the mainland."

"Betrayed by his own commander!" Lightfoot muttered.

The words pierced Imoshen's abstraction and, now that she understood the meaning of her vision, a wave of relief swept her. But this was just as bad. With Reothe and Tulkhan dead, how would she hold Fair Isle against the Ghebite King? How could she even think this, knowing Tulkhan faced execution and Reothe degradation before Gharavan had him killed?

She must harden her heart against their loss. Since the Ghebites invaded she had faced many grim choices. Her loyalty was to Fair Isle. But she could not let them die! Imoshen's head spun.

"Imoshen, my lady?"

Imoshen was startled to find herself on the floor, with Kalleen at her side and Lightfoot hovering over them.

Kalleen turned on the servants. "Stop gawking. Bring hot wine and food."

"What happened?" Imoshen asked.

"I sent for the Lady of Windhaven because you went white as a sheet and sank to your knees."

"Lightfoot says you've had a shock." Kalleen stood and brushed her skirts. "That is not good for women in our condition."

Imoshen fixed on this as she came to her feet. "I said nothing."

"No, but I have seen you push your breakfast away. You forget I kept you company through your last pregnancy, and I've experienced the same things with mine."

"Ah, a pregnant empress and an infant prince. What will become of the General's kingdom?" Lightfoot groaned.

"Fair Isle is my responsibility!" Imoshen snapped.

Lightfoot bowed in apology, but when he straightened, his eyes met hers, unchastened. "You are the T'En Empress, but you are still only one person and soon to be heavy with child."

He was right. Imoshen kicked the empty brass cylinder across the room in disgust. "Where have you put that damned message?"

"What message?" Kalleen asked.

Lightfoot removed the folded paper from inside his jerkin.

"Give it to Kalleen."

"But she's—"

"What? A woman?"

Lightfoot stiffened as he handed over the message. "I meant only that Lady Kalleen is not trained in the craft of war."

"And you are," Imoshen acknowledged. "I would hear your advice too."

As Kalleen read the message, her face grew visibly paler. "So this is what the vision and dreams meant. Can we buy their freedom? I know where—" She stopped abruptly, her cheeks coloring.

Imoshen used the old-empire signal for silence.

"What is gold to King Gharavan, when he has the resources of the Ghebite Empire?" Lightfoot muttered. "No, he wants revenge!"

Imoshen folded the message. "There is only one chance to save their lives, and I pray I am not too late. I must discover where the King is and sail in time to prevent Tulkhan's execution. Gharavan will want to make his revenge a public spectacle." She licked dry lips. Her experience in the Amirate made her bold.

"What if you fall into Gharavan's hands?" Kalleen whispered.

"Then I will die."

They both stared at her.

Lightfoot stiffened. "T'Imoshen, you have a responsibility to Fair Isle."

"Don't speak to me of responsibility. I have always acted for the good of Fair Isle. Just this once I will follow my heart. Kalleen, I lay this charge on you: you must keep Ashmyr safe. If I do not return, I name you Regent."

Kalleen was appalled.

Imoshen ignored Lightfoot's exclamation, turning to him. "As leader of the garrison, I name you Protector of T'Diemn. Commander Peirs I name War General of the army of Fair Isle. As Shujen of the Parakhan Guard, Drake serves you, Kalleen."

The young woman shook her head.

"Kalleen, Peirs, and Lightfoot will form a triumvirate of power. You three will serve the interests of Fair Isle until my son is of age to take an empress. A council of three, with majority rule."

The mercenary stared at her, as astounded as Kalleen was horrified. Imoshen supposed it was a long step from farm girl to regent and an equally long step from leader of a mercenary band to co-ruler of Fair Isle.

Imoshen strode to the table. "We must move quickly. Kalleen, send for the Beatific. I need her to draw up the legal documents." She frowned. "No doubt Engarad will want a finger in this pie. But which piece will I give her?"

Kalleen would have argued, but Imoshen sent her away. "Lightfoot, I want you to go to Deepdeyne. If that snake Haase is still there, I want him dead and his head spiked on the city gates."

This order was more to Lightfoot's liking. "He will expect this."

"He may, but these Ghebites always underestimate a woman. He probably thinks me cowering in my palace, terrified of the Ghebite King's wrath. Select your force and go."

He saluted her as he would salute the General.

When Tulkhan awoke, he found himself alone in the hot-spring cave. Shifting to ease the ache in his body, he realized the fever was over and the festering poisons had left his body. If his hunger was anything to go by, several days had passed. Where was Reothe?

Grunting with the effort, he pulled himself to his feet, bending almost double to avoid the low roof. The position triggered a memory. With the painful clarity of a fevered hallucination, he recalled finding Reothe huddled in pain.

Reothe's skin had been stretched over his bones so tightly that Tulkhan saw the pulse beating in his temple. When he asked what was wrong, Reothe had glared at him. "I took a life while we were escaping. The man's shade stalks me through death's shadow, and I am crippled on that plane." Dread had widened his eyes. "He comes for me again."

Tulkhan frowned as the memory faded. At that point he had believed they would both die. Then a third person had appeared, a healer with soothing hands. Those hands had packed his wound with herbs and forced him to drink a vile-tasting mixture. He could feel the bandages around his thigh, so it had not been a hallucination. Perhaps Reothe had died and the healer had taken his body away.

Painfully slow, Tulkhan limped to the mouth of the cave. He was stiff and hungry but he was alive, thanks to Reothe. And if Reothe still lived, where was he? Perhaps the Dhamfeer had left him to his fate. That made no sense. Reothe could have abandoned him many times. Shame scalded Tulkhan, for he would have abandoned Reothe. He had meant to. Yet when it had seemed there was no escape for him on the bridge, he had urged Reothe to save himself.

Tulkhan stepped out of the cave, blinking in the blinding light. Snow lay pristinely beautiful in the midday sun, individual crystals glinting like carelessly scattered diamonds.

Nothing moved, not even the air.

Tulkhan blinked and stared at a patch of darkness, which resolved itself into Reothe's face shadowed under the hood of a white cloak. He slid down into the hollow to join Tulkhan.

"When I woke and found you gone, I thought you dead." Tulkhan's voice rasped from lack of use.

The Dhamfeer pushed back his hood, revealing his narrow face, the cheekbones painfully prominent. "You confront death in your way; I, in mine." Reothe looked past him to the sky. "Haase's men have not come searching this way for two days."

"How many days has it been?"

"Six, I think."

"And the healer. Did I imagine her?"

"Is that bandage on your thigh a dream?"

"Then I didn't dream your suffering. When the soul of the man you killed stalked you through death's shadow, did the Parakletos come to your aid?"

Reothe's eyes widened, and Tulkhan was pleased to have startled him.

"Don't mention their name, True-man. They rule death's shadow, but they are capricious beings and I am no longer in their favor. Since that aborted attempt to take the Greater Pass, my mentors have abandoned me. More T'En riddles for you, Mere-man." Seeing Tulkhan's expression, Reothe laughed bitterly. Abruptly, he sobered. "I know exactly how many men I have killed, because I died a little with each of them. I am here now only because I have escaped death's shadow yet again!" Contempt narrowed Reothe's garnet eyes. "You True-men think yourselves superior to the T'En. You call us beasts. Yet you kill without compunction. Do not speak to me of this again!"

Heart pounding, Tulkhan watched as Reothe stalked toward the cave mouth. "You saved my life. Why?"

The Dhamfeer hesitated, then turned to face Tulkhan. "If one of the T'En saves someone's life, that person becomes their responsibility. They must see to it that this person is looked after in a worldly sense and if possible in a spiritual sense. But Ghebites' customs are different. Do you follow the Gheeakhan Code, General Tulkhan?"

He stiffened. "I hold my honor highly." That was why he had found it so hard to contemplate killing Reothe while under an oath of truce.

Reothe nodded, as if Tulkhan's reply confirmed what he knew. "Wharrd died in service to Imoshen, honor-bound by his Ghiad."

Reothe had saved the General's life knowing Tulkhan would be under a Ghiad to him. The General's head spun. Sunlight glinted on Reothe's closely cropped silver hair. Light flashed.

Tulkhan found himself facedown in the snow. Pushing Reothe's helping hands away, he came to his knees. The full implications of his position hit him. He was honor-bound to serve his deadly enemy.

"We must leave soon," Reothe said. "The healer won't be back. It is worth more than her life."

Tulkhan limped into the cave. "How did she find us?"

"Deduction. After we escaped from Deepdeyne, she guessed we would head for this place. None of my people will reveal the location of the hot springs."

Reothe unwrapped bread, roasted meat, and a flask of wine. He cut off a chunk of meat, offering it to Tulkhan. "Eat. You need your strength."

Hunger made Tulkhan's mouth water. He was honor-bound to serve Reothe, but did the Dhamfeer really understand what a Ghiad meant to a Ghebite?

"Don't worry," Reothe smiled sweetly. "I won't ask you to fall on your sword."

The meat turned to ash in Tulkhan's mouth.

"I have only one stipulation. Do not share Imoshen's bed."

A flare of anger engulfed Tulkhan, but he bowed his head to hide his fury, for under the Ghiad Reothe could ask for much more. He could ask for Imoshen.

Imoshen paced the map room. From information gathered, she knew that Gharavan was not in the Amirate. She longed to confront the little Ghebite King, but she would not make a move until she knew where he was. To set off too soon might mean Tulkhan's death.

Twenty

TULKHAN HID THE pain in his leg. He hoped walking was good for it; they had done enough, skirt-
ing upstream to avoid Haase's men. It had been on his
insistence that they had come back to Deepdeyne, and he
had not revealed how much trouble his leg was giving him,
not wanting to give Reothe any excuse to veto his revenge
on Haase.

Being under Ghiad to Reothe placed Tulkhan in a peculiar position. It was many years since he had followed another man's orders. Reothe could have refused Tulkhan his
revenge, just as he could have asked him to fall on his
sword, but he did not. Haase had to be killed and Reothe
understood the need to set an example. It was better to
serve out of love than fear, but sometimes a little fear was
necessary.

"The secret passage will get us inside Deepdeyne, but there
will be only the two of us against Haase and all his men,"
Reothe said. "Now, if my gifts were healed, I could slip in there
and bring out your commander without anyone noticing."

Tulkhan frowned. "And why would you do that?"

"Because I need you to help me hold Fair Isle, General." Reothe smiled disarmingly.

Tulkhan cursed silently as he headed up the slope to study
Deepdeyne. "You get us into Deepdeyne and I will do the
rest." He knew if he killed Haase, his men would surrender.

"Very well. We'll take a look at the defenses, but we'll wait until the small hours before dawn to strike."

They kept low so as to present no outline, though it would have taken an alert sentry to notice them from this distance. Once on the crest it was clear their care was not needed, for Deepdeyne was under siege.

Tulkhan was amazed to see that the encircling soldiers flew his own standard, the dawn sun. "Who?"

Reothe chuckled. "Imoshen, of course. She wouldn't let this insult pass. I expected as much."

Was Imoshen herself down there? How did she know of their capture? "Are you in contact with her, Dhamfeer?"

Reothe's eyes narrowed at the tone and term, then he smiled. Tulkhan was learning to dread that expression.

His back to a tree trunk, Reothe rolled up his sleeve to reveal the bonding scar on his wrist. "My gifts are crippled. But Imoshen and I are still bound in ways a True-man would not understand."

Tulkhan wondered if his original suspicion hadn't been correct. Perhaps killing Reothe would endanger Imoshen....

"Isn't that rider your mercenary leader?"

Tulkhan shaded his eyes. "Lightfoot! He'll know what's going on." The General plowed down the slope, limping in his urgency. Crossing the snow-covered field, he signaled the sentries, who gave a shout of recognition. His men charged out with their weapons drawn, running past him. Tulkhan turned to see Reothe surrounded by Ghebites.

Reothe held the General's eyes. Suddenly Tulkhan's mouth was too dry to swallow. He heard shouts and the sound of a rider approaching.

The horse pawed the snow, breath misting on the cold air as Lightfoot dismounted. "General? We had word...But I see report of your capture and execution was greatly exaggerated."

The mercenary glanced at Reothe, then looked a question at Tulkhan. Only the General knew he was under obligation to Reothe. He could deny the Ghiad and blame Reothe for the betrayal, ridding himself of the Dhamfeer.

"Reothe saved my life. I am under a Ghiad," Tulkhan said. Even Lightfoot knew the Ghebite term. To a man, Tulkhan's soldiers were appalled. "I am not awaiting execution nor drowned in this river because of Reothe. Put away your weapons."

Reothe's expression was unreadable. Did he think Tulkhan a fool for not ordering his death?

"Well, you are alive. This calls for a celebration!" Lightfoot filled the silence. "Come into my tent."

Tulkhan fell into place at his side. He had the men and the means to enter Deepdeyne. Before dawn tomorrow the dishonor of Haase's betrayal would be removed.

Suddenly, Lightfoot cursed.

"What?"

He lowered his voice. "I must send a fast horse with word of your safe escape. I only hope it reaches the Empress before she sails for the mainland to confront King Gharavan."

Tulkhan was astounded. "She wouldn't."

Reothe laughed outright.

The secret passage into Deepdeyne led through a damp tunnel under the river itself. The weight of water and earth above made Tulkhan's gut twist. Ahead of him Reothe led the way, dressed in borrowed mail a size too small. He carried a branch of candles, his weapon drawn.

"My parents saw to it that I knew the history of each of my estates," Reothe explained softly. "Deepdeyne's defenses are impregnable, but if the defenders wanted to make a sortie against their besiegers they could use this tunnel. Commander Haase will know nothing of it."

"Where does it come out?"

"In the old tower."

At last they came to a stone wall. Reothe removed a small plug and peered through. "Good. This wall should come down without too much trouble."

The men moved in and demolished it, removing each stone quietly. Tulkhan stepped through an archway that mimicked the arches on the surrounding walls. Barrels were stacked against one wall. Only an unlocked inner door stood between him and revenge. At this time of night, except for the sentries on the outer wall, all the inhabitants of Deepdeyne would be asleep.

"Do not hurt the locals if you can help it," Tulkhan told his men. "Lead me to the bedchambers, Reothe. We'll capture Haase before the alarm is given."

They searched the private chambers above the great hall, finding evidence of Haase's habitation but not the man himself.

Tulkhan returned to the great hall, where the men-at-arms slept, sprawled like so many dogs before the fireplace. Stepping carefully through the sleeping bodies, Tulkhan looked for Haase's sword-brother. He would know where the commander was. Tulkhan found them together.

The General signaled for his men to spread out. Weapons drawn, they stood over the sleeping men. Tulkhan had selected an equal number of his loyal Ghebites and Lightfoot's mercenaries for this attack. His soldiers had served with Haase's men. He knew it would not be easy for them to kill their companions-at-arms, but he hoped it would not come to that.

Holding his sword point to Haase's chest, Tulkhan roared, "Stand and face your fate, betrayer!"

The man awoke with a jerk, scrambling for a weapon before he knew who confronted him. Tulkhan gave him no chance, kicking him so that he flew into the wall. The startled cries of the men-at-arms faded as they woke to find themselves captured.

Haase glanced from Tulkhan to Reothe. He made the sign to ward off evil.

"What is the fate of a traitor, Haase?" Tulkhan demanded.

"No!" a voice roared.

Tulkhan spun to see Haase's sword-brother charge him, armed with a dagger. With precision, Reothe took his legs out from under him and sent the flat of his sword against the

man's skull. Even as the man was going down, Tulkhan
sensed movement and ducked. Death whistled over his head.

Haase had wrenched a long sword off the wall-
mounted display. It stood almost as tall as he. Tulkhan wondered which of Reothe's ancestors had wielded this grisly
weapon. Before Haase could regain control of the unfamiliar blade, Tulkhan stepped inside the range of the sword,
blocking it with the guard of his own. He drove his ceremonial knife up under Haase's ribs, straight to the heart. The
commander would die where he stood.

Dispassionately, Tulkhan saw him accept this.

Haase met Tulkhan's eyes. "Pray to Akha Khan, General, that you never have to choose between your honor and
your family!"

He toppled forward into Tulkhan's arms. Hiding his regret, Tulkhan laid the man's body on the floor. The General
looked up at Reothe, wondering what honor would force
him to do. Tulkhan straightened, cleaning his dagger. "That
is twice you have saved my life."

A fey smile lit Reothe's eyes. "By T'En custom, twice
over I am beholden to care for you and yours."

"By Ghebite custom, twice over I am under a Ghiad to
serve you."

"General?" Lightfoot prodded. "What will you have me
do with Haase's men?"

"First, there is a wrong I must redress." Tulkhan went to
the fireplace, where Haase's ribbons of office hung. The men
parted for him. He unhooked the three ribbons with the tip of
his sword. They slid down the length of the blade to the hilt.

"Come here, Reothe of the T'En."

Silently, Reothe approached Tulkhan and dropped to
one knee. But the subservient stance did not match the gaze
he lifted to Tulkhan. His mocking expression seemed to say,
*Do you expect me to be grateful to you for returning what is
rightfully mine?*

Tulkhan cleared his throat. "For hundreds of years your
family were the masters of Deepdeyne. You have proved a
truer friend than my own man Haase. I confiscate his estate

and return Deepdeyne to your care." He dropped the white ribbon over Reothe's head. "White to symbolize the purity of service to the people of Deepdeyne." He slipped the red ribbon into place. "Red symbolizes the blood you have shed and are willing to shed in their defense." As he let the black ribbon fall, his fingers brushed Reothe's short hair. It was soft and so fine that the sensation barely registered. "Black symbolizes death, which comes to us all."

As the words faded, Tulkhan felt himself to be more T'En than Ghebite. He recalled how Imoshen had first surprised him with this ceremony. Now he understood the significance. No matter how powerful you became, death awaited everyone, and the higher you rose, the more you served.

If he had been a Ghebite, Reothe would have kissed the naked blade Tulkhan still held; instead, he rose and met the General's eyes. Tulkhan read a reluctant emotion, quickly masked. Then Reothe stepped aside to stand just behind Tulkhan on his left. With a start, Tulkhan realized Reothe was honoring him.

Facing the others, the General sensed a shift in the balance of power. His men did not despise their general because he was under a Ghiad to the last Dhamfeer warrior. Somehow, Reothe's position at his back, their miraculous escape, and the taking of Deepdeyne had all added to the aura surrounding him. Tulkhan raised his voice. "Men of Deepdeyne, you have a choice. Swear fealty to me, or join your commander in death."

Late that evening, Tulkhan sat at the table in the great hall, where the fire had burned low. He had sent Lightfoot back to the capital with word for Imoshen, and all day the locals had come into Deepdeyne to swear fealty to their hereditary leader, honored by the new regime. Tulkhan had legitimized Reothe, but he could not leave him at Deepdeyne.

What was he thinking? He was under a Ghiad to Reothe. The Dhamfeer could do whatever he liked. Tulkhan's head ached. He dreaded returning to T'Diemn and Imoshen.

Reothe dropped a bottle of Vorsch beside Tulkhan's elbow. "Share a drink with me, General? I promise it's not drugged."

He sat two small glasses next to the bottle. Their solid bases rattled on the scrubbed boards.

"So, you have taken a liking to Vorsch?" Tulkhan dredged up an acceptable reply.

"No. I chose it because you like it." Reothe uncorked the bottle and inhaled the scent. "Though it does have a certain—"

Reothe's eyes widened at something behind Tulkhan. The General turned to see someone charge out of the shadows. A naked blade flashed. Tulkhan reached for his own weapon, but before he drew it Reothe lunged, his sword flying past Tulkhan's left ear.

Haase's sword-brother screamed. Tulkhan's chair hit the floor. The corpse lay twitching in a steadily expanding pool of blood. Several men who had been drinking on the floor below charged up the stairwell, weapons drawn.

"Who was watching Haase's sword-brother?" Tulkhan demanded.

A man stepped forward. "He was asleep a moment ago, General."

Tulkhan did not pursue this; instead, he glanced to Reothe, who was staring grimly down at the corpse.

"Throw him into the moat," Tulkhan ordered, denying the man the honor of a Ghebite warrior's burial. "And get out."

They dragged the man away, leaving blood smears on the floor. Tulkhan righted his chair and poured two drinks. "Again you have saved my life."

"You would have saved yourself. I acted on reflex."

Tulkhan considered this. "Yes. But I would probably have been wounded for my lack of wariness." The General wanted to ask Reothe how long before he suffered for the man's death, but his expression did not welcome confidences.

Reothe drained the Vorsch in one gulp.

The General watched the candle flame through his glass. He knew Reothe did not wish to discuss this, but Tulkhan had always thirsted for knowledge. "You killed him on reflex.

But I have known you to kill with forethought. Two days after you touched him, one of my commanders delivered your
message and dropped dead at my feet." Tulkhan shuddered
at the memory. He silently thanked the trick of fate that had
driven Imoshen to cripple Reothe's powers.

Reothe said nothing.

Tulkhan sipped his Vorsch. Before long Reothe would
lie in a delirium, hurting and vulnerable. Yet the Ghiad prevented Tulkhan from killing him. "You call yourself greater
than a True-man who kills and does not suffer for it. I put
this to you: The T'En are less than True-men because they
know what death is and yet they still kill!"

Reothe's face registered shock, then cold fury.

Tulkhan shrugged and poured himself another glass.

The Dhamfeer paced across the floor to the open
hearth. Placing his hands on the mantelpiece, he stared into
the glowing coals.

Despite Reothe's casual stance, Tulkhan's heart
pounded. If Reothe challenged him, he was entitled to defend himself by the laws governing the Ghiad.

Reothe stalked back. Tulkhan's body tightened in anticipation. His hand closed on his sword hilt. He knew the speed
of the T'En warrior's reactions. If he failed to block Reothe's
killing stroke, could he drag the Dhamfeer through death's
shadow with him?

Reothe came to a stop.

Tulkhan schooled his features, waiting for the first sign
of attack. Reothe stared down at him, the single flame barely
illuminating his face so that his eyes were dark pools.

The silence stretched until Tulkhan felt the tension
thrum through his body like a tightly drawn bow string.

Abruptly, Reothe gave him the old-empire obeisance.
"You are right, Tulkhan."

Tulkhan's skin crawled. How could Reothe make him
feel vulnerable simply by uttering his name?

With formal courtesy, Reothe topped up Tulkhan's
glass, refilled his own, and took his seat. The General had
to force his fingers to release his sword hilt.

Reothe sipped his Vorsch thoughtfully. "If I still had my gift, I would trawl your mind, True-man. You think differently."

Tulkhan repressed a shudder, grateful that this was impossible. Feeling he had the advantage, he pursued the point. "If your gifts are crippled, why does killing still affect you?"

Reothe stared morosely at the candle, playing casually with the flickering flame. He circled it, just avoiding scorching the remaining fingertips of his left hand.

When Tulkhan thought he had no intention of answering, Reothe spoke. "The T'En are different. This difference lies deep within our minds. Once I could have caressed the flame and wooed it to do my bidding. Now I am only aware that it exists." He saw that the General did not understand. "You know this flame will burn if it touches your skin, and you know how to put it out. Imagine that you have lost the ability to put out the flame, but it can still burn you. That is what Imoshen has done to me!"

For an instant Tulkhan glimpsed Reothe's agony, and unwelcome sympathy moved him. But he would not be distracted. "Does this mean your powers are healing?"

"If I'd had even a fraction of my gift, I would have known Haase meant to betray you. I would have smelled it on him!"

Reothe's revelation opened Tulkhan's eyes to the difference between a True-man and the T'En. Every time Tulkhan thought he was growing to understand Imoshen and Reothe, he discovered how much he still had to learn. "If your gifts are crippled, how did you survive death's shadow?"

Reothe laughed. "My gifts might be crippled, but I still have my wits!"

Tulkhan found this just as cryptic. He changed the subject. "Tomorrow we return to the capital. I'm under a Ghiad to you. Why don't you send me away on a mission I can't hope to survive?"

"Your men are loyal to you, not me. Even if you died, Gharavan might choose to avenge himself on Fair Isle. I need you to hold Fair Isle until I am ready to retake it."

As with Imoshen, Reothe used the truth like a knife to cut to the bone of the matter.

"Why tell me?" Anger closed Tulkhan's throat, making his voice a low growl. "Surely you must know I will kill you."

Reothe held his eyes. "Not until you are free of the Ghiad. How can you forget, Tulkhan? You are thrice bound by the Gheeakhan Code."

Fury and three glasses of Vorsch drove Tulkhan to speak before he considered his words. "Maybe I will kill you while you wander death's shadow!"

Reothe rose, graceful and utterly Other. "You will abide by your Ghiad because you are an honorable man, and that is why Imoshen loves you."

Determined to hide her misgivings, Imoshen greeted Reothe and Tulkhan in the map room. She stood on the far side of the table so that she could observe them. Tulkhan's broken nose was a visible reminder of how close she had to come to losing them both. She pushed the message across the desk toward the General. "Gharavan boasts he will take Fair Isle from you."

The force of Reothe's gaze was a physical thing. She knew that he was waiting for her to meet his eyes, but she would not give him the satisfaction.

With Wharrd's death, she understood what a Ghiad meant to a Ghebite. Tulkhan would die for Reothe. She wanted to be certain he did not have to. As for Reothe . . . what double game was he playing? Her gaze strayed to his face, and what she read there did not reassure her. Reothe's narrow features were even more sharply defined. If she had not known better, she would have said he had been deathly ill. His eyes, brilliant as garnets, blazed with keen intelligence.

When Lightfoot had explained Haase's betrayal, Imoshen cursed herself. If she had healed Reothe he would have known the man plotted treachery. Her lack of trust in Reothe had placed Tulkhan's life at risk. Once again she balanced on the knife's edge, unable to bring herself to trust Reothe enough to make him whole.

Tulkhan made a disgusted noise as he finished reading the message, which proclaimed his capture and ended with Gharavan's threats. When he passed it to Reothe without being asked, Imoshen marked this.

Reothe spoke to Tulkhan with the familiarity of a trusted adviser. "Does the little king have the ability to raise an army of sufficient size to do what he threatens?"

As she waited for the previous General of the Ghebite army to answer this, Imoshen marveled at how quickly Reothe had gained Tulkhan's trust.

"Gharavan might be able to raise an army of sufficient size. I could have done it."

"Then we face invasion come spring," Imoshen spoke, her mouth dry. Tulkhan had taken Fair Isle with less men. The strength of the army depended on the leader. Fair Isle's army was depleted, but Imoshen had General Tulkhan. His leadership might be their salvation. Reothe caught Imoshen's eye; their minds ran along similar paths.

Tulkhan's brows drew down. "What's this about Kalleen being made Regent?"

Imoshen gave a little start, surprised by the change of subject and the speed with which Tulkhan had caught up with events. "I see you have been speaking with Lightfoot. I had to make provision for the future of our son and Fair Isle in case I was killed confronting Gharavan."

Tulkhan met Imoshen's challenging eyes across the table littered with the letters of state and maps. She had held the reins of rulership since the day he sailed for Port Sumair, and she had not faltered. "But Kalleen? She is—"

"A woman?" Imoshen bristled.

"You would make a farm girl Regent?" he countered.

Imoshen came to her feet. "Do you object because she was born a farm girl or because she is a woman? If it is because of her sex, you insult *me*. If it is because of her origin, you insult *yourself*. You are the one who claims a person should be judged by their worth, not their birth!"

Tulkhan felt the overflow of Imoshen's gifts roll from her skin, making the little hairs on his body rise and his heart race. He wanted to bathe in that sensation. At her most T'En, Imoshen fascinated him. He found himself on his feet, glaring at her.

A slow hand-clapping pierced the roaring in his head, and he looked around to see Reothe mocking them with the Ghebite form of applause.

"Reothe!" Imoshen hissed.

He offered the old-empire obeisance and left.

"How could you give him power over you, Tulkhan?"

"He saved my life. I am thrice bound under a Ghiad to him."

Imoshen gasped, her fair skin draining of all color. "Thrice bound? This is fell news, indeed."

"How so?" Anger drove him. "What could be better— Reothe crippled and your war general forced to serve him?"

Imoshen's lips parted as if she would say something, but instead she only stared at him. He hated to see her distraught and ached to take her in his arms. "Don't play your tricks on me, Imoshen. I cannot be influenced by your gifts!"

Imoshen cursed in High T'En. "I would not stoop to influence your thoughts, but if his gifts were restored, Reothe would. When will you learn, General? *I* am not the enemy!"

"You don't need to tell me Reothe is my enemy."

"For now Reothe is your ally against Gharavan. To quote an old T'En saying, *My enemy's enemy is my friend.* And your half-brother's greatest ally is your lack of trust in me! If we are to leave anything to our son, we must unite to defeat Gharavan. It's nearly Midwinter Feast. We don't have long to prepare for war. What will the people of Fair Isle do?"

"They will fight or die."

"If only all life was that simple!" Imoshen sighed. She had been ready to confront Gharavan and risk death for Tulkhan. Her throat felt tight, and she moved around the table to him. "I thought I had lost you to your half-brother's thirst for revenge."

"Not yet. Not ever."

Yearning filled her; she stroked his broken nose. "Let me heal you."

"It is healed."

"I can smooth it."

"I am what I am, Imoshen."

She laughed, and the warmth in his black eyes illuminated her. "Why wear—"

"I will wear my broken nose until the day I die to remind me how close I came to playing into Gharavan's hand."

"I feared you lost!" She embraced him with all her strength. Tulkhan kissed her tear-damp cheeks. She wanted to abandon herself to his touch. She could feel the need in him, but Kalleen's door-comb sounded.

"I request an audience with the Protector General," she said formally.

Imoshen wondered what Kalleen wanted, but old-empire protocol forbade questions, so she left them alone.

Kalleen looked up at Tulkhan earnestly. "General, you must reason with Imoshen. I don't want to be Regent!"

He laughed. As if Kalleen would ever be Regent of Fair Isle.

"Please?" She caught his arm in her small hand. He was reminded of the women of his own race, but Kalleen was no subservient wife-slave. Her fierce will illuminated her. "Please, do this one thing for me. The decree remains in the Beatific's safekeeping. If anything were to happen to you and Imoshen, I would be Regent."

"Nothing will happen to us." He held her shoulders, feeling the fragile bones. Already she was big with Wharrd's child.

"You cannot know that, but the T'En can. Have you asked yourself why Imoshen has done this?"

Her words struck a chill in him.

"She has the Sight!" Kalleen whispered. "It comes on her without the use of the scrying plate."

"Imperfectly. She sees things and misinterprets them. Like Haase's betrayal." When Tulkhan slid an arm around the little woman's shoulders, he was surprised by a protective urge. "Do not fear, Kalleen. You will never be Regent."

Imoshen led Reothe down the path to T'Reothe's Courtyard to see the Malaunje children. Screened from view, they watched them play for a moment. Imoshen noticed Drake's covetous expression, making her wonder if he was sorry that the T'En gifts skipped his generation. She had never thought someone might court the T'En curse. "As you see, they are all well cared for and happy."

"I did not expect less." Reothe stepped around the screen. When they saw Reothe and Imoshen, the children dropped their colored balls and came running—all but Ysanna.

A little boy tucked his hand inside Imoshen's. "Will you show us how to do the fire trick, Empress T'Imoshen?"

"Just T'Imoshen," Imoshen corrected, and glanced at Reothe. "You have already been to see them, carrying tales, I see."

Reothe nodded. "Come inside."

Imoshen was reminded that their every move was watched.

A single door opened from the courtyard. Narrow fingers of afternoon sunlight pierced the deep-set windows, picking out imperfections in each small pane of glass. Imoshen liked the aura of age, the wood-paneled wainscoting, the rich wall hangings, and the T'En-sized furniture, chairs, and tables. Why hadn't she been born four hundred years ago?

Reothe led her to the huge fireplace, where wood had been laid but not lit. The children stamped their feet to warm them, shedding snow on the flags.

Imoshen knelt before the fireplace.

"Quiet now," Reothe ordered. "Watch and open your senses. Afterward, see if you can tell me how the Empress does this. Go ahead, Imoshen."

It felt strange to be encouraged to use her gift. A small child climbed into her lap and two more sat on each side of her. For the first time in her life, Imoshen felt truly accepted. She relaxed and reached for the power, welcoming the familiar taste on the back of her tongue. A rush of awareness traveled through her body, and she knew it would be easy to ignite a spark in the kindling. Like tripping a trap, she felt a snap in her mind. The children laughed, clicking their fingers in approval.

"Now," Reothe said. "Who knows how it was done?"

One by one they shook their heads.

"Ysanna?" Reothe asked. She glared at him. An older girl licked her lips but did not speak. Reothe looked disappointed. Drake made a sound in his throat.

Imoshen came to her feet, smiling on him. "How goes the Parakhan Guard?" He had been honored to learn she meant to leave her son and Kalleen in his care, though he had argued against Lightfoot and Peirs's involvement. He would have been happier to see the Triumvirate consist of Kalleen, himself, and the Beatific.

Before Drake could speak, Maigeth arrived. "Time to eat, children. Thank your T'En mentors."

Suddenly formal, the children lined up. Imoshen watched as they paraded past, giving the old-empire obeisance. They formed pairs behind Maigeth and Drake to walk to the hall where their meals were served. Imoshen caught the hand of the girl who would have spoken. When she probed, she felt the bud of her gift lying dormant, waiting to bloom. Imoshen squeezed the girl's fingers. "One day soon, Larassa. Join the others."

When the last two had gone, Imoshen turned to Reothe, who was watching her closely.

"She sensed something?" Reothe asked. He sighed. "I thought there would be some among them who could already use their gifts."

"Perhaps it is for the best that the gifts do not bloom until we reach puberty."

"My gifts were moving before then."

Imoshen recalled the Beatific's poisonous words. Had Reothe triggered his parents' joint suicides? It had to be a lie. "Mine did not start until I was a woman. And then the ability came on slowly, until..." She did not need to finish. Reothe had known her powers would grow with the birth of her children. "Is this part of what Imoshen the First wrote about in the T'Elegos?"

"The T'Elegos is waiting for you, as soon as you are ready to meet my terms."

"Terms?" Anger warmed her. How could he lay down terms when she had the power to restore his gifts? Suddenly she realized that she'd had a bargaining tool all along. Once she knew the secrets of the T'Elegos, there would be no need to fear Reothe's restored gifts. "Maybe I have my own terms."

She saw him accept this and understood he'd been waiting for this moment. He was more devious than she.

"And what do you offer me, Imoshen?"

Twenty-one

YOUR GIFTS RESTORED," Imoshen said. A muscle jumped in his cheek. It thrilled her to be in control.

"What are your terms?"

"Bring the T'Elegos to the palace and..." Here she paused, suddenly unsure. "Swear that you will not harm Tulkhan."

His surprise gave way to anger. "I saved his life. Do you think me so dishonorable that this counts for nothing?"

Her heart lurched. "I can only judge you by your past actions. You did not hesitate to cloak your form in that of Tulkhan's to come to my bed."

He flinched. "I did what I had to do."

"Exactly!"

"Would you respect me if I did not? How can you accuse me, when we both know you are using the General to hold Fair Isle? When the time comes and Fair Isle is safe, which of us will you choose, my Empress?"

Imoshen turned to the fireplace, thinking that Reothe had been reared in the royal household of the old empire, where the Empress's word was law. But this did not mean he would not try to influence her choice. His every action proclaimed his belief that she would eventually honor her vows to him.

"You are no longer that girl-woman I first met, out of

her depth in the Empress's court, Imoshen. I loved you then because I could sense the fierce flame of your being." His breath stirred the fine hairs on the back of her neck.

She felt him standing just behind her, not actually touching—but, then, he did not have to touch her.

"Shenna?"

Blindly, she grasped the mantelpiece and pressed her head against her hands. The heavy indentations of Tulkhan's Ghebite-seal ring bit into her brow, reminding her of her dual loyalties.

"Don't tell me you feel nothing. Events have come between us, but what we share goes deeper." He slid his arms around her waist. His lips brushed the back of her neck, sending a rush of warmth through her. A sigh escaped her as her body molded against his. She felt him smile.

"Heal me and I will bring you the T'Elegos," he urged, lips moving like living silk on her cheek. "It must be done in secret. Only the Beatific and the Master-archivist know the history still exists and they have no reason to consult it, so they do not know I have taken it. I promise not to kill Tulkhan until he has served his purpose."

Even as she spun to confront him, her anger dissipated. "You would not kill him. You are testing me."

He laughed. "I knew the day would come when I could no longer play you."

"You mock me. I was barely sixteen when we met. You've always had the advantage of experience. But I have only sought to do what is right."

"Whatever the cost?"

She shrugged. Without explanation, she went to the inner door, locking it, then she locked the courtyard door. Imoshen finally understood why she had chosen this hall. They were in a state of siege, the T'En. She was protecting her own. As she approached Reothe, her heart raced. The mind-touch was like an addiction, one that laid her open to his gifts. But it had also made him vulnerable to her, allowing her to cripple him. So much of what she did was instinctive, but she had learned a great deal about the use of her gifts in these last small moons.

He waited, intense and contained, as she joined him on the hearth.

"This could hurt. Close your eyes," she said, and without question he obeyed. "Open to me."

He took a ragged breath.

Imoshen stood on tiptoe to kiss his closed lids, first one, then the other, the healer in her bestowing this asexual blessing. She inhaled his breath as he exhaled, seeking his essence—that cool, bright spark she had known during their moment of intimacy.

The room, the fire, all sounds faded. She focused only on the pursuit of Reothe. Once before, when their minds had touched, she had not been able to escape the force of his will; this time she used her will to pursue him to his source, past the scarred landscape of his gift. At last she found him, trapped and bitter but still recognizable. Knowing that she had been the cause of his destruction tore at her.

As he welcomed her, his overwhelming emotion was one of relief. She felt as if she had come home, but it would have been too easy to remain there with him. Disciplining herself, she sought to repair the damage. She smoothed the scars that had barricaded his power, blocking its use. When this was half completed she broke contact, gliding away from him through the tortured terrain of his gift, leaving him stranded.

Imoshen returned to her senses to find herself kneeling on the floor before the fireplace with Reothe's head in her lap. She could see his eyes moving under the closed lids. Gasping, he returned to the waking state with bitter comprehension. Imoshen smoothed his fine hair, feeling its blunt ends. "Do you know what I have done?"

He pulled away from her. "You hold my gifts to ransom. Do you delight in your cruelty, Empress?"

"I had a good teacher, T'Reothe." She saw him accept this and continued. "When the T'Elegos is in my possession, I will fully restore your power. At least now you will not be so vulnerable to the Ghebites."

Imoshen crept on silent bare feet across the General's study to the fur rug before the hearth where Tulkhan slept. This was the third night he had not come to her bed, and she ached to touch him. Breath tight in her chest, she knelt beside him, admiring the line of his jaw.

Licking dry lips, she lifted a tentative hand, and her fingertips hovered above his chest. Suddenly, his hand flashed up and caught her wrist. With a flick he pulled her off balance and rolled on top, pinning her to the ground.

She bit back a cry of protest and wriggled against him.

"Ah, Imoshen," he whispered regretfully. "Don't do that."

"Why not?" When he did not answer, she pursued it. "Why haven't you come to my bed? I can feel how much you want me."

With a curse he sat back on his heels.

She knelt by the fire, suddenly fearful that he had discovered how she had partially restored Reothe's gifts. "What troubles you, Tulkhan?"

In frustration he flicked his heavy dark hair over his shoulder. "You know I am under a Ghiad, Imoshen."

Did this mean he could not sleep with her? Perhaps this was why Kalleen had felt rejected by Wharrd. "I don't quite understand. . . ."

"I think you do. Reothe has forbidden me to lie with you."

Imoshen's cheeks flamed. "He does not have the right—"

"He does, and more."

She met Tulkhan's dark eyes, seeing the regret and longing there. How Reothe must be laughing.

"There is one consolation," Tulkhan confessed. "He does not realize that if he asked I would have to relinquish you to him."

Imoshen snorted. "You could not relinquish me, because I am not your property, and Reothe knows that!"

His mouth opened, then closed. He shrugged. "I find it hard to walk the line between the Ghebite world and your world. Every day I grow further away from my people."

"And a little further from me, if Reothe has his way."

"I will not dishonor my Ghiad."

She stared at Tulkhan. The flickering flames sculpted his broad cheekbones, making his coppery skin glow. She wanted him to defy the Gheeakhan, but the warrior code defined him and she could not ask him to dishonor it. "How can you serve out the Ghiad?"

"I must save Reothe's life three times. A life for a life, Imoshen. It is the Ghebite way. If someone killed a member of my family I would have to take their life to avenge them. If someone saves my life I must repay that debt, and Reothe—"

"But three times?" Imoshen said. Now that she had partially restored Reothe's gifts, it would make Tulkhan's Ghiad harder to serve.

"What is it?" He was too perceptive.

Shaking her head, she went to him, kneeling between his thighs. "Reothe would know if you broke your word. He would smell your scent on my skin." She traced the line of his mouth with her fingertip, feeling the bristle of his jaw and the heat of his breath. "Kiss me before I go back to my cold, lonely bed."

Tulkhan swallowed.

Imoshen lifted her face to him and closed her eyes, concentrating on the touch of his lips as they explored hers. Liquid heat pooled in her core. Her breath caught in her throat. Everything was reduced to this one moment and him.

Breathing raggedly, Tulkhan pulled back. "Go now."

She did not argue, slipping away, her body sensitized but unfulfilled.

As the long Midwinter's Day celebrations stretched into an even longer evening, Tulkhan's eyes narrowed. Across the great hall, the Beatific was in deep discussion with Reothe. What mischief were they planning?

Lightfoot approached him. "I've been challenged to a practice duel. Will you stand at my back?"

Tulkhan grinned. He knew his men would not put up

with these civilized entertainments for long. If he had to sit through another session of dueling poets, never knowing when they would turn their razor-sharp tongues on him, he would not be answerable for the consequences.

"In the long gallery?" Tulkhan asked.

Lightfoot nodded.

"I'll be there."

Tulkhan came to his feet, weaving through the clustered townspeople, Keldon nobles, entertainers, and loyal Ghebites. This time last year he had shared the bonding ceremony with Imoshen, then they had slipped away together. He had felt a presentiment then that this would not last, and less than a year later he was fighting to retain Fair Isle.

His thirty-first birthday had come and gone with no one knowing. Even so, his True-man body would betray him, growing old while Imoshen was still in her prime. As if his thoughts called her, Imoshen met his eyes above the heads. She sent him a questioning glance, which he ignored. He was intent on clipping Reothe's wings.

"Beatific." Tulkhan acknowledged her, then addressed Reothe. "My men are giving a sword display. I thought you would like to see it."

"Swordsmanship?" Reothe grinned. "How can you honor it with this name when you wield plowshares instead of swords?"

Tulkhan recalled that Imoshen had once said much the same thing. "I suppose you think the knitting needles the T'En call swords are superior?"

Reothe smiled slowly, his challenge evident. The last time they had faced each other with swords in hand, Reothe had wounded the General with one of those knitting needles.

A rush of anger warmed Tulkhan. "I challenge you to a practice duel with Ghebite weapons."

"I accept. But not before you accept my challenge. Let me show you why a T'En sword requires more precision than brute strength."

"Very well. In the long gallery before the next bell!"

Tulkhan spun on his heel and stalked off, hardly aware of the revelers who parted for him.

"General?" Imoshen's hand closed on his arm. "Would you dance with me?"

He held her eyes. "Does your touch satisfy your curiosity? Can you tell what Reothe and I were arguing about?"

"I don't need to touch you to know you play games of male bravado. I thought we might dance to appease those who look for division."

Tulkhan fought the need to take her in his arms, to lay claim to her before everyone here, before Reothe. "You know I can't dance."

"So you say, but I've seen your sword work. You could dance if you chose!" She held his eyes, always a challenge. "Will I have the minstrels strike up a Ghebite pair dance?"

It was on the tip of his tongue to agree, but then he thought of his men waiting in the gallery and Reothe watching, planning to belittle him in swordplay. Wanting Imoshen consumed him. "No dancing. But you can kiss your husband good night, my wife." The words had barely left his lips when he realized his mistake. To Imoshen, *husband* meant master.

Her eyes flashed red with fury. But she surprised him by stepping closer. "Is it a kiss you want, General Tulkhan?"

That and so much more...

Imoshen lifted her face, eyes angry, lips parted.

Knowing others could not see her anger, only the supposed surrender of her lips, he kissed her from the depths of his soul. He knew the instant her quicksilver passion ignited. He groaned. Her answering gasp told him she was as shaken as he.

Dimly, he heard the music stop and recalled where they were. With difficulty he broke contact, lifting his head to draw breath. Imoshen smiled up at him like a satisfied cat. He recollected himself and took his leave.

Imoshen met Reothe's eyes across the crowd. Forbidding Tulkhan to make love to her had only strengthened her hold on the General. Reothe's garnet eyes blazed. She felt the force of his gift. The people between them laughed too loudly, spoke too quickly, responding to the rush of energy. But Imoshen withstood it and Reothe faltered, his hand going to the Beatific's shoulder for support. The woman's glare told Imoshen she had committed a breach of high-court etiquette.

Impervious to the Beatific's censure, Imoshen returned to Kalleen, who asked, "What was that all about?"

"Tulkhan and I do not agree on the roles of bond-partners." Imoshen opted for the simplest answer. "He called me *wife*."

Kalleen rolled her eyes. "Oh, Imoshen. You mustn't let him tease you. The General might be a Ghebite, but he is a good man."

Imoshen scooped up Ashmyr, who had fallen asleep in his basket, and drew Kalleen to her feet. She was a little awkward now with the weight of her pregnancy. "Let us escape while we can."

Heading for the staircase, Imoshen swayed with the weight of the baby and basket, but Kalleen lingered to look through the multipaned doors that gave onto the well-lit gallery.

When Imoshen focused on the scene beyond, her heart turned over. Tulkhan and Reothe were at each other's throats, swords flashing.

The slender T'En sword went spinning out of Tulkhan's hand and Reothe laughed, lowering his. "You see, it is all in the wrist, General."

Relief flooded Imoshen.

Tulkhan retrieved his blade. "Once more and I will get this right!"

Reothe saluted him.

Tulkhan returned the salute. "You know I'm only letting you disarm me because when you get the Ghebite sword in your hands the tables will be turned."

"Of course. Defend yourself!" Reothe lunged, coming perilously close to spitting him.

Kalleen gasped. "Tulkhan!"

Watching from the dark stairwell, jealousy stirred in Imoshen's breast. She had asked Tulkhan to teach her the use of the Ghebite sword, but he always put her off because, in his mind, a woman did not touch a weapon. Yet there he was, sharing this skill with the fallen rebel leader. How could Reothe be accepted by Tulkhan and his men when she, who had done everything in her power to support the General, received only grudging respect?

Frustration seared Imoshen. How long before Tulkhan revealed Seerkhan's sword to Reothe? She guarded the intimacy of that memory, aware that Reothe, with his insidious T'En charm, could take even this from her.

Tulkhan's sword spun away again, and Reothe saluted him. "Well done. It takes years to master this."

"Let's see how you fare with a Ghebite weapon." The General's men hurried forward with the weapons and he selected two. After testing them for weight and balance, he handed one to Reothe.

Imoshen watched as Reothe grasped the unfamiliar hilt, assessing its differences. She remembered the feel of the Ghebite sword in her hand the day she challenged Tulkhan in the snow-laden courtyard. The General should have welcomed her meeting him as an equal; instead, he had sought to teach her her place, and now Reothe wormed his way into Tulkhan's trust by virtue of his gender.

"I never thought to see it," Kalleen commented under her breath. "Only a short while ago they were ready to kill each other, and now they are sword-brothers."

Astonishment flooded Imoshen. She had been blind. Sword-brothers. That was why it was so easy for Tulkhan to accept Reothe—it was the Ghebite way.

Kalleen arched her back. "I don't think I can stand much longer. I'm for bed."

Still coming to terms with this revelation, Imoshen accompanied her. Anger powered her steps as she climbed the stairs. She must not let all she had worked for slip away, stolen by Reothe.

But Reothe was cunning; he monopolized Tulkhan's time. They rode the new defenses of T'Diemn together, they went hunting, and, as the days turned into weeks, Imoshen seethed.

Knowing that Reothe visited T'Reothe's Hall daily, returning via the narrow stairwell, Imoshen lay in wait for him. The sound of his soft footfalls made her body tighten in anticipation. She stepped out of the shadows.

"Imoshen?" he greeted her warily.

"When will I see the T'Elegos?" she hissed. "You have had the benefit of my part of the bargain for weeks now."

"I cannot leave T'Diemn without an escort of spies. Who would you trust with the knowledge that the T'Elegos survives?"

"Then when?"

"It is still several weeks until the cusp of spring. When the snows melt—"

"So it is in the Keldon Highlands?"

"When the snows melt, the General will continue his inspection of Fair Isle's defenses. I will collect more Malaunje children. Then I will retrieve the T'Elegos. Have patience, Imoshen. It is not what you think. Believe me, I've studied—"

"What have you studied?" Tulkhan asked as he rounded the bend in the narrow stair. Desperately, Imoshen searched for a distraction.

"Shields," Reothe said. "Come, I'll show you." He retraced his steps.

Heart thumping, Imoshen followed. Reothe led them past the entrance to T'Reothe's Hall through a dark connecting gallery to T'Ashmyr's Hall, built in the first century of T'En rule. If Imoshen had guessed correctly, the T'Endomaz dated from this time.

Reothe strode across the worn flags. First Throwback Emperor, T'Ashmyr himself had paced this room, planning his campaigns to consolidate his hold on Fair Isle. Dragging a chair against the wall, Reothe climbed onto it to remove a shield from the display. Imoshen hoped there was substance to Reothe's claim, because Tulkhan would see through fabrication.

"Here." Reothe tossed the shield to Tulkhan, who slid his arm through the grip and tested its weight. Imoshen caught Reothe's eye as he jumped down, trying to warn him to tread carefully, but his eyes laughed at her.

"Light and strong." Tulkhan turned the shield so that it glowed in the dim light. "Beautifully made. But what—"

"It's the shape," Reothe said. "Ghebite cavalry shields are small and round; this one tapers to a point. Your shields leave a rider's legs unprotected. Five hundred years ago, T'Ashmyr designed these shields. Tomorrow I'll meet you on horseback. Arm yourself as you normally would and we'll see which shield offers better protection for a mounted warrior."

"Done!" When Tulkhan grinned, his teeth flashing white against his coppery skin in the darkness, Imoshen felt a tug deep within her. She missed his touch. The more he withdrew from her, the harder she found it to resist Reothe's lure. He had not invaded her dreams, but she was sensitized to him. She felt him watching her. She knew if he had been in a room before her and sensed his essence on objects that he had recently touched. She did not know if this was deliberate or just a by-product of his half-healed gifts.

The General stood opposite her, barely visible in the twilight of the old hall, the shield in his grasp, shielded from her by his warrior code. Imoshen was very aware of Reothe only two steps away. Like victims of a spider, they were caught in a web of events and broken promises, bound by the fabric of their positions and personalities. Struggle as they might, Imoshen could see no honorable solution that did not include the death of one of these men, and that she could not bear. She dreaded to make a move in case it precipitated her worst fears. A silence of things left unsaid stretched between them. The air grew heavy with expectation. Imoshen licked her lips and drew breath to speak.

Three servants entered, armed with brooms, their candles held high.

"Empress," the first gasped. "We heard voices and feared—"

"Ghosts of T'Ashmyr's reign?" Imoshen laughed, surprised to hear how natural she sounded. "I'm afraid we must disappoint you. There are no apparitions here, only scholars of ancient weaponry." She glided over to them. "But I thank you for bringing light. We let our enthusiasm carry us away." Holding the candle high, she turned to Tulkhan. "Do you want to inspect the weapons?"

He hefted the shield. "Trial by combat will suffice."

As he and Reothe passed her, comparing cavalry-training exercises, Imoshen repressed a surge of annoyance. She hated not being in control.

Tulkhan looked up from his maps to see Imoshen sweep into the room. Radiant, imperious, and untouchable. He ached for what he could not have.

"Nearly spring, and new T'Diemn's earthworks—"

"Will progress whether I am here or not. I must review the defenses of northern Fair Isle," Tulkhan said. "I leave Lightfoot to oversee the work."

"And I suppose you take Reothe with you?"

"Of course!" He could hardly leave him here to stir up trouble. "Besides, Reothe is still looking for half-breed children. He has searched but a third of Fair Isle."

"When you go to Northpoint, take Reothe to the hospice. Eksyl may wish to accompany the children back here." She chewed her bottom lip. "Tulkhan, Reothe seeks to win your trust with the cavalry drilling and the new shields."

"Whatever his motives, my cavalry benefits."

Imoshen looked down, then up again swiftly. "Have you shown him Seerkhan's sword?"

"No." Tulkhan wondered why Imoshen seemed relieved. "It was torn from my hand in the Low-land flood. I meant to bestow it on my son, but I fear it lost, buried in Low-land mud."

"I am sorry," Imoshen said. "Will you teach me to use the Ghebite sword?"

He did not understand why Imoshen watched him so intensely. Perhaps she feared Gharavan would invade before he could return. "Lightfoot commands T'Diemn's garrisons. With his years of experience, you will not need to use a sword."

"I see," Imoshen said, as though he had failed a test. "I may not be here when you return. Kalleen's baby is due soon, and I will accompany her to Windhaven for the birth."

Tulkhan frowned. "Can't Kalleen have her baby here? Windhaven is too near the west coast for my liking."

Imoshen sighed. "You're a man and a Ghebite, so you cannot understand. Windhaven is where the babe was begun. Windhaven is the ideal place for the child's birth."

Tulkhan did not see the logic of this. "If she must go, then surely there is a midwife on the estate."

"I am her closest friend and trained for this task. Would you ask me to turn my back on Kalleen while she walks through the shadow of death?"

"What's this talk of death's shadow?"

"Have you forgotten?" Imoshen pushed the maps aside to perch on the table. "A woman must traverse death's shadow to bring forth life. There is a special place in the T'En afterlife reserved for women and babies who died in childbirth and warriors who died defending their homes."

As he listened intently, Imoshen felt close to the General. She wanted to stroke his broken nose and heal it, but he wore his scars like badges of honor and she must respect that.

He frowned. "I believe your place is here in the capital."

Anger made her voice grow thin. "According to the teachings of the Ghebite priests, females don't have proper souls. I suppose a woman lost in childbirth is mourned like a mare lost in foaling?"

He shifted uncomfortably.

"Well, General?"

"You won't like it," he warned. "Only after females have proved their worth by giving birth to a son are they accorded burial in the husband's family plot. As for afterlife . . . if the correct burial is observed, a warrior who dies in battle joins the great Akha Khan's host, riding the plains."

"And women?"

"There is no afterlife for women." He shrugged an apology.

Imoshen held his gaze. "And what do you believe?"

"Me? I have seen too many men die to believe there is an afterlife...at least, that is what I believed until I met the T'En. Now I question everything!"

"Questions are good."

"Answers are better!"

Imoshen smiled, then sobered. "Sometimes knowing is more terrible than not knowing." She thought of the Parakletos and leaned closer to Tulkhan. "What if I said I have walked death's shadow and know there is something beyond?"

"You are T'En. I am but a True-man. What is true for you may not be true for me."

Imoshen flinched. Perhaps they were destined to live apart forever because of the differences of their race, differences that stretched beyond death. Longing filled her and she stroked Tulkhan's jaw.

He pulled her across the desk onto his lap, burying his face in her throat. "I can't get enough of the smell of you. It haunts me. I left for the Low-lands wondering if distance would help me escape your strange allure."

Imoshen wrinkled her nose. "And did it?"

He shook his head. "I missed your voice, but not because it held some T'En trickery. Your wise words of counsel are what I value, even when they make me question the very assumptions by which I live. Ah, Imoshen. I would not leave T'Diemn if I had a choice." He cleared his throat. "But I must review Fair Isle's northern defenses. And I take Reothe with me because my father taught me to keep my enemies close by. This spring we face the final cast of the dice, Imoshen. We may all die and everything we've worked for will turn to dust—your T'En legacy and my plans for Fair Isle."

She was torn by the knowledge that what he said was true.

"I do not order you, I ask. Stay in T'Diemn, Imoshen. I fear for your safety in Windhaven."

"I can't fail Kalleen." She wished she could grant him this. "Tulkhan?"

"What?" There was a ragged edge to his voice.

"You were nearly killed the last time you left T'Diemn. I do not ask you to dishonor your Ghiad, but grant me this."

"Ask."

Unable to meet his eyes, she pressed her lips to his throat. "Stay with me this night and hold me in your arms. Nothing more."

Heart hammering, she waited for his answer.

It came in a bone-crushing hug. "You must think I have a will of iron."

She smiled, warmed to the core.

"I can't believe I'm *still* pregnant!" Kalleen complained. Nearly one small moon had passed and she was long overdue. She had been urging Imoshen to return to T'Diemn for days. "I swear I'm never going to have this baby!" Fanning herself energetically, she glared at Imoshen. "If you laugh, I will throw something at you."

Since they were seated under the apple tree in Windhaven's orchard and the closest thing was the remains of their lunch, Imoshen was not concerned. Ashmyr lay on a blanket on his stomach, trying to lift himself onto his knees. His eyes were fixed on a butterfly that had landed just out of his reach.

Chickens cackled contentedly and farmers sang as they worked in the fields. Soon it would grow dark and the workers would come in, hungry and tired. These last five weeks had been the most relaxed Imoshen had known since the Ghebites invaded Fair Isle. She was reminded of her own Stronghold and she longed to go home, but when she left Windhaven she would have to return to T'Diemn.

She decided it was time to broach a delicate subject. Perhaps Kalleen's baby had not come on time because it was not ready. The longer she carried the baby, the more likelihood of it being part T'En. "Did any of your family carry the T'En traits?"

"I know what you are hinting at." Kalleen levered herself up on one elbow. "My grandmother had the T'En eyes, but no one else. This baby—"

"Is late and getting later by the day. Face it, Kalleen. There is a good chance your child will be part T'En."

Kalleen threw her hands up in despair. "I just want to live a quiet life. I don't want to be Regent and I don't want this for my child!"

"We don't always get what we want," Imoshen said softly.

Kalleen had the grace to look down.

The singing changed to shouts of greeting, and Imoshen shaded her eyes to study the distant figures on horseback. Tulkhan and Reothe. Her body tightened in a knot of anticipation that was part pleasure, part dread. She rolled to her feet, hardly impeded by the weight of her pregnancy. She was nearly five small moons along now, but she had been bigger with Ashmyr.

"You must return to T'Diemn with them and leave me in the hands of Grandmother Keen." Kalleen named the local midwife. "After all, the Ghebite King will not halt his invasion plans for the birth of one baby."

Imoshen laughed and went to greet Reothe and Tulkhan.

When the evening meal was over, Tulkhan watched Kalleen lever herself out of her chair. She was huge. "Surely that baby is due soon. Will you present us with Wharrd's son tomorrow?"

"If only!"

"Kalleen is long overdue," Imoshen said, and Tulkhan

caught her exchanging a quick look of understanding with Reothe.

He hid his uneasiness behind a jest. "Should I expect to see the boy by morning, Kalleen?"

"What if it is a girl?" Kalleen challenged.

He shrugged, aware he was on thin ice. "So long as the child is healthy."

"Spoken like a true diplomat." Imoshen laughed and lifted her glass to him. "Have you left your soldiering days behind to take up diplomacy, General?"

"The gods forbid!"

They laughed and, as Kalleen went to bed, Imoshen dismissed the servants for the night. Tulkhan had the opportunity to observe her. Her loose gown only hinted at her pregnancy. But it would not be long before everyone knew he had been cuckolded and there wasn't a thing he could do about it.

Once the servants had gone, Imoshen turned to him. "What news?"

"I've ordered all the Strongholds' defenses improved and the towns' fortifications rebuilt. But if Gharavan's army made landfall under cover of darkness, they could get a toehold on the island and prove hard to dislodge. My spies report the Ghebites massing. Who is to say they won't sail around Fair Isle's southern tip and attack the east coast?"

"Gharavan is playing a cagey game," Reothe observed. "I wonder who advises him."

Tulkhan shrugged. "He has a dozen advisers, all eager to win his favor."

"But this delaying and deploying is not the act of a headstrong youth."

"Perhaps it is the act of an indecisive youth?" Imoshen suggested.

Tulkhan cracked a nut. "Possibly."

"You think it is only chance that his actions prevent us from anticipating where he will attack?" Reothe was not convinced. "Am I reading too much into this?"

"Whatever his motives, we know he *will* attack." Imoshen's eyes swept them both. "And we must be prepared."

Tulkhan felt a familiar pull.

"Will you return to the capital tomorrow?" she asked.

"Yes." He wanted to insist she leave Windhaven, but...
"Do you travel with us?"

"I don't know." She tilted her head, listening. "Ashmyr
has woken. I mustn't let him disturb Kalleen." She stood. "If
Kalleen has her baby tonight, I will come with you."

"Let us hope she does." Tulkhan could not resist prod-
ding. "Gharavan is sure to have spies on Fair Isle. You
could be needlessly risking yourself and my son."

Imoshen's mouth opened as if she might argue.

"He is right," Reothe said.

She glared at them both, then left.

Tulkhan met Reothe's eyes, seeing the mirror of his
own rueful expression.

"You should insist she return to T'Diemn," Reothe
said.

Tulkhan put his feet up on the chair, aware that Reothe
was baiting him. It was so easy to forget that they were enemies, seductively easy to lower his defenses. "You tell her."

Reothe laughed. "Never give an order you know you
can't enforce."

Tulkhan acknowledged the truth of this. "Then pray
Wharrd's child comes soon." He made a silent vow to watch
over Wharrd's son or daughter. He missed the bone-setter's
frank advice, though Reothe's knowledge had proved invalu-
able in planning Fair Isle's defense strategy.

Who would have thought... Here he sat in companion-
able silence with his most dangerous enemy, bound by the
warrior code—and gnawed by frustration.

Twenty-two

IMOSHEN STROKED ASHMYR'S back, alert for the first sounds on the stairs. All evening she had been observing the interplay between Tulkhan and Reothe, and it dismayed her to discover how the General had come to rely on her kinsman. She wanted a few minutes alone with Tulkhan, but when she heard the steps, there were two sets of boots and she seethed with resentment.

Imoshen paced the room. Ashmyr twitched in his sleep like a puppy and Kalleen showed no sign of going into labor. When she could not stand being closed in any longer, Imoshen crept onto the top of the stairs. The large moon was still up, but the little moon had already passed overhead in its quicker journey. Holding her hand in a beam of moonlight, she turned it over and over, recalling Reothe's words. Moonlight was beneficial for the T'En. He was right; she denied her T'En nature. Tonight she needed to feel the night air on her skin to clear her head.

Without stopping to put on shoes or a cloak, Imoshen ran lightly down the stairs and out into the courtyard. A dog whimpered in its sleep but did not wake as she let herself out the orchard gate. Her feet, toughened by going barefoot these last few weeks, flew over the grass as she headed for the knoll. This was a sacred place, whispered to belong to the dawn people and avoided by the locals. It was bare of trees and high enough for her to glimpse the sea.

The air was warm, with a foretaste of the summer heat, and lightning flickered like a fretful spirit behind the scattered clouds, illuminating them from within. The buildup of tension made her heart sing. She could smell no rain on the air. No release for the restless lightning.

Lifting her arms, Imoshen turned slowly. Her bare feet opened her to the power of the earth. Moonlight caressed her skin like a soothing balm. She was tempted to shed her clothing. Charged night air filled her chest, sharp and fresh to taste. Lightning flashed, and for a heartbeat the night was so bright she cast a shadow. A delighted laugh escaped her. Swaying to music only she could hear, Imoshen glided across the knoll.

"Imoshen!" Reothe's voice was raw. "I thought I would find you here, feasting."

She spun to face him, disconcerted. Lightning flickered. "Why did you follow me?"

"How could I not? You call me like a beacon."

She exhaled, acknowledging they were bound in ways she did not understand. Even now an awareness stretched between them. She could feel it drawing them closer. Trapped in a timeless moment, she felt as if there was nothing but this bare hilltop, the moon's lambent glow, and the lightning prowling the horizon. It enticed the T'En in her to forget her True-woman upbringing.

"No closer," she ordered, suddenly aware that Reothe stood within arm's length. "Why are you here?"

"You stand there, glowing with an inner radiance, and you ask why I am drawn as the moth to the flame?"

She touched his face, silvered by the moonlight, seeing the glint of the lightning reflected in his eyes. Her fingertips registered the silken softness of his lips, his hot breath.

Reothe caught her hand. She felt his kiss, the touch of his tongue as he tasted her. She yearned for him.

"You can try, but you won't make me break my vow," he told her. "I will not accept crumbs. It is all or nothing!"

"Then it can be nothing."

"How can you say that when we share this child?" He sank

to his knees, his arms sliding around her waist to press his face against her body. "Is our babe male or female?"

Reluctantly, she cradled his head against the pounding of her heart. "I believe it is not my right to touch the mind of an unborn child, so I choose not to know the answer."

She felt him smile.

"Your principles make you weak, Imoshen."

That familiar wariness returned. "I must do what I believe to be right."

He came to his feet, catching her hands in his. "When Gharavan is defeated and Fair Isle is ours again, I will come to you and you will have to make a decision."

"My decision is already made."

Reothe dropped her hands and stepped back. Relinquishing his touch was painful, but she would not give him false words of comfort. He stood before her, radiating intensity, so that if she closed her eyes she could still sense him. How could Tulkhan fail to realize that Reothe's gifts were returning? "Have you sent the T'Elegos to the palace?"

"Perhaps."

Anger sizzled through her. "Don't you want your gifts fully restored?"

"How do I know you will honor your part of the bargain once you have the T'Elegos?"

She laughed bitterly. "Surely you can't expect me to restore your gifts first."

"That would require trust, wouldn't it?" he whispered sadly.

"What would you know of trust, Reothe? You have stolen Tulkhan's trust of me." Her mouth went dry. "Is it true?"

"Is what true?"

"They say you and Tulkhan are sword-brothers." The baldness of her question made her wince and her cheeks grew hot. She strained to distinguish every nuance of his answer.

"You know the Ghebites." He shrugged.

She gasped. "I love him for himself, not for what use I can make of him. Would you take everything from me?"

"Name one thing I haven't lost!"

"Then it is true." Her blood roared in her ears. "You would use anyone and anything to gain your ends, even driving your own parents to suicide to be near the Empress!"

He grasped her shoulders. "Who told you that?"

Anger shimmered off his skin, leaving the T'En aftertaste in her mouth as she inhaled. She shook her head, regretting her outburst.

"Who told you?" His hands tightened.

She could have broken his hold as easily as blinking; instead, she placed her palms on his chest. She could feel the rapid beating of his heart, sense his pain and betrayal. "I wronged you, Reothe. I should never have repeated what I know could not be true."

"You say you know it is not true, yet you still doubt me enough to make the accusation!"

"I spoke in anger. Forgive me."

He backed away. "Why should I? Yet I forgive you everything else. You vow to bond with me, then take another. You say you love me in one breath, then turn me away. You make it clear you want me only for my knowledge of the T'En. Then you accuse me of murdering my own parents!"

"Please—"

"Please what? Forgive you again so that you can go on torturing me?" He cursed softly in High T'En and walked off.

Imoshen wanted to stop him, but her choice had been made the day General Tulkhan surrounded her Stronghold. If truth be told, she'd had no choice.

The door closed. Tulkhan sensed more than heard Reothe's cat-light steps across the boards. He schooled his breathing so that it would not betray him. He had heard Reothe leave and, imagining him in Imoshen's arms, time had passed with excruciating slowness.

He wanted to confront Reothe, but if he did he would endanger his Ghiad. Painfully aware, he lay in the shadow on his bed and watched Reothe stand over him, radiating violence.

When Reothe spoke, his voice was a corrosive caress.

"You have come close to death so many times, True-man. How does it feel?"

Tulkhan knew the danger had passed. "I am bound by the Gheeakhan code to serve you. What restrains your hand?"

"The knowledge that I cannot have your blood on my hands."

Tulkhan sat up and swung his legs to the floor. "Then our hands are tied."

"Unless something changes. She carries my child, General. Why don't you do the honorable thing and take a fatal wound in the battle?"

"Are you asking that of me under my Ghiad?"

"No!" Reothe stalked away and threw himself onto the window seat illuminated by a patch of moonlight.

Tulkhan crossed the room, ducking his head to accommodate the slope of the roof. He dropped into a soldier's loose-limbed crouch in the shadows. "How did Imoshen pass the Orb's test of Truth if she carries your child?"

Reothe turned, and his smile made Tulkhan's heart falter. "I went to her cloaked in your guise."

Tulkhan looked down, pleased to hear Imoshen's words confirmed.

Reothe's eyes narrowed. "Ask yourself this: Why was Imoshen willing to believe the lie?"

All night Reothe's words ate into Tulkhan's peace of mind. By morning, Kalleen had not had her baby. The General left Imoshen with the request that she return to the capital soon. Had she been his Ghebite wife, he would have simply ordered that her bags be packed, but Reothe was right. There was no point in giving an order he could not enforce, and after his restless night Tulkhan had begun to believe there was a lie within a truth.

When Imoshen heard the pounding hooves, she feared the worst. It had been five days since Tulkhan and Reothe had returned to T'Diemn, and Kalleen's baby had not come. A single rider hastened into the cold cellar, where Imoshen

and Kalleen were checking the state of last autumn's pre-
serves, as if that were the worst of their worries.

He gave the Ghebite bow and delivered a message cylinder. Imoshen opened it. As she read, her heart missed a beat
and her head spun with the implications.

"What is it?" Kalleen asked.

Imoshen folded the paper carefully, hiding her conster-
nation. "The General needs me to return to T'Diemn.
Come upstairs while I pack."

She picked up Ashmyr, told the messenger to go to the
kitchen, then sent a servant to the stables. Once in her
room, Imoshen dismissed the maid and threw garments
into her traveling bag. "I can't believe it. The Beatific is
dead by her own hand and Reothe is missing. T'Diemn is in
an uproar and Tulkhan fears Reothe has gone rogue! If
Gharavan gets wind of division he will strike." Imoshen
closed the tapestry flap and buckled up her bag, hands
shaking. "Will you be all right?"

"Go where you are needed." Kalleen hugged her.

An overwhelming sense of loss engulfed Imoshen,
making her eyes sting with an emotion that wasn't hers. It
was not a Vision but a presentiment of sorrow. She had to
return to the capital before disaster struck.

Tulkhan looked up as Imoshen walked into his map room,
Ashmyr in one arm, her traveling bag in the other. "How
did it happen?"

"Poison."

"No. What drove Engarad to this?"

"You tell me."

She dropped the bag and set the boy on the floor.
Ashmyr pushed himself up on his hands and knees and
crawled straight for the open fireplace. She darted past him
to adjust the grate, then turned him toward a chair.

Tulkhan watched in fascination as his son pulled himself upright and let go with one hand. "Look at that. He'll
be walking soon!"

"Not for ages yet. It makes no sense. Did she leave no note? Is Reothe still missing?"

"Yes." He frowned. He always had trouble reconciling Imoshen's role as mother of his son and head of state. In Gheeaba a woman might be considered a good mother, but she did not advise her husband. "The only communication the Beatific left is this, her final decree." Tulkhan pushed the document across the table. "It came into my hands after I sent for you."

"The seal has been broken."

"I read it."

"But it is addressed to me."

"It was addressed to the Empress," he corrected. She flushed. "Where is Reothe, Imoshen? What are the signs if one of the T'En goes rogue? I've put Murgon off three times. I swear that man is too eager for Reothe's blood."

But Imoshen gave no answer, intent on reading the Beatific's final decree. Her fair skin went so pale he thought she might faint. "Imoshen, are you all right?"

Dimly, Imoshen heard her name. Blood roared in her head. The Beatific was dead because of her. No, the woman was dead because she had tried to poison Imoshen's mind against Reothe. He must have guessed who had made the insinuations about his parents' suicide and confronted the Beatific.

Engarad had taken her own life in despair. Or had she?

Perhaps the Beatific had been right to suspect Reothe of driving his parents to their deaths. Could his partially healed gift be strong enough to drive a determined woman like the Beatific into a despair so profound she would take her own life?

Tulkhan cleared his throat. "It is a simple decree, unless you read something there that I cannot see. The Beatific named Reothe her successor. How much weight will this have with the Abbey Seculates? Could Reothe become the Beatific?"

Imoshen sank into a chair, forcing herself to think. "Reothe has not come up through the Church hierarchy, but his education equals the masters of the Halls of Learning. He was writing discourses on philosophy and obscure religious debates when he was fifteen." She tried to focus on the point. "When I appointed him Sword of Justice, I placed him in the upper echelon of the Church hierarchy among the ranks from which the next Beatific would be drawn. I...I did not foresee..."

The General came to his feet. "How can you tell if Reothe has gone rogue? Concentrate, Imoshen!"

When she lifted her eyes to his, Tulkhan read stark despair. She must believe Reothe had gone rogue. The General would have to order his death. All along he had wanted a legitimate reason to have the last T'En warrior executed, yet now he regretted it.

Ashmyr gave a crow of delight. Tulkhan turned in time to see his son take five tottering steps, then drop. "Look at that. He walked!"

"Impossible. He isn't a year old."

"I swear he took five steps on his own!"

Imoshen laughed. "Oh, Tulkhan. Let the poor boy be a baby. All too soon he will have to grapple with matters of state."

"But—"

"I'm going to consult with Keeper Karmel." Imoshen came to her feet, picking up the child. "The last rogue T'En was executed over a hundred years ago. I don't know the precedents. I need time to think!"

Tulkhan joined her. "I tried to persuade the basilica not to send for the Abbey Seculates, but they have already done it. They will hold the vote in three days."

"The Church needs a Beatific."

"But it leaves the abbeys without leadership if Gharavan attacks." Tulkhan noted that Imoshen stroked the boy's fine, dark hair as if seeking reassurance. "What is it? Do you suspect the Beatific did not write that message? It was not delivered to me until the evening after her body was discovered. Do you think Reothe forged it?"

Imoshen glanced around the room as if looking for the

answer. Two tears rolled unheeded down her cheeks. "I don't believe it!"

"Another thing I find strange. The Beatific did not strike me as a woman who would kill herself. Imoshen?" When she met his eyes, he realized she knew the answer, or thought she did. "Imoshen!"

She shook her head. "All I know of the last rogue's execution was what my great-aunt told me. The Aayel was a twelve-year-old child at the time. T'Obazim was declared rogue when he tried to abduct her. That was considered a sign of going rogue—rising up against lawful authority of the Church or the royal line."

"The Church recognized my right to rule Fair Isle, but Reothe continued to lead his rebels against me."

"I have reason to believe the Beatific had been secretly supporting Reothe in his struggle against you." Imoshen gave him an apologetic smile. "Another sign used to be if one of the T'En killed a True-man or woman with their gifts."

"We both know Reothe has done that, and in cold blood."

"As have I," Imoshen said softly. She nuzzled Ashmyr's soft head. "I don't know enough about rogue T'En. I must consult with the Keeper."

"But Reothe's gifts are crippled. Surely he is no more dangerous than a True-man?" Tulkhan asked. Imoshen's expression made him wary. "Is Reothe healed?"

"No. No, I . . ." She pressed her hand to her throat and took a deep breath. "I have felt his gift flare on several occasions, but I know he is not healed."

"Partially healed?"

She nodded reluctantly. Tulkhan took a step back, cursing. His elbow hit an onyx stallion. It toppled off the table and he caught it on reflex.

Ashmyr laughed. Imoshen smiled and handed the boy to Tulkhan. "Watch over our son while I do my research."

"I—"

But she was gone, leaving Tulkhan holding the baby. He

turned Ashmyr to face him, admiring the boy's brilliant
T'En eyes and pale skin, topped by hair black as sable.
Twenty years from now the women would be chasing him.

Ashmyr kicked his legs.

"You want to get down?" Tulkhan lowered him to the
floor, only to discover that the boy wanted to stand, his legs
planted wide. "Well, walk, then, and prove I am not a liar."

Holding on to the tips of Tulkhan's fingers, Ashmyr
walked across the room. With a laugh the General hugged
his son, Fair Isle's fate forgotten for the moment.

Imoshen stroked the polished wood of the library's shelves,
inhaling its scent, redolent with age and learning. Usually
this place made her feel at peace. Today she paced, waiting
for the Keeper's return. According to Karmel, the books on
containing rogue T'En were kept in the basilica's archives,
so when Imoshen heard a soft footfall, she looked up expecting to see the old woman. But it was Drake, and his expression was grim.

She gave him a wary smile and tried for a light note. "Do
all of the Malaunje children wish to join the Parakhan
Guard?"

"There are nearly sixty of them now. But I am not here
to speak of the children," Drake said. "I come on behalf of
someone who wishes to be heard by the Empress."

If someone felt they had been wronged they could present themselves to the Emperor and Empress, who would
hear their case without prejudice. The last thing Imoshen
needed was more complications, but she knew her duty. "I
am always ready to listen."

"Good. You must come with me now and you must
wear this."

Imoshen eyed the long silk scarf uneasily. Even though
she had appointed Drake Shujen of her Parakhan Guard,
his ultimate loyalty was to Reothe. Suddenly she knew who
wanted justice, and her heart raced. "Very well. But I tell
you that color does not go with my gown."

The last thing she saw was Drake's smile. "This way, T'Imoshen."

He took her hand, leading her to the back of the library, toward the secret passages. She had to believe Reothe would not endanger her life and that of their unborn child. Dry-mouthed, she stepped into the stale air of the dusty passages. Her body sang with tension and dread. Yet she could not deny Reothe a hearing. Fair Isle's system of justice was the one thing that made her people more civilized than Tulkhan's.

They traveled downstairs and underground, too far for Imoshen to guess where they were. When they came out in the open again, she could feel the gentle breeze on her skin and the air tasted fresh. They walked uphill for a little way before Drake stopped.

"We are here, T'Imoshen."

He undid the scarf and backed off. Imoshen blinked. The afternoon light had a pearly quality, making the distances soft and mellow. She recognized the delicate rotunda that stood on the outcropping overlooking T'Diemn. How ironic to think that Reothe would meet her here, where the Beatific had fired her poisoned barbs.

Drake retreated, and as Reothe stepped away from the rotunda's columns, Imoshen's senses strained to detect every nuance. Reothe greeted her with the old-empire obeisance of deep supplication, kneeling and lifting both hands palms up before bringing them to his forehead. Imoshen understood he was treating this as a formal request to the Empress. Feeling a little reassured, she looked down on his bowed head.

"Empress T'Imoshen," Reothe said. "I ask to be heard without prejudice or preconceptions."

"Then speak, for I am listening."

"I have been grossly wronged by one I trusted."

"Who is this person?"

"She was greatly admired and of high position."

"The Beatific?"

Reothe looked up, his recent suffering etched on his

features, and she ached in empathy. She must be wary; her love for him made her vulnerable.

"Imoshen, I am lost if you do not believe me. Engarad sought my destruction."

"But she is dead by her own hand and has named you the next Beatific!"

"So I heard."

"Is that the action of someone who would destroy you?"

"It is the action of a devious woman." He sprang to his feet. "I guessed she was the one who told you the lie about my parents' deaths, so I confronted her. That was when she revealed her hatred for me."

"I gave you into the Church's care because I thought she loved you."

"Hate is the other side of the coin."

"Is it?" Imoshen murmured, but he did not hear her.

"She thought to resume our old friendship."

"You were lovers."

"Once. But when Engarad realized I could not lie with my body, her feelings festered. She tried to poison your mind against me and nearly succeeded, yet all the while she turned her smiling face to me."

"Did you drive her to kill herself?"

"No! That is what she wanted you to believe. She wanted you to think I had gone rogue and driven her to her death so that I could take over the Church and regain Fair Isle!"

"You could be telling me the truth. Or you could have driven the Beatific to suicide and this could be a plausible lie."

His shoulders sagged and he sank onto the cracked stone seat, his head in his hands. "Then the Beatific has succeeded in destroying your faith in me, and she has given Tulkhan the excuse he needs to kill me."

He looked up, despair written large on his features. Imoshen took two steps back, fighting the need to reassure him. His compelling eyes held hers. "You can search my mind for the truth of what I say. I will not resist."

"You could cloak the truth from me. You are so much more practiced than I."

"Possibly," he admitted. "Then there is no reason why you should believe me."

She dared to touch him, tracing the line of his jaw with her fingertips. "So thin and pale. Where have you been?"

"In the passages. Drake has been bringing me food. I thought the General might have me killed."

"He sent for me straightaway."

"Tulkhan is an honorable man," he conceded, then caught her hand, bringing it to his lips. "I have given you many reasons to doubt me, Imoshen. I have done things that cross the boundaries of my own honor because I believed it was necessary, but I swear I am innocent of Engarad's death, just as I was innocent of my parents' suicide." He released her hand and knelt at her feet. "What is your judgment, my Empress?"

Imoshen swallowed. In the absence of a Beatific, it was she who would have to sign the Declaration condemning Reothe. The thought revolted her. "My heart tells me you speak the truth."

He wrapped his arms around her waist and she felt the heat of his flesh pierce her thin gown. Sinking to her knees, she held him close. This one embrace was all she would allow herself. His lithe frame trembled.

Relief filled Imoshen, for Tulkhan could have used the Beatific's death to frame Reothe, but he hadn't. She drew a little away to search Reothe's face, his hands in hers. "Tulkhan never suspected you of killing the Beatific. Why did you flee?"

"When they told me of Engarad's suicide, I wandered into the woods, stunned. Then Drake brought me news of her decree, and I—"

"So it is general knowledge?"

"The Church's high officials would have opened her decree, then resealed it. I went into hiding believing even if the General did not suspect me of her death, he would never let me become Beatific."

If Reothe became Beatific he would be more powerful than anyone but the Empress. Imoshen sat on her heels, heart racing as the implications rushed her. The Beatific was the embodiment of the Church, which worshiped the T'En gifts. "Originally, all the Beatifics were pure T'En, so you being a Throwback is not a problem. It takes a majority vote to elect a new Beatific. How many of the five Seculates would vote for you?"

"I'm sure I have the votes of the Seculates from Chalkcliff and Landsend. If you added your vote I would only need the General's, but why would he—"

"What of Murgon?" Imoshen asked. She longed to be free of the fear of the Tractarians. "He hates you."

"Because I was born a Throwback and he was born Malaunje, forever to suffer the indignities of his birth with none of the advantages. Murgon chose the Tractarian path to power because he had no alternative." He smiled at her expression. "I know Murgon. We were boys together. If I were Beatific of the Church, the T'En would not live in a climate of fear. It would be a public acceptance of the T'En, an honor for our race. It is for people like my cousin that I am trying to restore the T'En." Reothe's hands tightened on hers. "We must seize this opportunity!"

Her head swam with the force of his vision and she pulled back, unwilling to let him influence her decision. Dusting off her gown, she walked a little away. When she turned, he stood, waiting. "If I ensure that you are named Beatific, will you swear to protect the T'En, even Tulkhan's son?"

"You should not have to ask."

She held his eyes.

He placed his left hand on his chest, covering his heart. "I swear to restore the T'En. We will have a golden future."

"That was not what I asked, and it might be too much, too soon."

"It is only with a strong power base that we will be safe from True-men and women."

Imoshen gave a sigh of frustration. "As long as it is *them* and *us,* we will never be safe. Surely you see that since the Ghebites invaded there is no them and us, only Fair Isle?"

Silence stretched. He turned his hand over in entreaty. "Imoshen, we must not argue. We need each other."

"True. Tulkhan and I will endorse your Beatificship."

"Why should he give his approval?"

"The Church's power is more entrenched than his; it rivals that of the Empress. As Beatific you can bring the Church's massive resources behind the defense of Fair Isle."

"All the more reason for him to fear me as Beatific. Because of his Ghiad he is honor-bound to protect me, but he believes he has no such lever to hold over me."

Reothe's words triggered Imoshen's realization that they did have a lever over Reothe. She smiled. "Leave it to me."

Tulkhan recognized Imoshen's graceful stride as she crossed the stable courtyard. "Imoshen?"

She changed direction to join him. "What are you doing with Ashmyr?"

"He wanted to see the horses."

She rolled her eyes. "I suppose you were picking out a pony for him? Will he be riding as well as walking before his first birthday?"

"In my grandfather's time, when we lived as wandering tribes on the plains, children rode as soon as they were big enough to sit astride a horse. They fell asleep at their mothers' breasts, swaying in the saddle. The minstrels still sing of it." His eyes narrowed. "I thought you went to the library."

Imoshen caught his arm, drawing him away from the stable. She took him into the formal gardens to a pond with a central statue.

He planted his feet. "I am not a fool, Imoshen. You've been to see Reothe."

"Yes, I have seen him and he has not gone rogue."

"Then why did he go into hiding?" Ashmyr wriggled to be let down. Tulkhan handed him to Imoshen.

"The Beatific was Reothe's first lover. When she killed

herself he wandered off, lost in grief. It was only when he heard about the decree naming him the new Beatific that he went into hiding. He thought you would order his execution."

"I can't let him become Beatific."

"You need the Church behind you to unite Fair Isle and defeat Gharavan. If Reothe is Beatific, you will have that."

"Do you think me a fool? Once Gharavan is defeated, Reothe will use the T'En Church's power base to usurp me."

"He won't dare." Imoshen's intense eyes held his.

"Why not?"

"Because you will have power over the one thing he cares for more than Fair Isle."

Tulkhan's heart skipped a beat. Was Imoshen offering herself as surety of Reothe's support? Could he accept Imoshen on those terms? "You mean—"

"His child!" Imoshen whispered. "Acknowledge Reothe's child as your own and he will support you."

Tulkhan's head spun.

"Don't you see?" Imoshen gave an unsteady laugh. "He thought it would be the one thing to drive us apart. You could not accept another man's child. But it is the one lever he has given you over him."

"Imoshen." Tulkhan backed away to sit on the fountain's rim. "Reothe's child will be full T'En. Everyone will know it is not mine."

"Who says?" Imoshen turned Ashmyr to face Tulkhan. "Look at your son. Apart from his dark hair, he is pure T'En. Who knows what kind of children I will produce? Why do you think the first Imoshen decreed all pure T'En females must be celibate? Perhaps the blood of a pure T'En female is stronger."

"You could argue night is day, Imoshen. You say I can use Reothe's child as a lever, but that is an empty threat, because you would protect your children with your life!"

She frowned. "Surely you would not expect me to kill my own child for power!"

"Then what are you suggesting?"

"The same as what happened to Reothe. If a child is

orphaned they are given into the care of a relative. At ten years of age, Reothe was accepted into the Empress's family to be reared with her heirs." Imoshen sensed her argument almost won and joined Tulkhan on the pond rim. Ashmyr stood on tiptoe, dipping his fingers in the water. Imoshen turned the mechanism to make the central fountain work. Ashmyr gave a delighted squeal.

She smiled and met Tulkhan's eyes. "Fair Isle must be united to defeat Gharavan. The people know Reothe. They respect his leadership; that is why they were ready to follow him. But it works both ways. If he was leader of the Church, their loyalty would ultimately be to us, because the final veto for the Beatific rests with the Emperor and Empress. Reward Reothe with the Beatificship and he will have a vested interest in seeing that Fair Isle's power structure remains intact. Tulkhan, if you can offer the people stability they will support you in this, Fair Isle's hour of greatest need!"

Tulkhan looked down at Ashmyr's dark head as he stood between them and thought of another child who would come between them. "You ask me to accept a child who is not my own to use as a lever on my most dangerous ally. Desperate measures, Imoshen."

"It is time for the most desperate of alliances."

"I must think." He stood and turned away from her.

"You have three days until the Seculates vote. Would you rather Reothe became the next Beatific, or someone the Seculates select with their own plans? Better the enemy you know than—"

"You have a hard heart and a strong head, Imoshen." Tulkhan held her eyes. "Do you never doubt yourself?"

"All the time," she admitted, feeling the color rise in her cheeks. "But I am fighting for our survival. Remember this, General. Your son and Reothe's child are blameless. If we want them to have a future, we must hold Fair Isle against Gharavan."

She saw him accept the truth of this.

"What if the Seculates are against Reothe's appointment?"

Imoshen cloaked her surge of victory. "The last Beatific decreed it. The Seculates from the five great abbeys are jealous of one another. They will want to protect their interests." She sensed him withdraw as he stood. "What is it, General?"

"When I first laid eyes on you, I saw a dreaded Dhamfeer. But I thought, *She is only a woman, a girl at that. She is no threat.* I was blind. I will not insult you by saying if you had been born a man, you could have done anything!"

Imoshen laughed outright. "I did not choose to be born the last woman of the T'En, but I will do what I must."

"And damn the consequences? Reothe loves you, yet you have shown me the way to control him. Strangely, this coincides exactly with what you want. I can see through you, Imoshen."

She looked down, glad he could not know how desperately she wanted Reothe to become Beatific and win over Murgon and his Tractarians. When she looked up, the General was watching her from under hooded obsidian eyes.

"To all of them I am T'Imoshen, last princess of the T'En." She felt suddenly vulnerable. "But to you I would be Imoshen. Do not close your heart against me, Tulkhan."

He pulled her to him.

Tears of relief stung her eyes as he hugged her. Pinpoints of light spun in her vision and she pleaded laughingly, "Not so tight. I can barely breathe!"

He released her, letting her feet touch the ground. "I swear I love you more than is good for me, Imoshen."

Joy flooded her. She raised her face to his and found his lips, losing herself in him. She was not the cold conniving creature he imagined. She was this fragile, vibrant being enfolded in the General's arms.

They had nearly sixty Malaunje children living in T'Reothe's Hall now with Maigeth and Eksyl Five-fingers. It seemed Drake was always visiting when Imoshen dropped by. This afternoon he was teaching the older children how to fall without hurting themselves. Reothe stripped off his ornate tabard and let the smaller man throw him to show it could be done. When he rolled, cat-light, to his feet and laughed, he looked so young Imoshen ached for him. She had never known him as a careless youth.

"You have given us hope, T'Imoshen," Eksyl said softly, his eyes on the children. "Once a half-breed was welcomed only in the Tractarian branch of the Church."

"Tomorrow Reothe will become Beatific and the Church will honor the T'En. We live in an age of change," Imoshen said. In private sessions over the previous days, Imoshen had spoken with each of the Seculates and let it be known that she and Tulkhan approved of Engarad's choice of successor. No other candidate had been nominated and the vote had been unanimous. Imoshen believed this was thanks to Gharavan's threat. It was time for a warrior Beatific. "People will read about Beatific Reothe and General Tulkhan in their history books and think how interesting it must have been."

"But not so good to live through," Maigeth remarked. She raised her voice, calling the children for their midday meal.

As they lined up and thanked their instructors, Imoshen asked Maigeth, "Has Ysanna settled in?"

"I wish I could say yes."

As the others departed, Imoshen wondered what to do. If she singled the child out, the others would resent it. And for Ysanna's own safety it was better if no one guessed Reothe was her father.

"Dreaming with the Ancients, Imoshen?" Reothe teased.

She laughed, but that old saying reminded her that one of these days the Ancients would ask her to fulfill her part of the bargain, and she would have to, or forfeit Ashmyr's life. She must not falter when that moment came.

Reothe touched her cheek. "Why so serious, Shenna?"

But she shook her head, moving away so he could not use touch to skim the surface of her mind. "Seculate Donyx said something that made me think that Murgon—"

"Now that the vote has gone in my favor, I will win Murgon over."

"And how will you do that?"

"I will take a leaf from your book." He would say no more.

To witness Reothe's investiture, Imoshen wore an undergown of purest white samite with an overdress of silver lace, paired with an electrum skull cap inset with fiery rubies. She wanted to remind the Seculates of the old empire. The formal lines of the gown hid her pregnancy, but soon it would be impossible to hide the baby. She wished she could rejoice in this child as she had rejoiced in Ashmyr.

The church's choir filled the space under the great dome. On the dais, Reothe was flanked by his T'Enplars in full ceremonial armor. He wore nothing but a simple white robe, ready to accept the mantle of Beatific and all it entailed.

For once the sight of Murgon and his Tractarians did not make Imoshen's palms grow damp with fear. General Tulkhan stood at her side, resplendent in full battle armor. His eyes met hers and she smiled, wishing her great-aunt were here to see their plans come to fruition. She had traveled a hard path from captive royal to co-ruler of Fair Isle. Now with Reothe's investiture she would ensure the future of the T'En.

Reothe served warmed wine to the five Seculates, symbolizing that as he was Beatific, he served the Church. Then he accepted the mantle and crown of the Beatificship. But before the basilican choir could break into song, Reothe signaled for silence.

"I have sworn on my honor to serve the Church and Fair Isle, but I need an assistant to advise me in the role of Beatific." He walked slowly past the five Seculates. His eyes met Imoshen's for a moment and she saw he was laughing inside. When he stopped before Murgon, she understood. Like the General, he would keep his enemy close and make his success their success. "Murgon, cousin, will you accept this honor?"

Imoshen saw a muscle jump in Murgon's cheek. This was an honor he could not refuse.

Imoshen returned from the investiture to discover Kalleen's belongings in the hall outside her room. Joy filled her, for she intended Kalleen's child to be raised with Ashmyr.

"Kalleen?" Imoshen threw the door open. The little woman's stiff face made her falter. Kalleen's gaze swept past her to a servant who was cleaning the grate.

Imoshen placed her sleeping son in the small bed he had been using since he outgrew his basket. "Bring food and wine for Lady Windhaven."

The girl dropped a quick obeisance and scurried away.

Imoshen approached. "Kalleen?"

She lifted both hands before her in a defensive motion. "My daughter was born dead. Grandmother Keen said I will never have another child!"

Suddenly Imoshen understood her presentiment of loss when she had taken leave of Kalleen at Windhaven. She gasped in pain and Kalleen fell into her arms, sobbing fiercely.

When the storm eased, Imoshen drew her gently to the hearth chair. Then she poured water and sprinkled herbs in the bowl before bathing Kalleen's tearstained face.

The little woman sat, weak and listless.

"I should have been there," Imoshen whispered.

Kalleen caught her hand. "Six fingers, just like yours, but dead. Three days it took. I nearly died. They told me not to travel, but I had to see you."

"I will try to heal you."

"No!" Kalleen shrank back. "I never want to go through that again. It would kill me."

Ashmyr woke, saw Kalleen, and gave a crow of delight. Her face opened like a flower in the sun. But when she lifted the boy onto her lap, she winced.

"I will mix you something to dry up the milk and encourage mending," Imoshen said. As she measured herbs she listened to Ashmyr's happy sounds. Already she could sense the healing that was taking place. Herbs to heal the body, Ashmyr to heal Kalleen's heart.

As a midwife, Imoshen knew the journey through death's shadow to bring forth new life was fraught with danger. Her vision swam with tears, for she believed if only she'd been there she could have saved Kalleen's child.

A sound from the doorway made her look up to see Tulkhan watching Kalleen. From his expression, she knew he had heard the news. Unaware of him, Kalleen spoke, her voice bitter. "I said I did not want my child to have the T'En traits, but I was wrong. I would have loved her even if she was a Throwback!"

Tulkhan hastily backed out.

Imoshen smiled grimly and stirred the herbs. When they were ready, she handed Kalleen the cup. "You will feel weak and teary for a while. Drink this."

Kalleen took a sip, wrinkling her nose at the taste. "I don't feel weak. Wharrd, my child, and my family. Everyone I ever loved has been stolen from me. I feel *angry!*"

Imoshen squeezed Kalleen's hand. "You have suffered just as the people of Fair Isle have suffered, but we will overcome."

Twenty-three

IMOSHEN WAITED ALONE at the entrance to the ball court, trying not to recall those desperate hours when she and Reothe faced the Cadre. Footsteps warned her of someone's approach; prickling across her skin told her it was Reothe.

"So you have answered the General's mysterious summons too?"

"I gather you don't know what Tulkhan wants?" Imoshen was relieved to see that Reothe was equally at a loss.

Tulkhan opened the door and glanced down the hall. "Good, you are alone. Inside, quickly."

Curious, Imoshen studied the tabletop model in the middle of the ball court, recognizing Deepdeyne Stronghold in miniature. It was complete with tiny trees, river, and moat painted blue.

"What is this?" Reothe asked uneasily.

"I wanted you two to be the first to see this," Tulkhan said. He recollected the young man at his side and drew him forward. "This is Ardon, a fifth-year man from the Pyrolate Guild. He has been working with me."

Imoshen cast Reothe a swift glance. Ardon risked much. The guilds were notoriously miserly with their knowledge.

"For hundreds of years the Pyrolate Guild has been making star-birds and similar toys," Tulkhan said. "But I knew they could do more."

Reothe nodded. "So you set up the watchtowers armed with star-birds, ready to carry news of invasion. But—"

"But you mean more, don't you?" Imoshen walked to the table. "Why else have you built this model?"

Tulkhan took Imoshen's arm. "The demonstration will speak for me. Come."

He led them up to the first tier of seats and nodded to Ardon, who opened his coal pouch and lit a long string, which fizzed and hissed just like a star-bird's tail. The string trailed right up across the model toward Deepdeyne Keep.

"It is only a model, but—" Tulkhan's voice was cut off as, with a flash and a dull crack, Deepdeyne disappeared in a cloud of smoke. The General laughed, swung a leg, and dropped over the balustrade.

Imoshen leapt after him, Reothe at her side. Small flames licked at the paper trees. Imoshen's nostrils stung from the acrid smoke. The model's blocks were scattered over the tabletop. Deepdeyne's walls were breached.

Tulkhan smiled. "If only I'd had this knowledge when I was trying to take Port Sumair!"

Imoshen noticed Reothe's expression and knew Tulkhan had chosen this particular Stronghold for his own reasons.

"With the right mixture and placing, not even the greatest wall could withstand this!" Tulkhan announced, one hand on Ardon's shoulder. The young man glowed. "I call them my Dragon's Eggs."

"The knowledge must not fall into the wrong hands," Reothe said.

"Of course. Why do you think we've been experimenting in secret?" Tulkhan turned to Imoshen. "You are very quiet."

"Secrets have a way of escaping. If news of your Dragon's Eggs gets out, you will change the world. The greatest cities will no longer be safe from any barbarian with the right tools." She looked up into Tulkhan's pleased face and said the first thing that came into her head. "How typically Ghebite, to take a beautiful thing and turn it into a tool of destruction!"

"Today you think like a woman, Imoshen. I'm sure Reothe has the vision to see the application for this!"

Reothe met Imoshen's eyes.

"It is because we have vision that we hesitate to release this dragon of destruction," Imoshen snapped. "If Gharavan had this tool, all your work on T'Diemn's defenses would count for nothing."

Tulkhan looked grim. "There are only four people who know of this discovery. Ardon is sworn to silence, and we three..."

"I will say nothing," Reothe vowed.

"Imoshen? Think how the mainland kingdoms would fear Fair Isle if they knew of this weapon. Power protects."

"I am thinking of the T'En, who are feared because True-people fear their power."

Tulkhan threw up his hands in disgust. "At least promise you will say nothing."

"That I can promise without reservation!"

He glared at her, and she wondered how she could love him so deeply across divides such as these.

Imoshen smiled fondly. Tulkhan had been right about Ashmyr. With his first birthday only a few days away, he was already trying to run. Misjudging the slope, Ashmyr tripped and Kalleen scooped him up, spinning him around. He shrieked with delight.

Kalleen's body had healed and she laughed often. But when she thought no one was looking, she would sit and stare, her heartbreak clear on her face.

Gharavan still had not attacked, and when Imoshen had confronted Reothe about the T'Elegos, he claimed that while traveling with Tulkhan he had been too closely watched to retrieve it. But she could not complain about his appointment as Beatific. Since his investiture he had mobilized the Church's resources. In every abbey and every village, young people trained under T'Enplar warriors. It was the age-old problem: What kingdom could afford a standing army that might turn on those in power? Yet, when threatened, what kingdom could afford *not* to have a trained army?

Imoshen had appeased the Keldon nobles by convincing Tulkhan to admit a select few to his war council. Even now Woodvine, Athlyng, and the others were in the city, ready to take up arms at a moment's notice.

Imoshen arched her back and shifted her weight. She had been standing too long. Had she been a True-woman she would have had her baby by now, but it was almost midsummer and her pregnancy would drag on for another seven weeks.

The laughter faded from Kalleen's face and Imoshen turned to see Reothe approaching through the ornamental gardens, his expression foreboding. Hiding her trepidation, she crossed the lawn, meeting him under the clipped arch.

"As Beatific I must advise against the General's plan to tour the western coastal defenses," he told her.

Imoshen hid a smile. For Reothe to come to her, it meant he had been unable to sway Tulkhan. "General Tulkhan believes Gharavan's invasion is imminent."

"All the more reason to stay in one place, the better to coordinate the army when the attack comes."

"I suspect the General hopes to draw Gharavan out. The longer the delay, the more edgy our people become."

"You could be right. I might send Murgon with him." Reothe's voice became intimate. "I have a gift for you. It is a bit late, but for your birthday..."

Imoshen flushed, remembering how Reothe had risked his life to enter the palace on the anniversary of her eighteenth birthday. She rarely took out the T'Endomaz now, frustrated by her fruitless attempts to break the encryption. "Not another unbreakable code designed to drive me to distraction?"

He grinned. "No. The T'Elegos."

"Reothe?" She caught his hands, touched to discover he trusted her with this treasure.

"The T'Elegos is safely in its old hiding place in the basilica. And you would not believe what I went through to get it there unseen. Imoshen the First writes of events in the T'Elegos that would disturb True-people. Still, I promised you the T'Elegos, and when you have finished healing me, we will read it together."

"Must you remind me of our bargain?"

"I have taken a step toward trusting you, Imoshen. The next step is yours."

She opened her mouth to assure him of her good faith, but the basilica's bells cut her short. It was not time for the hourly bell. It was not a festival. It was—

"The signal! Gharavan has attacked!" Reothe darted onto the gravel path to get a view of the palace. As Imoshen caught up with him, star-birds leapt from Sard's Tower, informing all of T'Diemn that they were at war. She caught her breath, elated and terrified at once.

Reothe pulled her to him. "We've run out of time, Shenna." His fierce eyes fixed on her. "Promise me this. If I do not survive, look after the Malaunje children."

"Have you had a premonition of your death?"

He nodded. "The General is an honorable man, but he will have a moment of choice and I don't know which path he will take—honor or pragmatism. At least now you know where the T'Elegos is hidden."

"Reothe!" Only when faced with his loss did she realize how much she had grown to love him.

Tulkhan looked up to see Imoshen enter the map room with Ashmyr, followed by Reothe and Kalleen. His commanders shifted uneasily, annoyed to see women and a child invade the war council. Only Woodvine and Athlyng looked relieved.

"Where have they landed?" Imoshen asked. Two bright spots of color illuminated her pale cheeks.

Tulkhan indicated the markers on the map of Fair Isle.

"Windhaven?" Kalleen cried. "My people!"

"Who will meet them?" Reothe asked. "The nearest abbey is Chalkcliff. Their T'Enplar warriors can organize resistance and be there in two days."

"And so can we." Tulkhan was fired by a fierce determination that was not quite elation. He had spent many long evenings poring over the maps with Reothe, who had been able to suggest the best way to use natural features in defense and offense. Tulkhan knew he was lucky Reothe had not been Emperor when he invaded Fair Isle. The lack of preparation and incompetence of Fair Isle's defenders had been his allies in that campaign. How Reothe must have seethed to see his island thrown away by his own flesh and blood!

Tulkhan straightened. "Gharavan has chosen to make landfall only two days' ride from T'Diemn, which places the capital under threat. Peirs, prepare the cavalry for a forced ride. I want to surprise my half-brother with our speed."

Ashmyr gave a little cry, tugging at Imoshen's skirt. She picked him up, passing him to Kalleen. "Take him for now."

"What of my people at Windhaven?" she whispered.

"Dead, I fear. Gharavan chose to strike closest to our hearts. Your people, our people are already dead."

Kalleen paled and hugged Ashmyr as she slipped away.

Imoshen met Tulkhan's eyes across the littered map table and said no more, listening to the swift discussion of weapons, men, horses, time to travel, stores to bring up, where to meet, the innumerable what-ifs.

"Lightfoot will lead T'Diemn's garrison and report directly to Imoshen," Tulkhan said. "With the new city's defenses completed, the capital cannot be taken except by siege. But we will defeat Gharavan before he gets here."

In a flurry, the war council broke up. Suddenly Imoshen was alone with the General. "Two years ago you were invading Fair Isle; now you defend her."

"Two years ago I was the General of the Ghebite army, bastard son of the king. Now I go to defeat my own half-brother, who is not half the king my father was." His voice held regret, and Imoshen longed to comfort him.

"There are four outcomes that I can foresee," he said. "At worst, Gharavan defeats us and attacks the capital. If he does, you can hold out until winter. His army will have to prey upon the farmlands to survive. If we are defeated, torch the surrounding farms, bring everyone inside the city. He will be far from his lines of supply in a hostile land. Even if Reothe and I are both killed, enough resistance will survive to plague his every move."

A half sob escaped Imoshen, but he continued inexorably. "We may defeat Gharavan and return triumphant. Fair Isle will be ours. No mainland power will threaten us, because the mainlanders will be busy fighting over the carcass of the Ghebite empire."

"And the other two alternatives?" Imoshen asked.

He looked at her. "I believe you know them. Either Reothe or I may be killed. Men die in battle. I am under a Ghiad to serve Reothe, but I cannot be everywhere on the battlefield. I ask this: If Reothe dies, will you accept that it was none of my doing?"

"I know you are an honorable man, General." Imoshen offered her hand. "Touch me and feel the truth."

Dry-mouthed, Tulkhan let his fingers meet hers. Dropping the shields he had constructed against her gift, he felt the force of her love for him. It made the knowledge that he must ride off and leave her all the more bitter.

"All this and so much more could be yours if you would only trust me, Tulkhan." Her voice moved like a silken touch through his mind. He longed to bathe in her love and rise reborn.

Unable to bear the intimacy, he broke contact. "If I am killed and Reothe lives, fulfill your vows to him."

She shook her head, tears sliding unheeded down her cheeks.

"When a man faces death, Imoshen, there is no time for pretense. Fair Isle will unite behind Reothe. If I die, what is left of my people will have to follow the majority. I must prepare to ride now."

She stepped into his path, pale but determined. "When a man *or* woman faces death there is not time for pretense, General. True, I took you for my bond-partner because I had to. But I grew to love you. Won't you kiss me before you go?"

He held her face in his hands and touched his lips to

hers, savoring the impossibility of his love for her. Letting his guard drop, he accepted her questing mind-touch, sensed her surprise, then joy. But it was too much when he felt so raw and vulnerable.

He pulled back so that only their bodies touched. "You have taught me a great deal, Imoshen of the T'En. I would be the poorer for not knowing you."

Energy powering his steps, Tulkhan strode the palace corridors. He needed to remind Imoshen to keep Ardon under watch. Gharavan must not learn of the Dragon's Eggs.

In Imoshen's room he found Kalleen rocking his son to sleep, and in a flash of understanding, he realized that he was not fighting for glory or power but the safety of his hearth and home. Suddenly, all his years as General of the Ghebite army became a desert of destruction for its own sake.

Kalleen smiled and lifted a finger to her lips, pointing down the hall. "The library."

A group of chattering servants passed Tulkhan as he strode into the library, muffling his footsteps. The chamber seemed deserted, then he heard a sound from behind the great shelves at the far end. He was about to call Imoshen's name when he recognized Reothe's deeper tone.

As far as he knew, Reothe had gone to the basilica and not returned. A worm of disquiet prompted him to approach silently, his presence screened by tall bookcases. Through a narrow chink he saw a private nook illuminated by a finger of golden sunlight. Beyond it was yawning darkness, the entrance to one of the secret passages he knew riddled the palace. T'En architecture reflected its builders' minds—full of beauty, artifice, and deception.

Imoshen stood in the light, her hair and her skin aglow.

". . . have paid the highest price, Imoshen," Reothe was saying. "I have lain with you only the once—and that was by trickery—and now I won't even know my own child!"

"You can't be certain." The heartbreak in Imoshen's voice made Tulkhan flinch.

Reothe dropped to one knee, hands raised in supplication. "The dishonor of my actions sits heavily with me. Forgive my trickery?"

Imoshen did not hesitate. "You are forgiven."

Reothe kissed her sixth finger. When she pulled him to her breast, Tulkhan turned away, unable to watch. Now he understood Reothe's question at Windhaven. It was true that Reothe had come to Imoshen in Tulkhan's form, but in her heart of hearts she had loved her T'En kinsman when she had given her betrothal vows, and though she denied those vows to bond with Tulkhan, Reothe remained her first love.

Shattered, Tulkhan stepped back, the scuff of his boot betraying him. In a flash they both confronted him, weapons drawn, eyes narrowed. For a heartbeat Tulkhan felt a True-man's awe of the T'En.

"Tulkhan?" Imoshen's cheeks flamed as she tucked her knife under her tabard.

Reothe resheathed his sword.

The General cleared his throat. "Gharavan must not discover the power of the Dragon's Eggs. Have Ardon arrested for his own safety."

Imoshen's lips parted as if she might say something, but Tulkhan turned on his heel and marched out.

Imoshen waited on the palace balcony to accept the salute of the army. For the moment they faced the basilica, where Reothe stood, resplendent in the red and gold robes of the Beatific. He understood how to use ceremony to inspire devotion. Even the Ghebites were moved to join in as the massed voices of the basilican choir rose, weaving streams of exquisite sound. The beauty of it flooded Imoshen. T'Diemn was the jewel in the crown of Fair Isle, the pinnacle of T'En culture.

The blessing over, Reothe retreated to the basilica to remove his garments of office and Tulkhan rode around the square, the people breaking into spontaneous cheers as he passed. He stopped before Imoshen, saluting her. She placed her clenched hand over her heart, then opened it toward him. Smiling through her tears, she recalled the first time he had used that gesture, before words of love had ever left his lips.

Tulkhan wheeled his black destrier. It reared, walking on its hind legs. The people cheered, and when he let the beast settle she saw him smile confidently, ever the warrior. On his signal Tulkhan's army marched out of the square toward the north gate.

Only half a day had passed since Reothe told her the T'Elegos lay in its old hiding place. But she could not risk collecting his gift. With Reothe gone, Murgon ruled the basilica, and Imoshen dared not venture into the archives to retrieve the T'Elegos lest he catch her and discover its possibly damning secrets for himself.

The last of Tulkhan's men were still leaving when Reothe and the T'Enplar warriors appeared below her balcony. He was dressed in modern, lightweight armor, his only concession to display the red and gold of the Church's rich mantle. Behind Reothe the Keldon nobles waited, each with their own small army of loyal followers. Amidst them she recognized the stern matriarch Woodvine and Athlyng, Reothe's grandfather.

When Reothe saluted Imoshen with old-empire formality, her heart went out to him. He believed he faced death. His name left her lips as he rode out to collect the Church's army from every village along the way.

Imoshen waited until the last red and gold cloak had filed from the square, then she went inside. Her head ached and her back was weary. Remembering her naive question the first time she had delivered a baby, she smiled. What was the hardest, she had asked the new mother, the waiting or the birth? The woman had simply looked at her.

"Lightfoot," she greeted the mercenary. "I want T'Diemn secure. Send the new password to the lockkeepers and place lookouts on the hilltops. The people must be ready to vacate their farms at a moment's notice."

Having pushed his cavalry to the limit, Tulkhan rode into Windhaven after dark the following day. The destruction, illuminated by the light of the small moon, was all the harder to take since he had been eating in the hall and watching the local children play in the orchard only recently.

Tulkhan stirred the ashes, revealing hot coals. Scouts returned to tell him the Ghebite army was headed inland toward Chalkcliff Abbey.

As Imoshen greeted Tulkhan's messenger, she was reminded of Rawset's loss. This youth trembled with fatigue, his face stained by dirt and grime. His news was grim. Windhaven was destroyed. The General had gone to meet King Gharavan on the fields below Chalkcliff Abbey.

Imoshen nodded, aware of Kalleen's initial soft moan and now her silence. When the door had closed after the messenger, she turned to find Kalleen staring blindly out the window.

"I thought the people of Windhaven would resent me, a farm girl become their lady, but they didn't, and now I've failed them, just as I failed my child!"

Imoshen let Kalleen's tears ease, then took her firmly by the shoulders. "Is that what you really think?"

"No. That is what I *feel*!"

Imoshen kissed her damp cheek. "I've said it before, but I bless the day you fell at my feet!"

Kalleen managed a smile. "I still have the knife you gave me, and I remember how to use it."

Imoshen hugged her and prayed T'Diemn's people would not be reduced to fighting in the streets. She pinned her hopes on Tulkhan. Meanwhile, she had her own plans. Tomorrow morning Murgon would meet Lightfoot on the ramparts of the new city to discuss how the Church could help defend T'Diemn. Tomorrow the T'Elegos would be in her hands.

Kalleen picked up Ashmyr. "Time for your bath, my beautiful boy. Who will be one year old tomorrow?"

With a start Imoshen realized she had forgotten the celebration planned for the royal heir's first birthday. The

Thespers' Guild was going to perform in the square, and the palace would hand out sweet biscuits impressed with the first letter of Ashmyr's name in high T'En. She decided to go ahead with the celebrations despite Gharavan's attack.

The door flew open and a boy of about ten ran into the room. "You must come, Empress. Gharavan's army is in the city!"

"Impossible!" Kalleen snapped.

Spots of light danced before Imoshen's eyes. "Who told you this?"

"Commander Lightfoot."

Then it was true.

"He wants you, Empress. This way!"

Imoshen squeezed Kalleen's hand. "See to Ashmyr's bath."

"Imoshen?"

But she had no words of reassurance. Imoshen followed the boy from the room. As he led her down the long passages, the servants watched, aghast. Bad news traveled fast. Imoshen followed him up the steps to the top of the Sard's Tower, one hand under her belly to help support the baby's weight.

Climbing through the trapdoor was a tight squeeze. Lightfoot helped her to stand. As soon as she did, she saw smoke rising from the wharves, dark against the setting sun.

"The wharves!" Imoshen cursed. "The lockkeepers wouldn't let anyone through without the password. How could they overpower all seven lockkeepers without raising the alarm? We must turn them back, retake—"

"Too late. We weren't prepared for attack from that quarter. Dockside has been gutted," Lightfoot muttered. "They already have a toehold in the new city. People are streaming into old T'Diemn. We should close the inner gates."

Silently she thanked Tulkhan for restoring and reinforcing the defenses of old T'Diemn. "We will keep the gates open as long as we can. Muster the city's defenses, fight a rear-guard action."

"Street-fighting from house to house, townsfolk

trapped in their homes, fires and panic..." Lightfoot spoke from bitter experience.

Imoshen's spirits sank. If people saw her, they would take heart. "Have my horse saddled and call on the Parakhan Guard to escort me. The inner west gate leads directly to the docks. Is that the one we must hold at all costs?"

"Yes. But you can't risk yourself."

"I must be seen for my presence to be felt. Send for T'Imoshen the Third's ceremonial armor." Imoshen's ancestor had been Empress at the end of the Age of Tribulation, when a ruler could expect to lead her army in battle. The chain mail would cover her belly.

At dusk on horseback, it was a nightmare. People streamed uphill, carrying their most prized possessions. Members of the Parakhan Guard escorted Imoshen. She stood in the saddle, carrying a torch. It was symptomatic of the fall of T'Diemn that no one had thought to light the street lamps. As she had anticipated, her presence helped restore calm and order.

Leaving most of her guard at the entrance to the fortified bridge, Imoshen rode through the crowd, trying to estimate how many more people still had to get through the west gate and how close Gharavan's army was.

She hardly recognized the street as the way she had come the night Reothe had lured her to Dockside Hospice. Here the press of bodies was worse. Smoke flowed up the street as if up a chimney flue. Her horse snorted with fear and pawed the cobbles.

"Empress T'Imoshen!" the people cried, reaching for her. They were townsfolk, old and very young, no match for seasoned fighters. For the second time in less than two years, the people of T'Diemn saw their town invaded.

"Come away, T'Imoshen," Drake urged, and Imoshen realized the press of folk had flowed past her, leaving her with three of the Parakhan Guard facing an empty thoroughfare.

Shouts and running feet echoed up the smoky street.

From around the corner a burning building cast the shadows of people running.

"Imoshen!" Drake urged.

She quested with her gifts and remained where she was. Several young apprentices ran around the corner in a parody of Caper Night. This time they were armed with weapons of their trades dipped in blood, not paint. On seeing her they cheered, brandishing hammers and seamster's scissors sharpened to a knife edge.

Imoshen stood in the stirrups, holding the torch high. They trusted her, and she was going to ask them to die. "We must keep the west gate of old city open for as long as possible to let our people into the safety of old T'Diemn."

"We will hold it!" cried a girl, leaping onto a water trough to wave her butcher's cleaver. The others followed her lead.

Imoshen turned to the Parakhan Guard. "Will one of you stay to lead them?"

She was asking which of them would die at the west gate.

"I will." Drake urged his horse forward. "But you must go back now, T'Imoshen."

Imoshen met his eyes, recalling the earnest youth who had delivered news of the sack of T'Diemn. Then Drake had longed for glory; now he volunteered for duty in the full knowledge that it would bring him death. She wanted to refuse but could not deny him this honor.

Sad at heart, Imoshen touched the tip of her sixth finger to Drake's forehead, then guided her mount toward the bridge.

It was nearly dawn when Kalleen entered the map room at a run. "They just closed the last gate to old T'Diemn."

Silently, Imoshen bid Drake farewell and moved a barrier over the corresponding gate on her map of T'Diemn. Lightfoot met her eyes.

She hadn't slept. All night the baby had writhed within her, mirroring her agitation. The inhabitants of new

T'Diemn were camped in the streets of the old city, sleeping in doorways.

"If we need to reinforce the walls, we must have clear access to the ring road. The people will have to move off the streets." Imoshen remembered Tulkhan pulling down the houses that had obstructed this road. "Open the palace gardens. They can camp in the ornamental woods."

Lightfoot nodded.

"Empress?" A messenger stood in the doorway. "Their General is calling for our surrender in the name of King Gharavan."

"And who is this General?" Lightfoot snarled.

"Vestaid of the Vaygharians."

Lightfoot's expression hardened.

"Is he the one who thwarted Tulkhan's first attempt to take Port Sumair?" Imoshen asked.

Lightfoot nodded. "He was the one who led the attack on the plain outside Sumair. I thought him drowned."

"Apparently not." Imoshen straightened her aching back. "I will speak with him. Where is he?"

"He stands on west-gate bridge."

"Come, Lightfoot. Let us hear what he has to say."

Kalleen scurried after them, her little face determined.

Imoshen caught Kalleen's arm, lowering her voice. "I want you to take Ashmyr and go to T'Reothe's Hall. Tell Maigeth..." She faltered. How could Imoshen tell Maigeth she had left her son to die? "Stay there with them. If T'Diemn falls, you must take the Malaunje children and supplies and hide in the secret passages. I'm sure Drake has shared his knowledge of them with Maigeth. Stay there until Tulkhan retakes the city."

She only hoped the General was not already dead.

Imoshen and Lightfoot stood on the tower of west gate in the crisp light of dawn. Smoke from dockside had been blown inland.

"Empress, he has archers on the far defenses," one of her people warned.

"Will he order us killed if we show our faces, Lightfoot?"

He strode to the wall, signaling in an elaborate manner. Imoshen saw the same signal returned. She had to remind herself that Lightfoot and Vestaid were countrymen, part of the brotherhood of mercenaries.

Lightfoot beckoned and Imoshen joined him, looking down onto the bridge. No bodies littered the stonework, but there were bloodstains. The river ran under the uprights, gleaming in the early light. A man had stepped out of the shadow of the tower opposite.

She pitched her voice to carry. "I am T'Imoshen of the T'En, Empress of Fair Isle. What do you want?"

"I am Vestaid, War General of the Ghebites. Who is your Vaygharian lapdog?" he roared.

Lightfoot answered in his own language.

Vestaid laughed. "You choose strange commanders, Dhamfeer—a traitorous Ghebite whoreson and a disinherited Vaygharian merchant prince!"

Imoshen filed away the revelation about Lightfoot's past and raised her voice. "Make your point, Vestaid, my breakfast is getting cold!"

"Enjoy your hot breakfast, for I will have your surrender by nightfall, Dhamfeer."

"Talk is cheap, Vestaid."

"So is life!" He stepped into the shadow to haul someone out with him.

Imoshen knew that head of gingery hair.

"Rawset!" Lightfoot's gasp of dismay went knife-deep.

One of the emissary's shoulders hung at an odd angle. Imoshen's heart contracted. She felt the baby within her recoil in sympathy.

Rawset had escaped the flood only to be captured by Vestaid. This explained how T'Diemn had fallen, for Rawset knew the lockkeepers personally. Imoshen took a deep breath to slow her racing heart.

"Greet your friends, Rawset!" Vestaid urged, kicking him in the back of the knee so that he fell to the stones. Unsheathing his knife, Vestaid curled his fingers through Rawset's hair, pressing the blade to the emissary's throat.

Now that Rawset had served his purpose, Vestaid was going to kill him while they watched. Imoshen could not let this happen.

As she opened her T'En senses, everything went deadly quiet and the early-morning light faded to a dim twilight. She tasted fear on the air and extended her awareness, centering on the savage essence that was Vestaid, but the man was guarded against her intrusion.

Entwined with him, she felt the fragile essence that was Rawset. She brushed his senses and he welcomed her. They had mistreated him, tortured him, but nothing compared to the pain he felt knowing he had betrayed her. He craved her forgiveness. Imoshen gave it without qualification. He bathed in the pure flood of her absolution.

"He whispers your name like a prayer—T'Imoshen! It is clear the Dhamfeer cannot protect their own. Your marvelous powers are nothing but rumor!" Vestaid gave a bark of laughter, and in that heartbeat his guard dropped.

Imoshen found him susceptible. "You don't see because you are blind, Vestaid. Blind!"

Shifting her concentration to Rawset, Imoshen felt as if she was on her knees with Vestaid's knife at her throat. Vestaid's hold loosened as he staggered, his hands going to his eyes. She gave Rawset the impetus to act, urging him to spin under his captor's arm, to tear the knife from the mercenary's grasp, to drive it straight up under his ribs into his heart.

Rawset's satisfaction was hers.

Even as Vestaid's death cry rang out, a dozen soldiers surged forward, weapons raised. Imoshen felt Rawset fall under their blows. His pain was her pain. His death caught her ill-prepared, wrenching her senses.

Something buzzed past her ear. Lightfoot pulled her out of the arrow's path, bringing her back to the reality of her physical body with awful suddenness. From his touch, Imoshen knew the mercenary blamed her for Rawset's death. She had appeared all-powerful when she saved Lightfoot from execution in the Amirate. He believed, right or wrong, that she could have saved Rawset; instead, she had made him her killing tool.

All around them, men screamed as arrows flew true. But Imoshen felt only the after-echo of Rawset's surge of desperation as his life force left him. Imoshen's heart cried out at the injustice of it. Rawset's life was worth so much more than Vestaid's. "He died well, Lightfoot."

"Serving the T'En to the last!" he hissed, then straightened. "Take the Empress back to the palace. She has bought us time with Vestaid's death."

Without argument, Imoshen let the men lead her down the steep steps and into the cobbled lane, where the mayor waited.

"The Ghebites' war general is dead," she said. People cheered and shouted this news up the street and along the ring road. "Tell the townsfolk they are welcome to camp in the ornamental forest. We must have the streets free to send support to the walls where it is needed."

The mayor nodded his understanding. Imoshen recalled how she had distrusted him the first time they met. At least he kept a clear head under pressure. Together they walked up the rise through the streets of old T'Diemn to the palace. Her back ached abominably. She felt nauseous with the shock of Rawset's death, and the baby never ceased moving within her.

It took time to coordinate her plans with the mayor and palace staff, time to reassure people. When at last she closed the door to her private chambers, Imoshen found Kalleen placing fresh food on the low table before the fire.

"Where is Ashmyr?"

"Safe with Maigeth. I came back to see to you. Good news, I hear?"

"No, Rawset is dead."

"But the mercenary general is dead too."

Imoshen looked at the food. "I don't think I can eat. I don't feel well."

Suddenly something shifted inside her, making her bend double with pain. She looked down to find blood pooling at her feet. Kalleen gasped and Imoshen saw her own fear reflected in the little woman's face. She was going to lose the baby. Now. When she could least afford to show weakness.

With a moan of dismay, Kalleen led Imoshen into the bathing room and helped her undress. "I will send for a midwife."

Trembling with shock, Imoshen caught Kalleen's hand. "No one must know."

"But you could die!"

Imoshen closed her eyes, focusing on the force of the first contraction. It was not a preliminary warning, it was earth-shattering. She uttered an involuntary moan. "The baby is lying on my spine. Bring me my herbs. This is going to be fast and bad. Here it comes again."

Unable to stand, she sank to the floor. Kalleen left and Imoshen counted two more contractions in the time it took her to bring mother's-relief. Panting with the effort to ride the pain, Imoshen waited for the aftershock to leave her spine before trying to speak. "No point. I couldn't hold it down, even if we had time to mix up something."

Kalleen knelt on the floor beside her. "What do men know!"

Imoshen grinned, then went under again. It was going to be faster than the first, but, then, this baby was pure T'En and not due for another seven weeks. The babe was too early to live. Tears stung her eyes.

She hiccuped, then surprised herself by feeling the urge to push. No time to mourn, no time to grow accustomed to the loss. Her body was expelling the child.

"It comes," she warned Kalleen.

Her waters burst, and on a flood of pressure the child slid from her. Imoshen caught her breath, opening her eyes in time to see Kalleen lift the little body.

"So blue and still."

Imoshen moaned.

As Kalleen placed the infant on the blanket, Imoshen wondered if she could ignite his spark. Should she try? Physically he looked formed, but... Before she could decide, the contractions began again and the afterbirth was expelled.

"You've lost too much blood," Kalleen whispered. "I must fetch a healer."

"Give the babe to me!"

As Kalleen lifted him, he gave a mewling cry and Imoshen's heart turned over.

"By the Aayel!" Kalleen gasped. "He lives!"

"Cut the cord."

Kalleen did this, then wrapped the blanket around the infant and placed him in Imoshen's arm. Their eyes met, full of wonder and trepidation. To have hope was crueler than to lose the child outright.

"He breathes!" Imoshen marveled, wiping the grease from her son's eyes. His head turned instinctively to follow her hand. He would not give up, this one. Why should this baby live and Kalleen's die? She looked up to see Kalleen wrapping the afterbirth. "That must be disposed of safely to secure his soul in the temple of his physical body."

"But first you must clean up," Kalleen said.

Imoshen wondered how she was going to cope with an early T'En baby and T'Diemn under siege. Fierce determination flooded her. Just as this baby would not give up, she would never relinquish hope.

Twenty-four

THAT EVENING IMOSHEN dressed for effect. She had not torn with this birth, but she was still tender. Through the closed window she could hear the joyous pealing of the basilica's bells, announcing the birth of her son and celebrating the anniversary of the first birthing day of the royal heir. Those bells would carry to the mercenary army occupying new T'Diemn.

"The pearl circlet?" Kalleen asked.

Imoshen nodded and settled it into place so that the single large pearl hung in the middle of her forehead. Tonight people would be watching their T'En empress for any sign of weakness.

Ashmyr played on the floor by his new brother's basket, unaware that their lives hung by a thread.

"Are you ready?" Imoshen asked, rising and looking at herself in the full-length mirror. The lacings of the heavy brocade gown supported her back and pulled her body into shape. She felt strong despite the birth. Her skin looked paler than usual, her eyes very dark.

Kalleen picked up Ashmyr. "Come, let the people wish you happy birthday, my beautiful boy."

Imoshen cradled the new babe. Every time she looked she expected to find him cold and blue, yet he still breathed, no bigger than a small True-man's child, but pure T'En. Fine silver hair covered his body. If he lived, it would fall out. As midwife she had seen other early babies covered in this hair. This little life was frail as the candle flame that could be extinguished by a vagrant breeze, yet her love for him burned so fiercely it was painful.

In the hall outside, they joined Lightfoot. Palace staff lined the corridor, eager to see the new baby. Imoshen realized it would take a long time to reach the stables.

Serving girls rushed forward, but the master of the bedchambers called them back. Imoshen walked slowly, letting each person stroke the little six-fingered hand.

"A miracle!" they marveled.

Imoshen hid her fears. In the faces of the palace servants, she saw wonder and hope and understood what the birth of this baby meant to the people of T'Diemn at this dark time.

The Keeper of the Knowledge met Imoshen's eyes and stroked the baby's sixth finger. "Sacrare."

Imoshen's world shifted. She had never heard this High T'En word spoken. A Sacrare was a pure T'En child born of pure T'En parents. The last recorded Sacrare was Imoshen the First's daughter, who became the first Beatific.

"That word must not be spoken," Imoshen warned.

Cradling the baby in one arm while Kalleen held Ashmyr's hand, Imoshen greeted the mainland ambassadors who had been trapped in the city, the remaining Keldon nobles, the few Ghebites who had not accompanied their general, the guild-masters, and the town's elected council.

The mayor made his obeisance. "The streets are cleared, Empress. Though I fear the palace woods are full of families camped under blankets."

"Let us hope it does not rain. Come with me; we will tour old T'Diemn."

The mayor's eyes glowed. He was eager to bask in the reflected glory of the Empress. But he would not be as eager to share her fate if old T'Diemn fell.

Lightfoot waited in the stable courtyard beside the ceremonial carriage.

"Come with us," Imoshen said as she stepped up. Directly opposite her, Kalleen settled Ashmyr on her lap.

They drove through the palace grounds and out into the square to the festive pealing of the bells and cheering. Imoshen tilted the basket so that the baby could be seen, but fear gripped her, for if he died in the night everyone would despair.

When they passed the basilica, she beckoned Murgon, who would not look at the baby. "I want my son's arrival sung in the square by the full basilican choir. And tell the guild-master of the Pyrolate that I want fountains of lights pouring from the gate towers of old T'Diemn."

The town had celebrated Ashmyr's birth with these symbols. This child deserved nothing less and, besides, the encircling army would be aware of their celebrations. Vestaid had delivered death; the T'En Empress delivered life. Their attackers would see how the spirit of T'Diemn rose above their besiegers, unbowed.

That night Imoshen slept with her tiny infant on her chest. With every breath he took, she willed him to take another, and the long night passed.

When she sensed Rawset's soul questing for her, she met it squarely, expecting recriminations, but he did not seek to drag her through death's shadow with him. He wanted only to acknowledge her before making the final journey. Imoshen quested for the Parakletos, dreading their discovery, but they were amusing themselves with the hoards of lost souls and she escaped unnoticed, falling into an exhausted sleep.

All too soon she was awakened by Kalleen's indignant voice denying someone access.

"Who wants me?" Imoshen called.

After some furious whispering, the basilica's master-archivist and Keeper Karmel entered the bedchamber, accompanied by Lightfoot.

Imoshen sat up, cradling the sleeping baby.

"Your pardon, Empress," Lightfoot said. "This is the moment to strike. I know Vestaid. He would not have let strong men gather power beneath him. His soldiers will be leaderless.

These people claim there is a secret passage from the old town of T'Diemn under the river to the new town. We—"

"Trust the T'En!" Imoshen laughed. "We will send our people into new T'Diemn to strike when Vestaid's men least expect it. Give me time to get dressed."

Lightfoot's mouth dropped open. "You were delivered of the babe only yesterday. You can't mean to—"

"I most certainly do. Just imagine their dismay when they see me!"

Lightfoot gave this some thought. "I will ensure you have your own escort of Parakhan Guard."

"To keep me out of trouble?" Imoshen smiled sweetly.

"In keeping with your importance."

"You should have been a diplomat, Lightfoot."

But he did not smile and Imoshen feared she had lost him.

When the others left, Imoshen pushed back the covers. "We must hurry, Kalleen. I don't want to give Lightfoot any reason to question my ability."

"You'd rather he questioned your sanity?" Kalleen snapped.

"I will be fine. The farm women drop their babes in the morning and work the fields after the noon meal. I am no less capable than one of your sisters!"

"What of the babe? He's so small and fragile!"

"Don't you think I know?" Imoshen whispered. She undid the tie of Kalleen's bodice and opened the material to reveal her golden skin. "Hold him next to your flesh like this. He needs to feel you." She did not explain further.

"And if you are killed?"

"I will not be killed. I have too much to achieve to risk myself. My presence will be enough to dismay the attackers!"

"And then what?" Kalleen asked.

"We rid T'Diemn of these vermin and send word to Tulkhan."

The General stood in the stirrups, thinking it was clear Gharavan and his army had been through here. They traveled the countryside like a plague of locusts, destroying what could not be carried and murdering anyone unlucky enough to be caught. But they had not attacked Chalkcliff Abbey. "Have they gone inland and south to T'Diemn, or north?"

Reothe tilted his face into the wind. His nostrils widened, then narrowed, and his eyes closed in concentration.

Tulkhan watched this uneasily. "Surely you can't smell an army on the move, not with all these men around us?"

"Your kinsman has a peculiar stench," Reothe said softly. "He is half mad, and it taints his—" He used a word that Tulkhan knew to be High T'En, though he could only guess at its meaning. "I think they went west to the coast."

"That makes no sense. There is nothing of strategic value between here and the coast. He left Chalkcliff untouched, so he must be saving his strength for somewhere else."

"Send out the scouts," Reothe advised. "Don't assume he will reason logically."

Tulkhan had had enough examples of his brother's unreasoning hatred. "Very well. But he has delayed attacking Fair Isle until now and succeeded in dragging us up the coast then inland without confronting us. Why?"

"Perhaps it is to distract us from his true purpose. T'Diemn?"

"Can't be taken without a prolonged siege. We would come at him while he camped around the town and crush him against the city's defenses. I planned for that contingency."

"Then what?"

"I don't know!" Tulkhan seethed in frustration.

"This is where we crawl," Lightfoot whispered. "The passage runs directly through the west bridge, hidden within the roadway itself, and comes out on the riverbank below west tower. We'll be at our most vulnerable coming out of the tunnel."

Imoshen was content to let him take the lead. Even T'Imoshen the Third's light armor tired her, and the tunnel seemed interminable. Crawling under the roadway of the

west bridge, she marveled at her ancestors' ingenuity, and
cursed it. How her back ached!

At last she came to the exit. Light greeted her along
with the mercenary's strong hand. She swung down onto
the bridge's footings.

"Move along." Lightfoot indicated the shadows under
the bridge. "I'll secure the tower, then send for you."

Imoshen nodded and picked her way over the damp
stones, further into the shadows. Light came through the
broad arches, reflecting in the river's swiftly flowing surface.
Across from her the first massive pylon stood in semi-
darkness. Above the murmur of the river she could just hear
the furtive shuffling of her companions as Lightfoot prepared the assault.

Imoshen tensed. Something too large to be anything
but a man was crouched directly opposite her on the pylon's
footing. Opening her T'En senses, she quested for him and
met a mind too weary to shield itself.

"Drake!" Elation filled her. The figure jerked. Imoshen
crouched down so her face was illuminated by the light that
angled through the arch. "I'll get help."

Scurrying back to the tunnel entrance, she discovered
that Lightfoot had already left with his raiding party. She
found one man with a rope and several with sturdy arms.
They followed her unquestioningly. The rope sailed across
and Drake grasped it on his first attempt. He wound it
around his waist, then slipped into the river.

The current caught him immediately, swinging him out
into the center of the channel between the pylon and the
tower footing. But the rope was short enough, and growing
shorter as they hauled it in, to prevent him from being seen
by anyone on the riverbank or the bridge. They dragged
him out of the river, wet and shaking, barely able to stand.

"I did not think to see you alive, Drake!" Imoshen
hugged him. "You're injured?"

"My leg. Came off the bridge during the fighting.
Clung to the pylon since. What happened?"

"Vestaid's dead. We're about to break the siege." She

checked the wound. Infection was the biggest danger after being exposed to cold and damp for so long. "My people will help you back to old T'Diemn's hospice."

Someone called for her. She left Drake and went inside the tower, where Lightfoot's men held several prisoners.

"It was as I suspected," Lightfoot said. "Vestaid's officers have wasted time arguing whether to retreat, attack, or send for King Gharavan. Their men, released from the threat of Vestaid's discipline, have been drinking and looting. They fear Gharavan won't honor the contract. If we capture the officers, the men will lay down arms." He led her outside, where half a dozen horses waited. "Mount up."

Imoshen blinked in the bright sun as the Parakhan Guard mounted up around her; beyond them marched Lightfoot's garrison. As they headed down the street toward Jewelers' Square, it saddened her to see storefronts broken open and possessions smashed in the streets. The only mercenaries who were unlucky enough to discover them were quickly silenced.

Entering the square, they surprised four men on the steps of Jewelers' Guild Hall, cutting them down before they could close the huge double doors. On Lightfoot's signal Imoshen and the Parakhan Guard rode up the steps, straight into the hall. Their horses' hooves rang out hollowly on the polished wooden floor.

Vestaid's officers overturned tables and chairs in their haste to escape, but Lightfoot's garrison swarmed over them. They were caught and killed, or dragged back to kneel before Imoshen. It was over in a matter of minutes.

Her horse sidled uneasily. She tightened her knees to control him as she removed her helmet. The captured men muttered uneasily. "These are all Vestaid's officers, Lightfoot?"

"And a Ghebite lordling." He kicked a man on his knees.

"Who speaks for you?" Imoshen asked.

They glanced at one another. So Lightfoot was right; Vestaid had let no strong man rise beneath him. She met their eyes one by one. "Your choice is simple: surrender or die."

As Lightfoot had predicted, they surrendered. When the signal horn echoed across the rooftops, her own people on the walls of Old T'Diemn cheered.

Before long the gates were open and the defenders poured out, ready to restrain any of Vestaid's army foolish enough not to lay down arms. Imoshen watched all this from horseback, Lightfoot at her side.

That evening the people of T'Diemn celebrated in the streets. Imoshen was bone-weary, but her responsibilities were not over. Lightfoot waited for her at the entrance to the public hall.

"Are you sure this Ghebite would have been privy to their plans?" Imoshen asked.

"He's Gharavan's man, probably assigned to Vestaid's army to spy on the General. If any man knows what Gharavan plans, it will be him."

As Lightfoot strode into the great hall, the sound of their echoing footsteps told of its size. The lamps only illuminated the nearest of the slender twin columns, hinting at the majesty of the T'En architecture. A bound man stood alone in its vastness. Though he stood proudly among enemies, Imoshen could smell his fear. Terror crawled across his face as she approached.

"Kneel before the T'En Empress, Cavaase," Lightfoot ordered.

The Ghebite glared up at her, refusing to bow his head. "I would rather die than reveal King Gharavan's plans."

"Dying is easy," Imoshen told him.

He flinched.

Slowly she walked around him. Her own men stepped away. She opened her T'En senses and probed Cavaase, testing his resistance. Behind it was fatalism. "Were you there when they tortured Rawset? Did you watch while he screamed?"

She saw the sweat start on his forehead and noted how his color faded under his coppery skin. Again she probed, sensing panic and despair. "That is a crude way to get information, fit

only for barbarians. The T'En do not need to cripple the body
when we want something from a man's mind."

She came to a stop before him and leaned forward. Despite his terror, his gaze went to the rise of her breasts. She
saw him swallow painfully. He would not meet her eyes.

"If you resist me, this will hurt; either way, I will discover what I want to know, Mere-man." She was surprised
by an echo of Reothe's tone in her voice.

A muscle jumped in the prisoner's cheek.

Imoshen lifted her left hand, little sixth finger extended.
He jerked away as though she was going to strike him.

"Hold him," Lightfoot snapped.

"No." Imoshen waved the men back. "It won't be necessary. Will it, Cavaase?"

In that instant she sensed that despair overwhelmed his
will.

"You are mine!" She pressed the tip of her sixth finger
to the center of his forehead between his eyes. In a rush she
understood as much as he did. Gharavan despised and
feared the mercenary war general. Cavaase believed Vestaid
had meant to murder the young king and claim the Ghebite
empire for himself. He had not been sure whether to tell his
king this or bide his time and see who was victorious.
Gharavan's task was to distract the army of Fair Isle, evad-
ing battle until T'Diemn fell, and then he was to march into
the city and lay claim to it.

Imoshen broke contact, disgusted. She stared at the
Ghebite lord who was willing to betray his own king if it
was to his advantage. He blinked, his blank expression
clearing to sullen lines of hatred as his will returned.

T'Diemn was safe for now, but Gharavan still wandered
Fair Isle with a formidable army.

"I have what I need to know, Lightfoot." She rubbed
her back; it still ached with the aftereffects of the birth.

"I will decorate the tower of west gate with the prisoner's head," Lightfoot said.

Imoshen began to say no, then she looked into the
man's eyes. "I will ride past tomorrow morning. Lightfoot,

we must send word to General Tulkhan. T'Diemn has suffered because he did not anticipate this attack. I want him back here, ready to pay for this oversight!"

Lightfoot's sharp eyes met hers, but he did not reveal that this was out of character.

"Take this craven creature away; his will is broken." Imoshen did not have to tap Lightfoot's arm to tell him to stay.

After the others had filed out of the great hall, she said, "Arrange it so that Cavaase escapes. Don't make it too easy. I want him to think himself lucky to get away with his life. He will run straight back to his little king with the news of Tulkhan's discomfort. What do you think Gharavan will do? Run for the coast or attack Tulkhan from behind as he comes back to T'Diemn?"

The veteran narrowed his eyes. "He will attack. He won't be able to help himself."

Imoshen nodded. "I must send a message to the General. For all I know, Gharavan is already on his way here to claim T'Diemn."

A silence fell between them. Imoshen looked up to find Lightfoot's eyes on her. She raised an eyebrow. He shook his head and would have turned away.

"I have no hold over you," Imoshen said. "When this is over you may wish to return to your family."

"Forget what you heard. I cannot return. Twenty years ago my father declared me a dead man. My younger brother became heir to our merchant holdings and now has heirs of his own."

"I am sorry." Imoshen hesitated. "I am not all-powerful, Lightfoot. If I could, I would have saved Rawset."

"I have seen many men die. Rawset's death was one to be proud of." He rubbed his forehead where the sign of his servitude had been smoothed away.

"If I had known the man you are, I would never have imprinted you with the T'En stigmata," Imoshen said. "And I removed it when you asked."

"You cannot remove the knowledge that I could not

resist the T'En. It remains a stigma on my mind." Lightfoot gave her the bow of a Vaygharian merchant prince and backed away.

Imoshen frowned and rubbed the inner curve of the ring that Tulkhan had given her. Was there some way she could use the Ghebite seal to trick Gharavan?

Tulkhan stared into the fire, determined to precipitate a battle before his men lost heart. Raised voices made him look up to see a messenger dismount, his horse's sides flecked with foam. The man pulled two folded messages from inside his jerkin and handed them to Tulkhan. The first was addressed to him, the second was to Reothe; both were written in Imoshen's hand. As if the thought had called him, Reothe walked into the fire circle.

Silently, Tulkhan handed him his message and broke the seal on his own. Before he could begin reading, Reothe muttered under his breath. "Better for him to die!"

"Who?" Tulkhan whispered, aware of his men on the far side of the fire circle.

Anger and despair tightened Reothe's features. "Not only is my child a boy, but he has been born before time. If he lives, his gift will be crippled."

Tulkhan marveled that the child he had feared had been born without the T'En gift. Then the rest of Reothe's speech sank in. *Only* a son!

A T'En daughter would have inherited Imoshen's gifts. Reothe could have trained and manipulated her. Tulkhan recalled his intention to let the child live if it had been a girl. He had been blinded by his culture. He felt relieved that this male child might not live.

"What message does Imoshen send you, General?"

Tulkhan held the page to the firelight, reading with growing anger and astonishment. Wordlessly, he handed it to Reothe.

"We must return to T'Diemn," Reothe announced.

That had been Tulkhan's first thought. "It will be what Gharavan expects."

"The capital lies like a great beast with its underbelly exposed and outer defenses breached in key places, from what Imoshen writes," Reothe said. "What if Gharavan has another attack prepared for T'Diemn?"

Tulkhan stared into the flames.

"Are you considering breaking up the army to go on ahead with the cavalry?" Reothe demanded. "The foot soldiers can only travel so far in a day, and the majority are unbloodied. What if Gharavan doubles back and attacks the stragglers? Do you plan to let him butcher me and my contingent, then ride in to mop up?"

Tulkhan spun to face Reothe, ready to deny this, but saw that Reothe was deliberately provoking him. Once he would not have recognized this. Somehow Reothe had become his confidant, someone to argue strategy with, someone who knew him well enough to speak the truth and risk his displeasure.

"Even now Gharavan could get to T'Diemn before us if he pushed his army in a forced march," Reothe said.

"Until now Gharavan has been avoiding battle. But Imoshen has planted the misinformation that I am being recalled to T'Diemn."

"Then let him think you have been recalled, draw him after us until we find a place where the lie of the land gives us the advantage, then turn to face him."

This was what Tulkhan had decided, but he wanted to see if Reothe came to the same conclusion. "I'll let it be known that T'Diemn nearly fell and that the city is safe but vulnerable. We will give the appearance of returning to the capital." Tulkhan raised his free arm to clasp the T'En warrior's shoulder. "For what it is worth, I am sorry about your son." And he was surprised to discover this was true.

But Reothe would not meet his eyes.

Calling for paper and ink, Tulkhan wrote to Imoshen. He would return to T'Diemn as soon as he had defeated

Gharavan. Meanwhile, she was to stay safely behind
T'Diemn's walls.

Imoshen fretted. Somewhere between the capital and the
west coast, Tulkhan and Reothe would face Gharavan's
army, and the fate of Fair Isle—her fate—hung on that encounter. She feared only one of them would return.

Seeking comfort, she knelt by the sleeping boys. She
stroked her nameless son's pale cheek and his lips moved as
he sucked in his sleep. She raged at her impotence.

Imoshen threw open her chest and found the scrying
platter. She hesitated, recalling the imperfection of her previous attempts to steal a glimpse of the future. Her heart
might be tearing in two with fear for Reothe and Tulkhan,
but she would not let fate mock her by revealing a half
truth. Though it cost her dearly, she closed the chest.

Soberly, she went to her desk to reread Tulkhan's message but in her distraction she bumped the goblet, spilling
the claret, which gleamed in the candlelight. Imoshen fell
into that shimmering flame.

Sharply silhouetted against the molten gold of the setting
sun stood the jagged rock sentinel that guarded the mouth of
the River Diemn. Tulkhan knelt on the sand before his half-
brother. Gharavan's naked sword blade gleamed with reflected torchlight as he raised it to deliver the killing stroke.

The goblet continued to roll off the desk, clattering on
the floor. Her Vision had taken less than a heartbeat, but
she could not ignore it. Reothe was going to die on the battlefield and Tulkhan would be executed on the beach at the
mouth of the River Diemn! But not while she lived.

Imoshen opened the door of the bathing room. Kalleen
looked up from the tub, her face flushed, her long hair
pinned on top of her head. With a pang Imoshen noted her
beauty. It would not be long before some man tried to steal
her away. "I have to go to Tulkhan."

"The little one needs your touch and constant feeds."

Imoshen knew if she left the babe, he would die. "I saw

Tulkhan about to be executed. If you come with me, you could die."

Kalleen's mouth hardened. "I will see this out."

Imoshen nodded.

For the first time on this campaign Tulkhan was within striking distance of his half-brother's army. To lure him into attacking, the General had selected a campsite that appeared vulnerable. His hardened veterans and the Keldon nobles were camped on low ground by a lake. Their flanks were protected by lush green grass, which hid boggy soil, impossible for cavalry to cross. His unseasoned troops were held in reserve behind a ridge to the south. As soon as Gharavan attacked, Reothe was ready to lead a pincer attack.

Tulkhan had pitched his tent conspicuously on the low ground and spent a restless night expecting battle at first light, but none eventuated. Frustrated, he had sent scouts to discover Gharavan's movements. They reported his half-brother in retreat. With Reothe at his side, Tulkhan rode out to investigate.

"Gharavan leads us on a merry chase, but to what purpose?" Reothe muttered, riding through the deserted camp. Only wheel ruts, blackened fire circles, and trampled ground remained.

"I don't know, but I'm tired of playing cat and mouse. We'll confront him if we have to chase him all the way to the sea."

Reothe stood in the stirrups, studying the land. "The River Diemn lies to the south, and the sea lies one day's fast march to the west."

"Then we'll force-march the men and pin Gharavan between the river and the sea. He'll have to fight or drown."

All day they drove the army. That afternoon Tulkhan's scouts reported that Gharavan camped on the dunes at the headland. Satisfied, the General settled his forces into position. The feeling as the men made camp was optimistic.

Tulkhan stood on the last dune, staring into the west,

the sky lit by the setting sun. Gharavan's army was a dark shadow on the wide sandy flats.

"When the sun rises tomorrow, we face Gharavan and this thing is decided one way or the other!" Tulkhan told Reothe, who gave no answer. The General was sure something troubled him, but what could he say to the man whose death meant his future happiness?

Imoshen helped haul the boat up the sandy bank of the hollow, which was shrouded in twilight though the sky still blazed with the setting sun's light.

Kalleen handed a weary Ashmyr to Drake. They'd left Lightfoot to hold T'Diemn. He was none too pleased with Imoshen's plan but had agreed to hide her absence when she explained her Vision.

They unloaded the boat in silence. Imoshen climbed up the bank and pointed across the dunes. "That's Tulkhan's army, Kalleen. Stay here until I return. If I do not come back by midnight, go to the camp."

Imoshen hugged Ashmyr, who had fallen asleep in Drake's arms, then she stroked her nameless son's head and turned away. Determined not to look back, she walked along the riverbank.

If her Vision was to be trusted, Gharavan would be camped on the beach. Her plan was simple. She would make her way into his tent and kill him. According to Tulkhan, Gharavan was not a leader to inspire men. Once they learned of his death and Vestaid's failure, the Ghebite army would surrender.

As she approached she caught the scent of Ghebite cooking fires. Ahead of her, the sentinel that marked the entrance to the River Diemn stood stark against the setting sun, just as it had in her vision. But she was going to circumvent events by killing Gharavan tonight.

She noticed a man with his back to her, derelict in his sentry duties. To enter the camp she would have to assume the Ghebite coloring. In her heightened state of desperation, it

was not difficult to focus her gifts, and her skin stung with a
thousand prickles. Now she looked like a Ghebite, down to
the boots and cloak, the long black plaits.

A row of torches stood before Gharavan's tent on the
beach. Weaving through the campfires, she passed unremarked right up to the back of the tent. Freeing her knife,
she slit the canvas and slipped inside, but the tent was
empty. Imoshen fingered the knife hilt, looking about for a
place to hide.

Suddenly, a man thrust the flap open and marched in,
colliding with her. She spun him around, pulling his arm up
behind his back, bringing the knife to his throat. "Call your
king."

"Why should I betray my king?" he countered, and she
recognized his voice.

"You were ready enough to betray him for Vestaid,
Cavaase." Then she replayed his words in her head and
mimicked his voice, calling, "My king?"

"What is it, Cavaase?" Gharavan thrust the flap aside.
His eyes met hers. "You!"

Leaving his countryman to die, Gharavan fled.

Imoshen cursed. She should have guessed Gharavan
was a coward. But how did he recognize her?

Taking advantage of her momentary distraction,
Cavaase dropped and darted under her guard, bringing her
own knife to her throat. "I'd kill you myself if I didn't know
how much pleasure Gharavan will have slitting your throat,
Tulkhan."

It was ironic. In assuming a Ghebite form she had un-
consciously adopted the one she knew best.

Cavaase forced Imoshen outside, where curious
Ghebite soldiers gathered. "I have your traitorous half-
brother, my king."

"Bring the torches nearer, the better to see Tulkhan
beg!" Gharavan ordered.

Cavaase turned her to face Gharavan, who held his
drawn sword ready. The rock sentinel stood silhouetted
against the setting sun. With cold certainty, Imoshen

understood that she had precipitated the Vision. The absurdity of it made her laugh.

"You can laugh?" Gharavan roared, his blade flickering in the torchlight as he advanced.

She recognized the weapon. "Seerkhan's sword!"

"*My* sword. How do you think I felt, seeing our father give away what should have been mine?" He frowned, then grabbed her hand, dragging the Ghebite-seal ring from her finger. Stepping back, he held the ring for his men to see. "Our father never guessed he sired a traitor. But tonight I take back the seal just as I have taken back Seerkhan's sword, and tomorrow Fair Isle will be mine!" His hate-filled eyes settled on Imoshen. "I'll wash away the shame of your betrayal with your own blood, Tulkhan. Release him."

Cavaase shoved Imoshen so that she fell to her knees in the sand. Her head spun, superimposing the Vision over reality. Was it the fate of the T'En to foresee their own deaths? Would Reothe die tomorrow and their line be extinguished except for one sickly, nameless babe?

"Come, Cavaase," Gharavan ordered. "I give you this ring in honor of your service. And I award you my traitorous half-brother's estates."

The man accepted the ring triumphantly.

His duplicity revolted Imoshen. "He bears the T'En stigmata on his forehead. Ask him who he truly serves!"

"No." Cavaase rubbed at his forehead. "The Dhamfeer bitch touched me, but—"

"And sent you back to Gharavan to lead the army into this trap!"

Cavaase stared at her, squinting in the glare of the torches. Then his eyes widened in horrified recognition. He lunged for her throat, but two men held him back.

"Bring the torch closer," Gharavan urged. "I would see this T'En sign Tulkhan speaks of."

"That is not the General!" Cavaase cried. "I can smell the Dhamfeer from here. She wears his form."

"Look for the T'En sign!" Imoshen focused her will on Gharavan, for he was an easy target. "Do you see it?"

"Hold his head still!" Gharavan yelled.

"She's doing it. She's branding me," Cavaase cried. "It burns my skin!"

Gharavan's men restrained Cavaase, as the stigmata on his forehead grew more pronounced.

"Every word you have said, all you have done has been made known to your enemy." Imoshen let her voice persuade. "He has been the T'En's eyes."

She willed them to see the stigmata elongate, become a lid, and open to reveal a single wine-dark eye.

With a scream, Gharavan drove his sword straight through Cavaase's forehead, releasing the hilt as the dead man fell. His men stumbled away, and what little blood there was seeped into the thirsty sand.

"Look around you, Gharavan," Imoshen purred. "How many of them do you trust?"

Those men who were susceptible clutched their foreheads, others backed off. Gharavan snatched a sword from a man who staggered with his hands to his head, cutting him down. All around him, his men drew weapons against their fellows.

Imoshen retrieved her knife and lunged for Gharavan, who turned and ran. She darted after him. Around her, torches toppled, setting tents alight, and men turned on one another. Someone collided with her. She fell to one knee.

Gharavan leapt on her, hands at her throat. His weight forced her into the soft pillow of the sand. Stars spun in her vision. His knee on her chest drove the breath from her body. Her skin stung as the illusion left her with her ebbing strength.

"Dhamfeer!" Gharavan hissed, his grip slackening.

She gulped air, and her hand closed over the knife hilt half buried in the sand.

Gharavan recovered from his surprise. "Know this, sorcerous bitch. I'll choke the sense from you before I rape you. Then I'll hand you over to my men. You'll wish you were dead!"

Imoshen drove the knife up between his ribs. His grasp didn't falter. She twisted the blade. Gray patches swum in her vision. Which of them would pass out first?

Twenty-five

IMOSHEN FOUND HERSELF crawling through cool, silken sand. The damp air shimmered with pale light. Perhaps this was the elysian plane reserved for those who died protecting their fellows, but she did not remember traversing death's shadow.

Under her hands, the dune was threaded with silvery strands of runner vine, each perfect little star-shaped leaf bejeweled with dew. Looking about, she realized the world was cloaked by a pearly mist, and the night's events returned in a rush of revulsion. Imoshen tried to stand but her knees gave way. Then she felt the merest whisper of a questing awareness. Opening her T'En senses, she recognized Reothe. Relieved, she sank into the sand, concentrating on drawing him to her. Soon she heard the soft susurration of his boots in the dunes.

"Imoshen, what have you done to yourself?" His face swam above hers, familiar and dear. She tried to say his name but her throat was too tender. He frowned. "That necklace of bruises."

"I think I killed Gharavan," she croaked.

He leaned closer. "I cannot smell his death coming from your skin."

Tears of failure stung her eyes as others joined them.

"Carry her between you," Reothe directed, and she held

on to the broad shoulders of two men as they plowed through the sand.

"Reothe, what of Kalleen and the boys?" she asked.

He was right behind her. "Safe. She came to us during the night. Told us of your Vision and what you attempted."

Imoshen concentrated on staying conscious. She wanted to ask him if he had seen his son but would not speak in the presence of True-men.

People appeared out of the mist, their muffled voices alarmed but oddly disjointed as her consciousness wavered. When the General took her in his arms, she confessed, "I failed. Gharavan still lives and he has Seerkhan's sword."

"In safekeeping only." Tulkhan was secretly horrified to find her so frail. He ducked into the tent. As he knelt to place her on the bedding, his knees cracked. Imoshen caught his arm and he squeezed her hand.

Tulkhan sat back to let Kalleen bathe Imoshen's face with warm herbal water, removing the dried blood, but she could not remove the bruises. Imoshen swallowed, wincing with pain.

Tulkhan cursed. Under cover of this mist Gharavan and his army might escape. "Did you wound my half-brother, Imoshen?"

She nodded.

"We heard—" Tulkhan hesitated, recalling the screams. Despite Imoshen's injuries, he had to know how things stood in the enemy camp. "What happened last night?"

Imoshen slipped her left hand free from his. Trembling with the effort, she touched Reothe's forehead with the tip of her little finger. Reothe stiffened, his lids lowered over his eyes, shuttering his thoughts. His mouth narrowed in a thin line and he gave a soft exclamation of surprise.

Kalleen's small hand closed on Tulkhan's arm as her frightened eyes met his. He could feel the backwash of Imoshen's T'En gift. Kalleen picked up the bowl. "I can't stand this."

Tulkhan followed her from the tent, which was isolated

in a world of glowing mist. She threw the water onto the sand, barely visible under their boots.

Kalleen gave a sob of relief. "I thought her dead."

Tulkhan hugged her. "Even though Reothe insisted Imoshen still lived?"

He had wanted to invade Gharavan's camp as soon as the screaming started, but Reothe had argued against it, claiming it would place Imoshen at risk.

Tulkhan's fingers tightened on Kalleen's shoulder as the tent flap opened and Reothe stepped out.

"Well?" Tulkhan asked.

Reothe met his eyes, his own shadowed by knowledge Tulkhan did not want to share. He glanced to Kalleen, who slipped inside the tent. Reothe lowered his voice. "Imoshen lost consciousness while Gharavan was trying to throttle her. I believe only her T'En instinct preserved her life, cloaking her from them, driving her to crawl away like a wounded animal."

"But the screams, the fires?"

Reothe met his eyes, and what Tulkhan read there belied his words. "Mere trickery. The sooner we attack the better." Reothe inhaled. "The sea breeze will drive the mist away soon."

"Your gifts are healed."

"I never had Imoshen's gifts, never.... Did you know in High T'En the word for gift also means curse?"

Tulkhan repressed a shiver. Then he felt the breeze on his face as Reothe had predicted. "Time to move." He led the way to the tallest dune to see the headland revealed as the mist cleared. Gharavan had drawn up his army in a defensive position, with the river and sea curving around behind them so that they could be attacked only on two sides. "We could drive them back, force them into the river."

"You both think like landsmen," Reothe said. "By the time the sun is directly overhead, the tide will have gone out and the sand will be hard enough to send the cavalry in on his flanks. His defenses will crumble. We must divert him with the attacks he expects while we keep the cavalry in reserve."

Tulkhan held Reothe's eyes. "You have given me victory with this advice."

"You would have realized it when the time came."

"Still, I give you the honor of leading the cavalry."

A strangely painful smile illuminated Reothe's face and for a moment Tulkhan thought he would refuse, then he gave the old-empire obeisance of acceptance.

Imoshen woke to find herself lying on the mat with Ashmyr asleep on one side and her nameless son at her other breast. Kalleen was preparing food. Smoke drifted up to the hole directly overhead, playing in the shaft of noonday sun. It was peaceful except for the distant roar and shouts of battle blown inland from the beach.

"I—" Imoshen began. "My voice will never be the same. How goes the battle?"

"They will tell us when there is news."

Imoshen nodded. She did not want to discuss what was closest to her heart. Only time would tell if Reothe would die as he believed or if Tulkhan would be defeated by Gharavan's army and fulfill the Vision she had tried to circumvent.

The babe made a soft noise and she stroked his head. The fine silver down had fallen off, leaving his skin soft as silk and pale as milk. On Fair Isle it was customary for the mother to name her sons and the father to name his daughters. Imoshen had been waiting for Reothe to meet his son, to see if there was a name he preferred, but she had never admitted before Kalleen that the child was Reothe's. "Perhaps I should name him; then if we are all killed, at least he will die with a name."

"Imoshen! What have you seen?"

"Nothing, my gift has ebbed away. I am useless."

"Then you will just have to wait for the outcome like True-people do."

Imoshen winced. "I am sorry, Kalleen."

"Sorry doesn't mend a broken pot."

"But it may appease the potter."

Kalleen smiled despite herself.

As the sun approached the zenith, Tulkhan arched his weary back and flexed his sword arm. He had pulled back to the dune to see how the battle was going. Gharavan's army formed a solid core of seasoned men, who had succeeded in holding off Tulkhan's troops. His half-brother rode up and down behind the lines. Imoshen believed Gharavan carried a mortal wound, yet there he was in full battle armor.

The sea had retreated, leaving a wide band of hard-packed sand. Reothe had chosen to lead the cavalry that would attack from the sea flank. A second charge of Keldon nobles, led by Woodvine and Athlyng, would come from the river flank, where the tidal flats had been revealed. Tulkhan raised the cavalry horn to his lips and the signal rang out loud and clear.

Pride filled him as his men poured down from the dunes to form two spearheads. These outflanked Gharavan's army, aiming for the soft underbelly. Gharavan's own cavalry were hemmed in. Armed foot soldiers, no matter how well drilled, could not withstand a mounted charge.

He saw Gharavan attempt to send reserves, but before he could, Reothe's mounted division broke Gharavan's flank, allowing Tulkhan's foot soldiers to attack the less seasoned reserves.

Tulkhan kneed his horse. Now that it was clear the attack would work, he wanted to be at Reothe's side in the melee. If ever there was a chance to redeem his Ghiad, this was it.

Galloping down the soft sand of the dune, he felt his mount gain confidence on the hard-packed tidal flats. He followed the path his cavalry had taken, picking through the bodies, forging to the front ranks where he'd seen Reothe's red and gold helmet.

Rising in the stirrups, Tulkhan slashed at a defender. When he straightened, Reothe had disappeared. The General aimed for the place where he had last been. Now Tulkhan was in the thick of the battle—screaming horses, roaring men, and flying hooves. His own mount kicked and bit as he had been trained to do. For several heartbeats he fought with no time for thought.

At last the pace eased and Tulkhan wheeled his black destrier. A space had cleared around him. Reothe lay amid the fallen, one leg trapped under his slain horse, his sword shattered. Three men bore down on him, weapons raised.

Tulkhan rode down the nearest man, taking his sword arm off. A pike man lifted his weapon. A man leapt for the destrier's bridle. Tulkhan concentrated on keeping his seat. He broke the man's pike and kicked him in the chest, sending him onto a protruding spear.

Tulkhan's horse lost its footing, dragged down by the man at the bridle. The General jumped off his mount, coming up in time to block a killing blow. He followed through with a counterstrike, opening the man's belly. His horse rolled upright. It stood shivering and snorting as it pawed the ground.

In one of those odd moments of battle, Tulkhan found himself in an island of stillness. The fighting had moved on, leaving him and Reothe amid a sea of bodies, dead and dying.

"Your Ghiad has been served," Reothe said. The meaning of the words reached Tulkhan through the roar of battle and the pounding in his head. "This is your chance to kill me."

It was the perfect murder. When Reothe's body turned up with the slain, they would assume he had been killed in battle. Fair Isle and Imoshen would be his. Tulkhan saw the foreknowledge in Reothe's eyes. With a shock, he realized Reothe had suggested the battle plan and agreed to lead the cavalry charge, knowing this moment would come.

Time stretched impossibly.

Suddenly Tulkhan knew he could not kill Reothe. Silently, he extended his left hand.

Behind him, his horse snorted. Tulkhan spun. The man who had fallen on the spear charged him. There was barely time to bring the sword point between them before he was upon Tulkhan. The man's weight drove the blade into his body and carried them both down. His attacker was dead before Tulkhan could get out from under him. He rolled the corpse aside and came to his feet, disengaging his sword. If he had paused to slay Reothe, this man would have killed him. In sparing Reothe's life he had saved his own.

"That part I didn't see," Reothe said. "Free my leg."

Sweaty and soaked in the blood of the men he had killed, Tulkhan put his hands under the horse's rump and lifted. Reothe struggled out. Tulkhan searched the bodies for a sword, cleaned the scavenged weapon, and presented it to Reothe.

"Why didn't you kill me?"

Tulkhan shrugged.

A fey laugh escaped Reothe. "If you don't know, then I surely don't. Your walls are much too strong for my crippled gift!"

Tulkhan signaled his destrier, which picked its way fastidiously to join him. Another abandoned horse followed his mount. Reothe caught its reins, swinging into the saddle with care for his bad leg.

Tulkhan surveyed the beach from high in the saddle. The battle had turned with the tide. The defenders could drown or surrender. He would offer them seven years' service. By Ghebite custom, a surrendering soldier could accept death or service. While in service, if he refused an order his life was forfeit; if he survived the seven years, he was free.

"Gharavan's tent is down," Reothe said.

Tulkhan watched his father's standard fall. Seeing it trampled in the bloody sand brought him no joy.

Gharavan's army threw down their weapons. They wore the colors of Gheeaba and, despite everything, Tulkhan found he still thought of them as his men. He recognized many who had served him on other campaigns.

As he approached the ruined tent, soldiers dragged Gharavan before him. It should have been a moment of supreme triumph but, like the moment just past when he had looked into Reothe's eyes, Tulkhan felt no surge of killing lust.

They had torn the helmet from Gharavan's head and the armor from his chest. Tulkhan noticed blood seeping through his clothing and guessed the wound Imoshen had inflicted was bleeding.

"Tulkhan, brother!" Gharavan cried.

The General clenched his teeth.

Reothe urged his horse nearer and spoke for Tulkhan's ears only. "If he dies of the wound Imoshen gave him, she will suffer for it. If you don't kill him, I will. I already face death's shadow tonight, and I am skilled in that plane."

Tulkhan swung down from the horse, drawing his weapon. A soldier rushed forward, presenting him with Seerkhan's sword. Tulkhan took his grandfather's blade, feeling its familiar weight and balance.

Gharavan faltered. "Think of the blood we share!"

He would have fallen to his knees but Tulkhan's men held him upright.

"Let him go."

The men stepped back. Tulkhan became aware of numerous small wounds, making his skin sticky and limbs weary. He tossed his borrowed sword across the gap so that it speared into the soft sand at Gharavan's feet. "I offer you honorable death. Defend yourself."

Gharavan hesitated.

Someone in the ranks muttered, "He does not deserve—"

"Quiet!" Tulkhan barked.

Gharavan attacked.

Tulkhan deflected and countered on reflex. The huge blade cleaved Gharavan diagonally from shoulder to hip. He was dead as he stood. He blinked once in disbelief, then toppled, his blood soaking into the sand.

"The Ancients will be pleased. They belong to the land and they are eager for the life force of beings like us," Reothe explained. Imoshen's words returned to Tulkhan. *Conquerors come and go, but Fair Isle endures.*

"Throw Gharavan's remains in the sea," Tulkhan ordered. It was the ultimate insult to deny a proper burial. Before they could move the body, he reclaimed his Ghebite-seal ring and took Gharavan's in memory of the boy he had taught to ride.

Then he mounted his horse and rode through the

battlefield with Reothe at his back. It came to Tulkhan that Fair Isle was truly his, and the realization hit him: The Ghebite Empire was also his for the taking.

Restored by food and sleep, Imoshen soothed the wounded all afternoon, relying on herbs and stitching for the most part. It would have exhausted her to the point of death if she had tried to heal them all, yet it made her weep to turn her face from their desperation and let them die. She needed a hundred—no, a thousand—healers with her gifts.

Someone touched her arm and she recognized Woodvine, the woman who would have led the Keldon uprising.

"T'Imoshen, will you come this way." Woodvine led her through Tulkhan's men to the Keldon encampment. Silently, the iron-haired matriarch opened a tent flap.

Imoshen ducked to enter, recognizing Lord Athlyng on the low bed with his kin clustered around. She met Reothe's eyes briefly across the tent.

"Empress T'Imoshen," the others whispered, drawing back.

Lord Athlyng's pain-glazed garnet eyes focused on her. She knelt by his low bed. "I regret I cannot save you."

"I am ready to go. I have lived to see my children die of old age before me. That is a terrible thing." His gaze went past her to Woodvine and Reothe. "There are those who counsel war and death before dishonor. But I believe you see with vision beyond your years. Take the path of peace, Imoshen. You were given that name for a reason. Carry on her work." His breath rattled in his chest. "Reothe, are you there?"

"I am here, Grandfather." He knelt at Imoshen's side, tears on his cheeks. His long fingers threaded through the old man's six fingers.

"This time heed my advice, boy; take the path of peace. This Ghebite general is a worthy True-man. Build on what he has begun."

Woodvine tapped Imoshen's shoulder. She wanted to comfort Reothe but she came to her feet.

Woodvine held the tent flap open, meeting Imoshen's eyes. "With his passing the Keld lose a great statesman."

"We are not Keld or Ghebite or T'Diemn merchant," Imoshen replied. "We are Fair Isle."

Woodvine gave her the obeisance reserved for the Empress. "Athlyng was right—you see with vision."

Heart sad, Imoshen continued her work with the sick until she had emptied her herbal pouch. A little later she heard the pipes playing and knew Lord Athlyng was dead. Many Keldon pipes played that afternoon.

At dusk she returned to her tent to eat and to feed her smallest son. For all her talk she had not named him.

Tulkhan opened the tent flap. "Have you seen Reothe?"

"No," Imoshen said. "Is something wrong?"

Tulkhan shook his head. He let the tent flap drop and kept looking. After asking around the camp, he learned Reothe had walked to the dunes alone.

Tulkhan found the T'En warrior on a tall dune, wrapped in his cloak, watching the last of the sun's setting rays fade from the sky.

As the General joined him, Reothe met his eyes, then looked away. Tulkhan knew Reothe did not want to discuss what he faced when the souls of the men he had killed tried to drag him through death's shadow, but... "Wouldn't it be safer in the tent?"

"I take no pleasure in killing. I turned the flat of my sword on True-men, but even so I killed several, more than I could count in the rush of battle. Their souls linger after violent death. They cannot believe they are shades. But soon they will realize. And one by one they will come for me." His eyes were dark pools. "I don't want to frighten your people."

"Do you need food?" Tulkhan asked.

"I have my cloak and a water skin. You should go back."

Tulkhan stretched, working the kinks from his muscles. "I think I will watch the path of the moons tonight. When my people still roamed the plains, a boy on the verge of manhood took his horse, a blanket, and water, and left the tent circle.

"He meditated and waited for a sign. Eventually, he

would see an omen and know what his private name would be, usually a bird of prey, wolf, wild cat, or bear. After that, he would never kill one of those birds or animals, and if he was in trouble, he would call on them. By the time I was of that age, my people no longer lived on the plains. The priests assigned our private names."

Reothe did not ask Tulkhan his private name, for which he was grateful. He hadn't meant to reveal so much. Tulkhan studied the endless starlit night sky. The silence stretched.

"Do you expect a revelation tonight?" Reothe asked softly.

"May the gods forbid. I've had enough revelations!"

"I don't understand you, True-man."

Tulkhan smiled. Sometimes he did not understand himself. "I may not be T'En, but I have also been tainted by death's touch. I will stand guard while you walk death's shadow."

Reothe met his eyes, surprised. "It would be best if you returned to camp."

"Tell me stay or go, but tell me truthfully."

Reothe pulled the cloak tighter about his shoulders. "Stay, if you will."

Tulkhan was aware that some corner had been turned but he hadn't recognized the signpost until it was past.

In silence they watched the night deepen. Waves rolled onto the sand, their rhythmic roar hypnotic. Foam glistened in the light of the rising small moon.

The night was still, still enough for Tulkhan to hear Reothe's hiss of in-drawn breath. The little hairs on Tulkhan's body lifted in response to the unseen threat.

"Don't come too close," Reothe advised. He slid down the dune into the hollow, where he sat cross-legged with the cloak wrapped around him.

Tulkhan marveled. The Ghiad was over. Gharavan was dead. Nothing threatened his hold on Imoshen and Fair Isle but Reothe, and he was ready to protect him. Truly, life was strange.

Death had come close to them all, and Imoshen wanted Reothe to meet his son. She wandered the camp looking for him. One by one the Ghebites denied knowledge of his whereabouts. If it had been an emergency, she would have opened her T'En senses to search for him, but it wasn't, and besides, she was drained.

At last she came to a campfire at the far edge of the army. Only the rolling dunes, silvered by the moonlight, stretched beyond. She approached the men by the fire as she had done so many times. "I look for Beatific Reothe."

The Ghebites exchanged glances. One of them pointed out into the dunes. "The General and his sword-brother went out there at dusk."

Understanding rushed Imoshen. The slow burn of anger consumed her. How the men must be laughing. Presumptuous female. As if the General would prefer her to his sword-brother. She was only fit for bearing sons!

Furious, she returned to her tent. As the flap dropped behind her, she realized that Reothe would be facing the shades of the men he had killed, and a deeper jealousy consumed her because he had trusted Tulkhan before her.

The baby woke at dawn and Imoshen tended to his needs, marveling once again that he clung to life so tenaciously. Sleep welled up in her as he nuzzled into her breast. She took a deep breath of contentment, then wrinkled her nose. Opening her T'En senses, she identified the dusty, dry aftertaste of death's shadow.

Rolling to her feet with the babe still at her breast, she stepped through the tent flap to see Reothe lying pale and weak under the awning. His lids flickered and she knew he was aware of her. Suffering etched his features. All her anger evaporated and she smoothed the lines of pain from his forehead.

"Your touch is a balm," he whispered.

"I smell death coming from the pores of your skin. There was no mention of this T'En burden in the

T'Enchiridion. Does Imoshen the First explain how to cope with it in the T'Elegos?"

Reothe gave her a wry smile. "The T'Elegos is not what you think it is. It assumes the reader knows much, too much."

She remained unconvinced.

"If I told you that on no terms must you attempt Traduciation, what would you say?"

"First I must know what it is."

"Exactly."

Imoshen expelled her breath. "If only I had been able to break the encryption of the T'Endomaz!"

"With what I have discovered, I think that some secrets are best left undisturbed."

"How can you say that?"

"All my life I have carried the expectation and the burden of being a Throwback. My parents killed themselves when they realized there was no T'En mentor to train me. They could not face the thought of their son turning rogue. Everything I know I've had to uncover for myself. I am infinitely weary, Imoshen." He closed his eyes, his voice a dry rustle. "In the heat of battle yesterday I took the lives of True-men. Seven times I walked death's shadow as their shades tried to drag me into death's realm with them, and it was because of my T'En legacy that I was vulnerable. But I would rather that than kill without compunction."

In sympathy, Imoshen undid the lacing on Reothe's shirt, pulling it open to reveal his pale skin and the triple scars left by the Ancients' servant. She placed his son's soft cheek over Reothe's heart. "Here is a blameless life to bring your soul peace."

With great reluctance, he cradled the baby's downy head. Tears rolled unheeded down Reothe's cheeks. He lifted his son so that the little body hung from his large hands, vulnerable as a day-old kitten. "Because he came too early, our Sacrare son's gifts will be crippled, Imoshen. All his life he will suffer the mistrust of True-men and women, with no T'En gifts for his defense." Reothe kissed the baby's forehead. "I fear one day you will curse us for giving you life, my son."

Imoshen retrieved the babe, a fierce, protective fire burning within her. She recalled Mother Reeve's son. Like Reothe, she had made her own discoveries.

The sounds of the camp awakening came to her. Soon they would return to T'Diemn, to the responsibilities of their positions and the expectations of their people.

"Imoshen?" Reothe whispered.

"Ask, and if it is within my power I will grant it."

Tulkhan walked around the tent. Imoshen wondered if he had been listening. He towered above them, expression unreadable. "Will you ride, Reothe?"

"Of course." He rolled upright, and by the time he was standing he had shrugged off the pallor of death.

Imoshen rose with the baby in her arms. Tulkhan held out his hands for the child. Heart hammering, she relinquished him. When she had suggested Tulkhan use Reothe's son to control him, she had not actually envisaged handing the child over. Every nerve strained as Tulkhan turned the boy to the dawn sun. The baby's eyes closed in reaction to the light and his tiny arms came up. His six-fingered hands splayed out, then furled closed.

"There doesn't seem to be anything wrong with him," Tulkhan said. The baby looked ludicrously small in his large hands. "Truly, I am blessed. I never thought to have two sons. As princes of Fair Isle my boys will get the best education, and I will see that they are not ashamed of their T'En heritage." He held Reothe's eyes. "In Gheeaba a man names his sons. What do you suggest, Reothe?"

If Reothe rejected Tulkhan's overture, there was no hope for them. Imoshen realized this was the last thing he had expected Tulkhan to do. But so much had happened since he planted this seed of dissension.

Silence stretched. Reothe cleared his throat. "Do you have a name that means *One who will overcome*?"

"Seerkhan. It was my grandfather's name. He united the tribes. They say I take after him." Tulkhan smiled. "It is only right, since my son bears the name of the greatest T'En emperor of the Age of Tribulation, that this boy should carry the equivalent Ghebite name."

"Seerkhan..." Imoshen whispered. Images rushed her.

"Reothe," Tulkhan warned as Imoshen crumpled. "She's exhausted."

But this was not the reason for Imoshen's collapse.

"Will she be able to ride?" Tulkhan asked.

She pushed Reothe's helping hands away. "Of course. The T'En are a hardy race." And vulnerable in ways a Trueman wasn't.

"We leave for T'Diemn," Tulkhan said. "But first come with me."

When he ducked inside the tent to give the baby to Kalleen, Reothe turned to Imoshen for an explanation, but she could only shrug.

Tulkhan reappeared and led them through the camp to the last dune. Before them the sand fell away to the sea. The sentinel that marked the entrance to the River Diemn stood bathed in crisp morning light. Everything looked renewed. Imoshen sensed they hovered of the brink of many paths, but the imminence of the moment prevented her from foreseeing the outcomes.

The sea breeze blew her hair in her eyes and she flicked it aside as she turned to Tulkhan. "Well, General?"

He gestured to the central mountains of Fair Isle. "When I landed at Northpoint with my army, I never thought to pay so high a price for this island—my father, my half-brother, and my homeland. Reothe, you once told me that I was wrong to launch an unprovoked attack for gain. In those days I was my father's war general. The purpose of the Ghebite Empire was to expand. I...I am not the man I was. Fair Isle and the T'En—*you* two—have taught me much." His honesty was painful.

"None of us is unchanged." Imoshen could barely speak.

"I am weary of war and killing," Tulkhan confessed. "I

don't want to return to T'Diemn knowing I cannot sleep easy in my bed because the last two T'En plot my death."

"What do you want from us, General?" Imoshen noticed Reothe grow as still as a stalking cat.

Reothe gave a sharp laugh. "General Tulkhan wants a bloodless victory!"

Tulkhan nodded. "My army has been traveling nearly twelve years. My men are ready for peace. Your people have suffered; they, too, are ready for peace. Today we stand at a crossroads. We can return to the capital and further plotting, or we can make a vow to put our differences behind us. Build on what we have."

Imoshen's heart soared. Here was proof that she had not been mistaken in the General.

"I would make a truce with you, Reothe," Tulkhan said. "As Beatific of the T'En Church, you are second only to the royal house in power and prestige. If you make restoring the T'En your life's work, will that be enough for you?"

Imoshen felt Reothe's eyes on her, and her awareness spiraled down to this one moment. Her breath caught in her throat.

"Is this what you want, Imoshen?" Reothe asked.

She understood that if she said no he would take the path that led to Tulkhan's death. She could not unleash the last T'En warrior. To save the General's life she would have to deny her love for Reothe.

"Is this what you want?" Reothe repeated.

"Yes. It is what I want." The words left her lips in a rush.

Reothe faltered as if he might drop to his knees in the sand. Imoshen could not let herself go to him.

"You have her answer," Tulkhan said. "Reothe?"

He walked a little away, his profile to them. Tension radiated from him, rousing her gift so that she could taste Reothe's essence on her tongue. At last he seemed to come to a decision and faced them. "I never thought to be bested by the honor of a True-man, Tulkhan. You offered me a

compromise once before and I refused. This time I accept. Like you, I grow weary of death. I will make war no
more."

Imoshen's head spun with relief. At the same time, she
could not believe Reothe had accepted her decision. How
could he put her aside for an ideal? But wasn't that what she
had done when he had come to her at Landsend, offering to
help her escape? She had chosen to stay with the General to
ease the transition of power, never dreaming that she would
grow to love Tulkhan.

Numbly, she watched the General remove his ceremonial knife and turn the blade on his left arm. With a start
she realized he meant to make a T'En vow. She winced as he
slit the skin over his wrist, then offered Reothe the knife.
But Reothe refused it; instead, he lifted his arm and stared
at the old bonding scar.

Her mouth thinned as the scar opened. "See, Imoshen,
I once told you this scar would never be healed until we
were joined."

The extent of what she had lost made her gasp.

Silently, Tulkhan offered his arm and Reothe met it,
hand to hand, forearm to forearm.

"You have my vow," Reothe said.

"As Imoshen is our witness," Tulkhan said.

When Reothe dropped his arm and turned to Imoshen,
she felt the need in him. It robbed her of all pretense, and
she had to look away.

"I ask for a moment with Imoshen," Reothe said.

Without a word Tulkhan strode to the end of the dune
and put his back to them, arms folded. The wind played
with his long hair.

"Imoshen?"

She could not meet Reothe's eyes. He would see her
pain, and she had no right to inflict it on him.

"You love him?"

She nodded.

"He is the best True-man I have ever known. He will
bring honor to Fair Isle."

Her throat swelled with tears she could not shed. The bonding scar on her wrist throbbed, and she hugged it to her chest. When Reothe had risked his life to save her at Landsend, she had been torn by conflicting loyalties. Those same loyalties clawed at her now.

Reothe touched her cheek, turning her face to his. Tears lapped over her lower lids, sliding down her cheeks. "I misjudged you, Shenna. You do not have a hard head and cold heart."

"I do what I must."

"As do I."

"I wish—"

"No wishing. We must walk the path fate has presented."

"I don't believe in fate!"

He smiled with painful self-knowledge. "In the T'Elegos, Imoshen the First writes that a T'En couple rarely risked the deepest bonding because, though it enhanced their power, it left them vulnerable to each other. Already you have proved that true. I took a mad gamble when I offered the deep bonding in the old way, but I do not regret it." He took her left hand, lifting it between them so that their fingers entwined, wrists met.

She felt the warmth of his blood, and her own bonding scar stung. "What are you doing?"

"Amending our vows."

"I don't understand."

"There can be no other for me, Imoshen. But I can wait. Enjoy your True-man. Watch him grow old and die. I don't envy you. And when your heart is healed, I will be ready. On that day we will complete our bonding vows."

He pressed his lips to the back of her hand, then released her and raised his voice. "I'll tell the army to break camp, General."

Imoshen stared out to sea, hearing only the rush of the breakers, the cry of the seabirds. From what Reothe had revealed, the knowledge of the T'Elegos would bring as much sorrow as joy.

She knew when she was alone with Tulkhan on the dune.

"Imoshen?"

She looked over her shoulder at the General. He had aged since he took her Stronghold. Experience had marked his features with compassion and wisdom. "When I first met you, Tulkhan, you were a great war general; now you are a great statesman, one who will bring peace and prosperity to Fair Isle."

"Don't speak of Fair Isle, Imoshen. I know you became mine by necessity, not choice. Fate forced you to make cruel choices, but I had begun to hope that you might love me—"

A sob escaped her and she reached for him. They would have a few precious years together. She would not seek to know how many.

His arms tightened about her, and when he spoke there was a catch in his voice. "I did not know if you could love a Mere-man."

"Mere...nothing!" She held his eyes fiercely. "There must be no more Mere-man and T'En, only us and we."

"But what of you and me?" he asked.

"You know that I love you."

"But you love him too. And I have been second best all my life, first son of the king's second wife, supplanted heir. I must be your one and only. I would have it from your lips."

"I have renounced the last of my race. Doesn't that tell you how I feel?" She pulled back and searched his face. "My T'En heritage has always been denied by the people who loved me. On our bonding day you made me vow not to use my gifts. Since then I had begun to think you have grown less hostile. Can you accept me for the Throwback I am?"

She saw him hesitate, and her heart sank.

"If I have faith in you, then I must accept your gifts, but I cannot pretend they do not trouble me," Tulkhan admitted.

"Honest, at least," Imoshen whispered. "If truth be told, my gifts sometimes frighten me."

His eyes widened, then he smiled wryly. Wonderingly,

she traced his mouth with her fingertips. "Know this. For me you will always be the truest of True-men, Tulkhan."

He removed one of the two seal rings from his finger. "I want you to have this." His voice caught as he slid the Ghebite-seal ring onto her finger. "There were times when it seemed too much to ask for Fair Isle and your love." He kissed her palm and closed her fingers. "You hold my heart, all that I am, right here."

And she knew it was true. When he caught her face between his hands, they were both vulnerable. Imoshen opened her T'En senses and closed her eyes as she gave herself over to him, exulting in his love for her.

ABOUT THE AUTHOR

CORY DANIELLS lives by the bay in Brisbane, Australia, with her husband and six children. With more than twenty children's books and numerous short stories published, she set out to combine her two loves, fantasy and romance, in the T'En trilogy.

She holds a black belt in tae kwan do and is currently learning aikido and iaido, the Japanese martial art of swordplay.